C. I

Mermaid Adventures

The Mermaid's Apprentice

Book 2

A SeaRisen LLC Publication
2015

The Mermaid's Apprentice

Authored by C. L. Savage
Edited by Miriam Ball

Published by SeaRisen LLC
– Boulder Colorado
– SeaRisen.com

Cover Photograph by Sassafras Photography
– Superior, CO 80027
– www.sassafraspics.com

Cover Design by Mirela Barbu
– https://99designs.com/profiles/1328241

Stock art used in design:
– "Beach 31" by raindroppe, http://raindroppe.deviantart.com/
– "Croatia Stock 108" by malleni-stock, http://malleni-stock.deviantart.com/
– "Mountain Stock 1" by Lyfiar, http://lyfiar.deviantart.com/

Paperback: ISBN 978-0-9909258-2-8
E-book: ISBN 978-0-9909258-3-5

Printed in the United States of America

First SeaRisen LLC Printing October 2015

10 9 8 7 6 5 4 3 2 1

Table of Contents

Prologue .... *ix*

1 Windfall *1*

2 Sailing Blind *19*

3 Arrival, Papua New Guinea *33*

4 Charlie *37*

5 Taxi *43*

6 Ride to Town *49*

7 A Rat Eats My Apple *59*

8 Port, Papua New Guinea *65*

9 All Aboard *83*

10 Lost Sights *91*

11 Captive Imagination *107*

12 Fairly Fun *113*

13 Wanting to Fly *125*

14 Fresh Out *131*

15 Spider Island *149*

16 The Same Old Doom and Gloom *163*

17 Magic Carpet *191*

18 Sitting on Nothing *203*

19 The Gardener *219*

20 In the Spider's Lair *231*

21 Fumbling the Ball *253*

22 Have Us for Dinner 269

23 The Ghost of Future Present 291

24 Troubling Waters 297

25 Captured by Thugs 327

26 Cape Port 347

27 Being Human 361

28 The Garden of Gigi 385

29 Take Two 401

30 Bind Them Up 423

To Be Continued 431

About The Author 433

To friends, old and new…

Prologue

My name is Melanie McKenzie and I'm a mermaid (or the closest thing there is to the actual creature). I haven't always been a mermaid. In fact, most of my life I've only longed to be a mermaid, like many of my teammates and friends have. We swim on the local swim team at Goldie's Gym in Boulder, Colorado that's owned by my best friend Jill's parents.

What proof do I have that I'm a mermaid? Well, I breathe water, can speak any language, and have fabulous brown hair that cascades down my back in waves… And magic. I travel anywhere I can picture at a moment's notice and so many other things. It seems like I've been doing this forever, but it isn't so. Though being a mermaid isn't so much in what I *can* do, but in what I *actually* do. All without the benefits of a mermaid's tail. Gone was the myth of "get a mermaid wet and she sprouts a tail" because I'm wet nearly every day and I have no tail.

The journey to becoming a mermaid started four days ago, when my friend Jill had what she first thought was a dream where she was diving into a sunken pirate ship where she rescued a drowning man (who she later discovered was my Uncle Arlo). Then she woke up the following day in the gym's pool – underwater.

Jill began by telling us, her friends Lucy, Cleo and me, her story, showing us magical fish that she wore as a swimsuit. For some reason she couldn't do her magic, that of enabling us to breathe naturally and normally underwater while wearing the swim-team swimsuit we'd all been wearing. Together we exchanged our team suits for magical fish.

The fish-suit, as we'd begun to call it, looks like a regular swimsuit out of water, but while swimming, the fish can and do swim with us. So now we could experience mermaid life as Jill did. When we'd exchanged our suits for the fish, we were magically transported to an island in the South Pacific, the same location as Jill's dream, arriving underwater.

Ever since that day, I've had the fish as a swimsuit and began to experience physical changes. To begin with, my head hair became salon hair—perfect all the time. I've also become stronger and can speak any language known to man (as well as those of beasts). It was quite the laugh when a friend of ours was asking us what "grape" meant in French, but we thought she was asking us in English. At first we thought she was having us on, but she was speaking the word in French but we were hearing her in English, with her voice, perfectly speaking grape. There in France we unwittingly fooled the locals into thinking we were French girls.

How do we move about, from Boulder, to the South Pacific, to France in a single day? Magic, in a word. The basics of magic Jill taught me, the rest I've learned on my own. The magic used for transportation we call a "transfer" happens at the will of The Lord of the Water, like all magic. And according to Jill, he never denies our requests – and he has never denied me mine.

Prologue

Magic is the art of getting something done that wouldn't normally be possible. First you need to Attune, what I like to think of as mermaid vision, giving a view of everything around and connecting you to it as well. It is an intimate vision giving information so detailed that I would know if a woman was pregnant before she even knew. For a transfer, I attune to the person or place where I want to go. Then I need to gain Understanding. That is when I need to ask the Lord of the Water for help. He gives his permission and I gain the Understanding which makes the connection for a transfer and I see where I'm going, but I'm not there yet. With the connection, your self remains behind until you Practice it, enact it by stepping there, finishing the spell.

That's for doing a transfer personally, but many times the Lord of the Water does the work himself, with or without our permission. On our first swim to the South Pacific we had to ask for a way to be opened back home, since we'd been sent there by him. Jill has described being taken other places, without her asking, or trying to make a way of her own. It has yet to happen to me, a solo sending, but Jill assures me it will happen.

In Jill's first night swim, the one she thought initially to be a dream, she rescued my Uncle Arlo from drowning. He'd broken a leg and had an island fever that about took his life. While helping him, she'd learned of a people who served mermaids and our cause, they are called the Syreni. They lived on a large island in the South Pacific and Jill had left Uncle Arlo in their care while he recovered.

The Syreni have magic too. They use it to return those rescued back to their lives, with or without the memories of the mermaid that rescued them. Jill had debated whether she wanted this marine biologist to remember her or not. Since he was my uncle, Jill had given me the decision of whether he should remember her. Because Uncle Arlo is a researcher, a marine biologist and I knew his love at finding undiscovered creatures to share with the world, I felt he couldn't keep our secret to himself and so had asked the Syreni to remove the memory.

So it was with trepidation that I journeyed to the South Pacific with Dad and my friend Ri'Anne who swam with me on the swim team to help my uncle. He's unable to do his dives (because of his broken leg) and has requested Dad's help. In the past, Dad and I have been to visit, so we know his life. Back then I'd been an observer and now I was determined to be an integral part of his operation.

Giving Uncle amnesia of Jill's rescue may have been a mistake, though, because now I had to hide my talents from both him and Dad, as well as the rest of the world. I may be wronging Dad, even though I'd do anything for him. But what was he supposed to think if he knew, and could he allow me to do the things that I must? I didn't really want to hide, as I've accomplished great things as a mermaid and wanted to continue doing so.

Thankfully I didn't have a mermaid tail yet, so I could dive doing Uncle's research and not give myself away. It was my theory that mermaids didn't receive their tails until they'd earned one. And having only become a mermaid in the last few days, I guess I hadn't earned a tail and certainly hadn't displayed a tail. So there shouldn't be anything about me that set me apart from others.

I'm hoping my friend Ri'Anne and I can serve as Uncle's eyes and hands to help him with his research... *He needs us, not the least of which because we're excellent swimmers.* And I'm hoping to teach Ri'Anne to be a mermaid.

This trip is sure to prove interesting, swimming as a mermaid, teaching someone else to be one and all the while avoiding Uncle's notice. Who am I fooling? This trip is sure to be a disaster!

1

Windfall

Hurtling through the stratosphere at hundreds of miles per hour was mighty dangerous. So why, if I could cover that distance in an instant as a mermaid, was I doing it? I pondered the complexity of a mermaid life lived among non-mermaids while listening to the sound of the wind pass over the jet's hull. Or was that my skin? I really felt like I was out there, a fiery comet burning in the atmosphere, traveling faster than the jet, flying so fast that I split the sky, without the protection of an aircraft or a pilot to guide me.

"Melanie, you're far away," Dad said, pulling me from my thoughts and passing me the pretzels. "They'll help with airsickness." Then turning back to his magazine, he glanced at his watch and I saw it was 8pm, but it was really 1am at home. I wasn't at all tired, part of the strangeness of having slept in various places on the globe in the last few days. The flight telemetry on the back of the chair in front of me showed us southwest of Hawaii. Oh this flight was taking forever.

I took some of the pretzels and passed the bag to my friend Ri'Anne, who had graciously accepted to fly with me to the South Pacific at the last second. If not for her, I'd be alone on this trip, and I needed a friend. She was looking out the jet's window at the passing orange sunset colored clouds. I saw those same clouds, but I was out there with them, and closing my eyes to the sight didn't do me any good. I felt I was out there without the jet to protect me, my eyes tearing up from the wind.

Not eating the pretzels fast enough to please Dad, he took some of the pretzels from my hand and fed me, like the good papa he was. I was unaware of myself, still out there flying so fast, distracted because the people were moving backwards and talking funny…

"Melanie don't!" spoke an unfamiliar voice.

"Don't what?" Ri'Anne asked, her question pulling me from the vision. I hadn't said anything, though maybe it did sound like me. *Focus on Ri'Anne*, I told myself. Anything to get my attention to the here and now. Ri'Anne was looking out at the traffic of Denver. *Denver?* There were the sights and smells of the city and I was sitting in a car. The sight of it, the bustling traffic and the loud hum of the air-conditioner as the car fought the outside temperature convinced me that this was real. Its cool breeze so refreshing.

"What is happening?" I said aloud, freaking out more than a little bit. My friend Jill (the only other mermaid I knew who had stayed home) had told me of transfers that happened taking her places without her asking for it. This would be a first for me, and this wasn't so much a place, from the jet to here, but back in time! To our drive from Boulder to the airport.

Calm down Melanie. If it is happening, there is a reason for it. The one thing Jill and I had determined is that the Lord of the Water, the authority on all mermaid magic, had a purpose to sending us places. Like when we'd gone to the Amazon to help some villages unclog a river of fallen trees.

Turning back to me, Ri'Anne took my hand. "Are you alright?" she asked, her voice coming from far away.

With her touch, the here and there sensation subsided and I "landed" in the car with her. I closed my eyes, taking an uneasy breath. We were riding in Jill's stepdad Lucas's car, since he was giving us a ride to the airport. Lucas and Dad were in the front seats with us in back, Ri'Anne to my left.

"I hate flying," I admitted to her. "I always get sick." I was feeling a little of it just then.

Ri'Anne picked up on the conversation we'd been having at the time. "I was saying, do you think we brought enough stuff? What girl goes around the globe without taking the world with her?"

I opened my eyes to see Ri'Anne looking into the recesses of her backpack hoping to find the wardrobe that neither of us had with us. Still trying to ease my breathing, to soothe my nausea, I didn't speak and nodded my agreement.

Dropping her voice to a whisper, so that Lucas and Dad wouldn't hear, Ri'Anne continued, "You know, Coach Arden is getting upset that you and Jill keep missing swim practice." We can't help it sometimes, though it has been mostly Jill—she was gone for days at a time. "And this trip is going to play havoc with my chance of making the High School swim team." Coach Arden is Jill's uncle, and the reason that Ri'Anne was whispering.

Squeezing her hand, I whispered back, "I'm glad you came." Though really, missing swim practice was the least of my concerns. I know Coach Arden expected us to step it up this fall with our entry to High School, but that seemed forever away at the moment.

Looking at her near-empty bag in despair, Ri'Anne asked, forgetting to keep her voice down, "Your dad didn't pack for me, did he?" Dad had swung by Ri'Anne's place on the way to pick us up from the gym.

"No," Dad answered for me from the front of the car and Lucas added, looking into the rearview mirror at us for a second, "I got your dad to pack your things."

Ri'Anne and I looked at each other, saying at the same time, "We're in for an adventure."

Then, looking down out of her window, Ri'Anne said, "Look, I can see a sailboat down there. It seems in trouble."

The world skewed sideways and my stomach flopped. I'd heard Ri'Anne, but at her word I was suddenly looking at the deep blue of the Pacific Ocean. Not from the height of a plane in flight or even from our car, but I was seeing it from a seat on an abandoned modern sailboat. It was a beautiful boat of delicate curves and solar panels covering every empty surface. The boat could house a small family.

It was near to sunset and I shielded my eyes to watch, the sun just cleared the horizon of the Pacific. The first bit of fireworks highlighting the clouds with tinges of fire. I was tingling with magic, like I'd just received a carpet shock. Normally, magic is the art of getting something done, and here I was alive with it and not doing anything. I tried to figure out if I'd done something, but I really hadn't. Ribbons of colored confetti magic washed over and through me. It was changing me, I knew.

As I waited for the magic sense to pass, I thought of the past times when I'd felt this way before. Whenever the Lord of the Water used me, I experienced the world in a new way. Like when I'd spoken with the black leopards in the jungle, I'd felt similarly to this. And the first time, when I'd learned to breathe water on my own. All day I'd had that feeling, like I was being remade. But this time it was more intense and I could certainly use it. I'd never been out in the middle of the ocean on my own before. Seeing the rolling sea rise and then lift us up and then down into a dip, I had a new appreciation for the sailors of the craft. The wind caused the rope lines to sing from their tension. The sailboat was a toy in a giant's bathtub and the waves the giant kicked up smacked the boat for a spin, its main sail whipping across the deck, trailing its loose ropes.

Was I here to save the sailboat? It seemed its designers had taken care of a pilotless situation, like a specter at its helm, it was trying to correct its course, but then another wave crashed over and the boat disappeared for a moment under the water before it tried to right itself.

It all seemed so real but it couldn't be, and I tried to piece reality from illusion. Attuning gave me a detailed view of the water cascading over the boat and into every crevice where it spewed, flowing into troughs and wicked by the fiberglass hull back into the sea from whence it came. On its stern was its name, The Dancing Lady. Everything was as I was seeing with my eyes. At least with the water splashing over me, the nausea had gone away. It seemed this was real, I wasn't having a vision.

So, why was I on a ghost ship? There was nobody here.

At least the ocean was profoundly beautiful, and another wave hurled itself across the sailboat. The "ghost" steering the boat tried valiantly to head up wind, but the next great wave spun the sailboat to the side, causing it to run headlong down the great wave like a sled on snow before its sail whipped about causing us to skid sideways.

Perhaps I was here to keep the sailboat from disappearing beneath the waves, so I dropped off the seat and went for the tiller.

The main sail whipped across the deck, and I ducked it, and it slammed against its guiding wires. Again, the sea hurled itself over the boat, rocking it, threatening to capsize it. The tiller wheels whirled as it fought to compensate and the sailboat spun in place. Reaching for the starboard wheel, I was captivated by the sea as we rolled over the crest of an immense wave, watching as more giant waves rolled to the horizon.

A voice called to me from out of the wind, "Melanie, don't…"

I hesitated, pulling my hand back. In that moment of indecision, a wave crashed over the yacht and washed me into the depths. I struggled against the power of the water before orienting myself and drove for the surface.

I was almost run over by a swimmer and she stopped to stare at me. It was Ri'Anne, she looked at me under her in her swim lane, her eyes wide. When I surfaced, she said, "That's the second time someone has done that. Last week it was Jill. I know I saw her in the ocean somewhere, for a moment. Then she was gone. And now you."

"Um. Um," I babbled blinking back tears in the clear water of the gym's pool. The sudden sight of my friend, the pool… These "Melanie don't" moments were unhinging me. Ri'Anne noticed and put her hands to my shoulders to comfort me. *Ok, I'm home, none of it is real. I haven't left yet. It was not but a vision*, I tried to convince myself. Glancing at the clock, it showed 3pm, the time I'd arrived from Denver, *was arriving from Denver*. I'd really been in Denver helping Jill, on my way back here to meet Dad for the trip. But everything had seemed so real…

With a dozen people hanging out in the pool nearby, I couldn't explain now and told her, "Not here." I was wanting to share my *joy* with her, she had the same dream of being a mermaid, but there wasn't time and I saw Dad standing by the poolside. When he saw my glance, he lifted a thumb to get out of the pool. "Look Ri'Anne, I have to go. I promise, I'll …"

"You're leaving for the South Pacific again?" she asked wistfully.

"I'm out of excuses not to go," I admitted, affirming that I hadn't actually left. But then I had a rush of clear, vivid memories of the time aboard the jet, the trip to the airport and a sailboat in trouble made me doubt that thought. And Ri'Anne had been with me!

"Why wouldn't you want to go?" she asked. But then seeing Dad waving me over, she said, "Go, have fun…" Then Ri'Anne turned and swam down her lane. I wanted to tell her the whole story, but instead I dove for Dad, swimming under several swim lines to arrive at his side.

"That was Ri'Anne?" Dad asked when I slipped out of the pool. I nodded yes. He followed me to my things and my towel. He turned to sit and I sat next to him. "You know, Uncle Arlo suggested you bring a friend."

"Uh…" That means I wasn't imagining any of it. Struck with a wondrous thought I looked back at Ri'Anne. Maybe, just maybe, I could teach her to be a mermaid too! But there was trouble already with the sailboat, and did the plane crash? Was that why I was on the lone sailboat? Was I bringing my friend into danger? It seemed I already had.

"You seem alarmed," Dad said. "I thought you'd be pleased."

I put my arms around him as he expected and told him, "I am, Dad. I've had some other things on my mind," to put it mildly – and I already knew Ri'Anne would accept the invitation. Packing up my bag, Dad told me to put it in Jill's room. He had a pack for me already and I smiled, there was not much in it. Knowing the future was tricky business.

I shivered and Dad put his arm around my shoulder. "The air in here is a little cold, isn't it? Here have my blanket." *Blanket?* And he was passing me a blanket to wrap my legs. "Here, adjust your air, so you don't get so much." And he reached over me, and I followed his hand to the controls that directed the passenger air, back on the airplane again.

My stomach did one of those rolls and I gripped the arms of the seat. "Dad, I'm going to be sick," I said, and I got up, squeezing past him, trailing the blanket for a couple of steps in my rush to get to the bathroom. In the lavatory I stood to the mirror and looked at myself trying to hold on. Then, as my lunch came up I let it go into the toilet. I swore off flying. *We still have many hours left,* and I was sick again at the thought.

The jet heaved and I was slammed into the floor, and then the aircraft dropped and I bounced off the wall and onto the ceiling. My stomach rose up again, but I was on the roof as the jet plummeted. I felt a blast of refreshing air, it roared over my skin as I landed on my feet. Stumbling out of the aircraft's toilet I apologized to the steward, a hand over my mouth.

Ri'Anne was there waiting for me, grabbed my arms, steadying me. "You stink," she said.

"It gets better than this," I assured her. This certainly wasn't one of my better mermaid moments. "Hold me still, so I can do something about it."

Jill had told me that Attuning cleanses the environment – magic within magic. There were greater depths to everything. We'd learned in France that Attuning shielded us from the songs of sirens. So why not another effect that I didn't know of?

And Jill, the only other mermaid I knew, said it worked, so I tried. By Attuning, I had a sense of myself, the vomit that was stuck to me and my clothes, and it wicked away into nothingness. The same went for the mess I'd made in the lavatory, the passengers around me, and the woman with the infant and four year old boy. His spills disappearing, and our clothes freshening up, grime disappearing from under people's fingernails, and I felt the beating heartbeats of those nearby. Some were having fun, like

Ri'Anne, as the plane had its ups and downs, while other hearts like mine were scared.

Too much information! I cut off the view, letting myself relax, leaning on Ri'Anne. "There," I told her, feeling clean.

I was still wobbly on my feet and Ri'Anne suggested, "What you need are more pretzels!" Seeing me go green at her idea, she said, "Let's get you back in your seat." Though first she straightened my shirt and touched up my hair, thankfully all the goo was gone. Then she guided me back to my seat. At least for now the turbulence had calmed, and so I wasn't a reeking mess when I slid into the seat next to Dad, who gave me a little hug.

Ri'Anne looked at me after sitting and buckling back in, feeling sorry for me, but she was enjoying the trip. She said holding up the bag of pretzels to Dad and I, "Did you feel the roller coaster there? That was fun."

"Oooh," and I held my head. "Don't say that."

"Here Melanie," Dad said, handing me a sleeping pill. "It's a long flight anyway." He then tossed one back and took a drink of water.

"Good idea," I said, putting the pill in my mouth. But instead of it hitting my tongue, it fell through my jaw, and onto my neck – through my chest, through my body, chair, the floor and through the baggage compartment and I watched it go out of the jet. I felt a wind on my face. *Not again!*

Dad then handed me the water. But I put it down, not wanting water all over me. Another bump and I was gripping the armrests. I tried asking him, "Dad did you see the pill go through me?" But

I was gritting my teeth on the last part as I tried to hold myself still and I don't think he heard.

"What?" he asked with a yawn. "These pills, they're fas…" and he was out.

Ri'Anne said with a smile, "You poor things." Someday she'd be a pilot. "If you're going to be out, I'm going to listen to music," and she put on her earbuds and turned on the music loud enough that I could hear what she was listening to.

Then the jet jumped again, I was slammed into my seat and passed through it, my legs dangling and my feet kicking for something to stand on. Hanging by my forearms, my hands gripping the ends of the armrests, I decided right then and there to agree with Ri'Anne, "Poor little ole me!" The wind of the jet's passage blew through the cabin, and I felt it burn across my shoulders, whipping me out flat.

"Dad! Dad! Ri'Anne!" I screamed staring at the back of my seat and through it to my jeans and shirt, both hollow tubes that were holding the shape of my body before collapsing. I kicked through the food tray of the person two seats back, sending their stuff flying. But I couldn't find anything to stand on to try and regain my chair.

Then over the speaker system I heard, "This is co-pilot Hrendi," his accent was thick but I understood him, "We're encountering some turbulence, please buckle up."

"Turbulence!" I screamed as the jet dropped, shaking me loose and I tumbled out through the dozens of people behind me. I barely saw them before I was behind the jet and it was disappearing in the distance as I slowed. I had a moment to enjoy the twin pillowy sunset emblazoned cloud lines that were on either side of me, like the lanes of a white cotton "dirt" road, made by some sky chariot, before I was falling between them.

"Oh great," I frowned, suddenly noticing about 50,000 feet between me and the dark blue ocean below where the sun had already set. The sea stretched to the horizon in every direction. I stopped tumbling as I slowed, but then I was falling straight down, and you couldn't hear a sound. It was beautifully quiet.

"Yeah I know, right?" Ri'Anne said from right beside me, playing with her long straight blond hair, the wind from the window causing it to blow in front of her face. I jerked, feeling her so close. She was so cold. We were back in the car.

I had to get her away, but I had to thank her for saving me in the jet. *Err*, that she was going to save me.

"You're going to have a great time. Look," and I held up some fish. She reacted as expected, sliding away at seeing fish swimming in my hand. "You need these," and I held them out to touch her hand.

"Couldn't they be butterflies?" she asked. Her turquoise blue eyes wide open as the fish jumped to her extended hand, swam up her arm to disappear under her clothes. I knew they were making her a mermaid fish-suit, like I had received from Jill.

Jill had, when explaining her adventures, told us about the magical fish. We couldn't do magic while wearing our normal swim-team swimsuit. Clothing dulls the senses, like a glove, and that was the reason I wore fish most of the time. I was giving Ri'Anne the first part to being a mermaid.

I shook my head, "That wouldn't make sense."

"I know," she said with a shrug and an attempted smile. Holding up a case, she waved it, "A make-up kit, for a time aboard a boat," she made a motion of tossing it over her shoulder in the car. "I'll trade you it for some hair ties."

"Sure, I have plenty of those." Besides, since becoming a mermaid my hair hadn't been so fly away. "Want a shave kit?" I asked, feeling like I should trade her back, and I passed her mine.

"You won't need it?" Ri'Anne asked, putting away the trades I'd given her.

"The shave kit? I haven't shaved in a week," I said lifting a leg to show off my hairless legs.

She ran her hand over the leg, "Smooth," she "Ooo'd," saying, "I'm jealous. Think that'll happen for me too?"

I nodded. "It happened right after our first swim. As long as you want it," I added because it wouldn't happen automatically.

Wanting to be a mermaid seemed to be important for becoming one. But it had to be more than simply wanting it. I've wanted to be a mermaid my whole life, but nothing changed in my life until Jill had begun teaching me – showing me. I suppose it was like reading about being a ballerina, and wanting to be one, but never dancing with one. Then it would remain a dream.

"Want what?" Ri'Anne asked.

"I was thinking, what it takes to be a 'mermaid.' You must also experience 'these' things." I was whispering, so that Dad and

Lucas wouldn't hear. Though it was possible Lucas already knew, being Jill's stepdad.

"It can't be that hard," Ri'Anne said, brushing off my serious attitude. With her brush off, a blast of wind hit me in the face, my hair whipped behind me and I shut my eyes in response. "Close the window!" I yelled through the wind at Ri'Anne. But it was useless, because I could no longer feel the car seat beneath me!

Screaming did me little good, but I couldn't seem to stop. The wind blew tears from my eyes. My fall had turned to tumbling – my feet and hands hitting me as I spun. At this rate I'd beat myself to death before I splashed down. Then, remembering seeing others perform a jackknife dive in the movies while falling, I tried to get myself into a controlled fall, shoving my fists forward over my head and holding my legs out straight. It took all my will not to curl up into a ball. The tumbling slowed – it was working.

As I oriented myself, the fish of my swimsuit rippled, moving over me into new patterns. I was so glad to feel them, they were moving to help me. Showing me that I wasn't alone. The fish became wings under my arms, a helmet for my hair, a bird-like tail between my legs and goggles.

Finally able to see, I dug for the strength that came from being a mermaid, spread my arms and pried open my legs in an attempt to slow my descent. "Yargh!" It hurt, as the wings that the fish had made between my arms and body took the air. Then, like a flying squirrel, I began to glide and get a better angle that didn't have me going straight down in a dive that was sure to end with me going splat in the water.

In an uneasy glide, I found myself wondering how falling out of our jet served the mermaid cause. Sure, the wide Pacific Ocean was there before me in all its gorgeous blue glory, but I had a feeling I was going to plow a comet size crater in it as I became a bug on its windshield. All this way to come to my uncle's aide. At least I was doing it mermaid style. Plunging in over my head into a sea with no land in sight. That seemed about right.

Growing to take up the whole wide world before me was the incredibly beautiful dark sea. In typical mermaid flair, I had air to breathe in the mysterious way I breathed underwater. As thin as the air was, it wasn't so thin that I fell straight. Delighting in the "flight" I tried to do some rolls and then when my speed slowed and the ocean was much closer, I tried to snap out and truly soar.

Of course, I was without an engine. And, even though the air was filled with water molecules, I hadn't figured out how to swim through them as a mermaid. In the distance I saw what looked like The Dancing Lady, the sailboat that had been in the vision, and I aimed for it. But my downward angle was too great. My inept flying skills would have me plowing into the sea much further away than I had hoped. I covered my face with my arms just before I hit the water.

"Hey, it isn't that bad," said a young girl beside me. I had closed my eyes, but now uncrossing my arms I stared at the six-year-old girl beside me on the jetbridge, the walkway from the terminal out to our jet. I stood there in shock, expecting an ocean.

"Is your name Betsy?" I asked, getting better at this future past stuff. Playing with it a little by saying her name before she told me.

"It is, how do you know?" she said looking at me strangely. I remembered her telling me, but we've never met before this moment. Seeing that I wasn't going to answer her, she said, "I fly all the time."

She then went back to looking at her tablet like I didn't exist. It bothered me when people did that, leaving me standing there wondering if I should walk away.

"I hate flying," Dad said on the other side of me, and I glanced up at him. He was talking to the girl's father. We were standing still but my stomach was rolling, my dad looked at me in concern, finishing what he was saying to the guy, "I prefer my cab."

The girl was talking to me again and I struggled to hear her, "We fly a lot. It is perfectly safe." Then looking up at me she assured me, "It's not like you'll fall out."

Opening my mouth to tell her that falling out of a plane was indeed possible, "…"

"Melanie, don't…"

"Take care of your Dad, Melanie," Lucas said seriously as my world rocked.

Blink. We were standing beside his car at the airport departure lane. He was handing me my bag and then kissing me on the top of the head like I was still a little girl. I gave him a surprised look at his statement, but he'd turned to Dad to give him a hug. Then he turned to helping Ri'Anne, lifting her from the car in some ancient chivalrous gesture that she fell for, laughing at something he said.

What did he know? Jill said I was to keep things secret, but she had also said someone taught her. Jill's dad had to be in the know. So why the charade? Why go through the motions of keeping things a secret even from family? He was back into the car and gone before I could bring myself to ask.

Dad, who had packed my things, grabbed my attention saying, "I do wish I'd thought to bring you a hat. You know I'm a basket case when it comes to these things. I'll find you something," he promised. Then added, "If you'd rather wear that wrap for the plane trip, I'd be fine with it. Those jeans will be too uncomfortable when we arrive."

"The wrap is called a sarong, Dad," I said with a smile.

A friend of Jill's had picked us up the sarongs when Jill and I were in France, but Ri'Anne didn't have one. The sarong was a beach cover-up, not as a real garment, but I told Dad I was fine anyway. Though, I was probably going to wish I'd followed his advice. And like in France, what was I going to do when I spoke the language and he didn't?

I felt so out of my depth. "I wish Jill was here," I said, thinking out loud.

"Why?" Dad asked picking up our boarding passes for Papua New Guinea from the airline agent and handing one to each of us. Then he gave me a look that said, "Don't be insensitive," with a look at Ri'Anne to emphasize his point.

"Fine," I replied with my eyes. But Jill and I hadn't been apart in years. Somehow taking a flight halfway around the world seemed far away. Unless a serious need arose, we were going to have to not see each other until I got back. And to keep up the charade of not being a mermaid, with magical powers and whatnot, there would be no "sending" to each other. Sending, or bubble messages, was the mermaid form of text messaging, so to speak. Dad was right, I should be sensitive to Ri'Anne and not talk to Jill, or about her. It was going to be tough.

"Oh, she'd know what to do," I said, unable to keep my mouth from yapping, especially on hoisting my bag. It was too light. What was Dad thinking, going in unprepared like this?

"How so?" Dad asked, as we moved through the other passengers getting their boarding passes. "As far as I know she's never left Colorado. Though she'd tell you to figure it out for yourself." Dad was right, I should figure it out for myself. I couldn't run to someone every time I had a question or problem.

"Yeah, but sometimes Jill just knows," I said, still upset that I was without my best friend and now we couldn't even talk. Then we passed through security entering the tunnels for the tram to take us to our departure terminal.

2

Sailing Blind

We boarded the tram train and stood holding to the upright bars or to each other waiting for the doors to close. When they had, the radio announcement told us, "Now leaving for terminals A, B and C." Out beyond the tram, instead of walls of the tunnel I saw a green-blue sea, turtles and fish drifting lazily by. Touching the glass I could feel the cold sea on the other side.

With the lurch of the tram starting forward, a crack appeared in the glass and a tidal wave poured in – the water wrapped me about, pulled me out of the tram and into the sea. The deep blue sea where I'd fallen from the jet. Dad and Ri'Anne were gone. I was alone again, descending and trailing bubbles, each orb filling with air from the friction of my entry. My eyes adjusted to the dark and I was able to see forever. It seemed I fell even now with the seafloor far below coming closer.

When I came to rest I was lost in the tranquility of the immense sea, as it set to right all the mixed feelings I had on arriving here. It was everything I could do now to not transfer another fifty thousand feet straight up and experience that all over again. But then I saw the sailboat spinning far above me, a dark arrow in the turbulent turquoise sea and a clear blue sky above it. There should be some kind of metaphor for this, my fall, the sailboat, dad, uncle and the kid at the airport. Coming up from the depth, I tried to guess at what speed I must have been traveling at to come so deep. But math was never my strong suit.

Swimming up, I felt alive in a way I couldn't describe. The deep water was so encompassing, soft, warm, infinite and powerful. Gone was the airsickness I'd been feeling and with it the continual sense of incredible speed. Nearing the surface, the sea was rolling and a fierce wind plied it, just as I remembered.

The fish of my suit swam around me, reorganizing themselves from the flight suit they'd made back into their normal cute sea skirt and top – the cloth appearing to drift about me. I wasn't sure why they did that. In a pool they more resembled an actual suit, but here in the wild they seemed to prefer "pretty" over practical.

Watching the sailboat slide down a mighty wave, I rose up after it. It was listing to the side, looking like it might capsize at any moment. Then the wave was past and another smashed across it. I was amazed at its resilience. It fought off the wave, it hadn't yet been beaten by the tossing sea. But having taken on a lot of water it was close to giving up the fight. With this next wave it was tipping badly, one end of it underwater. It would capsize soon. As horrible as it seemed, I was loving floating in the rolling sea, riding to the top of giant swells with an endless ocean about me. It seemed incredible that anyone would sail to a place like this.

Here again, I was sure I wasn't here to observe. Swimming towards the boat I tried to determine how I'd get aboard. The boat swung around and I had to duck a smaller craft tied up to the back, a rough longboat with an old black engine – hijacker? Realizing I might be going into danger, I cast my vision through the boat, attuning to what lay within.

Three young twenty-something women, trapped aboard, stuffed into closets and bound. One of them badly injured… *beaten?* And nobody else. Water was in the hold, and I heard the girls cry out as the craft listed hard, swinging around its loose rudder, nearly heeling the sailboat over. One girl struggled simply to breathe as the air shifted angles in the narrow confines she was held in.

I was wasting time.

In an instant's decision, I would ride a coaster up and leap, as a dolphin might jump, to land aboard without being swept over with the wave. It didn't take much to dive down and then run up towards the surface. I catapulted up just as a wave was cresting to drive the boat. No, too high and I slammed into the sail, Ow! It was far easier than I'd thought, the leaping, and then I slid down, caught a rope and waited until the boom swung over the deck to drop. On landing, I thought I would skid across the slippery deck, but I thankfully stuck to it.

The boom with the main sail bounded off the wires and slammed back. Ducking it, I realized I had to get the boat under control or its own frantic throes would capsize it. I had to get it facing into the wind and then worry about the rest after. Going for one of the two tiller wheels, it took all my effort to restrain the spinning wheel and then begin to steer the sailboat around. It responded, but the craft was tremendously slow. The thing had taken on a lot of water and felt fat. I knew little about sailing, but knew enough from Uncle Arlo that sailing into the wind (and waves) would keep it from flipping. It turns out I didn't know enough, for tightening the sail only made it heel over more as I tried rounding on the wind. So I chose instead to flee with the wind. That too was a mistake as waves started crashing over the stern and into the cabin below.

Feeling the boat under some kind of control, the prisoners started calling for help and shouting instructions. I couldn't understand the directions, or more specifically, how to do what they said. I'd never sailed anything before. I'd only seen Uncle do it when I was a kid. I did the only thing I knew to do. I let go of the wheel and went in search of those who knew what to do. The room below was so flooded with barely any room to breathe that it was hard to believe the craft still floated. Fortunately, I didn't need air the way a normal girl did and dove under, seeking those who did. "Who needs help the most?" I called through the water.

"Help, who is that?" one asked.

"Never mind that! Help Jordan! She has almost no air! Forward and to port," the other said.

I went to the closet they had indicated. There was no air here, and the door was wedged closed. "I'm coming Jordan. Hold on and I'll get you out!" I called through the door. How did Jill give people air? She could share air with others so they could have air while underwater, but I'd not figured out how to do that yet.

Attuning to the girl, I felt her squeezed in vertically. I winced, sensing her injuries, and was tied up. I felt ill as I felt her incredible pain. How she kept going, I wasn't sure. At least there was air trapped in there with her.

Someone had jammed oars against each girl's door, keeping them closed. This had been done deliberately, but why abandon them? It didn't make sense. Why go to the effort of getting a beautiful boat forcefully from the owners only to abandon it? Hearing the swinging boom, I thought perhaps they'd been knocked overboard.

It didn't matter, in any case. I had to free these girls and worry about any others another time. Sitting with my back to the wall and my feet on the oar, I pushed with my legs until I felt I might knock the wall down before the oar gave an inch. But then it was moving and floated free.

Swimming to her door, I put my hand on it, feeling for her, ready to catch her when the door opened. "Ok, Jordan. I'm about to open the door," I spoke softly to her, feeling her take the encouragement. She nodded, and I wondered if she thought I could see her. "Take a breath, the cabin is full of water." Then when she'd breathed in and was holding her breath, I reached for the handle, saying "Hold on, here we go."

I needn't have bothered, the sailboat spun, sending the two of us tumbling across the room. Without the oar holding the door closed, it swung open under her weight. Knowing she needed my help, I oriented quickly, taking ahold of her and taking the brunt of her fall – she'd lost her air. I gave her air from my lungs in the only way I knew, mouth to mouth.

Then taking a breath myself from the water, I shared air with her again. I'd been taught lifeguarding techniques, but I'd never done it underwater before.

Her silver blue eyes surrounded by a halo of dark hair were big as she tried to fathom where I was getting the air. Then, I was grabbing her around the waist and pulling her out towards the steps. Bound as she was, she was no help, but I didn't care. I had strength for the two of us. The boat shifted, but I kicked through the water to compensate and then we arrived at the steps. A great load of water swept into the room, trying to bowl us over. I would have none of it and forced our way up through the temporary mighty stream, taking her with me to the top step.

She looked around at the sea on a level with the deck and looked to me, then down into the hold. She couldn't hear the cries of her friends for help, but I could. "Don't worry," I told her. "They live." Tears came to her eyes, and she nodded. Releasing her gag, I pulled it down over her chin.

"Thank you," she said hugging me as best she could. "Untie me, so I can get the lady turned into the wind." Right, exactly what I'd failed to do.

With want for a knife, I started in on her wrist's ropes, the whole time she was staring at me in wonder. I didn't blame her, I probably would have stared too. It took longer than I'd hoped, but at last the rope slid free. With her wrists free, she began working on her other bonds. Then the craft leaned hard on its side, sending her tumbling into me and then into the water of the hold. Seeing life vests and raincoats bound against the wall, I pulled a vest off and thrust it at her. Keeping her upright, I guided us back to the steps.

"Put the vest on," I ordered her. The last thing I needed was for her to wash overboard in her state without one. Helping her get it on, she looked wild with concern, wanting to get out to steer the craft, but I insisted. Then when it was tied in place, she frogged it out and across the deck. Washing with a wave and grabbing a rope, she slid into place at a tiller with practiced agility. Then I went for her friends.

The craft may have gone over with the next wave, but we'll never know. Jordan was the captain and when she got a hold of the tiller she began working miracles. Her friends were each in similar storage compartments, bound but had managed to remove their gags themselves. Sharing air once I freed them, I worked quickly to free their hands and then helped them out of the room. But first "a life vest," I insisted.

The last girl free, we went above. From there, I worked at freeing the captain's legs and their other bonds. Jordan had managed to lower the main-sail but it was billowing in the wind, another hazard, and she pitched the craft so as to keep its bow upwind. Waves continually crashed over the bow, but no more water was going below decks. I learned their names as Jordan shouted to them. Lorin, a long blond ponytailed girl, swung wild out on a rope to free the main sail so that they could tie it to the boom. Billy, curly brown hair escaping her French braid hauled sail on the jib.

Once they had the boat steady, Billy relieved Jordan, who came over and sat beside me. "Who are you? Where you from?"

I smiled and shook my head, asking instead "What do you need to do next?" I didn't feel like sharing. I knew I'd be leaving soon, but I wanted to make sure they were ok first. The jet was gone from the sky, and I needed to get back to it before it landed. Jill had told me to leave when the doing was done. I'd thought I'd understood her before, but now I knew. Jordan was speaking, "I'm sorry what?" I asked her.

She smiled at me, rolling her eyes, "We have to get the pump going. There's an electrical short somewhere. The Dancing Lady," she said, patting the sailboat with her hand and running her hands over its broad sides in love, "isn't done yet. Dad designed her. He'll be so glad to hear it really worked, though it was close. Another few minutes…"

"Are you sure you won't tell me…?" she asked, and when I shook my head no. "Fine, ok," she said, touching my knee and gave it a squeeze. "Let's try the pump first. The problem is it is down at the bottom." She gave me this look that said, I was going to have to be her air and did she really experience me giving her air out of nothing.

I nodded, "Sure. We can do that."

Then taking my hand, she led me back into the main cabin. Diving into the rolling waters, she shed the life preserver and stowed it, then guided us down to a hatch in the floor. Turning the handle, she lifted the hatch and gazed down. It was dark. There was no light. She wouldn't be able to, something – I didn't understand her hand gestures. Pointing up, she made to rise. I went up with her.

When we surfaced, Jordan said, "I need to get a flashlight. It's too dark, and unless you're an electrician I'm going to have to do this myself." I shook my head, and then she was kicking her way out.

In a moment she was diving back in. I dove with her. Giving her air at the door, we both went in feet first. We were down in a crawl space above the keel. She shined the light around at the things floating about. I could tell she was upset. They'd been robbed. Turning to me, she pulled me close and exhaled. I felt like an air bag suddenly as she drew on me, though it felt good to be giving someone life. Leading us down through the debris, we shifted things forward until we had a clear view of the pump. The pump wires were free, attached to another device.

From Jordan's expression I expected it wasn't theirs. Her eyes told the story. I was tempted then to get her to talk, but I wanted her to figure it out. It didn't look like a bomb, but I wouldn't know one if I saw one. Pointing up, we repeated our route until we were floating in the cabin.

There was a question in her eyes, "What do you think?"

I shrugged, "I don't know really."

"Well, I have to disconnect it and reattach the wires to the pump. I'll need the tools." Then breathlessly, she said with a lot of excitement, "I can't believe we're doing this. It's like out of a movie." Then she was swimming to the stairs out, dove and fished a chest out from a hatch in the stairs that I never would have seen. As I watched her swim about, I marveled at her hiding the pain she was feeling. Simply pushing it aside to do as needed doing. What an adventurer she made! I would love to sail with her.

"The tools are in order," she grinned coming back to me, showing them off. "So, they… never mind," and I watched her face grow dark for a second before she pushed it aside. "Let's go." Then we were diving again and skinning our way back into the hatch.

Arriving at the pump, she gave me the light to hold for her so her hands were free. Then embracing me, she gathered her air and then quickly set to undoing the bolts that held the wire clips. A couple quick turns and they were released. Surprisingly, the device didn't float free. Looking for what held it, we saw it was affixed to the hull by a couple angle brackets like the other devices seen about. No other brackets were missing, so what was this?

Seeing a rise of bubbles, I braced myself for Jordan as she held me again, giving me a sorry look. She had a real need. Second hand air must not be as good as real air, but it was all I could give her. Then she let go and bent to securing the wires to the pump's control box. Lastly, she gave a tug of the wires to be sure they were snug, then with a last exchange of air she surprised me with a private moment to really hug me. Staring into my eyes, trying to figure me out and then she kicked off the bottom to go up.

I followed her out, and then swam with her to the steps. Together we looked out of the cabin. Billy had the tiller and gave us a wave. Jordan jogged over, slid in beside her and said, "Let's hope this works." Then flipping a switch, she leaned out over the rear of the boat, scaring me.

Running my hands across the boom, I ran out to the edge to see what she was looking at. The water was only a couple inches or so from the deck as it bubbled away behind us. "There," she pointed to a hole.

It was at least a minute, and then she turned to look at the panel at the yellow light above the switch. "C'mon - work!" Then there was a dribble out of the hole, followed by a cough, and then a steady stream. "It's working!" Jordan yelled, getting up and dancing. Spinning me about a couple times, she stopped. "Let's hope it's enough."

"The solar panels Dad designed for us should provide what we need," Lorin said. "There's plenty of day left." Holding her belly as it made a noise we all laughed at, she added, "I'm starving." The danger seemed over as they started thinking about food, and the pump was busy getting the water out.

"I want some new clothes on," Billy said joining us. They were all wearing a variation of shorts and sailing shirts that dried fast.

"Soon," Jordan told them. Billy and Lorin seemed to take their cues from Jordan and relaxed. But Jordan was looking at me, then she was saying "Lorin, go see what can be salvaged for food. Billy, the hold has missing gear. See what we can recover from that," and she hooked a thumb at the longboat they were hauling. "Then let's cut it away."

I helped Billy draw the boat to the sailboat, then Billy leaped from the sailboat landing roughly, before nimbly moving through the boat peeking under tarps. She called, "It appears to be ours plus some other things!"

"It's much too rough to shift anything," I said to Jordan as we rolled over another giant crest.

She gave me a surprised look that I didn't get a chance to interpret before she said, "You're right," but I could see her wanting to get rid of the boat as soon as possible. It certainly would be difficult to sail with it pulling at them.

Lorin had come back and stood there looking between us holding a bag of dried apples, then she looked at Jordan and gave her a report. "It's too deep to determine what food stuffs we have for the long haul, but I did salvage some fruit." Then she opened the bag and shared. Hauling Billy back, we sat eating until the bag was empty.

Then Jordan sat next to me, so close that I turned to look at her. She had a pleading look in her face, but she couldn't say what it was. She only turned to look at the longboat. "What?" I asked her, but she wouldn't say. But her eyes were bugging out like she wanted to ask me a favor, but didn't dare.

I turned to look at Lorin, who shrugged. And then to Billy who hadn't seen the exchange. Billy said, "Let's get the longboat emptied before nightfall." I felt Jordan go still beside me. When I looked at her, she had gone white and had her eyes closed. I could see the wisdom in Billy's request.

"But the sea is so rough…" I started.

But Billy interrupted me, saying "We can do it."

I looked to them, Lorin didn't see what the fuss was about and Jordan nodded with the kindest face she could put on, but said nothing. They were looking to me for permission. Somehow I'd usurped Jordan's leadership, and seeing that they wanted to do it, I nodded, saying, "Ok."

"Thank you," Jordan said finally able to say something and squeezed my knee again. "Thank you. Let's do it!"

We hauled rope again, pulling the other craft near. And then with practiced ease, they moved it alongside the sailboat. We ran some rubber tubes between them so they wouldn't bang together and tied them bow to stern. In seconds Billy was over and unlashing tarps, folding them up and tossing them over. Then watertight storage containers were being passed over. They all disappeared into the cabin that had to be emptying out by now. Then when the longboat was empty, Jordan went over to double check pulling at anything that wasn't permanent.

"Good," she said happily. Then taking its ropes, coiling them, they kicked it away.

With the longboat drifting away, I felt a desire to dive into the ocean. But my heart desired to stay with my new friends. It was like that time in the jungle with Jill, then it was she that had known it was time to leave. I'd wanted to stay, but Jill knew when to cut and run. Yet, I found myself sitting back beside Jordan and listening to her and Billy hum a tune they knew. Lorin had the lights on, and I smelled food. In what seemed minutes, she was handing out plates. I tried to demur, but they insisted. When the plate was empty, I whipped my head about, staring at the sea. It was calling me and I couldn't stay any longer.

Putting down the plate and standing, I stood to the edge of the sailboat. I had their gazes as they sat with fork held in midair food uneaten. "It's time I left," I told them. Then before any of us could cry or they protest, I turned and dove in a long arc. I rose to give them a wave. I watched them go, and then they rode up a large wave and over it. That was the last I saw of them.

Turning, I dove into the sea, quickly putting distance between us. Then I was feeling the aircraft there beneath the sea, impossibly, but it was becoming more real to me than the ocean. It seemed to be floating there still in the water, but I knew it had to be traveling fast. Swimming to it and putting my hand to the top of the craft, my hand went through it and I pulled myself within. Most everyone was asleep, but a few were reading or talking.

Nobody saw me as I swam above their heads. Soon I was "swimming" into my seat, wriggling into my clothes under the blanket as the water became air. I was settling into my place just in time. The pilot announced we would soon be landing, waking Dad. He was still groggy from the airsickness pill he'd taken.

Ri'Anne gave me a look, asking with her expression "why was my hair wet?" but I had nothing for her.

Me? I wanted to sleep and I closed my eyes in an attempt to get a few winks. But there was a bump as the pilot put down the wheels followed shortly by the jarring bump as the jet touched down. Sitting up and holding my stomach I wondered if I was going to be ill again. Thankfully there were no more bumps.

Needless to say I wasn't going to get any rest.

3

Arrival, Papua New Guinea

Winding our way out of the plane, we were some of the last to disembark. I think Dad was hoping to hear from Uncle, but there was no word. The oppressive heat hit me first and the next I was overdressed. Dad had swapped to shorts and a Hawaiian shirt before landing.

"It's hot, Dad," I said waving air over my face, staring at the offending morning sun. We'd lost a day traveling west and at the speed of our travel it was now early. Normally an early riser, I now had another long day to get through before I could sleep.

"I warned you," and looking around he led us over between two baggage carts and told me to change. "You're wearing your suit?" I nodded. "You're always wearing that," and that was the last thing I needed, was for Dad to insist I ditch the fish suit. So I said under my breath, "Fish, something new," and I thought about a bikini in some colorful island design.

When I removed my jeans and shirt, I was surprised to see I had exactly that, and I was immediately comfortable in the island heat. Ri'Anne decided to dress down to her suit as well. I had my hip sarong to wear, but she had to wear her shirt the same way. Dad took our discarded things and stuffed them in a cart, never to be seen again.

Ri'Anne gave me a look, "Where did I get the suit?"

It's the fish, I mouthed. The fish I'd given her in the car.

"Um, where'd you get that suit? From Jill?" Dad asked me. "That girl has too many suits." That part was true. Companies donated suits to the gym Jill's parents owned, though they were mostly for the younger kids. I'd gotten to borrow a few. I didn't like deceiving Dad, but I couldn't tell him the truth. Actually, I hadn't said it was Jill's. He'd assumed it.

I stood next to Ri'Anne while she examined the colorful suit she now wore. "I wonder what they're saying," Ri'Anne said of the baggage handlers that were eyeing us while we changed.

I'd understood the handlers, but hadn't paid them much attention. "It seems mostly about work and us girls. I think they are impressed. Most American girls are weird to their minds. Mostly though, they complain of the heat and wish they could get out of the clothes the airlines make them wear, the same as us."

"You understand them?" she asked sidling up beside me.

I nodded. "Part of being a mermaid," I told her.

A couple bold baggage handlers came to offer to carry our packs. I was handing mine over, Ri'Anne about to do likewise when Dad picked them from us. “You can’t be too careful, Melanie,” Dad scolded me.

“It’s not like there is anything valuable in them, Dad,” I countered. “A few hair ties, some art supplies and a sketch pad.”

Getting between us and them, he guided us with nudges towards the terminal, repeating himself, “You can’t be too careful. Besides, where are you going to get those supplies here, if they are stolen?”

I nodded, true. But inwardly I wept.

Now I knew why he’d packed the supplies. He saw Ri’Anne and I doing art aboard Uncle’s yacht, not helping with the dives. I wanted to prove to him that we could help, but I hadn’t figured out how yet. Just a bit ago I’d been sailing in the beautiful sea, carefree and assured, on a mission sent, I suppose by The Lord of the Water, trusted to help those in need. Those older girls accepted me and had wanted me to stay, and here Dad’s behavior made me wish I could have.

About halfway between the terminal and our jet, which sat like a lonely bird, Dad stopped us give a few quick language lessons in between yawns. All of us were dead on our feet. The jet lag, Dad for oversleeping and Ri’Anne and I for not having slept at all. The lesson consisted of, “Yes, No, thank you and bathroom. Food and drink.” We each repeated what he said. “In this culture, women don't walk around unescorted and you should have a hat at the least. But we should be out and down to the docks quickly. It’s not like we’ll be visiting any of the villages.”

At the door, the man that opened the door said to Dad as we went through before him, “Father of daughters I feel for you. But your women are improper, get them covered or be cheated.”

"What?" Dad said in English and then the "thank you" he'd taught us, but it came out sounding like "Bread sandwich." Then he followed us in. I thought the man had been nice to warn Dad.

"What did he say?" Ri'Anne asked.

Dad shook his head saying, "I'm not sure."

My first test. Did I try to steer Dad into making proper choices. The problem was, what was proper?

By being last to arrive from the jet, we were stuck behind those that were delayed in security. Dad handed us a piece of paper that had some details, but mostly it was blank. "Fill in your name," he told us. Then he led us through other details like where we were staying, etc. Nor were we staying long. When we reached the desk, the clerk passed us through without a hitch. Then we were into the airport proper. It wasn't on the level with Denver's airport, but it had air conditioning and some market stalls to which Dad ushered us so we could purchase some items.

I tried observing what other American women were doing, but they apparently had no clue either. Though I did see one woman arguing with a vendor about the price. Is that what the man had been kind enough to suggest? The vendor was clearly overcharging the lady.

"Melanie, don't wander off," Dad told me. I'd stayed to see the outcome of the exchange. I had wanted to ask the seller what was going on. "The prices here are expensive," Dad complained, handing us each a hat and Ri'Anne a wrap to replace the shirt she'd been wearing as a skirt. I didn't really want to wear the hat, but I did as instructed.

4

Charlie

Above the noise of the crowds waiting for their planes, I heard a boy shouting, sounding really upset, “Let me go, let me go, let me go!” and I twirled to look who was being so abused. Look as I may, I couldn't see the kid. Then I heard the boy again, but it was a bird beating its wings trying to peck at a man for holding a strap tied to its leg.

“Oh isn't he pretty,” gushed Ri’Anne following my gaze. “Can we see?” she asked Dad. Dad paused a second, looking at his watch.

“We have time,” he nodded and we went to look.

Seeing the crowd he was drawing, the bird cried all the louder, and the man was at his wits end with the raucous bird. “I should just cage you,” he complained to the bird. The man looked like he'd just come back from a safari in his rakish gear and unshaven face. His curly, slightly greying hair curled over his ears. His sunglasses pushed back atop his head. He reminded me of an actor as I eyed his khaki shorts and brown leather sandals.

"Oh don't do that," I told him, leaning forward with Ri'Anne to gaze at the creature. I'm not quite sure what Ri'Anne saw in him, he was mostly grey, very fussy and not at all pretty.

Seeing the bird pecking at the man's hand again, I asked him, "May I?" holding my hand out to take the bird. I realized too late that I was overstepping myself, but I felt a need to fix the situation between the bird and his owner.

"He bites," the man warned.

"Hush," I told the bird. "You wouldn't bite me would you?" The bird turned on me at being addressed. Able to speak to all creatures, man and beast, had its benefits.

"Bite? I'd rip your…" and then seeing me, his voice changed octaves going through the roof before he squawked a, "No Madame! No, no – I'm so sorry. If it pleases you, it would be my extreme pleasure to rub my head on your cheek," he positively purred rolling his eyes and ducking his head embarrassed.

Ever since I'd begun to understand animals, having the bird talking like everyone else was normal. In fact I found animals the more reasonable. Humans tended to hedge and not say what they meant. Also animals knew me for who I was – somehow they knew me to be a mermaid.

Deciding to ignore his threat and embrace his wish to be nice, I held out my hand and told him, "Good, come here then." The bird tested its wings, and as the man gave him slack, he flew in a nice glide to my hand.

“Careful Melanie,” said Dad, “And nice Irish accent, by the way.”

Oops! The downside to being able to speak with any animal or human is that most times I didn’t know I was doing it with people because their words were all English to me.

The bird was hopping in my hand, preening and trailing the cord. Tossing out its wings the furthest it could, he gave me a graceful bow saying, “Madame, I'm a cockatiel, and my name is Charlie.” He then gave me an eye, still ducking his head slightly. Finally assured that I’d forgiven him, he pranced lightly up my arm to my shoulder. Sidling sideways, he stopped to rub my cheek with his head once, and then again just as he'd promised.

The man and the crowd were looking at me with wonder. “Now Charlie,” I said holding out my hand out in front of me, inviting him to it. When he'd flown to it and turned to face me, I asked him, “What seems to be the problem?”

“He, he, he!” Charlie exclaimed getting more and more upset with each word that he finally had to stop. Then with his gray wings snapping to his back said, “He thinks me a girl and keeps calling me Suzi!”

I laughed, “Really, all this fuss because he calls you Suzi?”

“And he thinks me a girl,” he added indignantly.

“It's not because he keeps you tied up?” I asked concerned.

“Oh no Mistress. He feeds me well, and he lets me loose most times. He's just thinking I may fly away in this place. I could make it really difficult on him. Oh,” Ri’Anne petted him. “Careful of the feathers Miss,” he said to her. Then a boy made a grab for him, but Charlie was quicker. He flew to the top of my head laughing raucously at the boy's attempt. Then from there he gave the boy a scolding from my forehead. With each word he walked down my nose. I was going cross-eyed looking at him.

The bird's owner stood to take Charlie back, "Come along, Suzi," and the bird rolled his eyes, giving me an upside-down look, "See!" Charlie pecked at the man's hand.

"Ow! Dang bird!"

"Easy, Charlie," I said, lifting him off my nose with a finger. "You be nice to him," I scolded.

"If you insist Mistress, but it would be so much nicer if he called me Charlie, hint, hint." Charlie was still hanging upside down off my finger.

I felt a tap on my shoulder that I recognized, "Melanie, let the man have his bird back," Dad told me.

Holding out Charlie, I told him, "Here sir, sorry."

Taking the bird gently, he stared in wonder that the bird didn't peck his hand. "What did you do, miss?" The man placed the bird on his shoulder, afraid at any second he would lose his ear. Charlie gave me a sour look and turned to look over the room.

"He just likes me, I guess," I said shrugging.

Charlie answered back, "Not anymore… Mistress."

"Charlie, cheer up and be a good boy, it could be worse," I said speaking to the man, but looking at the bird, hoping I would get the right translation.

"She's a he? And how do you know his name?"

I shrugged, "He told me, and shouldn't he know his own name?"

"Well, it used to be Screech! But I like Charlie better," Charlie explained.

"That was a wonder," Dad said as we walked off, leaving the man with his bird watchers. "I never knew you liked birds. What kind was it?"

"A cockatiel," I replied before I could guard my words. I was saying too much!

"And you know that?" Then Dad read my expression, "Because it told you?" I shrugged. What else could I say?

5

Taxi

We exited the air conditioning into the sweltering heat. It felt surprisingly good, but the air was clogged with pollution and I switched on my attuning to see if I could do something about that. Taking a tentative breath after a second, I encountered fresh air. I inhaled more deeply, "Ah!" Such lovely scents filled the air now that the smog was gone, reminding me of France.

Colorful flowers grew from big white circular planters on the sidewalk and from many trees on either side. Gathered around the planters or waiting under the trees people were leaning, waiting for friends and family with their luggage stacked at their feet. Heat shimmered off the pavement, and we stopped to view the empty waiting area before venturing into the sun.

Looking at his watch, Dad sighed, "Arlo should have met us." Flipping up his phone for the hundredth time, he looked for a missed call or text. Gazing off into the distance, I could see his mind whirling. Then he eyed the line of taxis waiting for customers. Dad loved taxis, and he smiled at getting to go for a ride, "I suppose we could catch a cab to the port. That would save a trip for your uncle," and he guided us towards the waiting cabs.

There was an invisible line, marked by a pole that had no signs, a line of people waited by it. To the left was clear of taxis, and to the right taxis were lined up into the distance with their drivers standing nearby, calling out to us. Another line marked the distance they'd go from their cabs, but this one wasn't obvious as some cabbies went further than others. Each was calling out their fare and how reasonable they were compared to their fellows.

Every time they hawked their prices, I felt uncomfortable. Analyzing the feeling, I realized I dreaded getting into any of their cabs. But Dad looked so excited that I pushed down the feeling until we reached the first one.

"Not that one dad."

"What, why? And don't say the bird told you. I've had about enough…" Then shaking his head, "Sorry. It's the heat."

On reaching the next one, it was variable shades of the dread. At one of the cabs I literally grabbed Dad's arm, looking down and not meeting the cabbie's eyes. When Dad questioned me, I could only shake my head. I couldn't explain why I was feeling this way. Except when I did look the drivers in the eyes, I saw shadows, but I couldn't exactly say that.

We'd left the airport proper, and Dad finally swung me aside. "Come on Melanie," he insisted. "We have to get to the port. Any of these will be fine."

"Not them, Dad," I insisted, but he was done with me.

"Melanie!" I turned, and Dad was talking with a driver. I came up, heard the man saying, "Sixty per kilometer," but not in good English, almost like he was intentionally trying to speak badly. Then, saying to himself in his native tongue, it came across loud and clear, "This be my lucky day. Ignorant tourists."

I gripped dad's arm hard. "Dad, not him. He's cheating us. He will go a long route and scam us. If we get there at all."

"Melanie, stay out of it! He says he can take us to the port. Hop in. And look, your friend with the bird is grabbing a taxi too. We'll be fine…"

"What was that about?" Ri'Anne asked as we slid in, she was looking worried.

I sat back, "We're going on a premature adventure." I pretty much was saying goodbye to our bags. At least Dad had our travel documents in his pocket.

Dad slid in on the other side, with me in the middle. "Melanie is just being a worrywart." I really hoped that was the case.

The driver sat down, shut his door and started the car.

On the way out of the city, in a way that looked like the right way, the driver said to himself, which I presumed was in his local language, "Kill the man, take their things and be back in no time. Nobody will know. Yes…"

He was laughing to himself, and when we made an obvious turn away from the city it was too late. When Dad finally said something, "Hey, the port is that way," I was thinking, *Poor dad, still trying to reason your way out.* We were in trouble, but the guy insisted even as we drove into the jungle, "This is short-cut," and laughed to himself as Dad leaned back, relaxing.

"It's a short-cut," Dad said. Ri'Anne stuck her hand in mine and I squeezed back. We rumbled over a bridge and then made a hard turn down towards the river onto a road that was barely a road down to a flat beside a churning river. He spun the vehicle around saying, "Wrong turn," but I saw him reach under his seat.

"Out," I cried, and pushed on Ri'Anne's door. It was easy for us, as the door flung open, we were on the outside of the turn – pushed out by the momentum. Ri'Anne and I poured out. Dad wasn't as lucky as the taxi came to a stop. Pulling Ri'Anne, I urged her, "Run!" We ran towards the trees for shelter.

"Melanie!" Dad cried, "What are you doing?"

I had a last view of Dad staring at a handgun, before Ri'Anne and I reached the trees. Dodging back through the brush, we came to a stop, panting from the fright. We stared into the seemingly endless jungle and leaned back against the closest tree regaining our breaths.

Ri'Anne screamed next to me, pointing up and falling to her butt. She curled up shrinking back from the biggest, hairiest spider I have ever seen descending on a web towards us, it had the face of a cat. I started to scream too, but its high-pitched hissy scary voice stayed me, "We comes Mistress. My sisters, we help."

Gulping, I with weak knees asked quavering in reply, "You'll help?"

Ugh, it came down to face height, did a 180 on its thread and looked right at me. "We help," it insisted. "Throw me. Please, I want to help."

Closing my eyes I held up my hand and it landed in my palm, eww. "There," it said skittering around on my palm. I bit my lip at the sensation. I'm surprised I didn't faint, I should have gone toes up. "Now throw me, and we do the rest."

Gulping, I opened my eyes and told it, "Hold on, and thank you."

"Thank you Mistress. Weeee," I pulled my hand back and it tucked into a ball and I threw it towards the car. In mid-air it unfurled and let out a strand to drift on the wind down to where it, and eww, other spiders were crawling towards and into the car.

"Get out now!" the man cried on seeing the spiders moving towards him. Then as Dad got out, the man put the car into gear, it spitting mud and rocks, roared up the road.

"I can't believe you touched it," Ri'Anne said when I helped her to stand.

"I can't either."

Ri'Anne and I came out of hiding. We stood next to Dad, "He was going to kill us," Dad said, defeated. "What was I thinking bringing the two of you along? When Arlo said he wanted you to come and bring a friend, I thought you would enjoy it. But now... He took our money and passports." Then there was a loud crashing sound.

Dad took off running, saying "Stay here." But after a few feet, he waved for us to follow, "Come on. I can't leave you here. Hurry!"

Soon we were passing him. "You're out of shape Dad," I said coming alongside him.

We found the car and a bunch of cat-faced spiders crawling on it, they looked pleased with themselves. Dad took off his shoe and moved in towards the car, but I couldn't let him hurt them saying "Dad, just our bags. Leave them alone, they helped us."

Giving me a look that said I was crazy, he paused and looked at the car. The spiders were crawling back into the forest. "They're leaving," he said in disbelief putting his shoe back on.

I came alongside the car, Ri'Anne right behind me, leaning on the taxi. Then Ri'Anne's eyes rolled up and I thought she'd give up the ghost as our spider hero crawled up her arm to her shoulder. "Thank-you Mistress, that was fun," it said.

Waving it to join its friends, I told it, "Go on and thanks!" and with that the spider jumped off Ri'Anne and ran off the car and back to the closest tree to scurry up it.

Dad was in the car and handing out bags. When we had them, he stopped to check on the driver. "I think he's alive, but the car is a wreck. We have some walking ahead of us." Dad had his hand on the guy's gun.

"What are you going to do with that Dad?"

"We're not out of this yet," he said taking the gun, putting it in his bag and climbing out of the car. Looking around, he put his bag over his shoulder and took off walking back to the road.

"Come on, I think it's this way," he said, taking the lead back over the bridge.

6

Ride to Town

"I hate leaving the car," Dad said making conversation. "I love driving old beat up cabs like her. There's something special about a taxi that has seen many miles. All of their passengers. I feel their history, my imagination runs wild with the thoughts of all the places it has been. You may talk to birds, but the taxi is telling me to go on with life, as it has said many thousands of times over the course of its life. It doesn't begrudge us walking away, but would welcome us back if it were ever to be put back into service."

"The taxi has to care for the drivers too," Ri'Anne said as she tried to cheer Dad up. "Helping the driver fulfill their dreams, raise their families and even carry some of the groceries. Sending their kids off to college and stuff," her imagination failing her as she tried to come up with other things a taxi did.

"Right," Dad said, letting us catch up. He put his arms around the two of us, as hot as it was. "We have the whole world before us now girls. I might get bogged down in the details of life, but never forget that we can go anywhere and do anything. Though always bring a friend. Life is best shared. And if you're fresh out of friends, make new ones."

All around us grew the verdant jungle, hot and steamy. I was glad we'd exchanged our clothes for the fish suits—they breathed well. I could just imagine if I was wearing the jeans I'd worn in the jet, I'd be dying. The road we were following paralleled the river and I wanted so badly to dive in!

"We could just follow the river to the ocean," Ri'Anne suggested.

"Sure, or swim in it…" I offered. It was a good idea, anything to get us back on track to meeting Uncle Arlo at the port.

"Through a spider infested jungle?" Dad questioned. He knew us girls so well, there were webs all through the trees down to the river. But with the recent experience with the cat-faced spiders, I was willing. "Besides," Dad added, "I bet when it rains the river floods. It would be too dangerous."

We left the side of the river as the road went further into the jungle and we grew quiet in the noonday heat. Then, on hearing the bustle of people, Dad picked up the pace and we came over a rise to see a wider road with people trekking along it. Dad looked excited, and hurried down to the road. Following along, we heard him asking directions, but none spoke English. And those that pretended to gave poor guidance.

It was difficult lettings us be steered wrong, but I'd already said too much already. At least they weren't trying to cheat us. It is just that nobody understood the other well enough, but without revealing that I understood, I couldn't help.

Of course, the people talked about the lost tourist with his two oddly dressed daughters, and that part I was glad to pretend to be ignorant of.

After following their guidance for about two hours, Dad grew unsettled, sure that we were going the wrong direction. But there was no going back. We'd made too many wrong turns to find the way now. It didn't bother Ri'Anne or myself, we were enjoying the sights. Seeing us, he asked, "How can you be so happy? We're completely lost."

"Because it's so beautiful Dad. And I've never been here before and maybe never again. We'll find our way eventually – so why worry about it?"

"You've been spending too much time with Arden. He loves the world too much."

I shrugged saying, "He is my coach. Besides, if you want me to stop…" I could see Dad getting upset. I shouldn't have provoked him.

"Melanie, don't put words in my mouth. You are much too compliant. I wish sometimes you'd argue with me." I raised an eyebrow at this, what would that solve?

He swung his fists at the air above him, and then came down to where he could be civil, saying, "No, I want you to remain on the swim team. Really, what are you thinking – quitting? That doesn't sound like you.

"Sorry, I'm so frustrated," he said. Putting an arm around me, he said, "You are right, though. It is beautiful here." Dad drew Ri'Anne in. "And we'll be ok."

"Beep, beep!" A flatbed truck came around the corner behind us, loaded with people. Many had their feet hanging over the sides, though a load of boys were perched on the roof of the truck. The driver called, "Ride anyone?" The locals were quick to load up when it came to a stop.

Dad gave a worried look, and then decided to risk it. "Come on," and he hoisted us up and then climbed aboard himself. "It can't get much worse and my feet are killing me."

Settling in the middle, Dad made sure we sat beside him. Then once the truck moved on, he sighed saying, "I haven't walked so much in ages." Taking off his shoes, he began to rub his feet.

A woman elbowed me, and held out a much-used container, "For his feet," she said. Taking it, I smiled thanks, and held it out for Dad.

"For your feet, Dad," I said to him, opening it to reveal a gray sludge.

"Very kind," Dad said to the woman. He dipped his fingers in and pulled out a heap of the goo. Then he handed me the container to give back to the woman. I watched as he spread the stuff over his feet. "Oh, ah. I feel better already."

"Thank you," I said softly, forgetting to use the "thank you" Dad had taught us. My feet were sore too, but more than anything I wanted to lie down and sleep.

The woman was young, short like Jill, relatively fit with dark hair that had been highlighted blond. She didn't take the "thank you" as expected and grabbed my arm, looking startled.

I pulled away. Even if I'd accidentally spoken her language, what was the big deal? Her eyes were wide, she dropped the container of goo staring at it, her hands shaking. Then she was looking at me. Muttering to herself she said things like, "It's not possible! Who does she think she is? She's putting me on," and then she realized I was listening to her ramble.

Moving closer, she whispered fiercely, "Who's your mother? Where are your kin?" Then when I didn't respond, she shouted, "I thought we were all lost! I thought I was the last, who are you?!" And more.

She was making a scene, and the others began saying in their own dialects, "What's she saying? Who is that? Why is she talking to the foreigners?"

"What did you do?" Dad asked tugging my elbow with a yawn.

"Said thank you. You told us to be nice," I temporized. Dad smiled and leaned back. "I'm gonna nap. I'm wiped. Don't go anywhere."

"You've done it now," Ri'Anne said from the other side of Dad. Now that he'd stuck out his legs, she stood and stepped across him to sit knee to knee with me. "Who is she?" she asked.

The woman was still carrying on, but softer, "Tell me, where you learn my language? Please, I must know. It's vitally important to me." I wasn't ignoring her, but it wasn't like I could answer her questions and get away with it.

"Hush mother," I tried to calm her, trying for an honorific. She went blue in the face, getting ready to screech again. Sensing that Dad was asleep I scolded her, "Hush, or I won't say another word."

Scowling, the woman knelt but was not cowed. "For three hundred and twenty years have I have walked this," and she swept her hands out to include the world. "Never in that time has a child spoken to me thus." Holding up a hand, she looked at my dad saying, "Your man sleeps." Then she examined Ri'Anne from head to toe and in conclusion said, "This girl, is she a friend? For she doesn't understand."

What the heck? Three hundred years!

Suddenly wary, who knew what an ancient such as this would know, or be able to do. Then the truck rumbled to a stop again and we all jerked forward as the driver braked. Then people were coming and going. There was no way to talk. Then we were on the way again. Dad was still sleeping. He'd slept so much on the plane, he should be wide awake. Or the stuff she gave for his feet had knocked him out, for he was asleep.

I looked over at her, "What did you do to him?"

"Me?" she said with feigned innocence. "The ointment is herbal, it relaxes the muscles."

"Nothing else?" I asked, knowing for sure there was something going on here. She didn't look a day over thirty. How was it that she'd lived so long?

"Well, you wouldn't talk while he was awake." I knew then it was something else. She'd given him the ointment before we'd talked in the first place.

"And what exactly am I supposed to be saying?" I asked exasperated. "You don't exactly come across as someone I should trust. Knocking Dad out. We've been robbed, almost mugged and we're a long way from home. I'm not in a trusting mood. But this is a beautiful country, and I'm glad we're getting to see some of it before we leave. Am I talking enough?" I was getting heated and tried to calm down by running my fingers flat over the sarong.

"I don't get it," she said. "You have perfect tonality, guttural soundings, and nasal consonants like you've spoken it your whole life, but I'm guessing it isn't your first language."

"Do you have to know?" I asked feeling my weariness. I had been awake for thirty-some hours and was feeling it. I didn't want to be having this conversation.

"My whole life, other than the early years I've sought someone that knows the old ways of our people. I've not heard my people's words from another since that time. Actually, I was pretty sure that even if there were descendants they would be speaking the tongue of the natives around them. Tell me of your people."

"My people? I come from the US of A. Beyond that you'd have to ask him who you put to sleep. And he doesn't speak this tongue as far as I know. Nor does my friend here," referring to Ri'Anne who was just looking at the rolling terrain and the green mist shrouded mountains. Along the way we'd rolled through a few villages where people got on and off. I didn't see anything resembling a city or even the sea or I would have awakened Dad to decide what to do.

"Well, I must be dreaming, for this isn't possible," she said repeating some of what she'd mumbled to herself.

I had to laugh at that saying, "Of course it's not, but it is. I didn't make the rules."

"What rules?" she looked at me in hope, to give her existence an anchor. I could only imagine living forever and not knowing why.

I shrugged giving her my best rationale, "That the impossible is possible, possibly."

"Well, in my travels," she went on to say now that we'd gotten past *introductions*. "I've seen some things that would surprise you, but nothing from myth or folklore. Nobody flies with wings, swims the sea, is taller than a building or can pass through walls."

I had to smile at how "little" she'd seen, since I personally had done two of those. But I turned the question on her, "And someone living for hundreds of years is normal?"

"Normal for me, so?" she answered. I had to nod and concede her point. If you didn't know better it might seem normal.

She was confiding in me, and I had to ask, "And do you go around telling everyone you meet? Because I'd guess that most of those that are that old don't say anything."

"You're right I never tell anyone." She shook her head and then looked at me earnestly. "You've disarmed me with your words. I'm addicted to hearing you speak. You speak with authority beyond your years. I want it to go on. I'd tell you anything. I've never met anyone like you, a child so, so… wise. It shouldn't surprise me that the answer to my life is to be found in a child." Then coming to a decision, looking at the sky, resigning herself to a future that wasn't of her own determination she said, "If it's not too much trouble I'd like to travel with you."

I frowned, thinking Dad wasn't going to like it. Then to Ri'Anne, she looked from the mountains to me as if sensing my attention. Putting the fingers of her right hand on my knee, she went back to gazing at the scenery.

Glancing from Dad to the woman, I asked her, "I'm not saying yes. It isn't for me to decide." Indicating it was Dad that made the decision. I wondered what Uncle Arlo would say. Deciding to cross that bridge when we arrived, it was no sure thing that Dad would permit it. Of Dad, I asked her, "But how are we supposed to communicate once he's awake?"

"You speak English?" she asked and I nodded. "Well, then that's settled," she said switching to English. Other than her accent, I couldn't tell a difference and that barely so. The problem with this language thing, everyone spoke English to my ears and it was hard for me to realize they spoke something else, including accents. And I spoke what I thought to be English, but they heard it as their language.

"That still doesn't get you accepted," I told her, "He, and ultimately his brother, my uncle, decide."

Holding up the can of salve she'd given Dad for his feet, she said, "I can be useful."

I shrugged. It was out of my hands but I felt like we'd just acquired another person, "Well, Uncle is a researcher. I'm sure he'd like to pick your brain. If you can prove your usefulness to him, I'm sure he'd let you along."

7

A Rat Eats My Apple

"No, absolutely not." Dad was putting his foot down when I explained.

"I can pay," and the woman who said her name was Gigi revealed some cash.

"Well, I can't stop you from following, but my brother is not very good with company. He mostly lives alone. We're along to give him a hand since he broke his leg in a freak accident."

"Aren't they all," Gigi said blandly, though I could tell she wasn't going to take no for an answer. I was intrigued by this "old" woman though that didn't mean I trusted her.

"What are?" Dad asked, not getting the rise out of her he had expected.

"Accidents," Gigi explained. "Nobody ever plans to have an accident. Freak accidents occur all the time."

He sighed trying to explain that her quest was useless, "Well my brother was diving a site and managed to break a leg, surface and get help. Then make it to port before succumbing to an island fever. It's a wonder he lived. Anyway, I'm sure he'll turn you away."

"So we're traveling by sea? I love water."

Dad gave up, and at the first decent-sized town he had us get off the truck and get a room for the night. He let the woman alone. I didn't blame him. I wasn't sure I wanted her along, interested as I was in her history. She was another reason to hide my abilities, when I didn't want to hide them at all. I kept attuning all day, afraid the woman might try a spell on me, but now that I lay to sleep beside Ri'Anne, I would have to let down my guard to get my rest.

As I lay there, I thought about sending to Jill for help with a bubble message, but I couldn't think of what to say. Then I sighed, thinking of Gigi in the other room. If a sending was traceable, then I'd be revealing myself to her and if attuning was, well – I'd been doing it when we met. So either it wasn't, or she couldn't tell. But I didn't want to chance it, so I let the desire to contact Jill go, and let myself wonder about Gigi and her people. Were they all long-lived like her?

Sleep claimed me quickly. Dad woke us in the morning early in an attempt to ditch Gigi. But she was up having coffee and offered Dad some.

"Well I've managed to figure out where we are," Dad said. "But that doesn't help us much. I've been talking with the proprietor. He did say there is a bus that will take us to the city. We have until eight, which gives us about an hour to look around before the bus arrives."

That time traveled fast as Dad wanted my picture in front of about every building, vehicle and animal in the town. I felt sorry for Ri'Anne, so far the trip hadn't been very fun. I wish she'd been included with the sailboat rescue, but she hadn't been and I was determined to include her in everything else that I could.

When I talked to her about how the not-so-fun trip was going so far, she said, "Are you kidding? This is great." Apparently I wasn't paying her enough attention. She went on to explain, "I could get lost in these hills and rain forests. The flowers are out of this world, there are so many colorful birds only seen in cages at home. And the traditional dresses that the ladies wear, well I wish we had them back home. I'm tired of 'fashion' dictating what we should wear. I'd love to have these native colorful outfits that the women wear."

"And ditch all your t-shirts and short-shorts you like so much?" I was clearly surprised.

"Oh definitely. This trip is an eye opener. We live in a little part of the world, and there is so much variety here." Talking about yesterday, she said, "I was observing some traditional girls our age on the ride down here. We'd be out of our minds to wear that back home. If I have the opportunity to return, I'm going to. Besides," she added with a sly smile, "you missed all the guys sitting at the front of the truck that wouldn't mind our numbers. You put them off though by the way you were talking with Gigi."

We were interrupted by the bus's bugle…

"Hoon-kah! Haaroo-gah!"

At the sound of a crazy circus horn, the bus arrived. Since Ri'Anne loved the terrain so much, I gave her the window seat. Dad sat across the aisle from us, and Gigi was somewhere else. Around noon, Dad passed out the lunch Gigi had cobbled together, proving herself already, determined to win Dad over.

Still suffering from jet-lag, my mind wandered and I failed to notice someone coming up next to me. "Excuse me, if you're not going to eat your lunch, can I have it?" asked a suave-sounding gentleman.

"Huh, what?" I turned around thinking the people behind me were talking to me…

"Miss, down here…"

A big ole rat, "Eeek!" I couldn't help it! I screamed and dropped the apple I'd partially eaten.

"I'm expecting you're wanting it back?" said the beady eyed rodent picking it up and gazing at me with meekness. His tone was so smooth it was hard to believe it was the creature speaking to me.

I shook my head no… Ugh!

"Thank you miss." His nose twitched and his whiskers wiggled – disgusting! His eyes misted over and then he reared back and took a huge bite. I gulped, feeling ill.

Then with apple crumbling out of his mouth, he said, "We'll be arriving at the port soon," and sniffed in a big whiff. "I've been smelling it for an hour." He hopped up to pat my knee, causing Ri'Anne to squeak, and he confided, "You should get off at one of the first three stops, after that it's the dumps. The dumps, oh!" He pretended like he'd swoon with the back of his hand to his forehead. "The fine meals, and the women…" Then he stopped acting like a cad and filled me in on what I would be missing. "Meeting my cousins from the city. We'll be up all night feasting on spoiled onions and potatoes. They have the ripest smell when properly taken off the vine for a goodly amount of time. Never understood how humans could throw them away when they are at their finest."

"Me either," I said trying not to gag at the thought. Months-old potatoes were the worst, and they crept up on you until you absolutely "Had to find that smell!" Their stench seemed impossible to clear out. I knew just what he meant.

"You sure you don't want a bite?" he said around another mouthful holding up the last bit.

"I'm good," I confirmed. "You are most kind."

Just then the bus came around a corner and a sea-scented breeze blasted us, and I thought to thank the rat again, but he'd dropped down and ran off somewhere looking for another handout. I couldn't help but laugh at the encounter as I put my feet up on the back of the next bench forward. I'd always thought spiders were the worst, but talking with a foot-plus tall rat took the prize. If only I'd thought to scrub his ears… they were kind of cute, but those teeth with food stuck between them and his whiskers... I shivered with the creeps.

8

Port, Papua New Guinea

Following the rat's advice, I convinced Dad to get off at the third stop. After our encounter with the taxi, Dad decided following my advice might be a good thing.

"Here, try some of this," Gigi said staying close to me. She'd been picking up supplies among the locals on the bus. Doling out a drop, she suggested, "Put it behind your ears and on your necks." Holding up the pint of unmarked liquid, "Eucalyptus oil for you budding actresses. You'll not only have the best tan when you get back to your friends, you'll not be burnt either. Some people chew their leaves too, but who wants to spit green?" I saw Ri'Anne's hand edge up tentatively. "Then here," and Gigi passed Ri'Anne a couple. "I think they taste nasty, so I was going to toss them. But you might as well. They're actually not bad when dried, either as tea or as a spice, but only barely."

"Quite a lovely place," she continued as we arrived at the water's edge. The boardwalk was pushed right up to the water. Boats were lined up on the piers in private docks to either side of us. It was going to be difficult to find Uncle Arlo in all of this. The port circled around to the right, going out wide and curving in like a fish hook, us on the long end near where you'd tie the line.

We started down to the right, it was slow going with the number of people meandering about. Several times we had to wait while a push cart wound through a narrow lane between the railing and the waterfront shops. Several times Gigi ducked in one to return a moment later with a small pouch that disappeared into her clothing.

"Mint," she explained to me once. "You can't tell by looking at me," and I think she meant by how thin she was, "I have friends that say you can tell someone is a cook by how big they are, but not me. I can't gain weight – and I've tried."

"Why would you want to gain weight? You're beautiful!" Ri'Anne asked her.

"Thank you dear, but beauty isn't always treasured, and often squandered. Sometimes you can get something with a smile or a pretty face, but I prefer people to respect me for my ideas and abilities." Gigi was lost in her memories somewhere. She tried explaining the errors of her past, "If you go the smile route, you have to follow it with more 'pretty' and less brains."

"I think we're here," Dad said, interrupting Gigi.

I looked at a long pier with a few of the larger yachts docked. Those that I could see were much nicer than Uncle Arlo's yacht. Uncle could have moored here, since he had the university's name to toss around, but the utilitarian The Lazy Cloud was nowhere to be seen.

Seeing Dad start down the pier, I could tell he secretly wanted to check out the boats. He'd never quite forgiven himself for not taking a job on the sea. Tired of looking for The Lazy Cloud and Uncle, Dad was daydreaming – he longed to have one of these boats to spend days on the sea with no city in sight.

"Will you look at this one, wow," Dad said as he stopped at a luxurious cruiser. Pleasant music was drifting down from well-hidden speakers. It looked like a relaxing way to spend retirement.

"Would you like to come aboard?" asked a man aboard the yacht, sitting up on hearing Dad.

Dad looked around, we'd neared the end of the pier and there was no sight of Uncle Arlo or The Lazy Cloud. "You know, that'd be great," Dad said. "And thanks. I haven't done so much walking in ages. I'm a cab driver from Colorado. This is my daughter Melanie and her friend Ri'Anne. And this is Gigi."

"Hi," we all said climbing aboard. Everything was new and beautiful.

Gesturing for us to make ourselves comfortable, he opened a simple ice chest and pulled out some water bottles and handed them out. "Name's Enrico – I don't get many visitors. What brings you down to Papua New Guinea?"

Glad to plop down on a lounger, Ri'Anne and I folded up our legs and relaxed while Dad filled Enrico in on our journey. Gigi sat with us, using some of her foot ointment herself. "Can we try some more of the oil?" Ri'Anne asked her, to which she smiled, pouring some out to each of us.

"Your skin is so nice," Ri'Anne said to me as she applied the oil to her legs and shoulders. "The Colorado air still affects mine. But this humidity will help. By the time we return we should be like new."

Eyeing the glamorous yacht, I asked them, "You think you could live like this?" I was trying to figure if I could, because reportedly mermaids lived their lives in and around the sea. It seemed a little much to me.

It was like Ri'Anne read my mind, "Mermaids live in rivers too," she said. "If we were mermaids," she said for Gigi's sake, "we wouldn't have to live wasting away life at sea stuck on our mega-yachts."

Enrico overheard Ri'Anne, "It isn't so bad Miss, if it is what you like to do. If you write, or love the sea, it talks to you. I love what the sea is saying, most of the time, that is, when it isn't furious with a storm. Though that can be fun too if you have an ear for it."

"What's it saying now?" Gigi asked him from behind us.

"I've been trying to figure that out. There is expectation. Look to the birds," and he gestured about. From our elevated view we could see birds in panoramic display. "If I were watching them alone, I'd say they were searching for the queen of the birds, ready to welcome her. But the sea… Last night the fish were leaping, dolphins followed me in. But the water, even quiet at port is speaking. I've never heard this verse before and I'm intrigued."

Dad laughed, "If you keep up this prose, you'll have the girls listening all day. We've had a few experiences where stuffs have been talking to us as well."

Enrico smiled, "I'm not going for eloquence, but understanding. It is low tide, but the water is in at its highest depth. I'd planned to sail at high tide tonight, but I think I'll wait to see what the water is saying."

Dad looked at the posts nearby the boats, "Hmm, it's low tide? You're not worried?"

"The lines are in, only the port jets keep me docked. It uses fuel, but if it were a wave I'd want to move out at a moment's notice. Look, see the other boats? They're doing the same." All of them had their mooring lines in, sitting snug against the dock by their side facing thrusters.

I shook my head, "No, it's not a wave," I said before I could reign the words in.

"My daughter Melanie," Dad said by way of an apology. "Prophet and mystic. If I'd listened to her yesterday… well anyway, she tried to warn me before we took a taxi…"

"Then what?" Enrico asked me, cutting off dad, and Gigi sat forward not wanting to miss my next words.

How to get out of this, then I remembered what he'd said, "Maybe it's a sea lord or something," I said fidgeting.

Enrico sat back sipping his drink. "Hmm, a sea lord. Can I use that?" he asked me.

"For what?" I asked suddenly suspicious.

"The ocean is in, the sun glistening off the waves, awaiting its Sea Lord. The world awaits breathlessly. The sea birds soar ready to greet the Sea Lord upon her return." He then coughed into his fist, "Or something like that. I write, didn't I say? It doesn't make much sense with waves and no wind, but it sounds trite."

I gasped when he began his poetry as he called me out, and then I grew mad. I was letting it all out, right from the start. What was the matter with me? Why couldn't I keep my big mouth shut? If I told him no, then I'd have to have a reason why. I was so in trouble.

"Do you have to?" Ri"Anne asked when I'd gone silent.

Enrico looked from my down turned face to Ri'Anne, and then back to me and to her again, "No," he drawled. "I don't have to. I'm just intrigued by the possibility. I write fiction, and, well anyway, if you'd rather I not…" and he waited but I said nothing and gave him no indication one way or the other. Anything else and I'd be lost.

"Ok then," and he switched back to what he'd been talking about, giving no credence to his verse. "Anyway, as I was saying, I haven't figured out what the water is saying. It's good to know it isn't a wave. I think I'll go tie up." He looked to me, but I kept my eyes down.

"Could you use my help?" Dad asked.

"Sure," and the two of them went to do that.

"What's a sea lord?" Ri'Anne asked out loud, trying to keep Gigi from asking it. "Is that a god or something?"

"Unlikely," Gigi said casually, but I wasn't fooled. "Enrico was talking about a queen of the air. I think Melanie was just adding to the mystery. I thought his make believe fiction fit eloquently to the mystery of the sea being in when it shouldn't be. But I've seen all sorts of weird things. A sea being in instead of out is no big deal."

"I don't like being called a mystic," I gulped out, glad that Gigi was making light of it instead of plying me with questions.

"Don't you worry dear," Gigi said. "I've known people that just know things, not able to say how they know it. Or afraid of what people might think if they said." Then she said, nudging me, "But you can't blame people for being curious, how you know. Just be careful with what you say."

"Well, the words are out before I can stop myself," I said still upset. Gigi was making sense, making me feel less like a freak and more a natural part of the world.

"Well then, you'll have to learn to be less bashful when the questions come. And realize they aren't trying to hurt you. People are drawn to truth, and when you utter a word like that it cuts through all their theorizing, and you'll get questions." Looking the way Dad and Enrico had gone, Gigi continued, "Or you'll get people like Enrico. He is entrusting his life at your word. But enough of that. I feel like I've picked the right group of girls to hang around," and she put her hands on each of our shoulders and gave us a little hug before sitting back. "One thing for sure, you don't live boring lives."

"But our lives are boring," Ri'Anne emphasized as we turned to face Gigi. "Swim practices, swim meets, and school. All of it boring."

"And life aboard yachts, visiting exotic locations and if I read you right – you'd love to swim with the dolphins he mentioned," she said with a smile.

"Ok, so not boring," I said in relief, joining the conversation, glad the awkward focus on me was gone.

I couldn't help knowing what I knew. I'd just read the sea at Enrico's word of the wave. In a second I'd known the reason of the false tide, and knew it would now go out. It had only come to say "Hi," just as Enrico had said. I wanted to curl up. Why would the sea come to say hi? Who was I?

Gigi leaned back in her chair, putting her arms behind her head relaxing. Closing her eyes she said, "From a flatbed truck to a yacht, it's best to roll with life. It's odd I know, but life is full of surprises. I'd not trade the flatbed for a yacht, but I do know when to enjoy either. I wonder what we'll be doing next. Oh, you mentioned swimming," and she looked to us. "So you two swim?"

"You can't tell?" I asked showing off my bikini top. We laughed, but for different reasons. Ri'Anne and I knew only swimming.

"Not really," Gigi said closing her eyes again. She went on to explain, "Many people sport the suits but won't go in over their head." Then she laughed again, "And some won't even get their feet wet."

"Well we do," Ri'Anne said with a big nod. Leaning back beside me she added, "I've been a swimmer all my life. It can be boring to just go up and down lanes, but I find it's a great place to think. I'm hoping to dive into the beautiful waters here like Melanie promised." She looked up to me for reassurance and shaded her eyes from the sun.

"There will be plenty of that, and more," I assured her. "If I can get Uncle to use us primarily, we'll see more of the underside of the boat than the top side. I'm sure Dad won't mind sharing the dives. As you can see," I said with a wave, "we've arrived. Once we get going on The Lazy Cloud you'll see. Soon we'll be diving every day, so much so you may get sick of it."

"Never," Ri"Anne promised.

"I'll hold you to that. We won't be diving in shallow water, but going down tens of feet where creatures large and small lurk. I can hardly wait to study them as Uncle's eyes and hands."

"Do you have to be so dramatic?" Ri'Anne asked gulping at the thought of creatures.

"But that is why we are here," I said trying to ease her fears. "But you won't have to if you don't want." I couldn't imagine my mermaid pupil's fears and did my best to put a positive light on them. "The fish are colorful, as are the coral and the plentiful plants that grow down there. You should see the great kelp forests. If you get lost, just go up."

"I don't think I could ever get lost in a forest," Gigi said, her eyes far and away.

"Me either," Ri'Anne said with an understanding smile. "I could spend endless days in a forest."

"You like plants?" Gigi asked and the two of them began a discussion that bored me.

In minutes I'd completely tuned them out as they went on and on about the varieties of plants, where they grew, what they liked, the kind of soils and so on. I had to flee for my life.

Hearing the water lapping the sides of the yacht, I removed my sarong, kicked off my sandals and went looking for a way into the water. Looking out over the bay, I didn't see the many boats anchored out on it. I soaked in the presence of so much water near me. Water was never boring for me, and it was time I put my feet in. I reached the stern, looking for a ladder, or some way down. There was a place for a ladder, but it was missing. With a sigh, I had to settle for sitting on the end of the boat and letting my feet dangle ten feet up from the clear turquoise water.

I saw fish swimming about, but they were staying deep in their game of tag. How I longed to lay on the bottom and watch them play over me. I imagined myself with my arms behind my head as Gigi had been, my hair floating about in a halo and a dozen tiny fish playing hide and seek in my hair while others played tag. I heard tags of, "You're it," "Got you," and "Found you."

"Hey sister, careful you're about to fall in," interrupted a pelican sitting out on a post nearby. I was sliding forward and only caught myself from falling by an arm. Swinging by the one hand, I put my feet on the boat's side and walked my way back up.

Jumping, I plopped down again on the edge. "Thanks," I said to the pelican and looked at the post he sat on. It was old and rotting away. The top no longer flat, grass and a couple flowers growing in the cracks. A single board remained of what might have been a dock that came out from the pier.

On the board several seagulls were sitting, looking delirious. While I watched one circled in to land next to the post and begged of me a, "Fish." There wasn't room for him, and he bumped the one next to him outwards. It hopped sideways echoing "fish" and bumping the seagull next in line. This repeated outward to the end of the post until the last seagull tumbled off the end, squawking her request for "fish." She then flew up and over them all to land closest to the post to start them all bobbling along again until another dropped off the end again. I was laughing myself silly at their antics.

Ri'Anne, hearing me laughing, came and joined me. She and I sat shoulder to shoulder, laughing for a little while at the seagulls. Then I noticed some kids watching from the pier, "Hey, I don't suppose you could act a little frightened of me?" I asked the birds.

The pelican shook its head, "No Ma'am, I'm not gonna run. Besides, with you near there will be fish and we love fish." To which the seagulls echoed him, "Fish, fish."

"Are you talking to them?" Ri'Anne asked, looking back and forth between us. And when I nodded, she asked "What are you saying?"

"Well, those kids over there are watching – and I asked the seagulls and pelican to pretend to be afraid of me. But they won't," and I gave a pouty face. "They say fish will come about if I stay around."

"And do they?" Ri'Anne asked curiously.

"I'm not sure, really." It was true, I'd only been doing this a few days. It was hard admitting to it though. "I've not noticed it before."

"But you have spiders, birds and the rat," Ri'Anne said. "Coming about, that is."

"True. I suppose," closing my eyes I felt to see if the fish were still below. There were quite a few under Enrico's yacht, hiding from the birds, but basically right under us.

"There are, aren't there?" Ri'Anne asked when I didn't say anything upon opening my eyes. I nodded. "Ok, well – how about you ask your friends where your uncle's boat is?"

"That's a good idea. I should have thought of that. But first, I want to ask how did your talk go with Gigi?"

Turning her head so that her long straight hair rolled off her shoulder she said with sunshine in her eyes, "I like her. She knows so much about plants. But mostly I like her because she believes in fairies."

"Fairies?" My eyebrows went up. "Not mermaids…?"

Nodding she looked down at the water between her feet. "Yeah, fairies. I've never really admitted it, but fairies are really cool. It's too bad you can't become one, like you can a mermaid."

I didn't want to discourage her, but this was news to me. "If you could choose?"

She looked at me, smiled and shrugged off the thought. Taking my hand, "I'm here to be a mermaid," she said quietly. Squeezing my hand she added, "Fairy stories are for little children, and I think they are cool. Can we leave it at that?" Then she nodded towards the birds, effectively ending the discussion.

Turning on the birds, I thought about what I'd say. I decided I'd describe it to them, "Hey, I'm looking for this boat…" I had an image of The Lazy Cloud, Uncle's converted yacht into research vessel in mind. "We've been searching…"

"I've seen it, Miss," said a yellow-legged seagull floating above my head before I could describe it. He'd picked the image right out of my words somehow. Then he did it to me as he flew to join the others, asking "Is it *that one* out there in the bay?"

When he said "that one" I knew exactly which one out of the hundred vessels floating in the bay was the one he thought it to be. Turning to look for it, I couldn't see it through the other nearby yachts.

"Thanks," and I told Ri'Anne. "It's over that way, but it doesn't really matter. I can't say I know to Dad."

Ri'Anne turned on me excited, "But it's cool that they knew and could help. That could prove useful."

"You're right, it could," I returned her smile.

"Fish, fish?" the seagulls started up including the one that had helped me.

"What are they saying now?" Ri'Anne asked.

"About the only thing they ever want, fish. It seems cruel to lure fish in for their supper."

"And the fish already here?" she asked.

"I think they're too big. I'd bet the seagulls would want smaller ones," and I held up my thumb and forefinger to indicate a short fish.

"Like herrings," Ri'Anne said. I kind of had a mental image from her too of a tiny fish that swam in large schools.

"If I can find some…"

I'd never really tried to attune very far before. Looking under the yacht, and around me had been about all I'd done. And it turns out, about anything beyond that and I was starting to feel light headed.

"Ooh, I don't feel so good," I said holding my head. "Ow, and spots."

"You don't look so good either. Here, drink some water," and Ri'Anne put a bottle in my hand. I couldn't even see it.

Trying to sip at it, I felt it more enter my body through me. "Oh," I uttered as the spots disappeared and my eyes snapped open.

"Um, you didn't even drink it," Ri'Anne said pulling the empty bottle from my hand. She was looking at it and me. "You're weird. Want another?"

"Please," and she went to find one.

Returning in a minute with an open water bottle. "I think it was yours anyways." I made a grab for it, but she held it back, asking "Can you drink with a finger?"

"I think so," I said tentatively and she held the bottle out for me to put a finger in. When Jill, Cleo, Lucy and I had been thirsty one time, we'd stuck our hands in a stream and I'd felt the cold go all through me. I'd stopped being thirsty too, but I hadn't told anyone.

I wasn't sure that I wanted to display another ability, but I was craving water so badly now. "It seems," Ri'Anne said as we watched the water disappear from the bottle into my finger like it was a straw. "You use water like it was…"

"Like I was a mermaid?" I said shrugging my shoulders.

"Yeah. Hmmm, well did you find the fish?" I shook my head no. "Well, let me see if I can get you more water."

Looking over the side of the yacht she added, "If only…" *I could go for a swim.*

"I know, right? But it can't be helped." Shrug, shrug.

She was back a minute later, carrying several sloshing bottles. "I filled up the other two, and got Gigi's, your dad's and couple other empty ones I saw. Ok, stick your fingers in and search."

It was much easier, but I couldn't just zoom out everywhere. I had to narrow my search for just the herrings. Even then I was melting into Ri'Anne when I found them.

"I found *some*, and…" I was talking to empty air as seven birds took flight arrowing out over the bay.

Watching them go, I felt Dad come up, "Been talking to birds?" He paused smiling, and then leaned against the stern of the boat on which we sat putting his arm about us saying, "It's ok. I like that my daughter is odd. This trip is good for you, and if you like I'll talk Uncle into giving you dive time."

"Oh yes, yes, yes!" and I was up on my knees hugging him when I saw he meant it.

He was smiling when he pushed me back, holding me by the shoulders, and then he wiped away tears I didn't know had come with his thumbs. Looking past me to the bay and the seagulls flying away, with the big pelican leading the way, he had an unasked question.

"They mostly talk of fish," I hedged leaning in for more of his hug. If he was hugging he wasn't going to be upset.

"And off to get some I imagine," Dad added. I'm glad I hadn't brought the fish here, there would be some serious explanations required as I looked up at his face. Continuing to look out over the bay he was smiling.

"You make a new friend?" I asked as I leaned my head against him.

"I think so," he said.

His arm around me felt wonderful, but I had to ask, "Dad, why haven't you contacted Uncle?"

His arm went stiff, and then he decided to confide, "I didn't want to worry you. My phone broke when the taxi crashed with our stuff inside. I haven't been able to make calls since." And I hadn't brought mine, leaving it in Jill's room. We'd left from the gym.

The others joined us on that. "Would my ship's radio help?" Enrico asked. "He could be out there listening. Otherwise, I have a phone somewhere."

Dad didn't look like he wanted to impose, but Enrico insisted. So the two of them went up to the steering deck to see if they could get ahold of Uncle Arlo. I felt the cold place where his arm had been, but I looked forward to getting aboard The Lazy Cloud. Enrico had been nice and this had been a welcome break, but it was time we found Uncle and began the research we'd been brought here for, especially since the university in Boulder paid all our expenses.

9

All Aboard

"Jeb, is that you?" We heard Uncle Arlo over Enrico's phone. Dad had come back carrying it. They'd been trying to reach Uncle without success, but finally he'd answered. At Dad's affirmation, Uncle continued explaining why he'd been slow to pick up, "The command deck is a long way away on a boat this size for a guy with a broken leg." After a short exchange we agreed to wait for Uncle to arrive. When he finally found us, he got right down to business.

"We might as well eat here before heading out on The Lazy Cloud. The load I requested is waiting to be delivered, and I have a bunch of samples to offload. Then there will be boxes and containers to stow." Patting his leg he added, "With this leg, Jeb, I'm more in need of your help than ever. Now who are all these people?"

Uncle Arlo, the same stiff upper lip as I remembered, failed to take me under his arm. I'd wanted to hug him, but I ended up drifting back to stand next to Ri'Anne. When they'd handed out social graces, they'd skipped my uncle. If only I had a way to make him nicer. Ri'Anne took my hand and she gave me a sympathetic glance.

Jeb introduced him to Enrico, Gigi and Ri'Anne. Standing next to Ri'Anne I hoped to hear Uncle open up about us doing some dive work, but so far all his praise was directed at Dad. Surprisingly, he didn't give Gigi a cold shoulder, probably because of his need for helpers.

"Is Enrico joining us...?" Uncle directed the question at Dad. Then to us, "Get your things girls – we have a dozen stops to make."

I ran to get my stuff, pretty excited that we'd finally get moving. When I arrived back with the others, they'd decided on a place to eat and Enrico was offering a bag to Ri'Anne. "Swimsuits and things – my daughters are grown, but I've been holding onto them for no particular reason."

But Dad wouldn't have it, "Thank you, but we can't," and he wouldn't let us accept the gift. "You've been more than kind, Enrico." I saw Uncle turn away, not wanting to contradict Dad's decision, but I was having a hard time with it. Dad noticed. "You have more than enough, we're blessed already." I agreed on principle, but Ri'Anne and I could certainly use the clothes. Even if I was wearing all that I'd brought with me, it would have to do.

"What's the problem?" Gigi asked having come up on the heels of that conversation, being more sensitive to my feelings than the others.

I shook my head, pushing back my hair and lifting my chin, "Nothing. Everything's fine." I wouldn't show that there was any disagreement between Dad and me, and smiled to be sure that Gigi knew that.

We said our goodbyes, since Enrico wasn't joining us. I think Dad shutting him down on the gift put a halt to the goodwill feelings. We started walking to the restaurant that they'd picked out. Before we had gone far, I slipped my hand into Dad's and said so only he could hear, "I thought you said we should make friends…" hoping he'd go back and invite Enrico (and perhaps get those suits…).

He did glance back, but instead of going back for Enrico, he disengaged his hand and fell back to walk beside Gigi. That didn't go as planned. If the two of them were making friends, though, did that mean Dad had accepted her?

I had to step it up to join Uncle and Ri'Anne, who were discussing computer stuff.

"Because of the accident, I forgot to turn off my deck cameras. The night of the accident, I couldn't sleep and had been up late. I'd left the cameras on to record the brilliant moon and then went to sleep. I only discovered it today, when I had an alert that my computer storage was low. I'm going to have to delete the whole file, and that bothers me. I hate deleting research."

"Mr. McKenzie…"

"Call me Arlo," Uncle interrupted Ri'Anne. "With both Jeb and I, you should call me by my first name."

"Storage is cheap," Ri'Anne continued. "You should be able to find a bigger drive than you currently have for cheaper than you last paid. Even here in this port. Then you can go back and look at your moon footage anytime you want."

"Hmm, I hadn't thought of that. It's just that I don't get computers that well. If you can install it…."

"Sure, I can do that," Ri'Anne said. She gave me a wink, glad that she was able to fit in.

"This place is beautiful, isn't it?" Uncle said as he posed before a statue. We were walking through a plaza looking at all the flowers. Dad had borrowed Uncle's ever-present camera to get some pictures of us.

"What have you done with my uncle?" I said to him. "My uncle never sees beauty unless it swims."

He squeezed my shoulder and gave an uneasy laugh, "I'm celebrating life. When it is almost taken from you, you learn to see the flowers. I'm trying to see the good all around me and take things as they come. It is true dear Melanie, I'm an intellectual. Don't worry, he isn't gone. For you and your friend I'm trying to unbend. Though don't expect miracles. Still, I aim to involve you. If your dad agrees, I can use you and your friend. Think of it as self-serving, if you must. I'm useless with this hurt leg here."

I turned under his arm, hugging him close, being careful not to hurt him. Looking up into his eyes, "You're not having me on?

Ri'Anne and I are expert swimmers." *Hint, hint,* I wanted to add. But his offer was already ten times what I was expecting.

"And I'm out of shape," Dad admitted, looking up from the camera screen. "You should use Melanie as lead diver, along with her friend." I gazed at Dad in awe, I could hardly believe my ears.

Then I heard the uncle I knew, "We'll go over everything when we're under way. And we'll have to work close you and I, and you already know most of what I look for from previous trips. But you and Ri'Anne will also be setting up the equipment too." He paused to be sure I was serious. His equipment was important. "I'll be relying on you."

He could have given me a discourse on the workings of the universe at that point, but I didn't hear anything else. I was probably crying and smiling from ear to ear, but I didn't notice. I felt amazed, all my hopes for the trip seemed within grasp. If my theories on what it took to become a mermaid were true, and if Ri'Anne was to become a mermaid while we were here, we were going to have to swim and swim a lot. There was only so much I could teach her while we were dry.

After a whirlwind of shops, people and the sights, we were sitting. Apparently we'd ordered, because they were setting a chicken salad in front of Ri'Anne and me to share. Leaning her head close to mine Ri'Anne asked, "I overheard before, we're going to get to do most of the diving?"

"Yes we are," I told Ri'Anne, excited all over again.

Chewing on my salad, I heard Uncle ask Gigi, "What's your story?"

"Hmm?" Gigi said, petting a green shoot she'd pulled from her outfit, like it were a pet. The air around us filled with the fragrance of mint. Finally realizing Uncle Arlo had asked her a question, she twisted the shoot between two fingers, such that the leaves twirled.

"I'm a bit of green thumb. I love plants," Gigi told him and I felt Ri'Anne stir at overhearing her. "There is something about them that resonates with me. Plants are the world to me, and they can be made to spice up any dish. I can cook, if you have a need for that."

One thing for sure, I couldn't cook. I saw the two men's eyes rise at that. Jill's mom had told me once, the way to a man's heart was through his stomach. I laughed, seeing her catch their attention with so simple a thing. And the trick with the mint, that was something to be envied as well. What could I pull out of my hat, a fish, as I did for Ri'Anne in the car? She'd been shocked by the display of magic. I should have something natural like a shoot of mint.

Gigi didn't need to say another word, she had them with the cooking bit, but she added, "I can tidy things up a bit, if need be, too. In fact, I'll be hard pressed not to. I tend to get carried away with that. But I'll keep out of the way, I promise, and not interfere with any of your experiments, or whatever you are doing."

She had them won already, but she liked the opportunity to talk. So telling them a bit more about herself, "I've traveled the world over, been to many a port. But, I'm always looking for new weather, distant seas and lands. All my life I've been searching, seeking a past that was lost to me. Someday I hope to find that piece to my puzzle that will explain my wandering way. I'd greatly appreciate being taken along. I can haul sail or mend shirts."

"Can you teach me to cook?" Ri'Anne asked fingering her hair and looking at the mint.

"Of course," Gigi said. "It would be my pleasure."

They started up a conversation on plants again and I tried to stick with her. Ri'Anne could make a dead plant sit up straight. She said, "I see plants as an extension of life. There is just something, especially in the hard cases, in seeing them revived and take to the air. And that's the trick. Plants don't need just water, soil and sunlight, but air. I like to think that air is their true element, where they take shape. I see them and their wings…" and that's about where she lost me. I had little interest in plants, and really only in those that flowered – but give me those already potted. I liked the instructions that said, "Just add water."

"Really?" Gigi asked. "I've never thought of it that way. Why, that is… the things I've seen. The Caddeous Turnip of the Jamaican Highlands, why I've always thought its leaves resembled wings."

It seemed Gigi had fit herself in, even Dad had warmed up to her. I saw them chatting and laughing at things as we packed up Uncle's supplies to be brought aboard The Lazy Cloud. Now if I could only wrap myself around the idea of sharing how I knew what she wanted to know. A time was coming when that would happen. Was I prepared to share all? By Uncle admitting her aboard, I felt lost – sure that I'd end up revealing myself to both her and him.

10

Lost Sights

We decided to spend the night in port and to get a fresh start in the morning. Dad found a deck of cards, and we stayed up late playing games and talking. It was a fun night with all of us happy and together. After games, I ended up sitting out under the moon looking at the bay, watching the silver of the moon create interesting swirls in the water. I wondered what it would be like to sleep underwater with the light of the moon all about, but instead I descended to the room Ri'Anne and I were to share, trying to be sensitive.

In the morning, The Lazy Cloud lay out twin curlers as we gunned it out of the harbor, at first heading south, but eventually turning east. We were out of the port before the sun rose and had an eye blinding sunrise through a few clouds scattered on the horizon. To top it off I was bleary eyed, feeling like I could have slept all day, not having fully recovered from the flight here.

Yet I was happy, standing at the prow, with the wide sea before me. I wanted to be running my hands through the water, but the yacht was too large for me to simply lean over and run my hands through the wake. So I had to make do with putting my arms on the railing and feel the water via attuning. I could feel its great depths, watching with an inner eye to its sand dunes, rocky outcroppings with fish staring at the alien dark shadow pass overhead as they discussed the current events of the day.

Captivated by the undersea world, I didn't hear Uncle come up, but I felt his shadow as he leaned over the railing beside me. "One of my favorite parts of an expedition is the first part when you leave port," he said being vague. "There's something mesmerizing about the sea. It might seem flat, but it has so much variety."

I'm sure he meant the above-sea view, and the seemingly endless view of it we had. I smiled, but I couldn't take my inner mind from what I was seeing. It looked like we were in a fast plane, skimming over the depths of an undersea kingdom. But it was good to see him happy, though I knew his mind was on returning to his research.

Uncle had revealed at dinner last night that he had a number of leads he had to skip on his previous trip. He'd told us how he'd healed up on a surprisingly modern island. (Syreni Island, thanks to my friend Jill, who rescued him). We were on our way to the first of those dive sites now. It was hard to sit through him telling us the story of how he'd nearly drowned, made it to his yacht, with a broken leg and suffering from a fever into port. It was a lie, a memory implanted by the magical Syreni people at my request. I felt horrible listening to him tell it, wanting to tell him the truth. I hate lies, and had never thought that is what would be happening when I'd asked them to alter his memory of Jill's rescue. I'd been thinking they'd just remove the parts of her, but of course either his mind had filled in the blanks subconsciously or they'd filled in the gaps for him.

And what could I say, *Jill and I are mermaids!* or that we'd decided he didn't need to know the truth, and to be alive should be enough? But I knew my uncle. If he got a whiff that anything was amiss he'd chase it down until he unraveled the truth. At least right now he was relaxed with the port disappearing behind us.

To get my mind off the ill memory, I turned to Uncle, "How about we dance… To celebrate?"

He guffawed, "You're kidding me. With this leg?" And seeing that I hadn't thought about it, he put his hand to my elbow, giving me a turn towards the deck. "You dance, and I'll watch." He tried to be formal, bowing over my hand, but it wasn't working and we both laughed.

Returning the bow, I knew I would accept the dance before I stepped away from the railing. Then a bow to Dad, who waved from the command deck. Ri'Anne was up there being given an introduction to driving the big yacht.

I felt the sea's twirl rise up from my feet as I set them, twisting and spinning out a leg, with my arms above my head. Taking a step, the wind caught my hair and the waves passes us, spinning me like a top. In seconds I was leaping, then came down awkwardly and stumbled. With a little laugh, I stepped back twirling and came out of it, trying to keep from stumbling again. It came more naturally after that.

Uncle expected I'd be wild, dancing around the boat or something. Now, not some time in the future. Putting wings to my feet, I leapt with the sea spinning up through me, I floated and danced around the yacht as a water spout, and then through his study back to the foredeck. He caught me a couple times as I spun his way, and I found myself looking over the railing, then he'd toss me back to the center. When my legs were wobbly I sat beside him on the couches set out front. Together we watched the sea go by.

Catching my breath and sweating profusely, I really wanted a swim. It was as good as a time as any to ask, "Uncle, can we go for a swim? I've been longing to get in the water since we arrived." I'd had the short swim while helping those girls on the way here, but really I wanted to swim laps in a pool and get as exhausted as I could swimming. That was probably out until I got home, but a good swim would be nice.

"What now?" he asked looking about in every direction, nothing but the deep blue sea. "We'll be near swimming waters in a little while if you can wait."

"Sure," I sighed longing to be in the water and it so close. Uncle went to join Dad, and I went back to leaning over the railing. We were moving too fast for my taste. I would have liked to experience the sea onboard a galleon like Jill had found sunken on her first expedition. It would be so much slower, and you could feel the ocean's wind and not that which was created by moving with a motor. Climbing way up into the ropes to haul sail, to see the sea from such a height. Ok, maybe not way up. But sailing on a boat such as the girls I'd rescued had, from the comfort of the deck was the way to go.

"Why you smiling?" asked Ri'Anne coming to join me. I leaned over, gave her a hug and gazed into her eyes that reflected the blue of the sea and sky, "I was imagining sailing this in the days of old."

She wiped her arm across her forehead with an expression of disgust. "There were so many sicknesses in those days. Me, I'm for a modern craft like this one. This is grand!" she shouted, getting up on a railing and leaning into the wind. When I joined her up there she said, "This feels like flying. I've always longed to fly. In my dreams I'm always flying."

"Always?" my eyebrows going up at that. "Occasionally in one of my swimming dreams, I'm swimming, but looking at the bottom it appears like I'm flying and then suddenly I am. Really though, I'm gliding because eventually I land. I try to jump, flap my arms or something to regain the flight but it never works. Normally though, I'm swimming."

"And no wonder," Ri'Anne said leaning into me. "You're a mermaid."

I looked around to be sure we were alone. Sound carried over water, but there was nobody and the wind was too loud for us to be heard far.

"What about Jill?" I asked back. My friend was the real thing in my opinion. I'd learned everything from her.

"I only know what you've told me, and not much at that." She frowned at this. "You, on the other hand, like being one, but hide it. I suppose rightfully so, I couldn't imagine having such a secret."

"Well, you're here to learn more. If I can ever get us alone anyway. I'm trying to find ways to help Uncle without giving up the knowledge. I don't need to be one of his experiments. Did you know every 'magical' person out there is always being captured? Think of Tinkerbell in a jar."

Ri'Anne frowned again, then added reluctantly, "That is true of every hero in every story, being bottled up somehow. But you're forgetting one thing. They get bottled up only to escape and save the day! You need to decide if letting your uncle know is worth the risk."

I shook my head, "I didn't go through all this trouble to keep the secret to then just …"

Suddenly the yacht's engine cut off and we leaned way over the railing, windmilling our arms to keep from going over. We started to laugh, but on hearing yelling we looked back, then got down and went to look.

"It's over there!" Uncle was pointing back the way we'd come, and Dad was turning the yacht about. "What happened?" we asked coming to join them.

"This leg!" he complained, slapping it. "I lost my balance, tried to use it, and pitched over in pain, dropping one of the cameras overboard. We have to retrieve it if we can. I threw my hat overboard to mark the spot."

I climbed up to the command deck to have a look. "There Dad," and I pointed out the hat that had landed upside down and was floating like a bowl.

"Good eyes," he said smiling stepping away from the wheel. "Ri'Anne, steer us close and I'll get the dive gear." He turned to go.

Coming down behind Dad, I told him, "I can get it Dad." I'd left Ri'Anne to use her new skills with the yacht. I had only to remove the sarong that was on over the fish suit. Out of it in a flash, I leaped out into the water.

"Melanie!"

I pretended I didn't hear him. The undersea world opened to me a thousand times more vivid than trying to view it from above. This is what I was here for and it had been too long… I laughed at that, diving down into the depths. It had been a day… a whole day since I'd been wet. But then I was brought up short by what I was seeing. Instead of the endless sandy beach I'd seen before, there were tall coral pillars and a kelp forest growing in between. Plus, it was deeper than I'd gone before.

I tried to find the camera by attuning, casting my vision all about. I felt the seafloor through the kelp but it wasn't directly under the hat. I tried imagining the direction we'd been traveling but I was turned around. And what did Uncle's undersea camera look like anyway? I could be seeing it and not know it. I tried remembering previous trips, but it had been too long. And it wasn't like the bottom was devoid of human junk. Plus the coral grew in crazy random shapes down near the seafloor.

Sighing, I heard the yacht coming around. It was time I surfaced, to get "air." Even if it was for pretend, I couldn't stay down indefinitely and give away my secret the first time I swam. I suppose it was good that I didn't find it on my first try. That would be too much, pointing another finger towards me. After the predictions, it might be better to let Dad, or better yet Ri'Anne have her day in the spotlight. Before going up, I couldn't help take an extra gulp of clean "fresh" air – the sea air tasted sweet on my lips; I flashed around to swim upwards.

Jill might be able to locate it faster, but this would be good practice for us. I just wish I knew how to share air for Ri'Anne, as Jill could. It had to be an ability I had as well. Jill had tried to explain how she did it, saying it came from her heart. It didn't make a lot of sense to me, so I would dive without a scuba tank, but Ri'Anne would be restricted until I could figure it out or until she figured it out for herself.

Arriving at the hat, I almost got a sea-buoy anchor in the face. "Sorry," Uncle cried as I surfaced lifting the hat. "The buoy should help keep us in one place. The hat has probably drifted some too," Uncle said looking dismal.

When I swam close he put the ladder down for me to climb. When I grabbed ahold, he asked, "What did you see?"

I handed off his hat saying, "It's all coral and kelp down there."

He wasn't happy at that news. "We'll find it Uncle," I said trying to encourage him.

Arriving on the big aft deck, I saw Dad suiting up. His belly sticking out of the wetsuit. I frowned to keep myself from laughing, but he saw anyway. "Hey," he said laughing at himself, "It has been a while. I've lost my beach body… So what?"

I said nothing. It had been a while since he'd done much of anything. He liked his work, being a cab driver, working his own hours and was able to leave at a moment's notice. I smiled seeing Ri'Anne come up to strap on a tank. Uncle turned to help her. Dad tried to get me to wear a tank, but I demurred. There was no way I'd put one on. There was such a thing as being discreet, but that was over the top in my opinion. Dad insisted.

"You won't have to pretend to go up for air," Ri'Anne said as I helped her don her flippers.

"I know, but…" I could stay down the whole time, she was right. At least this trip I wasn't restricted to The Lazy Cloud to watch while everyone else had fun. Going back to Dad I let him choose a tank for me.

"It's too big," I complained knowing I didn't really want to wear it. Then realizing where I was feeling the real discontent, I looked over my shoulder at the horizon. "We don't have much time. There's a storm brewing."

Dad gave me a glance, then asked, "How much time Melanie?" There was nothing to see yet, so I shrugged. I just knew we'd see one before nightfall and said so.

"She's been having these premonitions," Dad explained to Uncle when he wanted to know how I knew. That was enough for Uncle to get Dad to help batten down some things.

While they were doing that, Ri'Anne nudged me asking, "Can't you do something about that?"

"Like what?" I asked accepting a sandwich from Gigi who'd just come from downstairs.

Gigi held up a bowl of potato chips, played catch with those that tried to fly away in the breeze. Just as she'd catch one, some more would fly out of the bowl. Laughing, we tried to catch them with our mouths as they flew by. Before the bowl was empty, I grabbed a handful still dancing in the bottom of the bowl.

Chewing on some of the chips, Ri'Anne tried to nudge me more, but I really didn't want to play weather wizard. I was having a hard enough time as it was with everyone looking at me when I knew something without being able to explain how I knew. Suppose I did "magic" the weather, then they'd think I was trying to draw attention to myself, because of my "failed" prediction. This mystic stuff was complicated enough as it was. Besides, I didn't know enough of the consequences to attempt something like that on a whim. Thankfully Dad returned, coming down from the command deck, so I didn't have to try.

Dad sitting on my left effectively ended the conversation. But then he was looking over my shoulder with concern. "What's that?" Dad asked pointing towards the yet invisible storm. "Gigi, can you hand me the binoculars," he asked holding out his hand.

We turned to look but I felt it before I turned. There was an awkward pole cruising along at a slow pace, but I sensed the displacement of water beneath the surface by a giant cigar-like black tube. Nobody expects to see a submarine.

I didn't have time to beat myself up for not sensing it because Dad asked, "Anyone done anything illegal lately?"

I shook my head slowly, unsure. They wouldn't be looking for mermaids, would they? The sense of guilt had me wondering if mermaids were legal. What if it was legal to hunt down mermaids? I about flipped out right then, but Uncle interrupted my thoughts.

"We have official status," Uncle said coming to stand beside Dad, being handed the binoculars to have a look himself. I was feeling terrible. I was endangering us all. But Uncle continued logically, overriding my feelings, "If they are USA, they wouldn't be stopping us anyway. We're in international waters." Which left about every other country that had subs.

"So do we dive?" Dad asked, eyeing the clouds suddenly appearing on the horizon. The wind picking up sending more chips flying from where they had landed.

Uncle looked up from where he'd been eyeing the submarine's periscope. "You better. The buoy has a transmitter, but it will probably be dragged a little by the storm. And I want to retrieve the camera before then."

"What about the camera, does it have a transmitter?" asked Ri'Anne pulling her hair back into a braid, a few strands of her hair whipping around her face. Uncle looked at her, thinking. Did Uncle think her suggestion stupid? I would be upset if he said anything of the kind, but then he said drawling out a, "No, but it was recording. We might be able to see what it is seeing."

"So it has a transmitter," Ri'Anne corrected him, "if we can see its broadcast. Won't it have a GPS stamp on the recording?"

"Now that's good thinking," piped in Gigi handing out more food.

Growing restless, I picked my mask up saying, "You'll sit here all day," I complained and fell over backwards over the side of the yacht. "Melanie!" Dad scolded me again. Uncle said with a smile, elbowing his brother, "She takes after me." I had to laugh at that as I turned my vision from the yacht to the seafloor and the patrolling submarine.

I knew the submarine wasn't here by accident, but until it proved itself to be unfriendly I would treat it with respect. Underwater, my strength to search was stronger and I felt along it, and read the name on its hull, the Victor, but there was no American flag. It was a silent beast, having crept in but I knew of it now. It had warned us of its presence, so they were probably friendly.

Then I tried to swim and felt a weight on my back, like I'd grown a turtle's shell. Or a rock was resting on me and I tried to shrug it off. Feeling for it, I felt the dive tank's straps. The mask was floating beside me along with the tank's mouth piece, I'd forgotten about them already. I should be using them. Picking up the mask, I glanced through it, knowing I would be doubly restricted in wearing it. The mouth piece made me want to gag as I tried to use it. "Only if I have to," I said, hooking them to the tank strap, which I didn't need while I was alone, or the mask.

I wanted the gear gone, but Dad would be coming and he'd insisted. The deep blue was all around, and I swam a little ways waiting for Ri'Anne to join me. Seeing a pair of tiger sharks gracefully cruising through the top fronds of the kelp, I waved to them calling them over, "Hey guys – What's up?"

I was so lame, but how else did you talk to anyone the first time? Though I did get their attention. Their steely eyes swiveled on the sides of their heads to spot me, but they'd already begun their graceful turn to rise above the kelp and then they swished over to swim by me. "Up? We're bored. The same endless blue," said the dominant female of the pair.

There was a splash above, and I "saw" Ri'Anne drop in. Her entry startled the sharks and they scattered. Halting my dive I waited for Ri'Anne to catch up. When she arrived I noticed her eyes wide behind the mask as she started at the sharks hovering out of range. She made mumbling noises behind her mouth piece pointing at them. I squinted, trying to give her air. There was something I wasn't understanding and I shook my head. "I'm not sure how to share. Sorry," I said.

The sharks circled back to swim by Ri'Anne to snap quick circles beside me. "Want to help us look for a device my uncle dropped overboard?" I asked them. Then of Ri'Anne, I told them, "My friend here is new to being a mermaid."

"Of course Mistress. I'd do anything to change up my patrol. Grab on," they advised as they pulled up alongside and I reached out for a dorsal fin. Ri'Anne followed squeamishly, her shark waiting patiently until she took hold, and only because me and mine were disappearing down ahead of them.

There was another splash above, and when they sprinted off, we were in for a wild ride before they calmed. By the time Dad oriented, we were obscured by a million fish, and then we were down into the kelp and coral. I felt bad for ditching Dad, but there would be more dives.

On calming, the sharks offered, "We'll spread out looking around. Where should we be looking?"

"Oh, by the anchor." I'd lost track of the anchor. The kelp made it impossible to spot it, and so I had us rise again above it to find it. "Ah there," and I pointed at the pale rope descending from the buoy. "Ok," they said, "When we find it we'll drop you off." Down we went again through the thriving community of fish.

It was a little unnerving to see us swim through a school of bullet tuna and see one snapped up with but a side swipe. "Here Szzarrs," and the one I rode batted with its tail another tuna, "Thanks Skizzers dear," the other replied chewing down the snack and dragging the witless screaming Ri'Anne, she trailing a stream of bubbles. We'd have to exchange tanks or she was going to run out of air.

I thought the tuna would make for the other side of the ocean with the sharks on the prowl, but they seemed to trail us because they felt safe with me. Which, in the end, made them easier targets, but the sharks said when I asked them to be nice, "No worries Mistress. Wait, oh," and she did a one-eighty. "I thought I saw a flash below. Let's go look."

Once down in the kelp it would be easy to get lost, but the sharks seemed to know right where they were. Then we were over a small clearing, and there at the bottom of it lay the camera. "Wow, perfect!" I let go my ride and dove for it.

I worried at first that it might be filming me, but then saw it was face down, recording the bottom. At least now it wouldn't be giving away my secret. Picking it up, I turned it on Ri'Anne, who was gesticulating wildly. "What?" I asked. Then I saw a black cloud descending towards us, and then saw it for what it was - a weighted net and I was right in the middle of it and it was carrying Ri'Anne down with it.

I had about two seconds. Not enough time to save her, but I kicked hard suddenly slamming through two pairs of hands reaching for my arms.

Why I didn't sense them, I didn't know, but I attuned them now. Normally, I could outrace a speed boat, but weighed down as I was it was difficult, but the net was only so big and I coasted out beyond its reach. What was this about? I turned off the camera and clipped it to the tank strap and began getting out of the tank harness. In my struggle, men moved in towards me in the forest of kelp.

Knowing they had Ri'Anne, I decided I'd best be "captured," but it would be on my terms. All sorts of ideas came to me, then out of the blue came the pair of sharks charging at the men. Before I could react, they each had a guy by the leg, and suddenly it was a mess. Time slowed, and I kicked, cruised around and out of the enclosing circle of men again. The sudden appearance of the sharks surprised everyone, me included. Steel darts began flying through the water. The men had something else to occupy their attention for a time.

Watching the action I forgot to keep track of Ri'Anne and went in search of my friend. I felt her and swam in her direction, finding her being escorted towards the submarine. Catching up to them wasn't a problem, they were slow as molasses compared to a mermaid. Debating a rescue, I gave up on the idea upon seeing Ri'Anne using a buddy mouth piece of one of her escort divers. Ri'Anne had run out of air, she'd been frightened since the first moment.

It was all my fault really. I shouldn't have roped those two sharks into joining us, but I'd been missing unfettered mermaid companionship. The sharks accepted me, no questions and no demands. Their reward for being friendly to me, was to have spears shot at them. They were probably dead back there. It was fairly obvious as the trailing pair of divers turned to watch over their shoulders at me, that they were nervous having me trail them. They swam up to a hatch, and soon they had Ri'Anne inside. I felt her go in without a protest, then it was closed and they began swapping water with air.

The men guarded the hatch, but I had no intentions of fighting them. I sensed the other team coming and turned to watch them bring their injured with them. I felt truly bad for that, but they should learn that mermaids weren't to be trifled with. The team of eight swam past me, giving a half-hearted attempt at chasing me down and trying to shoot me with a net. I was too nimble for them, and at last, giving up, they went by pairs into the hatch.

I didn't doubt that they were recording everything, but there was nothing I could do about that. Once the men had gone in I began to feel around for their command center. I didn't know subs, but really, all I had to do was wait for them to bring Ri'Anne somewhere. Should I go in, grab her and exit? Instead I went back to examine the site of the fight.

11

Captive Imagination

Getting the mask off was a mercy! Oh air! Sweet air. Ri'Anne didn't think she had it in her to be a mermaid, she liked air too much! But she would try, because Melanie wanted her to.

When Melanie had proposed the idea of being a mermaid, it had seemed sweet fiction – but now who wouldn't believe after what Ri'Anne had seen? Ri'Anne had wanted to be a mermaid, like almost her whole life! Well, that or a fairy, but since there were no fairies out there wanting to teach her, it seems she'll become a mermaid.

Ri'Anne had been looking forward to the dive, too. Seeing Melanie handle spiders, talk with birds and now a pair of sharks, it was so fantastic. She was all set to learn it all. It was everything and more that Ri'Anne had ever imagined being a mermaid was. And seeing Melanie swimming without a mask, not drawing on her tank for air, amazing!

Ri'Anne's first view of the submarine after the chamber swapped the water for air looked at first like her dad's garage – equipment everywhere. But where you'd park a car was a pool with a woman in a red one-piece suit looking at Ri'Anne. It seemed hard to believe Ri'Anne was on a submarine. It looked like a normal room – like the pump room at the gym.

It became apparent that her captors didn't speak English, and by hand-gestures they wanted her fish suit off. They were not even giving Ri'Anne privacy to change into the sweats that they put in front of her. Ri'Anne had grown used to the fish being a suit, so she'd forgotten they were fish and they simply disappeared on her when she attempted to remove them. The fish of the suit would not become her captor's property, leaving Ri'Anne with no choice but to slip on the sweats as quickly as she could. When the thugs wanted to know where the fish went, at least that is what Ri'Anne thought they meant, she couldn't say – she had no idea.

They led Ri'Anne to another room that looked more like a storage room. A single guard stayed there with her. They'd injected her a mild sedative when she freaked out in the water, and it was starting to wear off. It had a side effect that Ri'Anne was having troubles with, because it didn't seem to be going away. Ri'Anne could see Melanie somehow, apparently no one else could, standing and talking with someone. Drawing close to her, Ri'Anne could almost hear her.

Ri'Anne jumped up and went to hug her, to cry in her arms. Melanie seemed so sure of herself, but then she stepped towards Ri'Anne and walked right through her like a ghost. Ri'Anne was left standing there, confused. Turning about, she saw the wisp that was Melanie fade away, turn right and walk through a wall.

Ri'Anne's guard had stood too, perhaps to pull her back, but Ri'Anne was left staring at the spot Melanie disappeared. Was this a mermaid ability she'd not heard of?

Then Ri'Anne was seeing Melanie again, she was trying to "talk" to Ri'Anne, but she couldn't hear her. But this wasn't the Melanie she'd been swimming with. Melanie was wearing a silver and pink swimsuit. Had she changed fish?

Melanie's holographic face grew frustrated, seeing that Ri'Anne wasn't hearing her, so she turned and motioned for Ri'Anne to follow her. This time Ri'Anne didn't rush after her, but stood up – stretching. Eyeing the guard, the guy not much older than Ri'Anne, Melanie walked off through some racks. Ri'Anne followed, but when she rounded the corner Melanie was nowhere in sight. "C'mon Melanie, give me a break…" Ri'Anne whispered, hoping her friend's ghost would hear and come back for her.

Fidgeting, wondering if the guard was going to come look for her, Ri'Anne waited, and waited. So far they'd treated Ri'Anne pretty well, but it was true, *people want to capture mermaids.* So she was their captive, and Ri'Anne smiled at their ignorance. Ri'Anne, a supposed mermaid. She wasn't going to tell them she wasn't – at least she was being treated kindly. Besides, would they have believed her had she denied it? Who ever heard of a mermaid requiring air tanks and flippers?

Seeing a warm light further back, Ri'Anne went to investigate. Rounding some stacked brown sacks, Ri'Anne saw a line of planters filled with plants being attended by a researcher. She hadn't known there was anyone else in here. Ri'Anne drifted over to observe. He had a pretty nice garden of vegetable plants, but they were starved for attention. The poor fellow wasn't even talking to the plants, and had a handful of Q-Tips which he was using to try and pollinate them with.

Seeing him drop nearly all the pollen from one flower, Ri'Anne reached forward and caught the drifting fruit. "Careful," she told him lifting the dust, and with a finger brushed it into several other waiting flowers. "There you go beautiful," Ri'Anne told it. "Oh, you need some water, here," and before she knew it Ri'Anne was alone tending the plants. Give her plants any day over sharks and fish.

The plants started to hum to the attention, and Ri'Anne hummed right along with them. Hearing a hand shovel fall over, Ri'Anne turned to see three pairs of eyes watching her. "Oh, sorry," She said backing away. But she couldn't help but watch over their shoulders as they bent to take her place and she looked longingly at the greenery wanting her place back.

When they cleared out, and her guard changed, Ri'Anne went to sit among the plants. Sitting in the artificial light was nice, but the plants were popping out their fruit. She'd just pollinated them! What were they using for fertilizer? Now the plants needed pruning badly! Looking about for some snips, the place was bare – they'd left her nothing sharp. Well fingernails could prove just as useful. Judging the plant by its balance, Ri'Anne examined how they were growing. This one here falling over, its spine in pain. Snipping off a long sapping branch, the plant righted itself, then over here another overly long stem. A quick cut, encouraging the plant to hum again, its song soon came forth and it was reaching for more light.

What to do with the clippings? Crawling among the plants, Ri'Anne put them up her sleeve, figuring she'd do something with them later. The plants were strengthening, growing up and out – all with proper care. But they kept her busy. The guard came and watched Ri'Anne for a while, before returning to his post. She hardly noticed as one plant after the other kept trying to grow lopsided. Then before Ri'Anne knew it, sitting back and wiping sweat off her brow she observed ripe fruit on one plant. Then another was joyfully singing, sounding so much like a "ding" in a video game that she smiled. One after another, the plants "dinged" as they brought forth ripe fruit.

Looking for help, Ri'Anne wondered where the gardeners were. Surely they'd come to relieve the plants of their fruit, and begin another planting. But she was all alone with them.

Remembering the guard, Ri'Anne came out of the stacks of supplies. He looked up and she asked him, "Hey, can you help? The plants need harvesting."

"Baskets, there," he said pointing at a small stack of buckets, burdened under a pile of other things. She sighed, he spoke hardly any English.

"These will never do," Ri'Anne complained examining the baskets. "They're too small. The melons alone are the size of pumpkins. We'll need more… Can you get more? More, bigger?" And she tried showing with her hands. Reluctantly he nodded. Deciding Ri'Anne wasn't going anywhere, he turned and left locking the hatch behind him.

12

Fairly Fun

Waking, feeling exhausted and fried, I looked at the time. I'd only meant to get a short nap in. *Oh Melanie, leaving your friend Ri'Anne to rot while you sleep!*

Sitting up, I worked my hair into a braid. I couldn't be recognizable if seen. I readied myself for taking on a submarine and its crew. I really couldn't get over my giant-sized boldness.

Going out on deck, the yacht still pitched from the after effects of the storm. With an easy slide as if I'd been born at sea I reached the railing and gazed into the mist that shrouded us in a fog-bank. The sea as it lapped the sides of the yacht the only sound. *I should be long gone and back by now with Ri'Anne.* Looking at the water, I begged, "No splash," and made to leap over when I felt a hand take my arm.

"Melanie, I got it…"

And there was a bright flash when her hand touched mine. It had been a girl's hand on my arm, and the voice… It really sounded like me. When my eyes cleared, I was no longer on the yacht.

Surrounded by metal, I looked behind me because what I was seeing before me was impossible. It seemed I was sitting on a shelf, having instantly appeared on what had to be the submarine. The room was huge, about it walked giants, or I was very very small… They made booming sounds with their voices, sounding like thunder when they spoke. Echoing about me was the sound of water.

It took me a minute to get over the shock, and in that time nobody even noticed me sitting there. I decided I was tiny, mouse sized – hopefully these sailors sailed without cats.

Then I stood in alarm as one came my direction and floated right off the shelf up into the air! This isn't right, but unable to stop myself, I was drifting into the room. Backpedaling, I swam to hide behind a dive mask. This was too unreal.

"Hurry it up! The girls are gearing up. We must be in place before they dive," one of those in the room barked.

Girls? Horrible kidnappers! *Leave them alone!* I shouted at them in my mind.

I dropped back in fear as the giant's hand reached for me. Did they hear? Flinging myself against the back wall of the shelf, the hand grabbed the mask and withdrew. I swam to get behind another, but then hands were grabbing for that one too.

I attuned, hummed, whatever I thought might help in hiding, narrowly escaping time and again as masks were handed out. My hope was that they weren't looking for a pint sized girl hiding amongst them. Then they were entering the airlock, leaving me alone in the room all by myself.

Sneaking out to the end of the shelf I knelt surveying the room. An endless pool spa sat quietly. Testing this floating bit, I put one foot over the edge and then swam out into the room. Almost like swimming, but not quite. I coasted further than I would have in water and I didn't move myself by using arms and legs. It seemed to me that I had wings, they doing all the work, even gliding. If I wanted to go a direction that was the way I sent, much like a hummingbird. Even down required a conscious action; I wasn't falling.

Then there was noise, I flipped and swam back to the shelf not quite having got the hang of things, swimming being my first thought. Someone entered, a woman. Suppressing a sigh, I now had to wait for her before I could explore and find Ri'Anne. Returning to the shelf edge as the woman moved about the room so I could keep her in sight, I ducked to hide near the edge of the shelf when she turned about. Then she began to remove her sweatsuit top and I glimpsed a red swimsuit. I relaxed seeing that she was here for a swim and not looking for a stowaway. Once she was in the water I'd be able to move about again. Kicking off the pants she dumped them on a chair and knelt by the pool and adjusted some controls – then she slid into the water as the pool responded to her request. With the woman face down in a relaxed freestyle swim I could now search out my friend.

Ri'Anne, where are you? I tried sending to her, hoping she would hear. Never having attempted to talk to her in this way I wasn't sure what to expect, but I was desperate for my friend. I held out for an answer, but there was no response.

I'd have to find Ri'Anne the old fashioned way – with magic. Attuning, I sensed some the souls of the great sub about me out to about thirty feet and pushed harder to almost fifty feet before giving up – there were few women and none of them were Ri'Anne. Feeling faint I let go the sense and leaned against the shelf edge until my vision cleared. The water in the oh-so-close pool pulled at me like a magnet.

Without water I couldn't reach far. That also might be the problem with trying to reach her mentally. Even though I floated, it wasn't in water. Looking over at the water I heard churning in the pool, I wanted so bad to use it for my need but I couldn't risk being discovered. I would have to wait until the woman left, and then use the pool.

Looking around the edge of the shelf, the woman was swimming in place, her red swimsuit at odds with what I thought was a Navy sub. As far as I knew women didn't serve on submarines, but she seemed comfortable.

Maybe I had these people wrong, they hadn't said they were going to kidnap girls – but from my experience… No, it didn't matter what their current intentions were, they'd kidnapped Ri'Anne and had made a grab for me. If they had wanted to talk, they could have done so without all the thuggery!

All riled up and unable to do a thing about it, I searched about for some way to express my anger and caught sight of the racks of gear. I should check them for Ri'Anne's things.

Holding to the edge of the shelf opening, there were enough odd hiding places for a girl a few inches tall to hide in and left the shelf for one. Coming out around a pipe, I saw the tanks. Just a quick swim through the center of the room…

Kicking, I pinged off a tank all the way across the room in an instant and dropped, arriving before I could finish the thought. The tanks rattled in their holds, but the one I'd nailed fell out of its holding and crashed to the floor, pushing me down with it – nearly cutting me in half on the floor grating.

Oh my head, "Ow, ow, ow, ow." I was seeing stars.

"Is there someone there?" said the woman climbing from the pool.

No, no one is here! Go back to swimming, I urged the woman. Then there were bare feet walking above me and I was looking up at the giant woman. I giggled and then swam under a pipe in alarm.

Reign it in Melanie! Could this get any worse? Though, it was just too funny seeing the woman so big. If only women were so large in real life! We were always so tiny.

"Done with the pool Raini?" asked a new voice, a baritone. *Great, now there are two of them!* I didn't dare look, but crept along beneath the pipe afraid of any sudden bursts of speed or at being seen by them.

"No, but I thought I heard something. And this tank is dented, and it fell out of the rack..."

"Well if you're not going to…" said the guy impatiently.

"I'm not done yet," she said giving up on her search. She finally left and I saw her feet returning to the pool. The water splashed as she got back in.

Coming out from around the pipe I looked up and saw the grating clear above me and rose to look about. There was a fellow sitting on a chair with a towel draped over his legs. He was watching the woman swim.

From there I looked at all the tanks, working slowly along through them. But none was the tank of Uncle's that Ri'Anne had been wearing. I grew desperate on not seeing it. It had to be here! Well, her flippers and mask should be around here someplace too.

About to go look, I noticed the big red light over the airlock flickering. The divers were returning! I wanted to be able to watch and quickly decided the tanks gave enough hiding space. They also provided a view of the room and I could go down through them to the area under the floor if needed. Swimming behind one, I hid behind its air valve to watch.

The light went green, and the airlock door opened. The first thing I heard was Ri'Anne crying, "I don't know anything!"

Shocked, I reeled back, grabbing the air knob before I floated off. Then the divers I'd seen carrying her off entered the room with her between them. Together they removed her gear and she wailed between them, and then they were fingering her fish suit.

In seconds other sailors came into the room, followed by an officer that I thought might be the captain. "Sir, one of them evaded our nets." It was the first words I heard Ri'Anne's captors speak.

"And why is that, Varctor? One teenage girl against the lot of you?"

Varctor didn't look happy to be making excuses, "They had help. Two sharks attacked us, and we had to let her go before others were drawn to the blood."

"Sharks helped them? Really, that sounds far-fetched. I hope for your sake that you speak true, Varctor, my friend," the captain said patting Varctor's rough shaved cheek.

Then the airlock light started blinking yellow. "Close the lock," the captain ordered. "Take her to storage C, and get her something warm to wear and out of that wet suit. Raini help her." He spoke to the woman who had been swimming, but had been standing in the pool at their commotion.

The captain looked at the door in anticipation, "Maybe they succeeded where you failed Varctor. An opportunity blown, nobody was to be wiser for it. Now that yacht knows."

"But there is nothing they can do about it," Varctor spoke up.

"True. Once your divers are back, get prepared for another dive. We have that job I spoke to you about."

The woman handed her sweats to one of the guys to give to Ri'Anne. Then I felt a sensation and noticed Ri'Anne's fish returning to me. I wished they had stayed with her, but then she may have given up my secret by keeping them. Happily I greeted the fish, assuring them that Ri'Anne would be ok. *No, we'll get her out of this mess... Wait and see,* I responded to their worried vibes.

Hearing booted feet, I looked up and saw Ri'Anne was leaving dressed in the sweats escorted by her captors, and I decided to chance following. Diving for the floor, I skirted under the many boots I saw above and hopped over the hatch lip and then back under the floor grating.

Leaving the room I was suddenly glad to be leaving. I had no desire to see the sharks' handiwork on the men that would be coming from the airlock. They had bought my freedom with their lives! I hit my palm with my fist, mad all over again.

Breathe...

But what was I doing here now? I had that feeling I'd felt on the jet, scattered about. This had to have already happened, but here I was experiencing it. Was this a vision? It seemed so real.

After drifting through an endless series of tunnels filled with pipes and conduits, they put Ri'Anne in a large room that looked small at first, but on exploration discovered that it was quite large and packed with supplies. But underneath the grating it was clear. I found this vantage the best. They could make more use of their storage space if they didn't put everything above the floor.

"Stop crying Ri'Anne!" I comforted my friend, coming up around front of her face, but she kept staring off into space shocked. At least she quieted, I took solace in that. "We'll get through this!" I tried talking louder and waving my hands but she couldn't hear or see me.

Perhaps the guard wouldn't see or hear me either, though the woman had heard me knock over the scuba tank. That had been real enough. I would have to be careful. Deciding to test it, I floated out away from Ri'Anne into the middle of the little space they had. The guard ignored me but Ri'Anne stood to follow. Good it was working!

Um, how about this way and I swam slowly down a narrow isle between stacks of goods, being sure not to lose Ri'Anne. Seeing light ahead, I rounded the corner and saw some fellow gardening. He looked up and before he could focus on me, I dove into some stacked cans and hid.

Hearing a soft footfall, I looked out from the cans and saw Ri'Anne staring at the light. *No, not that way!* Ri'Anne was transfixed by the light, and she went closer to kneel down beside the plants. *Bugger them!* They'd captured my friend for real now!

There was nothing I could do but leave her and return to the airlock for her gear. At least now I knew why I couldn't find them before, but arriving at the door to Ri'Anne's cell – it was closed!

Ok, not a big deal… You're a mermaid Melanie!

Closing my eyes, I attuned, but other than seeing only a little bit around me. I couldn't see the other side of the door. *Water, I need water!* I'd forgotten to get water.

The plants need water! Yes, and I flipped about and zipped… And plowed into a bag of potatoes, blasting right through them into a crate of lard tubs. Ugh! I felt like a bee caught in honey squeezing my way out of there.

Yuck! I was covered in white sticky lard and mashed potatoes. Though I smelled pretty good, *lick… yum!* Yes, lick it all off… *Just a little salt and pepper please.*

When my belly was full I realized that it was going to take all day getting this stuff off of me like a cat. With a hand to my head, I scolded myself… *You're a mermaid Melanie!* Attune the stuff off! *But it tastes so good...*

With a huff, I attuned and with a sigh saw the good goo disappear. Now clean, but terribly parched, I was almost driven mad by the feeling of the moist plants on the other side of these supplies. The haphazardly stacked potato sacks had me near to passing out as I climbed up through them. There was no straight way through.

Heaving myself over the last sack, I glanced down into the light. Ri'Anne and the gardener were gone from the plants. Where had they gone? The question went unanswered as I saw water dripping into a near full watering can. The heavy, full bodied, deeply cold, plunking water drops pushed aside my conscious control and I zipped… *woah!* right into the water, the can tumbling over. *Quick, absorb the water before it escapes!*

Stumbling out of the watering can, the floor was amazingly dry. I'd absorbed it all. I felt wonderfully fat!

Now to make use of the water. Picturing the room with the pool, I saw the pool and went for it. But it was in motion when I arrived and the pumps started drawing me in...

I tried zipping, even a little zip, but I was being sucked backwards! Looking back I could picture whirling blades pushing the water around to the front side. Turning on a mermaid kick, I did manage to hold myself still in the water, for a little while, but I was tiring.

Angling upwards, I rose to the surface kicking with all I had… And bounced off the ceiling and through the floor grating with a gong-like sound as I dented a pipe in the floor that suddenly let out a load of steam.

Smart going Melanie!

It's not my fault!

Talking to yourself isn't going to get you out of this, think!

Steam was quickly filling the room, then there was an alarm going off. *Quick, Ri'Anne's gear!* There they were, on a bench… And blood all over the room!

So where was I to store Ri'Anne's stuff while I worked on getting her out? To stash it where it wouldn't be found. Somewhere underwater, and my thoughts went to the island sea where Jill had taken us on our first swim. It seemed ideal, and I knew I could find it. Grabbing the gear, I had to make four trips, being mouse-sized…

Arriving to grab the last flipper, I knelt in exhaustion and a plastic tub smashed down atop me.

"So what do we got here Marin?" said a giant dude staring down at me. "I think I've caught a fairy."

Panting, I blinked back black dots, eyeing the behemoth. "I'm no stinkin' fairy! I'm a mermaid…" but he couldn't hear me. Falling down to sit, I lay back to take a breather. I'd never felt more exhausted in my life. I probably had it in me to do another transfer, but I had to take the remaining flipper with me! …And it was outside the tub.

"Put a weight on it and help me with this!" replied Marin, and the guy lifted a wrench and put it on the tub.

"Like that's going to hold me, stupid thug!"

I was wasting my breath. Nobody could hear me. I was so mad, but too tired to do anything about it. Laying there felt too good, and I slept… *No!* But then I was dreaming...

13

Wanting to Fly

In a second there was a hand on her shoulder and Ri'Anne jumped with a scream. Melanie was standing there with a finger on her lips. "Where did you go?" Ri'Anne asked, but Melanie only shook her head. Taking her by the hand, Melanie took a step and disappeared. Pulling Ri'Anne after her. They went from standing in a submarine to looking at the greatest aquarium known to man. The "room" they were in was dark, except for the soft white disc they stood on and around them was the sea in all its glory.

Ri'Anne grabbed to hug Melanie from behind as she began to cry. Ri'Anne thought from the stress and excitement, and put her head on Melanie's shoulder to comfort her and feel her nearness. She'd never missed anyone so much in all her life near to tears herself. The submariners had been kind enough once she was their captive, but captivity never was fun. It reminded her too much of being grounded.

Melanie wiped back her tears, then taking a breath asked, melting back into her, "How on earth did you get the guy to leave?"

"Um, their garden needed harvesting," Ri'Anne said. "He went to get help, buckets or something."

"Perfect," Melanie said turning around in her embrace, and gave Ri'Anne a squeeze taking her breath away. "Good thinking," she said wiping her tears with her shoulders. "I've been waiting this whole time for that break. I'm exhausted. Let's hope they don't discover you're missing for some time. Anyway, you need to ditch those sweats. We have to swim down to that rock there and get you back into your dive gear. Surprisingly, nobody knows you never made it back aboard The Lazy Cloud, but that won't last."

Seeing Ri'Anne alright seemed to cheer Melanie, but there was something Melanie wasn't telling her. The pain she'd first read as stress went much deeper, she felt guilty of something. Maybe she thought she felt responsible for her being captured.

Trying to distract her, Ri'Anne said, "I saw you in the sub several times, but you… Why did you leave me?" Ri'Anne was hurt and it came out in her voice. She wanted to apologize for the way she sounded, but she couldn't help it.

Dropping back, Melanie held her at arm's length. "I haven't… I didn't…" and she looked confused before hitting on something. "Uh, was it the dream? No hold on, you haven't, of course... I guess I have to…" Shaking her head as first one thought after another came to a close before she stopped herself, forcing a smile saying, "Another *time*." She was holding Ri'Anne firmly staring at her trying to impart with the word all that it meant, as if what she said made total sense and it made none. But it did help her over being hurt, with Melanie's steady *We'll make sense of this one day,* attitude. "Right now we need to get you back to The Lazy Cloud before you're missed!"

Then she was holding the fish out for Ri'Anne to wear, but they wouldn't join with her. Wondering why, Ri'Anne removed the sweat top and discovered the branches she'd pruned had taken over that job. It was the same for her swim shorts. Ri'Anne was secretly glad to see that the branches had flowered, real flowers that smelled lovely. Her top was several pink and purple orchid like flowers. A thin tattoo-like curly vine wound itself down her left side, making the top appear to be flowers of the leafy bottom.

"So this is where you got them," Melanie said finally puzzling something out, but her words puzzled Ri'Anne. Melanie wasn't making much sense at the moment and Ri'Anne would just have to wait until she explained herself.

"It's lovely," Melanie continued with a wink of her former joy and Ri'Anne beamed happiness to hear her approval. "If it works for you, then it works for me. Anyway, your gear," and Melanie pointed to the nearby rock. When you're ready, hold your breath, we'll get you suited up and returned to the yacht."

"You don't give anyone time to get settled do you?" Ri'Anne was all mixed up. "I need a break."

Shaking her head no, "I can't. It's costing me keeping us here like this. There will be time when you're back aboard."

"Ok, sorry – I didn't know." Gulping back her feelings and wiping her eyes, Ri'Anne said "I'm ready," and she took a breath.

Taking Ri'Anne's hand, Melanie turned pulling them out of that place and suddenly they were in the water. The transition was quick, it wasn't like jumping into water. They were completely and wholly submerged all at once. The water felt thick compared to the clear air they'd just been in.

But in it they could "fly" down to her gear. Ri'Anne smiled at the thought. The time spent with the plants had made her feel more in tune with nature, and fairies were good with plants. At least with swimming it was sort of like flying.

It seemed unfair that Ri'Anne had to wear the gear and Melanie didn't, but Melanie assured her she'd be breathing water on her own in no-time at all. So with a happy smile Ri'Anne let Melanie dress her with the pack and fins. She helped Ri'Anne get the air going first. Having breathable air, Ri'Anne "sat" putting on the flippers and other items. She didn't ask how Melanie had retrieved them from the sub, not sure she wanted to know.

Ri'Anne marveled at the fish that were attracted to Melanie. From everywhere, fish were congregating and playing nearby. They were so beautiful and Ri'Anne was glad for them, since they helped distract her from her troubles. Ri'Anne found herself wanting to be Melanie for a little while. The feeling didn't last long though, because she got to thinking about the sharks. Ri'Anne knew they were Melanie's friends, but they weren't hers and never could be. She'd seen them attack the divers, and that had been too frightening.

Still with the colorful, playful fish near, Melanie let her have a chance at quiet time sitting together, their legs touching. They both needed that time together to rest against one another. Sitting there, Ri'Anne's heart quieted and she was able to let go of being grabbed and taken someplace she hadn't wanted to go. Even if a part of her wondered what became of the harvest, the plants had been innocent in it all.

"Let's swim," Melanie suggested. "We'll go slow. I need to stretch my legs."

The gentle swimming helped more, especially because it seemed as if they flew over the landscape. In her heart Ri'Anne was soaring, floating on a breeze. Imagining herself a tiny fairy, she darted forward, dipping, arching over and turning back. Enjoying the moment, Ri'Anne repeated the maneuver, adding a spin at the end. If only it was true flight, but it was good enough.

"Ready to go back?" Melanie asked after they took up swimming together again. Nodding, Ri'Anne held out her hand for Melanie to take and guide her. Wasting no time, they went from that sunny sea to a deeper and instantly familiar one.

How was it that Melanie moved them around like this? It must be incredible to be able to do so and Ri'Anne reaffirmed her decision on wanting to be a mermaid. She enjoyed swimming on the swim team, and their friends had stopped talking about wanting to be a mermaid – but she knew they still all privately thought about it. Noticing the tall kelp forest, Ri'Anne wanted to swim down and be among them. There had to be a way to be mermaid and plant lover at the same time.

"Alright," Melanie said, "Go on up. I've adjusted your air tanks to be about right as if you'd been using it for a while." Melanie clipped the camera to Ri'Anne's tank strap. "I have to go another way." Then she gave Ri'Anne another surprising hug, gulping back an unexpected sob, then dove down and away before disappearing in a flash of light.

Ri'Anne pondered that for a second, before realizing she was under all alone. Swimming quickly for the ladder, she climbed up. Melanie's uncle was there to greet her and help her out of the gear. It was fun to see him light up on seeing the camera. Thankfully he didn't ask about Melanie, and free of the gear, Ri'Anne dove down the stairs to the lower area. She was surprised at how glad she was to be back aboard.

14

Fresh Out

I dreamed. I'm Melanie the mermaid, with a mermaid tail and everything. Floating in an endless sea, the night's lights causing flickers to highlight the waves. My friend Jill was talking to a star. I tried to tell her stars couldn't talk, but she ignored me. I dove, feeling the fish I'd known as my swimsuit swirl out, creating a ball gown for me.

Then I found myself on a rock in the sea with Uncle sitting in a boat beside me. He was telling me that if he could get me into the water bottle he held, he would help me be rid of the fish swimming around my legs. I tried telling him that it was a mermaid tail. But he'd have none of it, scooping them up one at a time until they were gone.

Then there was a hand shaking me awake, "Melanie wake up. It's a bad dream, wake up!"

It was Ri'Anne, and at her voice I peeled my eyelids open, "Ri'Anne!" I threw my arms around her, "You're all right! I am so glad to see you, but…" and I looked around at our room. "How did you get here? Tell me about it!"

"Hold on," she said pushing me back and looking into my eyes, "You got me out."

"I did?" I asked confused, and then remembered tiny me. But that had to have been a dream… and I'd been trapped at the end of it.

"You did. You came and got me…"

I hugged her again, "I don't remember, but at least you're all right. But I had this dream where I was this tall," holding my thumb and forefinger out wide. "I was on the submarine looking for you. I saw you, but it was so confusing."

"Tell me about it… It sounds like you were a fairy," Ri'Anne inched up closer.

"Well, one of the thugs who captured me said I was one… but I denied it. Anyway, it's fading away. Let me see what I can remember…"

I tried to recapture the feeling as I told Ri'Anne the dream. How I'd felt at finding everyone giant-sized. The unexpected and incredible bursts of speed that kept getting me in trouble. We had a laugh when I told her about being covered in mashed potatoes and licking them up…

Hearing Ri'Anne make a grumbly snort sound, I realized I was talking to myself and Ri'Anne was asleep on my shoulder. The longer I talked the more real it seemed, but I still didn't remember rescuing her. Though if Ri'Anne said I did, so I must have.

Closing my eyes I wondered what it would really be like to be only a few inches tall. I'd gotten in so much trouble. Smiling, I drifted asleep.

I awoke to hearing Ri'Anne singing in my ear. It sounded like a song I might hear from "A Midsummer Night's Dream." Peering at her with one eye open, I hoped she would lullaby me back to sleep, but the tune was too lively for that; full of ups and downs, twists and turns. Surely she was dancing in her dream.

Flipping over, I tried to go back to sleep, but she snuggled in close carrying on with her tune. *This is no use!* Pulling myself up, I peered out of the starboard window. It was pre-dawn, and with my interest I felt the sea calling.

"Only a short swim," I told it. Standing up, I stretched and then remembering my own dreams did a quick double count of my fish. Interesting, there were more than when I'd given Ri'Anne some. Smiling, I imagined I could have the gown like tail they'd made for me in the dream. It bothered me more than I wanted to admit that I didn't have a real mermaid tail, because isn't that what it meant to be a mermaid – the tail?

Getting up, I snuck out of the room so as not to awaken Ri'Anne. Gigi was already up, and she gave me a little wave as I headed up the spiral steps to Uncle's study. Seeing Uncle's maps laid out, I glanced at one, trailing my fingers over them wondering where he'd been.

But that really got me back to my dream. Would Uncle really try to take the fish from me? And what would it mean if I lost them?

I didn't know. I wanted to think that my mermaid-ness didn't depend on a bucketful of fish, that it was deeper than that.

Coaxing some out onto my hand, I glanced around to be sure I was alone. Running my fingers over their backs, I asked them, "What would I do if I lost you?" They swirled around my hand and wrist, delighting in being with me and giving me bumps with their version of hugs. It seemed strange their loyalty and versatility if the dream was any indication. Oh how I wanted a mermaid tail, would they make me one?

Feeling the rays of the sun on my shoulder, I glanced up and looked at the clock. Stretching, I wondered where the time had gone. My back hurt from bending over. Pulling Uncle's charts near, I wondered what it would be like to be a true mermaid in one of his research dives that he described in his notes.

Hearing an appreciation whistle I glanced up in surprise. There was Uncle sipping at some coffee. "You steal my heart, Mel dear, seeing you at my charts." I flicked away a tear that came to my eye, surprised at being called "Mel," and quickly made sure the fish were hidden. He came alongside pretending not to see me teary eyed, and looked over what I'd been studying.

"You'd promised a swim," I said pointing down at the charts. "But I want it somewhere we can help you too." Anywhere I could test my new idea with the fish! "What about here? It's not far and Ri'Anne and I can get practice setting up a site. But I'm confused by your marks on the map, what are these?"

"Hmm. You two could use the practice, for sure. I meant what I said before too, about you two helping." Flipping some of the charts about, uncomfortable at his own niceness, he went quickly on, "Ri'Anne really has proven herself recovering the camera. It sure surprised Jeb that you two took to the water so fast, but I like it. I'll want more of that, going forward."

Then he looked at me, being sure that I was taking him seriously and he wasn't displaying any human tendencies. I hid the joy I felt at his earlier happiness, my toes being the outlet for the dancing I wanted to do. I nodded, trying to be serious, grouchy and business like. "Right boss," I said with a salute, spoiling the feeling.

Lining up the chart with his notes, he ignored me saying, "The markers are previous dives. The area around here speaks of ancient cities, but I've yet to find the civilization and its remains." Gesturing at his notes, "I've found old pottery shards and the like. Not enough to request a formal investigation, and that is what we are here to find, among other things."

Out of nowhere Uncle decided to open up. "As often as not Melanie, life throws you a bone." Leaning back against his table, he explained. "I thought myself unfortunate to get lost, unable to plot my way or navigate as I was used too. The island I ended up sheltering near was the most beautiful island I'd ever stepped foot upon – totally unspoiled. You could have hiked the glorious paradise and swam in the beautiful lagoon fed by a freshwater waterfall that I found. You would have loved it.

"Unspoiled land is vital to my research, and next to impossible to find true locations where people live in harmony with the land. Here I'd thought I'd found the real thing, and then I'd found the galleon I'd described before. Aboard it were treasures I haven't even begun to understand. But I forgot my true purpose, overcome by artifacts.

"I probably could have spent the next five years cataloging the wreck and the sea life that made it their home. But I had to go and get greedy and dig up those material treasures. I should have left them for those that love those things, but I had thought that if I didn't take them with me, I wouldn't be able to find my way back, and them possibly being lost forever distracted me.

"Oh, I curse my greed. It's everything to a researcher to be the first with a find, but it was my doom. Because now, as much as I go over these charts to find the island and my way back, I cannot find it. I was lost and found it. Now that I'm not lost, I cannot; it's a mystery, one that I'm not fit to discover."

I asked him why and he explained, "None of my instruments worked then, except the cameras. I've gone through them, but as I was saying to Ri'Anne they don't show location, but I always knew where I was before. That's next on my shopping list, dive equipment that has GPS."

"But other things worked, right?" Dad asked coming in, sipping at some coffee too and carrying a pot. He refilled Uncle's cup.

"Thanks Jeb," he said taking a sip of the coffee, his eyes looking over the charts as he explained. "Sure, the motor and the lights were all working fine. It's as if all the satellites had been removed from the sky. Which of course isn't possible, so I've ruled that out. Especially since they are clearly there now." He showed us the sea plot on one of his monitors. It had everything from sea depth to water temperatures, and it showed our exact location on a global map.

Theorizing, he added, "Maybe a sun flare had disrupted communications for a couple days, but I've read nothing about that in the news." Throwing up his hands, "I'm at a loss to explain it. Still, I know it is out there and with enough perseverance I'll find it again."

"In the meantime there are plenty of sites to dive," Uncle continued. Tapping a chart and saying to Dad, "Melanie and I were just discussing one. Let's head towards this island."

While Dad went up to get us under way, Uncle tapped the chart. "Look. We'll be here in a bit. Study these," indicating a long chain of shallow reefs. "It's a set of reefs with excellent diving potential. I've scouted them before, but it could always use a going over again. There was a lot of activity in this area over the millennia, and considering what I'd found at the 'island,' I'm sure to find more evidence of their travels elsewhere. One can hope anyway. If you and Ri'Anne want to have your swim and clean up then, you can have the top deck to yourselves. Jeb and I can get the gear ready for the next dive." Funny that he didn't even think of Gigi. The woman had absolutely no interest in swimming. The yacht had a shower, so it wasn't absolutely necessary, but who'd want to shower when you could swim in the ocean?

At the smell of breakfast coming up from below, Uncle and I went to the aft deck to sit and wait for the others. Dad returned after setting the autopilot. Ri'Anne came up, sporting a new beautiful island flowered swimsuit and slid in beside me, she looked subdued, still in shock from the abduction and rescue. I tried some humor saying, "You were singing in your sleep." All the while eyeing the swimsuit, hoping she'd explain.

"I was singing?" she asked a little surprised. I nodded, "You must have been dancing in your dream."

A twinkle came to her eyes and she admitted she was. "I think your dream of being a fairy inspired me." Fingering her new swimsuit, she said, "We have to do something about getting you a new suit." And that was it, no explanation on where she'd gotten it!

Then, breakfast was laid out and we were talking about the dive. Misunderstanding Ri'Anne's idea on a new suit, I thought I might try and get Uncle to get us to stop so we could shop. I still wore the same fish design that I'd worn from the airport. Even if I was perfectly comfortable in it, a change is good for a girl. Thinking to ask Uncle, hoping he was in the same mood we'd had before lunch.

I trailed after him, back to his study. I breached the shopping plan with him, "Uncle, any chance we can make a stop among one of the many tourist trap places among these islands to pick up some islander clothing?" Uncle stopped in his tracks and I almost walked into him, he stood with his back to me, crutch under his arm. "Ri'Anne and I have been forced to wear the same things for three days now." Which I realized, I'd just lied to him – Ri'Anne had a new flowery suit, as of this morning. I should ask her about it since she wasn't going to explain.

Uncle turned around and it looked like I'd sucker punched him.

My mouth wouldn't stop once I'd started, even though my heart wasn't in it anymore, "As much as I could live in a suit, some change of clothes would be nice."

His face went through a wide range of emotions, but I could tell he was hurt by the request, "Do we have to Melanie?"

I debated, realizing I should have gone through Dad with the request. He'd made the decision to not shop in Papua, after all. "I'm sorry. I shouldn't have asked," and I turned to go.

"No, hold on. You were right for asking, but the timing couldn't be worse. You should have gotten something while we were in port." Seeing my expression, he guessed at its cause. "Jeb forbade it?" I didn't blink, nod or anything, but he read me anyway. "Why would he do that? Gave one of his 'we're fine' speeches?" Holding up a hand palm towards me, "Don't answer. You do yourself credit by being loyal to him."

He temporized, "I have tons of things you can borrow. I know they aren't girl things, but I have shirts galore that are long enough for short girls like you two. Will that do?"

I bit my lip. Technically I was fine wearing the same swimsuit. But I nodded, because I thought I'd be fine with whatever he had, if only for appearance sakes. That was all that mattered.

"I have an idea. Here," and he dug into a bucket of old shirts he used as rags. "Let's see if we can unbend your dad a little. Why don't you exchange your suit for this. If he sees you in rags he might 'spend' a little." Holding it up, he examined it, and then seeing it too full of holes he switched it for another, once colorful, now-faded rag. It had a few long gashes on the back, reminding me of tops that had no backs. "Go ahead and change into that," he said tossing it to me. Then he turned the request around on me, "You're going to get a rash wearing that suit all the time."

I stepped into the bathroom to change. That didn't go as planned. Uncle was losing his gratitude quickly for Dad and I coming all this way. It was understandable, he'd been cooped up thinking about his work for a while, and we were here to help him get his work done. No, that's unfair, but now that we were here he wanted to get on with his work – and we were a part of that.

I officially switched to his shirt, but what to do with a suit that wasn't a suit? The fish hid themselves somewhere. The shirt was big, comfortable, ratty and ugly – the perfect rag.

Looking at myself in the mirror I wasn't sure if I should laugh or cry at my appearance. "Perfect" mermaid hair, bright complexion – nice fingernails. I felt like a waif in an Oliver play. I needed some dirt for my cheeks because I looked too good for the shirt. It was even complete with stains. Just great. If Dad didn't have a fit, I was sure to. At least it didn't *smell* bad.

Coming out of the bathroom, Uncle frowned at my new dress. "You make that look good, now twirl. Hmm, it needs a belt. Come here," and he pulled out some scissors, snipped by my waist a couple times and then pulled the snips tight. There was a slight rip, and then, "Ok, that'll do. Here, give me those, I'll drop them in your room." With feigned gladness I gave him the sarong hoping he wouldn't notice the fish-suit not being in what I gave him.

I leaned back over to study the charts as he'd instructed. But after a bit, I got bored with the wide sea passing us by and walked to the sliding door to the deck and let myself out. I'd promised myself a swim on awakening, but now that possibility was gone and I had to make do with leaning out on the railing as Ri'Anne and I had done the day before. I opened my hand before me, coaxing the fish out onto it. It was a second before they appeared, and only a couple appeared. Waiting a little longer I realized, I had only two fish.

Standing there stunned, I wondered, *Where did they go to? What was I to do without fish?* My whole existence as a mermaid went back to when Jill gave me them. Feeling like the floor had been pulled from under me I gripped the railing tightly. Was I going to be able to breathe water without them?

I had a feeling, these two were alone with me.

"You guys don't have to disappear," I told them suddenly weak in the knees and stepping down from the railing, knowing I couldn't ask them to stay. Their job was to be a swimsuit for me. "What am I to do?" I asked, but I didn't expect them to answer; they'd never yet spoken to me.

Did they just shrug? Fish shrugging without shoulders, that made me smile, but I knew if I let these two go I'd be without fish completely. I almost tipped my hand over dropping the fish into the sea beneath me, feeling fatalistic. But the fish were my only link to decency, and what would I do if Uncle said, "Go get suited up," and I had no fish? Looking at the two of them, I knew they wouldn't be enough for a full swimsuit. So what was I to do?

I had to keep them. Could they be jewelry? I had no bracelets or rings, that they could disguise themselves as. In my pack I had a whole pocket full of unused hair ties and barrettes, would that work? I hadn't used any in a while, my hair behaving better than any hair tie ever could do for me. I'd changed since deciding to be a mermaid, not having to use hair fasteners only one outward sign of the change, but now I needed one – if only so a fish could disguise itself as one.

Attuning to Ri'Anne, she was in our cabin braiding her hair. I composed a bubble message, asking her, **Can you bring me my bag? Please hurry,** I emphasized, giving her my location.

She met me in the study, my pack over her shoulder. I sat holding the fish, one hand cupped over the other.

"What is that?" she asked in a hushed whisper, eyeing my hands and coming to the table I sat at, sitting across from me. But really I could see she was wanting to ask how I'd talked to her.

About to reveal the *how*, I uncovered my hand and gasped, there was a single fish remaining. And it was the smallest of the two. I was astonished at seeing the one. They must need to be needed.

"Put a barrette in my hair," I told Ri'Anne hurriedly, afraid the last fish was going to go the way of the others. "I'll explain in a minute," and Ri'Anne grabbed out the fastener and stood behind me, fingering my hair and combing it until she had it layered just the way she wanted it to be. *Oh girls!* I complained inwardly, knowing I would have done the same.

"There," Ri'Anne said, patting the barrette into place, and then resuming her seat. "Now what?" she asked, looking out the panoramic window that gave us a view of the passing sea, the waves tossing off sprays as the open sea wind whipped along their tops. but her face said she'd ask openly about the sending if I didn't explain soon. I would get to that. First though I needed to keep the remaining fish, or be fish-less.

Looking at the fish, I pictured the barrette in my hair and asked it, “Can you be the barrette? Please, I need you to stay.” I was pleading with it. “Afterwards, you can be a swimsuit too. If only one can be...” Before I finished speaking, the fish swam up my arm and then my neck to my head. Out popped the barrette onto the floor. When I lifted my hand to the spot, I could feel a barrette.

With a surprised look, Ri’Anne watched the barrette dance as it bounced across the floor. The roll of the yacht causing it to slide under the chair. “What was all that about?” Ri’Anne asked bending to pick up the fallen barrette and putting it back in the bag.

“You saw what Uncle gave you, and what he ‘said’ he gave you?” I leaned back, I could relax now. I felt if my mermaid existence was wound up in these fish and now that I’d kept one, I could go on.

“I saw,” she nodded. “He said he was giving me your skirt and suit, but when I got to the room it was just the skirt. Which of course I would have thought it a complete change in direction had you given him a pile of fish.”

“Well now I’m left as you see me. My fish have disappeared. I guess they go away if not needed.”

Sliding open the window a crack, I let the breeze blow through my fingers. The wind blowed over my skin and through the holes of my “new” shirt. “I do hope they return, but if they don’t I’ll have to figure something out and soon.”

Closing the window I told her of my failed attempt at getting Uncle to stop. “At your suggestion, I tried to talk Uncle into stopping so we could buy clothes, instead he insisted I wear his things and gave me this shirt."

"That's not bad," Ri'Anne said, stepping around the table to run her fingers over the shirt and through its many holes. "Actually, I kind of like it. He said we both could use his things?"

I nodded, "There's more of these in those buckets," and I waved at the one with the rejected rag hanging out. Continuing I said, "I tried convincing him we needed a change of outfits. He agreed, insisting we'd get a rash wearing the same thing all the time."

"You're concerned with a rash?" Ri'Anne asked laughing. "Think of this as an opportunity," Ri'Anne said fishing through the buckets, deciding on the one that Uncle had at first rejected, saying "This will look good over my suit." Then turning back to me, she finally noticed my troubled expression and raised an eyebrow. The first time she'd seen me in doubt. Giving up at least for the moment her desire to learn the sending trick.

It took me a little while to figure out what to say, but finally I was able to put words to my feelings. "I cannot imagine going on as a mermaid without the fish. They are as important to me as breathing. Magic is hindered by anything non-magical worn as clothing. With this simple shirt, I feel less effective."

"But you don't have to remain without a sea suit, as I was trying to explain at breakfast. Take for example my swimsuit," Ri'Anne said laying the shirt she'd picked out over her suit and comparing it to the blooming vines that were her top. "These," she said tracing the flowers with a finger, "came from plant cuttings. It seems you were right on becoming a mermaid, by doing mermaid things. If having these vegetable plants bloom and become a swimsuit for me is any indication, your magic is becoming my magic. There's no way they'd bloom so beautifully on their own otherwise."

"They came so easily for me, and I'm a beginner. I'm betting you could get a suit from about any fish. As a larger-than-life mermaid you should be wearing the sea, not just a few fish. Sea snakes, eels, octopuses, sharks, and every growing plant is yours for the picking. Have an aquarium for a swimsuit! If you're stuck on fish, even the water itself should be your clothing. I'm betting if you put your mind to it, you could get the fish to move across the suit as if it was a real fish tank."

Ri'Anne suggestions were supposed to encourage, but I wasn't so sure. I couldn't help but think the fish Jill had given me were special. In more ways than the fact that they'd been given to me by my best friend. What was I to tell her? That I didn't treasure her gift? How could I go on and wear any ole fish?

While I struggled inwardly, Ri'Anne tried on the shirt, and spun about. Something moved under her shirt like a snake, my eyes opening wider and wider until I caught sight of the vine flowers of her swimsuit spiraling up and out of several holes in the dress length shirt. With mouth agape, I gasped, the pain of my fish having abandoned me gone for the moment. The vines were casting little flowers with shrouds of leaves out of the holes. "I think they like it."

"What? Oh!" The flowers complimented the shirt, and more of the vine grew catching up her hair to disappear only to flower beside her ear. Ri'Anne's fingers brushed the delicate flower. It and its vine enjoying the attention. "You're going to get me into trouble," she told it and plucked it off her ear and snipped it from her neck, pulling it out of her hair by its long stem. Looking for somewhere to toss it, she shrugged and slid it up her sleeve, where it rejoined the rest of the suit.

With my jaw in hand, I did an imitation of a fish out of water at her antics. My thoughts catching up to what she'd been saying, I wondered aloud hoping what she'd said was true, "So you think the first chance I swim around fish, they'd join me?" She nodded, not having thought it strange that the plants were "swimming" around on her. "Oh, by the way we could test that later," I mentioned Uncle's plan for our swim. "Uncle says we'll be near some reefs where we can swim and clean up."

"Which of course leads us to your dilemma, so you don't have to hide." Ri'Anne continued and my head popped up at that all ears for any way out of the situation. "We need to involve your uncle. He needs to have 'magical' experiences that don't point at you, but include us."

Standing up, I frowned at that, seeing several obstacles. "Uncle's not dumb, he's liable to come to the conclusion that either you or Gigi are responsible unless I give him a specific reason to think it's me. He doesn't know either of you, and Gigi is the mysterious lady of fortune. What did you have in mind?"

Seeing that we were arriving at our destination, I turned for the doors forward. Going out front, Dad was slowing the yacht as we were headed in towards a large island. Ri'Anne came out after me asking, "How about during our swim you get some seagull to talk to him. I know we're supposed to be 'bathing,' but we can mix business with pleasure."

She continued as we sat on the soft white fake leather sun couches, the breeze no longer cold as we slowed to a gentle cruise to navigate through the reefs. "Your uncle and I were talking earlier. He has a bunch of cameras to put on the bottom of the boat. Perhaps we can involve him then. We could use the practice, and during it, you can have some 'fun' talking to him as a bird."

"That's going too far. I could swim, or bathe, and do the camera thing," I thought out loud, pulling my feet in beside me, to lean on my arm as we talked. "But he'll know it's me for sure."

"Plant the barrette fish on him," she suggested leaning back on her chair and stretching out her legs to cross her ankles. "Surely it can modify what he hears."

I shook my head, my life was crazy enough, but this, "You really think that will work? And, it's my last fish." I thought my life would come to a halt if I gave it away, or I might stop being a mermaid and told her so.

"You're being silly. Don't worry," Ri'Anne coxed and pushed away my fears. "At least until we go swimming, or try one of the other ideas we were just talking about. The problem is, we can't be wearing suits when we come out, or they'll wonder where we're getting the change of clothes."

"Ri'Anne, do you really have to think of everything?" I complained. A moment ago she was forgetting details.

"It's not like you didn't think this was going to happen." Honestly I hadn't. Seeing my expression, she added, "We don't have to, but it was your idea."

No. Really it had been Uncle's. Normally he didn't think about anyone than himself, but in this it was really smart. Us girls did need time to ourselves. Only by accident had Ri'Anne and I spent any time in the water together. General swimming among the reefs, I had a lot of hopes pinned on this swim; getting Ri'Anne comfortable on her own as a mermaid. Well, and now planting Uncle's devices.

"You know," she said picking at her fingernail polish, "This could work. You get him talking to a seagull, and before you know it he's talking to us, mind to mind. He'll think it's all him."

I hated to be a spoilsport, "But, what about when he tries to do it with others?"

"You're saying it won't work?" I shrugged, she was right I didn't know. I really didn't know how long it took for someone to learn our ways and adopt them. "Well, until your uncle figures it out. How about it only works when we're swimming?"

I saw the hole in that immediately, "How is that supposed to make him think it is him and not one of us, if it is bound to us?"

Then it was Ri'Anne's turn to complain, "Do I have to be the one to think of everything? I say we give it a try." And that was that.

15

Spider Island

We passed away the remaining time until our bath time, enjoying the island view and preparing for our fun. The island was a pretty place, with some hills or small mountains draped with green, a living thriving paradise. There wasn't much in the way of a population, at least none that I could see. But I knew that was true for a lot of these islands. The soil was too sandy to support a lot of people.

"Sometimes it's the local chieftain that has the authority," I was telling Ri'Anne.

"You sure know your way around. It must be nice to have an uncle with a fabulous yacht to cruise in," Ri'Anne was saying, but she didn't sound jealous. I used to consider it a pain to "have" to come on these trips, while Uncle filled my head with trivia.

"You know," Ri'Anne continued, "If we're going to do the seagull talking bit together, you're going to have to show me the trick too."

Sure, why not? Ri'Anne was already picking up on things quickly. **Well, to do it,** I explained in a bubble message, sending the whole time. Her eyes grew real big hearing me in her mind, knowing for certain she hadn't imagined it before. Jill had made it clear, I was to be cautious sharing magic, and Uncle had cameras all over the yacht. **You have to believe it works, and seeing me do it helps – but you're going to have to want it too.**

"I do want it," Ri'Anne said aloud.

That's close, I sent having heard her thought too, **But use your mind only. Speak as if you're saying it aloud, but don't.**

Like this? Oh… and Ri'Anne fell over. I jumped up shocked and ran to her side. She was attempting to speak, "Water…" she croaked, barely audible.

Water, right! I should be teaching her in water! Amateur mistake.

I ran to get us some water bottles. Returning I poured some on her face, my hands shook and the water splashed all over her, some managing to find her mouth. Licking her lips, she held out her hand for the bottle. Because of the shakes, I nearly dropped the bottle. But then she had it and was sipping at it. The water was disappearing faster than she could possibly have been drinking it.

Mermaids out of water, she sent clearer. Then held out the empty bottle for another one.

It gets easier, I told her. I wasn't feeling parched at all, but remembered my need when searching Papua's bay for fish. Being immersed would be better. **But, it still requires effort – not just water.**

Let's clean, she suggested sitting up feeling better, her brows knitting together at the effort to talk this way. **It'll give us a chance to use lots of water,** she explained at the sudden change in topic and the unusual request. I laughed at that, and together we went in search of a pail and some brushes.

Dad suggested the deck hose. Once we had an unlimited supply of water in which to play with, we worked on letting one another see through the other. We were both going to try and let Uncle use our hands and feet, as if we were unaware of it, or at least see through our eyes. We practiced it until we were sure we could "let" Uncle be us, but ended it in a water fight. **Hey,** Ri'Anne sent, ** We have to save 'bath' time for later... ** And then she was blasting me with the hose until I gave in.

We arrived, and the anchor went down. Then there was a loud whirring noise coming from the back of the yacht. By the time we arrived, the back of the yacht had split open to drop away to form a swim deck. "Nice work Dad," I said to him as he came down from the command deck, slipping my hand into his. Together we ogled the unexpectedly delicate stairs down to the fanciful wood deck that was bare inches above the waterline. "I never knew The Lazy Cloud had such grace," I said to Uncle, who leaned against the railing beside us.

"Never seems worth using it when I'm alone," Uncle admitted. I managed to slip him the remaining fish. Where it went, I didn't know, but I advised it to hide so well even he couldn't find it. Having it on him, I immediately sensed his presence.

**Do you feel the fish?* I asked Ri'Anne in a bubble message, and she gave me a nod.

Unaware that Ri'Anne and I were talking mind-to-mind, Uncle kept talking. "It's better than a ladder, but it has one too for the lazy…" Were Ri'Anne or I the lazy types? he asked with his eyes, "No?" And we both shook our heads. "Good." The swim deck was only a few inches above the waterline. I'd lifted myself from pools with higher sides than that. "So we can do this little operation of yours, and you can maintain your privacy at the same time."

I wanted to say, *except for the cameras we'd be installing.* So far, if he was thinking this way, then I had to assume we'd be ok.

Our plan was moving ahead. The seagull we'd picked flew back to perch on the winch after being driven off when the swim deck was lowered, and it dodged Uncle's every attempt at shooing it away. I could hear the seagull, and through the fish sent Uncle everything it said, doing my best to imitate the seagull's mannerisms.

"I swear, that thing is talking to me," he complained and Ri'Anne laughed almost giving us away. "It calls me a dimwitted landlubber," which had the rest of us laughing. Out of all of us, he was the least likely to be called a land lover.

We ate lunch while Gigi made the aft swim deck presentable. It had been years since it had been opened.

"We can start," Uncle said, holding up some boxes the size of credit cards. "By affixing these to the hull, I won't feel nearly as helpless and can help guide the dives. And if a camera goes overboard again, we can use their strength in the search."

These nearly invisible cameras were to go under the waterline of the yacht so he could see downward. No more swimming with sharks down under. It was difficult anyway, being a mermaid in present day – there were cameras everywhere. I had to hope the magic of a mermaid extended to them as well. Besides, Uncle wouldn't always have me around – he needed every tool at his disposal.

After lunch Dad and Uncle made themselves scarce, to let Ri'Anne and I have a little time before the camera operation. Stepping down to the lower swim deck we joined Gigi in setting up folding chairs. Then she surprised us by laying out fabulous swim suits.

"These are from Enrico, back at the port," Gigi told us. I wasn't sure whether I should be delighted. "Your dad might not like it, but they are mine and you are borrowing them, if he asks." She then gave a wink and went up all the steps to the weather deck, above the command deck, carrying a chair so she could sit and read in comfort. There was nothing up there except antennas.

Sitting and putting my feet in the water, Ri'Anne rummaged through the suits. Easily adapting to the change she said, "At least now we don't have to explain where we're coming up with any odd swimsuits."

"I suppose," but they didn't fit with our plan. And taking one look at them and I knew I'd never wear them. The thought of any one of them touching my skin gave me the creeps. I was too much of a mermaid now.

Seeing my expression Ri'Anne asked, "What's wrong with them? They're beautiful. You don't like second hand clothes? I thought you did…"

"It's not that." Pulling my arms within the t-shirt of Uncle's, I turned it around to look at the tag, a hundred-percent cotton. "It has to be the fabric, nylons and the like make my skin crawl. I need all natural."

"And that is why we are here, to experiment in that area. But they give us cover, not to wear mind you, but if I have say blue flowers one day," she said holding up a like top, "and orange the next, I can point to them there if I need an excuse. That's all."

Pulling off the shirt, I was feeling moody. I didn't like my emotions, feeling out of touch, because I'd been abandoned by the fish of my suit. Looking at my dark Greek legs, I lifted them up out of the water to verify they were still smooth. I was filled with doubt without the suit. Did the fish of my suit make me a mermaid? Feeling my legs, they were still silky soft, and when I dropped them back in the water, I felt the water rise up within me. Cupping some water with my hands, I pulled it up to, well to cover myself. But the whole boat rocked as I drew on the water, Ri'Anne stumbling. I instantly let go of the water and caught her.

"What was that?" she asked, deciding to take a seat beside me before she fell over. I shrugged, not wanting to explain it, but I think the water I lifted thought I was pulling the boat down, the best I could figure. It did make me feel slightly better knowing there were unexplained watery puzzles going on about me. I think I'd regret the day I didn't learn something new.

Ri'Anne sat beside me, removing the cuttings that made up her suit and they cracked into green dust and blew away. So that's what happened to plant coverings. My heart dropped at seeing the dust blow away – my fish must die if removed too. I wanted to cry and did. I'd begun to think of them as lifelong friends, to think of them as gone for good was difficult.

"Hey," Ri'Anne said bumping me with her shoulder. "Remember, fish come around when you're near. They'll come, and you'll be dressed like a princess again."

"I think I prefer the rags look," I admitted, thinking I might be too old to want to be a princess anymore.

"Well we do make them look good," Ri'Anne said with a winning smile. Then pulling her legs up, she said, "That tickles." And then looked aside at me, "The fish are nibbling on my legs. You know," she said thoughtfully rubbing her legs. "I haven't shaved since we arrived, and my legs – they're smooth!"

Feeling them too, I had to smile at her smooth skin. *Ok, so the magic isn't gone. So why did the fish have to leave?* It didn't make any sense to me, but then I really didn't know the hows or whys to being a mermaid. I barely understood that I was indeed one, and mostly because others told me. My mermaid companions had always been creatures, affirming to me my choice in doing what I did. But now I realized I was going to have to slip in, fish or no fish, and be a mermaid.

Ri'Anne had slipped in and was looking at me from where she rested her chin on her crossed arms. It was one of our favorite things to do at the gym, to hang to the edge of the pool and listen to coach in exactly that pose. Now Ri'Anne looked cute, and I wanted to join her, but I couldn't get over the fact that I was different without the fish.

"C'mon," Ri'Anne said taking me by the wrist and pulling me in. "I want to swim!"

I dropped down about five feet and turned into a seated position, Ri'Anne joining me… "I can breathe and talk!" Giving me a quick hug, she sat beside me, drinking in the experience. There were fish, but not so many, or of the size to be our swimsuits. "So there are fish, but why don't they 'join' us?" Ri'Anne asked.

I dove deeper, wondering exactly that. Ri'Anne turned to follow, and we drifted down to the colorful coral and the thriving community of life there. With the sea life all about me I no longer felt alone, and I did tell her, "They are with us." I answered her. "I think it is because I resent them leaving that I can't bring myself to open myself to trusting them again."

Hopping over some shallows, we dove over them into a deep pool. Ri'Anne said as we went over, "Don't you think it goes both ways? Do you think they might resent you abandoning them?"

"But," I said as we treaded water, "It isn't like I intentionally gave them up."

Ri'Anne tipped her head back so that only her face showed above water, saying, "Seemed that way to me. I thought your uncle was giving me fish in the sarong, even if that isn't what you thought was happening." I couldn't help affirm that is what I'd intended everyone to believe, or at least for Ri'Anne to pretend to believe. Apparently I'd gone overboard on the issue, and had really given away the fish.

"So what do you suggest to get some back?" I asked as we aimed for a shallow area to rest.

"Invite those around us. There are so many pretty fish here," Ri'Anne examined the coral mere inches beneath us, waving at all the fish whose scales rippled like gems. "I'm sure they'd join you." Gentle waves rippled across us in the shallows, the golden sun making the water as warm as bath water.

Turning my heart on the idea, I didn't even have to ask, suddenly I was surrounded by suit-sized fish. They came out of the coral and swam in close. But they remained fish as we stood to go sit by a tall ridge reef that lay exposed to the sun. Its hard surface had eroded under wind and weather, but it gave us a tiny bit of shade. The fish of my hopefully new suit swam the inch deep water to rest against my sides.

I sat down in the shallow pool of water that existed there. Looking over at Ri'Anne who was sunning herself in another puddle, playing with a handful of reeds. It didn't take me long to figure she'd rather have plants for a swimsuit, and I needed to know how she handled that so easily.

"How do I get the fish to become magical fish?" I asked, joining her in her pool. "Your plants do all the magical stuff that I'm used to."

"Have you tried singing to them?" she suggested looking at me, and I looked at her, startled. "All mermaids sing, don't you know? Don't look so surprised." Smiling, she leaned in close, our eyes inches apart, "You have such a lovely voice."

"But, but," She was right with the mermaids singing thing. Part of the fantasy we'd grown up with was that mermaids sang like angels, with pitch perfect voices and knowing every song.

"Sing to them?" I asked thinking out loud. The funny thing was, I liked singing, truly, but I didn't think I was very good.

I knew there were melodies in the sea, the sun, wind and stars. I did feel them. The sea was the loudest to me. I found the sea alive with the sound of music. "But, what to sing?" I asked her.

"Be magical," Ri'Anne suggested. "Think of the fish shimmering us in radiant glory, princess gowns of living color."

Laughing at Ri'Anne, at her princess one-track mind, a melody did come to mind. But I'd have to make up the words. I almost didn't sing it, thinking I might not be able to carry it through. But the sea was right there with us, and I needed the suit. I had to give it a try or continue to go without a suit and that wasn't acceptable.

The wind carried in the sound of the sea, and I let that fill my heart. Waves were lapping at our feet, and crashing on the reef beside us, and I kicked my feet to their timing. Above us the radiance of the sun basked us in its glory, but it was from the water I lay in that I sang to the fish,

"First off, I'd like to say I'm sorry, fish of the
sea, in the beautiful waves, sparkling in the
sunlight. You could choose a life different
from mine.

I apologize for not considering you. How
can I express your incredible talents that

have no tale? In a sea with wonders that
leave me breathless…

It seemed the melody was enough as it came from my heart. The fish that had been gasping for air in the shallows, stirred at the first notes. Waves of water rippled up over me, carrying some of the fish until the water and the fish covered me as a patchwork, worse than my "holy" shirt. I drifted off with the words when this was happening, but continued to hum the tune that was alive in my heart, and slowly the fish rippled and became one garment. When it "snapped" to me, to be like my old suit, I stopped.

Turning to Ri'Anne and in surprise, I saw the fish and water had done the same to her. Together we basked in the glittering suits, we both sat up seeing that the fish stayed with us. Standing, Ri'Anne wanted to see what the song had done for the fish, noticing that they did indeed stay with her as she stood. Twirling about, "Do we have to call them fish suits?" she asked.

I shook my head, "What do you suggest?" I asked her back.

"These are mermaid suits," she declared and our fish flashed as bright as the sun.

"Woah, too bright!" I shouted shielding my eyes with both hands as our suits quickened, gaining the intelligence my previous suit had displayed. I'd thought the fish-suit they'd made was fine, but with Ri'Anne's words they shimmered, at first becoming a sparkling leotard of glittering scales, but the shimmer continued until the scales were as small as glitter becoming a swimsuit. Hers were all gold, making her look like she had gold skin.

Ri'Anne dove in to swim out to where it was deeper, but stayed between the two reefs. Diving after her, I caught up saying "I like mermaid suit better. But what are we going to do when we're installing the equipment?"

"Scatter," she said gesturing wildly, fingers curled like claws as if she was the controller of puppets.

Huh? What? Then on seeing our fish disperse and the suit disappear, I realized she was talking to our fish. They spread out to resemble the sea around us with the "normal" fish swimming here and there.

"How is that going to help?" I asked, wondering if we wanted to appear in garments so fine.

With a toss of her hair, she looked at me with her head tilted, "I'm confused. Didn't you want them gone?"

"I do," I said trying to copy her head tilt. "It just seems we're back to the problem of being…"

"On our own, just us, what?" she asked, still confused and turned to splash the water before her, running her hands across the top of the water.

Leaning back, I kicked my feet in the water gently, tilting my head until my ears were in the water – I floated. "I was afraid they'd left me again. Sorry."

Pushing a wave to pass over me, she said "No worries. They are all around us, mostly unseen – but you shouldn't worry. They'd never leave us."

"How can you be certain?" I asked, lifting my head to look her way. Ri'Anne was more confident than I was and comfortable in her skin. But that wasn't what was bothering me, I was still skittish, afraid that the fish might leave me.

Lifting a hand so that the water rolled off her palm she said, "It isn't in their nature to abandon us. Just like my plants, they want to be needed." Then she went back to making pancakes of the water ripples with the palms of her hands.

"So how'd the fish know to do that?" I asked sinking to the bottom to gaze at the undersea world.

"You taught me," she said looking down at me through the water.

"I did?" I asked popping up in surprise. I hadn't told her anything of the kind.

"You said to picture what you want. Well I did that with the 'scatter.' Saying in essence, be 'invisible' to a casual look and not to attract attention. As you can see, or not see, they are doing what is needed. Words help aim the magic," Ri'Anne summed up. I guess it was like when we are speaking, carrying a message in the words to another. How the seagull had told me where The Lazy Cloud was while we were in port and I'd told them where to find the fish, never really saying where. I'd known and they'd known. So knowing what you wanted, just as I'd always used with transfers, did the trick. I was so glad Ri'Anne was with me. I was pretty sure I'd not have understood it on my own.

"Good thinking," I told her. I was thankful too that we had figured out the trick to having fish join us. I hadn't imagined it could be so unnerving to be without my mermaid clothes.

In a change of topic, she said "We should practice with them." Standing to the top of the tall reef, she dove off into the deep water on the other side. I followed after her, and we curved out of the cove, she using more mermaid swim speed than I was used to. I could see her delighting at the newfound freedom. When I caught up to her, we twined, spiraling around one another.

"It's working," Ri'Anne said pleased. "The fish spiral around with us," and we weren't making it easy on them.

I laughed, enjoying it as well, shouting happily, "Nor are the fish confused about which of us to follow." Then spinning away from each other, with our hands out as if they were wings, we twirled as fast as we could becoming little spinning tops before gliding in lazy spirals enjoying the wide warm sea. I was glad to have the fish back, but they didn't make me a mermaid. I was narrowing it down in what it meant to be a mermaid and I was one in spite of the fish of my original suit having left me.

16

The Same Old Doom and Gloom

The clear aqua waters went on forever and I wanted to swim in them for all time, getting lost in the moment. Ri'Anne coming out of her twist, her fish creating a flag behind her as they streamed after her, suggested that we should be getting back to our chores. It was to be our first real dive for Uncle, though it was going to be practice.

The seafloor was much deeper than was apparent, the coral reefs thick and tall, creating a maze to dive through. Seeing some things Uncle would want to examine, I went to capture them. The first a tiny starfish that had odd spots, whose name incidentally was "Spotty." Then there was "Jarmin," the two-headed eel.

Hoisting myself up onto the swim deck, I had a moment of trepidation. Uncle hadn't seen Gigi's suits yet, so how was I to explain mine? But at least now I could go boldly to him in the suit I wore. *Wrap yourself in a towel,* I told myself.

I found Dad in Uncle's lab, instead of Uncle. He was cleaning up a statue that was covered in layers of crustaceans. It was quite impossible to tell what the statue was supposed to be. He pointed me out onto the front deck where I found Uncle reading.

"Bring me more, Melanie," Uncle begged getting his first real samples in weeks. "These are great," and I beamed at his praise.

Coming back with handfuls of this and that for him, he dropped them in baggies and labeled them. "Ok, that's enough," Uncle said at Dad's prompting, Dad reminding him that it was our swim time.

"You have your swim, don't come back for an hour or more. No wait," and he looked at Dad. "You can do that after we get the equipment installed…" Hurrying on before Dad could interrupt him he said, "Then you can have the rest of the day, deal?" I waited on Dad's nod before I agreed, and then ran back into the water to go find Ri'Anne.

We returned and sat on the end of the swim deck, our new suits shimmering in the sun. Uncle made extra noise coming up on deck, alerting us to his presence, but it wasn't needed. When we didn't hide, he slowly looked around and discovered that we were dressed in our mermaid suits. Our "new" suits passed for extravagant girly beach wear, of the kind Enrico had bought for his girls. And that we could pretend to wear from now on.

"Good," he said setting down his box on a chair. "You're ready."

It was time to put Ri'Anne's plan to work. And it was about time for the magic to affect my family. Since songs helped bind sea life to me, I hummed a few bars of the song I'd been singing on my lips hoping it would do the same for him now.

Fire raced over us, and I knew another mysterious "mermaid" change was begun. It had started with the song, but now was alive in a new way as we got ready to include Uncle in our mystery.

Ri'Anne said with a smile, eyeing the seagull we'd chosen, "This is going to be fun." She was feeling the fire too.

"The sockets will need to be cleaned," Uncle told us, holding up a pair of brushes. Then he was handing out flippers, masks and snorkels. I felt like I'd been slapped. It was such a shock, but then I had to wake myself up from my mermaid fantasy. Uncle lived in the "real world" where there wasn't magic or singing to fish to become clothing.

"Mind if I free-dive Mr. McKenzie?" Ri'Anne asked. I silently cheered at Ri'Anne's boldness.

"But, you should at least use a mask…" he suggested, suddenly uncomfortable with talking to Ri'Anne. I couldn't only guess at the cause, looking at her. The mermaid changes she was experiencing made her particularly fetching in her gold suit. Her eyes and complexion were radiant. If I'd known Uncle was weak for girl charms, I'd have tried that ages ago. He'd always seemed indifferent before.

"We'll be ok," I told him, and Ri'Anne giggled. **A little much,** I sent to her and she dropped into the water before she could embarrass herself further.

He looked miffed, sure that we were now wasting his time by not using gear. But then he uncrossed his arms and said, becoming gruff again, "You still have to find the places to put the devices and clean them off," and passed us each a brush.

We'd be alone on opposite sides starting at the bow and working our way aft. We both gave him a thumbs up, and Ri'Anne sent to me, **Let's do this. And remember, let him experience us slowly, so as not to freak him out.** I smiled, thinking Ri'Anne was taking to this quickly. She'd be a right 'ole mermaid in no time.

Inhaling like we needed to hold our breaths, we dropped under and swam under the yacht past the huge propellers that were sitting idle. I couldn't help but add extra space between them and myself as I passed. Swimming at normal speed, kicking along I opened myself up, letting the water fill me with a sense of the sea about me. I attuned to Uncle and let him feel what I was feeling as we'd practiced; the water on my hands, shoulders and feet, and a semblance of what I was seeing, Ri'Anne doing the same, we coordinating together. Knowing it would be a shock, I ignored his reaction and let it continue. Then, when I judged I'd been under long enough, I went up for air.

It was pretty easy to include Uncle, and I felt almost like he was there with us in person, swimming along beside us. It was his presence that made me feel that way, and he was tentative at first, thinking it was purely his imagination getting the better of him. But when it continued, and he experienced our thrill at experiencing the sea, and he began to accept the dreamlike wonder. When I came up for air again, I felt him want to wander forward to speak to me, to confirm that it was real. He became frustrated that he wasn't mobile enough, and then became relieved that he had us to do this for him.

Patting the side of the yacht, I dove down again, going down deep enough to check Ri'Anne's progress and to try to match my effort to hers. This was really in an effort to let Uncle "keep" us working at the same rate. He knew where we were connected to each other, but I still had to pretend that I didn't know that he knew, and so I ducked under the bottom of the boat to check on Ri'Anne. Being a part of the swim team, we were both good swimmers and it was sorely tempting to swim over and join her. But we'd decided to keep to ourselves.

I felt Uncle's impatience at my dawdling, strangely enough, and I turned to continue onward. Going at a normal pace, the swim seemed to take forever, but it wasn't that big of a boat and I arrived. It didn't take us, Uncle and I, long to find the spot that the device was to go on and I felt Uncle's elation when I saw it.

He was taking to this all too quickly. Then I felt him wanting to use my hands, because I wasn't going fast enough for him, but that wasn't a level to which I wanted to go. I didn't want to become a remotely controlled robot. Again, he became frustrated that I resisted him, but then he eased up by finding that he could be more effective guiding rather than controlling. He had the two of us to do twice the work faster than he could do alone.

The brush made quick work of the algae in the small indentation, and then I worked on cleaning up the power and communication contacts. When Uncle was satisfied, I knew. Then he wanted me to move onto the next one. The first had been the easiest to find, and it took Uncle a time to find the next one. We actually ended up finding the third one first. It hadn't been that long since he'd cleaned the bottom of the yacht, I could hear him complaining inwardly. I had a feeling, given the opportunity, he'd be using the two of us for that purpose.

Finding the second one I got to scrubbing it out. I'd stopped feeling Uncle's direction and guessed he'd tired out. These abilities could be taxing on anyone as I myself had experienced several times. Once I had the five camera sockets cleaned out on my side, I was tired too and wanted to stretch out in the sun. I swam back along the side of the yacht to the swim deck. Ri'Anne had beaten me to it and she was up on the deck getting the devices. Uncle was asleep on one of the chairs.

Ri'Anne sent to me, **When he wakes up, let up and make it weaker. We've alerted him to the possibility, just try to be sensitive to him wanting more.**

"Within limits," I sent back. "I forgot to anticipate it, but these abilities don't come without costs." He would need water too. I went to find him a bottle of water, and set it by him for when he awoke.

"I don't know the first thing about this," Ri'Anne said, making conversation. We were up on deck trying to do Uncle's work as well as our own.

"Well, let's leave it for Uncle then," I said wearily, sitting down on an empty chair. She hooked a thumb forward, and together we replaced the devices in the kits and then went to the bow to relax on the cushions there.

"Installing the cameras is more tiring than I'd like to admit. Especially scrubbing out their sockets," Ri'Anne said rubbing her shoulders. "Can you?" she asked, asking me to give her a shoulder rub. Sliding in behind her, I worked at loosening her up. Playing my hands over her shoulders and back, she moaned as her stiff muscles were worked out.

"Here," Ri'Anne said picking up a brown bottle she'd brought out, "Use the oil that Gigi picked up in port." And when I uncapped it she said, "All over, I want to smell like that."

"All over?" I asked holding the open bottle over her head.

"Obviously not all over," she said, pushing away my hand, which made me spill it on her face. She wiped it off with her hand and turned to get me with it too.

"Hold still," I complained trying to work her muscles, getting it in more places than intended because I still had the bottle uncapped and we were now facing each other.

Leaning into me she pushed me backwards and took the bottle to work on me. "My turn." But I was ticklish and she wouldn't leave me alone. What began as a massage ended up a wrestling match as we slid on the now-oily couch, neither able to get a grip on the other before we gave up laughing breathlessly, laying all a tangle with arms and legs intertwined, gleaming in the sun.

"That was fun," I said breathlessly and Ri'Anne "Uh-hum'd" too, soundly sleepy. I was right there with her. "Though I wish Uncle had his cameras on to record it – I'd love to review it."

"They're on all the time," Ri'Anne said and I looked to her, she was twisted to her side with her head on her hands, studying me. "We were talking. He said he needed a new hard drive when he picked us up. You don't remember? Anyway, he said that leaving them on was easier than forgetting to have them on when needed. He picked up some software to help him go through the recordings, skipping repeated material for the 'good stuff,' he called it."

"So they're recording us right now?" I asked sitting up, "I'm not sure how I feel about that."

Ri'Anne laughed, "You are being silly. You were just saying you wished they were."

"Half wished," but she was right. I knew being Uncle's research assistant meant being observed. Especially now that we were putting cameras on the underside of the yacht. And his focus wasn't on us, but on his fish. "I'd like to be selective on what is recorded and what isn't, but I'm sure we're safe in his hands." At least while he thought we weren't mermaids.

A shadow passed over us, but birds were always circling, so we failed to notice a semi-transparent golden eagle circling to land on the railing before us.

"You two are a *sight*," said an attempted baritone that broke on "sight" to tenor. Recoiling, we held one another, surprised – thinking it Dad playing a joke with the intercom, but the angle was all wrong. Then the thing shimmered and became gold with white highlights, leaping from the railing to glide the few feet to our couch. We reactively pulled in our feet, but having our legs tangled together we didn't get far. He landed just short of our toes.

"Sea Lord," he said as he gave me a bow with his wings wide, and then to Ri'Anne, "Lady." Then walking up Ri'Anne's leg, he climbed the hill of our combined legs, and then with his sharp claws descended her leg, somehow managing not to so much as scratch or slide on her oily leg to drop off between us.

He then set to lecturing us, "What are you two about? Do you not have duties?"

Indignant at being scolded unexpectedly for taking a breather from a hard morning of work, I shot back, remembering how Shrremmm the orca-sized sand shark had quivered before me, "Hold on a second Mr. Eagle, …" He held up a giant claw that looked ready to rip open my chest and my words slid to a halt.

Because Ri'Anne was protected from his claws, naturally, I thought I was too. Apparently I was in error. His words confirmed it. "I don't answer to you Sea Lord, shepherd of the sea and all that lays within. We are allies, but at the moment I see a couple fools."

Turning from the threat of raking me across the chest, he lowered his claw and instead walked up onto Ri'Anne like she was a tree, he perched atop her hip. Jumping from the perch, he flew off around the yacht and then came back to land. Ri'Anne and I hadn't moved and he landed back onto her hip in a grip that should have hurt. Why wasn't he carving up her delicate skin the same as he threatened to do to me? Even on accident, she had to be getting scratched, but there wasn't a mark on her.

Continuing as if he hadn't stopped he said, "Teaching humans Sea Lord ways can be dangerous." And here I thought he was rebuking us for playing in the sun. He meant us teaching Uncle and I felt a chill run over me, remembering Jill's warning not to share our magic. I nodded to him. He was right, we were playing the fool, but it was too late to stop it.

"What could he do?" Ri'Anne asked, she figuring it out at the same time as me.

The eagle looked down at her, his words were kind when he spoke to her, not the rebuking tone I received. With a shrug he said, "Death and destruction. What else do humans do?"

"Isn't there hope?" she asked, rising up on her elbows trying to be on an eye level with the very tall eagle that was standing on her.

"Hmmm," he purred. "Hope, yes – Yes, hope. Hmmm." You could hear him purring deep in his chest as he thought that through. "Perhaps if you let hope have its perfect work, there may be a way out yet."

Because he figured we weren't that smart, he added, "The world has to end sometime." Then he raised his wings, began to flap them and flew off. We watched him for a little ways, but then he went fully invisible and was gone.

Looking at one another, we both rolled our eyes before I remembered that Ri'Anne had been talking with him and I got all excited for her and tackled her with a hug. We were back to wrestling again, grabbing up the oil and soaking ourselves all over until we were a sloppy mess.

With Ri'Anne's forearm pressed into my mouth, her weight pinning me down, I got to tasting eucalyptus. Running my tongue across her skin, her eyes went from serious as she held me there, to laughing. "Stop it!" she complained but I didn't stop. "Ok, you win," she gave in and rolled off of me getting her arm free of my mouth. Seeing me lick my lips, she said, "You're impossible."

"I'm just happy that you heard him," I said smiling and rolled to lean on her, looking down into her face.

With our noses touching, our eyes looked into one another I felt her breath on my lips as she said, "Yeah, I did didn't I? So what do you think he meant by the end of the world?"

Leaning to the side I put my head on her shoulder, "Oh the same old doom and gloom," and we both laughed.

"That's what we ought to name him," Ri'Anne continued to laugh. Pressed as we were together, I smelled the eucalyptus oil on her neck and felt complete in our gooey oneness. "Seriously," she continued after a minute of my silence, "What do you think he meant?"

I sat up to look down at her, "Nothing. I don't take a random bird, magnificent as he was, as anything important. It's the Lord of the Water I answer to. The bird said he was an ally, not in the same chain of command." Seeing that Ri'Anne wouldn't let it go at that, I sighed and looked off at the ocean. "I'm of the opinion that we be careful of Uncle. But at the same time we can't stop, we must continue. You were right that we needed to include him. Let's just hope we're doing the right thing."

"He did say to let hope have its perfect work." Sitting up so that we were shoulder to shoulder, she asked, looking at me while I still looked to the sea, "What do you think that means?"

"It means," I said leaning into her until we fell down together again, "to not give up hope."

"So," she said after "oofing" from me landing on top of her again, "we let hope refine our decisions. So that we temper what we do or say, and 'hopefully' we get something good from it?"

Hearing the sound of Uncle's voice talking to Dad, where he still worked on the statue in the study, I looked at the oily mess we'd made. At least it would come up quickly in the salt air. Feeling Uncle desiring to have a have a look through me, I felt Ri'Anne stiffen at the contact too, and I let him have his way, keeping in mind not to let him overextend. But it turns out he only wanted to know where we were and he let go the connection.

"Whew, the smell and what a mess," said Uncle coming up behind us. Holding his nose between his fingers, "You two need a bath – weren't you just taking one?" He was leaning against the cabin and shading his eyes from the bright sun under the awning. "Wait, let me see. Yeah, I think I saw you swimming. Give up on the equipment already?" I blushed for a second, but then pushed that down. There was nothing wrong with the two of us having fun.

"Exactly," I whispered to Ri'Anne sliding across her to sit facing the railing. Standing, I turned to lean against the back of the chairs, putting myself between Uncle and Ri'Anne. He seemed to have awakened from his "nap" in a foul mood.

Turning to look out at the sea, Uncle moved past me to sit around the other side of Ri'Anne, waving for me to resume my place beside her. "Ignore me," he said. "I'm going to relax. I feel like I've wakened from a coma."

Sliding back over Ri'Anne, I moved in beside her and when I leaned down to face her again she gave me a stare. It took me a second to understand it. It was with his "coma" comment. She was reading into it quicker than I had, like she had with the eagle. I thought she meant he needed water to operate. Looking into her eyes I saw worry, but then she whispered so only I heard, "Hope."

"You know," she began, not being silent, letting Uncle hear her talking, "I'm starting to like this. I hope we get to spend more time swimming in the days to come." Then when she finished, she ran her fingers through her hair and eyed mine. "Your hair is so nice," she said struggling with a tangle. I helped her with it, using my oily fingers to good effect until the knot came loose.

Uncle was silent and I glanced over at him. He was smiling to himself, and I knew he was content with the sea. I'd never seen that look on him before. He loved the ocean. In that moment I wished his love for the sea would transfer to me. Though it was childish to be jealous of the ocean.

"Uncle, we should leave you," I said sitting up, taking Ri'Anne's hand and sliding to the end of the couch. If I couldn't be a part of his love, I wanted to let him have the sea to himself. It was the wrong thing to be doing, but I couldn't seem to stop myself.

'Huh?" he asked, looking over at me and Ri'Anne. "Forgive my rudeness. I can't abide slack hands, but here I am sitting idle too. But you've seen Melanie – it isn't in the charts! A madness has overtaken me and it won't be solved by getting the cameras installed. Though that is in part, but since this trip began nothing has gone as planned – that is it in whole. My life spent seeking mysteries and when I'm in the midst of one – I hate it! There, I've said it.

"I'm not giving up – no! No, not anyway or anyhow. We'll track, search, but it will probably be dumb luck again that gets us to the Island – just as it was the first time. Until then we have a good part of these turquoise waters to explore. It is fantastic, true, and I should be content – but when you've had a taste, a sample of something simply too good to be true – it is hard to go back to the simple living I've enjoyed."

His eyes took us in, and I knew he wasn't seeing me as the "brat" that had come along with Dad, but as his niece, the closest thing to a daughter he'd ever have. "Don't go," he requested bluntly. It was the nicest thing he'd ever said to me and I smiled in response as my heart thumped loud in my ears. "I'm enjoying your presence," he admitted, "even if forever more I'll be reminded of this moment by the smell of eucalyptus."

What could I say to that? Except to stay. Ri'Anne gently pulled me back onto the couch and we got to playing with one another's hair again. In a different mood, I got to feeling the motion of the sea, the sounds of the sea birds who'd returned to float in the air above us and the gentle lapping of the waves against the boat's sides. Knowing now that Ri'Anne liked my singing, I let the sea's melody find my lips. Ri'Anne put her chin on my shoulder, humming along. "That sounds like the sea," Uncle commented. "You have a gift for that."

Together she wove in the sun with the sea. The tune awakened something in me, and I took on the part of the water's song as an individual melody. Ri'Anne delighted in the sun's magnificence. We felt at peace as the birds of the air came to sit on the railings, and it seemed as if they were crooning along with us.

Uncle touched our shoulders, getting our attention, "I don't want to break the mood, but could we get those cameras installed? I'm too tired to assist, but I'll be up calibrating each one as you get them placed."

"Sure," we said, getting up and returning to our duties.

Walking down the steps to the sea onto the swim deck, Ri'Anne said, "That was nice."

I agreed, "I was afraid he was going to remain awkward forever."

"No I mean… Well, I mean that too, but we've been wearing the new 'mermaid' suits, and nobody has even noticed or said anything. Either they aren't concerned with how we appear, or there is something else going on."

"Well, they heard us singing – that has to be it. At least they weren't complaining," and I put my fingers in my ears to demonstrate.

"Ha, you only think you sing bad. I think it was wonderful, especially the birds. You had them singing a wonderful counterpoint."

"I thought that was you…" I wasn't really sure.

"Well, don't take credit if you don't want to," Ri'Anne said. "But I want to thank you for this trip. Today is the first time I have felt the whole thing worth it. Do you think we'll spend more time like this?"

"One can only hope," I said, sitting down to dangle my legs in the water. "It depends on if Uncle continues to works us to nubs. I'm not sure if I'd prefer that, honestly."

"A mix of both would be my preference," Ri'Anne said handing me the first of the cameras I was to install, and I dove under to go affix it. It didn't take me long to miss having Uncle's guiding influence. I could feel him now in my heart, a result of the song I imagined. The songs were good for bindings. He knew how to attach these things intimately, but I had to make do with putting them on by feel. It wasn't terribly complicated, they could only go in one of two ways, and only one of them was right. The device snapped into the spot, becoming flush with the hull.

Sensing faintly Uncle's elation as it went live on his monitor, I wished he could be here too. But he was the instant scientist wanting me to move aside so he could test it. Then he used its power to see the seafloor below. I didn't wait around, but rose up for air and then swam back for another device.

Working from aft to bow, we soon had an empty box. It was easier and faster to simply attach them than it was to clean their sockets. Uncle waved us up to show us what we'd done. He was delighting in the readings he was getting from the things. He showed us the close ups of us, and then the sea floor, in accurate detail and then us swimming beneath the yacht as we installed the other cameras. It seemed to me to be nothing more than movies, but he said they were not and showed us the other things he could do, though the scientific jargon made no sense to me. He tried explaining, "It's measuring temperature, of you and the sea, and cataloging what it sees and compares it with what it already knows. See, the two of you each now have separate entries. Soon, I'll have the whole yacht wired such, with all my instruments feeding into it."

"Uncle, let's practice putting out your other sea cameras and equipment, so you can calibrate them too." I really didn't know what he had just explained, or what it meant to him. I did gather that he was excited about it and in a way that made me feel good for a job well done. But I did understand one thing all too clearly, having those underwater cameras on all the time meant that we "mermaids" were up a creek. Fortunately, he considered us no different from others, just regular people. As long as he had no reason to doubt us, we should be fine.

He gave us a nod as he made another adjustment, and the three of us went back to the swim deck. Ri'Anne and I carried the plastic tubs filled with his devices, and placed them so Uncle had them within easy reach.

We slipped into the water, Uncle sitting beside the edge handing us each a piece of equipment. "These," he said holding up one of four tripod-like devices, "set up the computer grid. It can be done with just one, sophisticated as they are. They help me map out the research area to have more in place. So, Ri'Anne I'll have you place the first one, roughly over there," and he pointed out a ways from the stern. "Then Melanie, when Ri'Anne's is in place, yours has an indicator, so follow it to the spot it gives you. The closer you get, the closer it is to bright green."

He then explained what could cause us difficulties. "What could hinder it is the shape of the seafloor, like drop-offs or rising cliffs. So you'll place it the best you can. Then the two of you will repeat that for the final two. When you're done, you'll have a rough 50-meter square grid, like this," and he showed us. It was a simple dial that spun to a 50m mark. "One last word of advice, is to be circumspect. We don't want the devices wandering off – either by other divers or sea life getting curious. Hide them."

Ri'Anne swam out roughly to where he'd said. I imagined it would be easier with a specific item to map, like the sunken galleon Jill had found that I'd gotten to explore with her. The advice to hide them was a good one and probably why we were putting out more than one. He wouldn't lose his computer grid if one was stolen.

My device was and on the indicator light went red. Ri'Anne had hers placed. Getting mine in place was a game of hot and cold as I swam out to the top right corner of the grid. Finding the place of greatest green, I set the device down in a cranny on the seafloor and flicked it to the monitor position. The green light went dark. Setting a bit of sea grass over it, I looked at the place. Without knowing where it was, it would be hard to find. Good, and I turned to swim back to the yacht.

Ri'Anne was just leaving with the fourth one. She was faster than me, and she shrugged as she swam off, clearly enjoying herself. Uncle handed me the first of the cameras. "We'll be placing them so that they cover everything from at least two vantages so that we can track whatever moves, and whatever is found specifically on the grid in three dimensions." It was a lot like placing the grid monitor, only once I found the place, I had to spin it until it faced the pre-planned direction. After a couple of those, I started to get the hang of it. I was anticipating the direction the camera should face, and it went faster."

Then there were other devices. But when I returned, I noticed Uncle was tired and he about bit my hand off with my confusion asking him again to explain the latest device's placement. They didn't have the nifty glowing LED's that the cameras and grid devices had. It was older and of Uncle Arlo's own creation.

"Go easy with that Ri'Anne!" Surfacing after putting it out, I could hear Uncle bark at Ri'Anne.

Swimming over to the yacht, "Uncle!" I barked back, getting his attention, jumping up and putting myself between him and her. She was crying. To the both of them I said, "We're done here." Then to Uncle. "This was supposed to our 'private time.'" I stood there with crossed arms as Uncle went up and left us alone.

Ri'Anne had reigned in her tears, "Thanks. You think this is a good idea? We've already had some time." She was looking at the setting sun. In the southern hemisphere in their winter it set early. Seeing that I was determined, she grabbed up a pair of Gigi's suits and got them wet and set them aside.

"That's good thinking," I told Ri'Anne. They'd be our cover in case anyone checked on us. "And we have to get in some beach time. C'mon!"

Together we dove in and took off away from the yacht. "Scatter," Ri'Anne said. "I want my bath time." It didn't need to be like that, but I'd let her learn, as she probably already knew. My fish disappeared at the thought of joining her. I'd never needed to banish my fish for true bath times, and I realized that was another puzzling thought to why my fish had left me before. Since they could do this, why had they left?

We passed several skinny islands that were mostly trees and plants growing in the coral, and finally settled on a tiny sandy island. Sitting, we talked and basked in the deliciously hot sun, the flower fragrant sea breeze keeping us from melting. The sand was brilliantly white and so fine that it stuck to us until we dried off. "You know, I can't see the yacht," Ri'Anne covering her eyes to the sun as it neared the horizon. "Are we lost?"

Looking back, what I thought was back, I only saw the open sea. Standing, I turned in a circle, and then sat, "Yep – we're lost." Though I wasn't ever truly lost, able to go anyplace I'd been before or to anyone I knew if I could make the connection. Right then I didn't care about returning.

I looked at my hands, "Sorry, but after Uncle's outburst… he really got under my skin. I know he wants things done perfectly. But he shouldn't be yelling at us."

We sat for a bit, and then I noticed Ri'Anne playing with some diamond-like crystals. "What are those?"

"Our fish," she responded. "I think I killed them," and she rolled them around on her hands. "Haven't you noticed that our suits have started to flake away?"

I hadn't. I had thought it was dry sand falling off. They weren't all dead yet, but our shoulders bare and the rest patchy. "It's a good thing we're having 'private' time," Ri'Anne laughed brushing off more dead fish.

"They're drying out?" I wondered aloud. "But they were fine when we were sunning on the yacht."

"I think then we were using the oil, and they lived beyond the sea," she said getting up and walking to sit in the water to splash her fish. "I think they can sense that I like plants."

"It isn't your fault," I said coming to sit and do the same. There didn't seem to be anything I could do to halt their death. Attuning was ineffective and so was the water or singing. All the feelings of before tried to come on me again, but I pushed them away. My sense of being a mermaid was not in jeopardy anymore. Being without a suit wasn't horrible, since we could make a new one when we went swimming again.

"How come they don't say anything?" Ri'Anne asked, looking at anther handful of her suit's fish. Those on her palm were looking sick and weren't swimming. "Are they just going to die off?"

"I've never had my swimsuit fish say anything, though I usually know if they want something. And they've always understood me, even my intentions. I'd thought after singing to them that they'd respond to be like my old fish." But pulling out a bunch, I held them in my hands, watching them. "They seem listless, confused," I said. "What is it guys?" I tried asking them. And they gave off a vibe that pulsed with anger.

"Oh!" Ri'Anne put a hand to her head. "I feel ill. There is some kind of taint on them, and they are broadcasting it. Please stop it," she asked them, falling to her side, and then she sighed in relief when they did. Her skin had turned a pale white.

"They feel anger. Do you think it is Uncle's being upset at us?" I asked turning to face her concerned. "The anger is affecting them," and there was a sudden rash of them falling off the both of us.

"It's my fault," Ri'Anne groaned fighting against the negative vibes the fish had been throwing off. "I shouldn't have dropped his gizmo. My fish will be all dead soon."

Attuning to her, I couldn't sense anything wrong. "Mine are dying too," I chipped in, but without a sure answer, maybe she was right. Still, I wouldn't let her feel guilty over whatever was happening. "It doesn't have to be Uncle. It could be the submarine guys aware that we gave them the slip."

"What do you know of the magic that you have?" she asked in a gulp, and then she was looking blankly to sea. That'd taken a lot out of her just asking that.

"Um, you know I haven't taught you any, right?" I asked, but then I got to thinking. Speaking mind to mind and breathing underwater weren't so much magic as they were abilities. Magic came from asking the Lord of the Water for something special.

Pushing herself up with one arm, she splashed herself with more water. "Everything you've been doing is magical to me. See it from my perspective. But, what I'm getting at – something is twisting your magic. I would have testified when we were on the yacht everything was perfectly fine, even if the fish appeared differently out of water than the previous ones. But after the eagle's visit, it has gone sideways."

Hadn't she been hearing me? "We haven't done anything differently," I said moving to her side so she could lean on me.

"It is all different to me." But then with a look of her eyes, I saw she had heard and asked me, "Do you think we should continue with your uncle?" Ri'Anne asked. "It can't be those guys of the submarine. As much as I'd like to lay it at their feet. We've only been teaching your uncle. He has a connection with us now."

"You were right from the beginning. We need him on our side. If we can effect a change in him so that he becomes 'mermaid' like, then he should treat us fairly when he discovers us."

"You're saying 'when' not 'if.' "

Picking up a clamshell, she held it up and it popped it open. The creature on the inside spit on her. I fell back laughing. It apologized after it saw Ri'Anne's face, not at all apologetic about it.

"It's sorry…" I told her, but then I saw her pull a lumpy future pearl out of it. "You can keep it, it said. I think it's laughing at you," and I had to laugh along with it.

"Very funny," she said hauling back and pitching into the water. Smiling with a gleam in her eyes, the illness she was feeling faded away. She got up to go find more clams to throw. Her back was bare, there wasn't much left of the suits on either of us.

"Let's swim" I suggested. "We can explore while we still have light." If I didn't get in the water soon and attract more fish, I wouldn't have a suit and all mermaids need "mermaid suits." It may be a death sentence for them, but they did volunteer and I needed them.

All that was forgotten when we took to the water. I was always amazed at the infinite variety of coral found underwater. There were fissures where hot water came up, and the coral was brilliant in red and yellow. Tiny green fish swam all through, feasting off whatever was coming up from below. Tentacles appeared from the coral and I had a first-hand view of being at the mercy of a plant. It captured a poor fish and dragged it, struggling, to its hidden mouth. I shivered wondering what I'd do if that was me. Brrrr, plants… No mercy at all.

"How come you're so concerned about your appearance?" Ri'Anne asked, for once not enraptured by the voracious plants about us. I was happy to swim on, over and through a large cluster of coral that changed to green and blue colors. "You can get new fish at any time, or something else if they aren't working for you anymore, such as these colorful coral."

"But they're plants," I said. "You saw the success I had with them."

"You wrong us Mistress," spoke up a thousand coral voices. I'd mistaken them for plants. Ri'Anne laughed at my expression. I halted in my swim and looked at the coral, their tentacles waving gently with the current. Nervously, I dipped my hand to run my fingers through them, afraid at any moment they'd grasp a finger and try to drag it within. But they giggled at the contact.

I frowned at my quick condemnation of them, "I'm sorry," I told the beautiful sea creatures. How could I leap so quickly to thinking of them as evil? They were living their lives and making the world around them more beautiful just by doing what they did. I should be doing that too, but instead I was dealing with my own life breaking down. The suits dying on us were compounding it all.

Explaining to RiAnne, "These mermaid suits decaying by an external source bothers me. Last week Jill was attacked by something, we're not sure what. But we thought it could have been a Siren. Add to that list something that affects our suits and

I don't like it." Then seeing I wasn't answering her, I tried asking her "Why aren't you bothered?"

"Oh, because I'm enjoying myself and this is a lot like what I pictured we'd be doing, as 'mermaids.' I never pictured mermaids having fish for suits." Picking up a pair of sea-shells, she held them up, "Most mermaids use these for tops, if they're wearing anything other than hair – at least in the pictures people make of them. I feel more a mermaid now than before." Our suits were mostly gone, only a few speckles giving us any decency at all. It was nice to have her perspective, but that didn't make me like the idea more. Maybe if I was older it wouldn't bother me so much, but I had enough issues without adding being a typical mermaid. I liked who I was. The fish that joined us on the swim hadn't stopped to make our suits yet, and now I understood why. She was celebrating 'mermaid' life and for now I joined her in it. Anything to help her become more mermaid-like.

I should be happy for her and worked at changing my attitude. With the decision to accept her as she was, I started to enjoy being as we were too. Maybe on this trip we should have more private swims, if she enjoyed it so much. But for me, I wanted to get back to working with Uncle and that meant a suit. For now I let go the remaining fish before they'd die on me and let Ri'Anne pick the time and place for us. Ri'Anne circled about me, tossing her hair back and arching to do a backwards summersault. Twining about, she led the way and I joined her in her water dance.

"Before," Ri'Anne rested an arm on a small above water reef, "we wore one thing the whole time – never having to switch it up." Coming up beside her, Ri'Anne showed how we could do it her way. "Now, pick a frond," and she snipped some colorful underwater plants. Then twinning them in her fingers, humming to them, they grew and blossomed. Laying them over her arm, they flowed to cover her chest. "Now you do it…"

I copied her, but the stem of the plant wouldn't cut with my fingernails. Ri'Anne helped, and when I had it in my hands, the twirling didn't help. It stayed limp and unmoving. I tried humming, which got it to wiggle, but not grow or flower. Placing it on my arm, it didn't know what to do.

"Why's it work for you?" I asked a little upset that the plant ignored me.

"What would you get more emotional over, a gift of a fish or a rose?" Ri'Anne asked in return.

"A fish," I said before I even thought about it, and then realized she'd gotten me. Girls were supposed to like flowers. Uncle always brought me tropical fish. He bought my love with them, and I looked forward to his visits.

Ri'Anne smiled knowingly, "See… Fish like you, so go with where you are strong. Still, don't be limited by thinking of only fish. You could wear the coral like a Mexican dress, or how about that starfish?" The beautiful five point ridged starfish crept along scouring for food. "Or these sand dollars on this ledge. Get the true mermaid shelled bra with them…" Ri'Anne laughed at my expression.

"Ha ha," I laughed right along with her. So I needed both the starfish and the sand dollars. Thankful that Ri'Anne was helping me have a mermaid suit, I humored her and decided to try something other than fish for a suit. "May I?" I asked the starfish, petting its ridges with a finger.

"Of course sweetie," said the aunty sounding lady starfish, and she scooted onto my hand.

Picking her up, I sang her a little tune, "*You be my gown and I'll go to the ball…*" adding in my love of the sea.

"Oh that tickles," the starfish giggled becoming liquid caramel flowing from my hand to take up residence as bikini shorts – patterned with a dozen white starfish stars. Its arms became the suit's bow ties.

"Cute," Ri'Anne said.

"I'm not done yet," I said as I hovered over the sand dollars. Feeling more confident, I asked them, "Care for a ride?"

"Me, pick me!" said the lot of them.

"I only need two," and I picked the cutest of the bunch, sang them the song and they became like ghosts until they settled into place as my white shelled top, complete with straps.

"I don't know how you do it," Ri'Anne said with a whistle, "But you managed to upstage me. Add a few flowers in your hair and you'd look like an island princess – but you'll have to learn to talk to the plants as you do fish."

"You're beautiful too," I told her not liking the idea at all.

"Just keep a lookout for something to add to your ensemble, and we'll never be left wanting." Ri'Anne emphasized.

Then Ri'Anne went with a bit of kelp for her shorts, and we held a little memorial for our old fish. Dressed in different items from the sea, I could no longer think of my suit as a fish suit. I'd have to use the more appropriate mermaid suit. And even if Uncle was the source of what affected the suits, Ri'Anne and I could always come up with something appropriate to counter the effect.

17

Magic Carpet

Swimming through a narrow canyon within the coral, I looked up through the clear holes to the surface at the underside of a sailboat. Some kids were playing in the water nearby on their rubber raft, but they didn't see us. Their laughter carried down to us.

Rounding a corner, the undersea floor dropped away and we floated down to swim among great blue fish that were hiding from the swimmers. Diving through them, we threaded our way through some tall kelp, up a red horned ridge and looked on a beautiful vista of every color imaginable. An oasis of sea life.

I half expected to see a mermaid as we swam down into the picture perfect garden. Matching colorful fish swam with us, and then separated as Ri'Anne saw a tunnel through the coral cliff that rose before us and swam for it – I followed after. A burst of fish exploded out of the tunnel around us. I didn't think anything of it, though I should have been more aware of the rising bubbles. But there were always bubbles rising here and there that I paid them no mind.

Dipping into the tunnel, we swam down easily, coasting among the thriving coral. The two of us enjoyed the swim. We were on a group of divers before we were aware of them.

My first response wasn't the smartest, "Um, hi…" I said waving.

"Fish cover us," Ri'Anne reacted and suddenly the fish were back, large and small coming between us and them. "Come on," RiAnne said, grabbing my hand and turning us away. I swam with Ri'Anne, she ducked around the tunnel entrance laughing.

"That was quick thinking," I said over my shoulder, holding to the coral to look back. "Oh," there were a pair of swimmers chasing after. A dozen fish kept getting in the way of one of them trying to photograph us.

Melanie! Ri'Anne called with a bubble message, she'd swam on.

Coming! I sent back, hightailing it towards her. She didn't stop to wait. Even though I was faster, it was a while before I caught up. Pulling up short, I looked behind us and said, "Ok, hold on. I think we've lost them."

"Whew, I'm worn out. My heart is racing a mile a minute," Ri'Anne said, catching her breath. Together we rested, then she started laughing. It was catching and together we laughed away our fears.

Laughing at the situation, I shared, "You should have seen the two swimmers that were trying to photo me. Each time they'd try, the fish would suddenly appear before the lens just as they clicked the switch. Poor things."

"The divers?" Ri'Anne asked confused.

"Huh, no – the fish. They weren't getting a chance to be photographed in their full glory."

Together we went to the surface for a look. "I think that is the island, but I don't remember seeing homes…" Ri'Anne said.

"And there is no sign of The Lazy Cloud. I can't believe I'm lost. Though if that is our island, we should be able to go that way around the island to find The Lazy Cloud, but it will be dark soon." The last bit of the sun remained on the horizon coloring the clouds bright orange up to purple. The orange clouds looked on fire. It was a glorious sunset.

"And a dozen other yachts and boats," Ri'Anne said.

"Yeah," I said. "They've come in for the evening." There was even the smell of food drifting on the air.

"What do you think we should do?" she asked.

"I can bring us back aboard The Lazy Cloud…" but it sounded like a cop out as I said it.

"Not to mention your uncle would record it."

"Oh, the cameras," I'd forgot. He didn't used to keep them on, and now we'd installed the new underwater ones. "We could beg for food."

"Come up like seals and beg for scraps?" Ri'Anne clapped her hands together like a seal.

"Actually, I smell… food."

"Stop it, you're making me hungry," Ri'Anne complained. "We can make for the island. If we can find someone with a phone or a radio, we can contact your family. All natural like."

"Good idea," I said and together we started swimming towards the island, I was hoping to find a small and hopefully deserted beach to sleep on.

The sound of a propeller travels incredibly far underwater, so I wasn't initially worried when I heard some. Other boaters were making for the island for the evening. We'd been swimming together, and because of the boats I thought it wise to go deep, but I found I was alone. Feeling for her, I had a glimpse of her treading water in a colorful forest talking to a pair of parakeets that fluttered just out of reach. Then jet skis were racing overhead, the pounding noise as their hulls slapped the surface as they crossed over waves grabbing my attention.

Watching them blaze trails above, I was annoyed at their noise. My tranquil mood I'd been feeling since we'd found new suit items was gone. I'd been pleased to be wearing more sea creatures than just the fish I'd worn from the beginning. I wasn't alone in my anger, the sea life around me regretted their appearance. Now I wanted to send a wave at the riders, anything to get them to go away. A pod of dolphins out in front of the riders squeaked and clicked their surprise at the noisome water scooters.

Hearing the alarms of dolphins, I rose up and went for a closer look. The jet skis had come across a pod of dolphins playing in the shallows, probably riding the waves. Getting closer I saw they were circling a pair of dolphins. The riders were they unaware how much they terrified the dolphins. "Hey, over here," I called to the porpoises.

"We can't," they called back. "They come between us… too fast." They were being driven back into the shallows, full of sharp coral. What can I do about it? I could rise up, and create some waves in an attempt to scare off the riders – but would that really work? The jet skis were called Wave Runners for a reason, and their drivers might enjoy it.

Diving under, I swam their way, afraid myself as the water grew shallow. In that time, the jet skis were driving in only a few inches of water, scaring the dolphins into beaching themselves. I heard their cries of terror and I forgot my own.

Getting close, one jet-ski passed only inches above me. I felt the pull of its water intake, but then it was gone. Jumping up, I ran for the dolphins. By me jumping up, the surprise caused the next driver to swerve away. Running to the dolphins, I squatted down beside them. "Hold still," I told them and both of them quieted immediately. I attuned to them to examined them, feeling through them. So far they'd sustained only minor scrapes, they'd be ok. "You're bleeding, but the cuts are minor," I reassured them.

I'd become accustomed to the normal fish that shadowed me. Quite a few suddenly leaped upwards around me to unknown heights. My mouth was dropping when I heard a loud **crack** sound – a shot rang out and one of the jumping fish exploded right before my face. *That shot was meant for me!*

"You missed her, you idiot! I'll get her…" he said reaching for his weapon.

"Melanie… don't…" and I hesitated, though my mind rushed like a waterfall. I thought of ways to get back at them from electrifying the water around them, maybe killing them if their vehicles blew up to physically knocking them down myself.

A bright flash of light at my feet drew my attention. Glancing down, a line or seam glowed before my toes and ran out to either side of me. Bending at the knees I fingered the seam, above it rippled and the light spread out stronger along the seam of what appeared to be a cloth edge. Peeling it up, the sea over it became two-dimensional, like a picture, but pliable like silk. What could I do with this?

Maybe not something so rash, something I'd later regret. *Perhaps a wave with this?* I'd been thinking about making a wave before, but doing it with my hands as I'd always done, but thought the jet skis might escape. With the cloth I knew I could flip it out and create a wave. How was this better than my quick wave hand motions? But as it came up to either side of me out a ways, all within it came to a stop stuck in a moment of time trapped within the canvas. Ah, I grinned as I held the riders in my grasp. There would be none to escape me.

All of this happened in seconds, now I looked at the rider who had taken aim at me and the other that had failed. The anger still burned, but now I wasn't going to kill them. The "Melanie don't" had guided me to the better path – I would give them the ride of their life. I smiled back at the riders, they frozen in the cloth I held in my hands like a god holding the lives of people in my hand. I'd never imagined the sea as one piece of felt, to be wrapped up, folded or flipped out. The water had come away from the bottom. It weighed nothing, only the ends of where it still held to the bottom gave it tension.

Flipping the cloth was going to create a wave, and I wondered at the size of it. Looking behind me at the dolphins, I saw that they and the sea behind me remained normal. But before and to the sides I held the sea and everything it. "Ok, here we go." Bending my knees, I rose quickly and gave a heave upwards. The sea cloth rose up to some 15 feet before it went out from me. Then time for those in my cloth sped up until it was its normal self.

It was just like I'd predicted. The riders simply tried to ride out the wave by driving in to it. But some of them were surprised and were sent swimming. Urging the wave higher, I flipped the sea sheet again, going for a greater height. The wave crested 30 or more feet high, and the roar of it as it went out from me was awesome as it gained speed and magnitude. All I saw after that was flipped vehicles and swimmers being washed away, their weapons floating down to the seafloor below where they'd never harm anyone again.

Dismissing the riders, I put down the sea and it became one with the part behind me. Again, water rippled around my feet, as if nothing untoward had happened. I dropped down to sit with the dolphins again. "Tell me your names," I told them to get their mind off of the pain.

"I'm Sezi, Sea Lord. They're gone?" asked the one closest to me. Having driven themselves into the shallows nose first, they hadn't seen what I'd just done.

I wasn't sure I could explain it, so I nodded looking around to be sure and saying, "Yes, they're gone." In fact, there wasn't any sight of them, like I'd erased a chalk board of their presence. Giving a slight grin, I asked, "Can we get you out now?"

"Yes please Sea Lord. I'm Dezi, but I don't think I can back out," said the second dolphin.

Ri'Anne surfaced next to me. "Oh," she said coming out to sit with them.

"Dezi and Sezi," I said introducing them to her. "Do you think you can help me lift them?"

"Lift, as in carry?" Ri'Anne asked, nodding her head and flexing her skinny arms like she was a body builder. "Let me at them," she joked.

"No, silly," and I grinned moving around in front of the dolphins. "Let me show you," and I suggested Ri'Anne come around to my side. When she joined me I showed her, "Like this," and I reached down, finding a seam, and I peeled it up and began lifting. "Help me," and Ri'Anne grabbed the cloth. Working my way around, we peeled up an oval section of the water on the top of the reef. The two dolphins were squealing in delight as the water rose around the rocks they had been stuck on to lift them free. The dolphins weighed nothing in the sheet. We were careful to carry them level.

"Um, what are we doing?" she asked holding the sea cloth in her hands. "Could we fold them up in this?"

I had to laugh at that, "Let's not get carried away. We're only freeing these two, then we'll put it back." But it really did seem that we could roll it up – but I'd save that experiment for some other time

"They can't see what we're doing can they? I'm not sure that I'm seeing what I'm doing," Ri'Anne admitted with trepidation in her voice. "Honestly, from one perspective it seems as if the sea has risen a few feet, but just where we're holding it."

"I see that too," I reassured her. Looking down on it, it did look like we carried a pool. But my fingers told me we held a thin cloth.

Together we walked the water cloth towards deeper water. "Just a little further. There, now down." Speaking to the dolphins when we had them level with the rest of the sea, "There you go you two. Off to join your friends."

We watched them go, they saying their thanks and then Ri'Anne and I put the sea back. Seeing it back in place, she shook her head. "When you said, 'come and be a mermaid with me,' I had no idea it would be like this."

"Me either," I admitted. "But they shot at me…"

Taking my shoulder, Ri'Anne turned me to her concern for me in her expression, "Who shot at you?"

"Some jet ski jerks. They were frightening Dezi and Sezi into beaching themselves. I went to help, but when I was checking them out – well. I'm not sure what happened, but it seems a fish sacrificed itself when whoever it was shot at me. It leaped out of the water, and the bullet hit it. You'd think the bullet would have gone through it to me. Maybe it was deflected. Anyway, when that happened I flipped the sea at them…" and I shrugged. I didn't want to explain how I'd nearly lost my temper, but some of it was reflected in my eyes.

Ri'Anne laughed, "You make it sound so normal. Remind me not to get you mad."

"Agreed," I answered with a grin. But then I frowned, "Think Dad and Uncle will be ok from the wave?"

"A wave?" Ri'Anne asked.

"I said I flipped the sea at them, yes a wave. Well, two. The first wasn't big enough," and I shrugged again. "Anyway, we'll have to sleep on the beach," and I put my head on her shoulder, feeling weary. Flipping seas was tiring.

"As long as we have it to ourselves," Ri'Anne said and she put her arm around me, helping me down into the water. "You give yourself without limits. I like that about you, but you should learn to hold back some." I gave her a weak smile as we swam off from there.

It was late as we trod up onto the beach, having spent the remaining light waiting for a couple to have their walk on the beach and to get back in their boat and return to their yacht. Even then, we went for another deserted cove that had enough of a sandy beach to enjoy. The sky was going through its last phases of twilight, the stars were bursting out over us. Walking out onto the beach, we sat and looked at the sea.

"Good night," I told Ri'Anne as I felt the exhaustion I was feeling rise up and I drifted off to sleep as the sea sang me a lullaby. Tomorrow we'd have to find some way of contacting Uncle. It was the issue we'd had in the Papua New Guinea port all over again. But now we had no city nearby and I didn't trust the yachts that drifted out where we'd been swimming. That's where those jet ski jerks had come from.

18

Sitting on Nothing

"Yawn," bright light through my eyelids wakened me roughly. Opening my eyes to daylight, I sat up to see Ri'Anne staring out at the calm waters of the new day. "I could have used more sleep," I said to her gaining her attention. It was then that I noticed she was wrapped in a new flowery outfit. Seeing me sit up, she tossed me a ripe fruit. "Oh… Ah," and I held my forehead from a sudden headache and a remembered dream that faded away, leaving only an image of Uncle. I think he was trying to find us.

Eyeing Ri'Anne's outfit, her fish were gone, replaced by flowers like she'd worn from the submarine. My eyebrows rose in question. "Living things like me," she said shrugging. Sitting down beside me as I sat up, she waved it off and said, "What can I say?" Which was true, she'd always liked plants, but that they liked her, what did that mean? Was it like fish liking me? Another mermaid quirk of what you liked liking you, so I was hesitant to ask about the fruit, wondering if she'd "grown it," but then – why not? "And the fruit?"

She waved at the jungle behind us and said, "They grow back that way some. Ripe for the picking." Then she fingered my sand dollar top, "These comfortable?" They were drying up too and she dusted bits of them from me.

"Not so bad," I said, still holding my head, "They don't feel like hard shells."

"This magic has benefits to be sure, but they die too quickly. Mine were all gone when I woke, but flowers had sprung up overnight to cover me. You know I think it's the Eucalyptus oil Gigi gave us that are causing them to die," but that didn't make sense and said so. "Then I can't think what else could be causing it. Let's get you something to replace those sand dollars. I saw some spiders, back that way..."

"No," I protested as she dragged me to my feet. "You don't want to cover up?" she asked misinterpreting my reluctance. I hadn't gone that far into embracing mermaid life as she thought. Besides, we were planning on meeting people today. I definitely needed a swimsuit.

"No, the other thing," I responded not wanting the touch of a hundred legs crawling across me.

"Oh, you mean the spiders," Ri'Anne said turning to lead the way. "Well, you were the spider lover the other day."

"Lover is stretching it." I whimpered starting to follow after, feeling sudden pain, and dropped to my knees. I could feel Uncle searching. If only I could give Uncle what he wanted, that we come home – but we had to do it natural like. Fine a phone or a computer with internet. The headache was tripling with his pressure and it was taking all my effort to resist him. “Hey wait up,” and I got up to stumble after her.

Ri’Anne had disappeared, and I called for her. “Over here,” she replied and I ducked under a fallen over tree with moss hanging to the ground and came up in a grotto. She waved to me from the other side, and then disappeared again. Oblivious to the jungle with its many animals making merry, I brushed through some bushes and happened to glance down at a sudden flash of color. A butterfly was settling in where, oops, my sand-dollars used to reside.

Standing beneath the orange tree, I showed Ri’Anne the butterfly top I now wore as she climbed up to pluck us some ripe juicy fruit. “Oh!” she exclaimed hopping down to examine the suit. “But look…” it was flaking away already. “The black anyway, the color seems to last longer. You didn’t sing to it did you?” Shaking my head I realized it was too late now. I had to overcome my reluctance of the spiders, and sing to them! I shivered all over again imagining tiny legs crawling on me in my sleep.

“Ok, so…” she continued not noticing my inner struggle. “On a positive note, I found closer spiders…” And Ri’Anne was eyeing my suit, afraid to say a word. I didn’t look, afraid to know what she was seeing. Hauling me to my feet, she said, “This way…” and we were marching back into the jungle

Then we stopped and Ri’Anne pointed up. Filled with trepidation I looked. Great webs stretched through the open air in the trees above. “Come on, it’ll be fun,” she said and stepped to a root and started climbing. I was never much for climbing trees, but I followed Ri'Anne, who was quickly disappearing up the tree.

About twenty to thirty feet up I became frozen, afraid of heights and looking at my feet. From that angle, I saw my suit – it was intact, and actually holding together. Ri'Anne, *the prankster,* making me think the suit was dead. But it wasn't that bad, though it would need to be replaced soon; almost completely dead. It had to be the fish I'd given Uncle, poisoning ours through his sendings. It had been going so well, I wondered what had changed. The starfish was gray instead of brown, and it felt brittle, and the colorful butterfly now had the appearance of a powdery moth.

"Over there," Ri'Anne called leaning out from above pointing out handholds to get me moving again. Grabbing a hold where she said, I started moving again. Upon reaching her, she advised, "Don't look down," and then she scrambled up, leading the way.

Don't look down, great thanks! She had to go and say that. I knew I was much higher than I wanted to be.

Then I got to thinking, I'd glided from a jetliner to the sea below from a much greater height! What was the problem? But now there wasn't a sea below to catch me if I fell. I hugged the branch I was on for a few minutes and Ri'Anne returned. "We're almost there," she said pointing.

"Why couldn't the spiders come down to me as they had before?" I complained.

"Because climbing is half the fun," Ri'Anne admonished. She may be enjoying it, but the higher I got, the more afraid I became.

"Nice climbing mistress," said a raspy drowsy voice when I stopped next.

Eeek! What was that? Trembling and afraid to move, I replied to whoever spoke between my teeth, "Thanks."

The creature, I was betting it was a creature, continued saying, "If you were a little lighter I would love to carry you."

Um, what did I say to that? What was I talking to? Attuning, I searched about me. I saw the grimy bark in all its variations (with tiny bugs crawling right under my fingers!), the spiders out to my right, their big gooey nets dripping with dew with a couple of bird-sized catches hanging from them. Above me I saw them, big giant creepy fruit bats with glowing eyes droopy with sleep hanging upside down. I almost ran screaming from everything (Why did I leave the ocean?), but for the open air beneath me. Another moment attuning and I could see saliva dripping from their fangs, felt their hearts at ease as they swayed in the gentle island breeze. Too much information! But I didn't dare stop watching them in case they changed from friendly bats to something else.

"Why didn't you mention the bats?" I complained to Ri'Anne when next she made her appearance. I still hadn't moved. She looked up and then back to me, asking, "What bats?"

"What do you mean, what bats?" I said pointing up without moving anything else. She shook her head saying, "There's nothing there."

"What?" I said, "I can see them clear as day." But when I turned to look with my eyes, there was nothing there. "Why can't we see you?" I asked them, for there were nine of them close enough to touch.

"Climb a little further," they advised, "and you'll see."

Climb further, "Yeah right," I complained. Ri'Anne looked at me funny, she hadn't heard them. "Do I have to?" I asked them. They nodded and glittering *dew*, yes dew, dripped from them to the ground below. Reluctantly I started up. *This is dumb Melanie,* curiosity was sure to kill me.

"Where you going?" Ri'Anne asked me, "We have to go that way," she pointed out towards the spiders.

"Up," was my one-word reply. Ri'Anne followed after, and then passed me with the agility and fearlessness of a monkey. I watched her go, and then the air rippled around her like a pond in mid-air and she disappeared into it! I could see she was in the place with the bats. A solid transfer point! *But where were we going?* I wondered as I followed after.

I had to see the place for myself and kept my hands moving. Passing through the same pond in the air thing, I felt fire go across me in a ring from head to feet, slow as I climbed through what felt like a translation. Then I was beside Ri'Anne and together we gazed at a beautiful waterfall in the distance that hadn't been there before, and to our right was the glorious sea. It was crystal clear and its waves dazzling in the sunlight. And around us many, many bats!

"That doesn't look like the sea we just left," Ri'Anne said. "Much too clean, though I had thought it clean before." Breathing in with her nose, she exhaled with a smile. “Mmm, wow. I could live here.”

I knew what had happened, but felt like pointing out the obvious. “Also, there aren’t any yachts at anchor out there,” and there had been quite a few when we’d left the beach. “I wonder what else is different.”

Ri’Anne noticed the bats, greeting them, “Hey fellas.”

“Hey bright one. Thanks for coming,” one of them said.

“At least we’ll be invisible to any trouble that may be seeking us,” and I smiled real big. She looked at me, thinking me daft, and then asked, “Is that another skill you haven’t taught me?”

I shook my head, “Isn’t it obvious, we can see the bats now. If we couldn’t see them before, then we’re alone here with them now. We should be fine.”

“That doesn’t make sense, why are we safe?” she asked.

I wanted to explain, to show her. The fire on the way up was telling. “The fire you just felt, that was a transfer, we’re someplace else that looks similar enough.”

I thought about trying to explain it in more detail, but I hadn’t taught her magic. Noting the specifics had been my best attempt at explaining that sometimes The Lord of the Water took me places without me requesting it. This portal was similar. I had to wonder though, was it a natural occurrence or had someone made it? And if so, for what purpose? Which made me wonder how I might make one.

I'd read about a similar portal once in a book. Kids had gone through a wardrobe into a fictional land, lived there for several years until they were adults only to go back through and still be kids in the "real world." Could this be like that? But this was no wardrobe, but a tree in a jungle where anyone could find it.

"I'm sorry," Ri'Anne said when I'd gone silent. "When you say we're somewhere else, do you mean we did that thing you do – taking us someplace else?"

"I didn't do it, but yes…" I started to say.

But she interrupted me asking, "Will we be able to go back?" She was suddenly afraid we wouldn't get home. "If we go back down, will it go back the other way?" I shrugged, I was pretty sure that would be true – but I didn't want to test it yet. We'd just arrived.

"My first guess?" I asked. Ri'Anne nodded, sitting down on a branch to listen, swinging her feet out over the open air. I said "This is my first guess. I think we're in a 'Neverland' kind of place."

"Like in the movies, with Tinkerbell?" Ri'Anne asked, suddenly interested, her voice rising in octaves. When I nodded, she gushed, "That's great. I can't wait to meet her. Do you think we will?"

I shrugged saying, "I hope not. She's always causing trouble."

"Tinkerbell is misunderstood," Ri'Anne said defending the fairy. "I think a fairy could help us. A little of their dust and we'd be right as bees."

Whatever that meant, I didn't want to talk about it. Seeing if I could steer the conversation back on track, I said, "So, we'll be able to move across the island free of sendings until we want to reverse it."

Turning to look at me seriously, she said, "I bet the 'island' your uncle is looking for is here too. That's the reason he cannot find it. It is in this place."

That was a leap, but it was a good guess... "That makes sense." I thought about that some more. We were all remarking on the island being too perfect. An untapped paradise. "There probably aren't satellites here then too. Uncle was saying that was a reason for him being lost. There hadn't been anyone or anything. Well, except for the sunken galleon."

"Sunken galleon, like a pirate ship?" Ri'Anne asked intrigued by the idea.

Afraid she'd start thinking Peter Pan thoughts again, I hurried on. "That's what we all thought, but the likelihood of that is small. Besides, who wants to run into real pirates?" We were all romanticized by the movies about pirates, but "Real ones are cutthroats and robbers."

"And mermaids drown their victims," she said looking at me. "How many people have you killed?" she asked really interested in knowing.

"I'm a nice mermaid," I shot back.

"Except the navy divers you left to be shark food." Ri'Anne had to go and remind me of that, which made my stomach flop over remembering the bloody room from my "dream." It seemed the only thing I remembered real well, except everything had been so huge. But she had a point, mermaids were not known for their kindness either.

"What is it?" Ri'Anne asked. "You've gone green. Are you ok?"

"I'm remembering that dream," I said blinking back the feeling.

"When you'd been a fairy?" It all came rushing back, me going to go find Ri'Anne. But I'd never left the yacht... "What I'd give to have such a dream," Ri'Anne dreamed, her eyes going blank as she looked inwardly at her vision of being a fairy. Apparently she'd envisioned it before and was back there in a flash.

I let her have her moment and then asked her, "So, if we are truly invisible here, what do you think our next move should be? The first thing I want is to get out of this tree, but if we go down here we'll go back through to our world."

A gleam of wickedness flickered in Ri'Anne's eyes as she looked beside her and said, "You're not going to like this. But, you're going to have to crawl to another tree, go down that way, and pick you up some spiders along the way."

Chills ran up my spine, my fear controlling my words, "I've changed my mind. I don't want spiders. Maybe you can give me a pretty flower." *Spiders, heights – no way!* No matter how much I'd gone out of the way for them.

With an unusual trill of laughter, Ri'Anne almost fell off her branch. "You're a riot Melanie, but there is an upside. We did get to discover this place." Snapping off a leaf from a vine, she twirled it in her fingers. Just like before, it grew to unusual size while I watched, and started to grow down her forearm, which with her other hand she unwound and held it out to me.

Gratefully, I held out my hand and it wound onto my arm, and snaked from there onto my body. Ri'Anne was humming, sounding like a bee in flight, and the plant was responding. By her magic, the vine blossomed into twin flowers which took over for the butterfly, which fell away. Tiny blossoms in a leafy wreath took up sanctuary as shorts, the starfish relieved of duty. When she was finished, I felt like an elf in the colorful green outfit.

"There. You make a pretty Peter Pan," she said with a bright smile, her teeth glowed like the sun. "You just need a hat," but I shook my head no at the idea of a funny green hat. She went from glistening sunny teeth to the biggest frown I'd ever seen. I thought she would fly off and have a temper tantrum. I couldn't wait to bring her out of this place.

I also wanted to complain about being called Peter Pan, but I'd done enough of that and so resorted to the age-old phrase, "Thank you." It felt good receiving from her. I didn't begrudge her the ability, I knew I'd picked up things differently than Jill had. Ri'Anne's gift with plants was coming in handy. Someday it might save her life.

Her frown disappeared, and she stood up and put a straight finger under her chin struck with an idea, "Well, if not Tinkerbell, I bet we meet a fairy." She fell back, crossed her feet before her and said, "This is going to be a great day!"

Looking over to Ri'Anne, my eyes expanded in surprise. Was it my imagination or was Ri'Anne sitting in the air, "Um, what are you doing?" I asked her, pointing afraid any second that gravity was going to take over and send her plummeting to the ground.

"Huh?" she looked back at me, totally at ease. "Ah, I love trees. So comfortable," and she 'climbed' backwards onto her perch, which was only air, and now she was suspended out over the ground. "Seriously," she said pointing, "if we head towards the falls..."

"Ri'Anne," I said my voice shaking, I was shaking. She turned to look at me. Asking, "What's wrong?" She was losing patience with my fear of heights.

"Ri'Anne! You're flying…"

"Am not," she denied bewildered, and then looked down, her eyes going wide. "But this is impossible," she said, pulling her feet in to see she wasn't touching the tree. Rapping her seat with her fist, "It seems hard."

Accusing me with a glare, she asked, "Can you fly?" She thought I was holding back from her, but I shook my head no.

"My attempts at flight have not gone very well," I admitted. I'd fallen from the jet, not flown from it.

Reaching out, I crawled to the edge of the branch before where she was seated and felt outwards. I was expecting my hand to flop through the place she was, but I could feel the air, it was solid "ish" like water and sort of like a step to stand on.

"Come on," she said making a swimming motion backwards, suddenly not interested in me anymore. Squinching my eyes closed, I did my best air crawl. I had to follow after Ri'Anne or lose her forever. Now I had both hands out on the air floor. It was not possible, and I almost drew back. But if I expected her to swim with me and follow without question underwater, the least I could do was do this with her. I shook my head. This was no mermaid trait I'd ever heard of as I took to the air.

Eyes still closed as my left knee crawled out onto nothing, I gulped air when my right knee came free. I turned around and looked back. I was sitting in the air. Sure, there was a wide branch below I could fall onto if suddenly I dipped, but I didn't dip.

This felt so familiar. I'd done the same in the dream I realized, but it had been a dream!

"Ok," I said to myself. "Let's try standing." I know I looked dumb on all fours.

Turning away from the tree I looked to Ri'Anne, who was comfortably sitting feet together, like she sat on a floor. But she was some 15 feet out and seven feet up in the open air. Climbing to my feet, the breeze was causing me to drift and I thought I might fall. Caught in the island breeze, I was slowly drifting away from our tree. Standing was kind of tough, even though the air floor was solid, I couldn't see it. Leaning into it, I thought about the dream, then I'd sat more and moved from that point of view with my legs dangling. When I thought about it, I wasn't wobbling, but it took some getting used to.

Jumping off from where I "stood," I shot past Ri'Anne and did a summersault midair, "pushing" off a ceiling of air with my feet to glide softly back. My swimming skills came to the fore unconsciously, but they weren't for flying and did me only a little good. Pulling from the dream I was able to float down to join her, and I asked her, "How is this possible?"

Catching my hand, we drifted together, but she was surprised at my question. "You're asking me? You're the mermaid."

I sat across from her, and it took all my concentration to keep from floating away because of the wind that was even fiercer above the trees. I was definitely out of my element. I reviewed everything I'd ever been told about mermaids, and everything I'd heard. Flying was never a part of their lore, ever.

"How easy is this for you," I asked Ri'Anne, "to not move relative to the ground?"

"We're not standing still," Ri'Anne said looking down and around. "The tree we climbed is that one over there," she said pointing out a tree that to me looked the same as all the rest. I wouldn't have known which one it was, but because she knew I knew, because I had it from her word.

Pointing out the snaking dark waters below us, Ri'Anne said, "Oh, and there's the river. What do you think we should do?" We had drifted higher up and we could see over the top of the falls to a short valley spreading out to a rolling set of hills.

I thought aloud, "If we're to pick a direction, I say away from the beach…"

"Melanie, we're procrastinating. We have to go back to your dad and uncle, no matter the consequences. We're literally drifting further and further away, and the longer we stay away the harder it will be to go back."

"So no flying?" I asked, not sure how to give this up. But Ri'Anne was right. We had to face them.

"No more flying and you showing off you're a mermaid," she agreed.

I wanted to counter that, "We are mermaids," but that seemed presumptuous. It didn't seem true anymore. I pushed aside the thought, *of course we're mermaids. What am I thinking?* What we were doing was a different kind of mermaid thing. If she didn't want to be a mermaid, I couldn't make her want to be one. I knew she had been shaken up by the sharks, but her encounter with the Navy had actually helped. But then all this talk about fairies and now we were flying had sidetracked the issue.

Seeing as how Ri'Anne was guiding our decisions, I asked her, "Ok then, so what do we do, scout the island with my sight?"

Ri'Anne shrugged, "It's your ability, you decide. But why not check out that mansion over there, obscured from the sea by the trees. They might have internet."

19

The Gardener

What we saw was a mix of run down shacks and a palatial private residence, with a sturdy dock. It was in the real world, but now Ri'Anne was seeing it too. I was happy for her, but so many changes.

"What, no towns?" Ri'Anne asked holding out her hand, "Let's not fly down to them but use your thing."

There could be, I thought. Taking a hold of her I pulled us across to be underwater near the residence.

Exiting the water up onto a perfectly swept beach, our footprints were uncommon even in the wet sand. A beautiful mansion, shrouded in perfectly trimmed trees. Beside it, hiding in its shadow, were the shacks that we'd seen before arriving. "What a strange world," Ri'Anne said. "I'm glad to be back and all, but such opulence beside squalor seems unfair. Do you think we'll be well received?"

"I doubt it," I said laughing at my attitude. Glad to be wet and on the ground. "I suppose it depends if they want visitors, but by the looks of the beach I'm guessing they don't like their sands disturbed."

"Then let's oblige and walk above them, like this," and she stepped onto the dry sand, but not quite, for she didn't sink in. Fly without leaving the ground? I followed after. We weren't quite walking on the ground, but who would be able to tell? At least we were leaving their sand undisturbed. Whoever maintained the sand would appreciate it and I was glad for that.

I bumped into Ri'Anne when we passed the rows of trees carefully planted to hide the residence from the beach. "What?" I asked looking around her.

"Shhh, tigers," and she pointed at a pride of Bengal tigers lying in the shade beside a small flowing river between us and the cultivated garden surrounding the home.

"Oh, they're beautiful," I said stepping around her. She reached for my shoulder trying to pull me back, but it was too late. One of them lapping at the small stream of water looked up.

"Hi," I said to them with a wave. "Mistress," replied a few, and then the two yearlings got up from where they lay and charged across towards us. Ri'Anne squeaked seeing the giant creatures bounding easily on their great paws, but I doubt she was noticing their playful attitude. I bent to one knee to receive their hugs.

The first bowled me over as it landed on my shoulders with his front legs. I was up laughing, rolling over to pet him. The young tigress batted her sibling aside and landed with a plop before me. Her fur was warm and I ran my fingers under her jaw and scratched her soft brow.

Ri'Anne knelt tentatively, and patted the young tiger that had tackled me. "I've always liked cats," she said, "But why are they so friendly?"

"Mermaid thing, like all the animals we've met. They like me." I got up to a squat, scratching them both on the head. With a nod to the house I said, "I think we should get going."

"You really think they'll have a phone that we can use?" Ri'Anne asked, as we walked towards the stream between us and the house. The closer we got to it, the less it seemed natural, which didn't mean anything, but there didn't seem to be any way across.

Kneeling beside one of the great old cats laying on a rock, sprawled out enjoying the sun, I asked it "How do we get across?"

"Mistress, hmmm. Errr, I guess you can swim. Nobody comes this way. We're to deter visitors, but generally we lay about all day since nobody comes."

I raised my eyebrows at this, "You're here to scare off people?"

"Or eat them if they are too slow. This collar itches," she said, pawing at the thing that was so cleverly disguised that I hadn't seen it. Rubbing my hands under it, I noticed an electronic device built into it. "What do you suppose this is?" I asked Ri'Anne.

She was sitting some five feet away with her feet in the water, "It's probably an electronic fence device," she said. "Otherwise they'd probably wander off. It would explain the lack of paw prints on the beach."

Coming to sit beside Ri'Anne, I told the cat "Thanks and goodbye."

"I've heard of people having private zoos," Ri'Anne said looking around. "But they don't have a wide selection. I see colorful birds in the trees on the other side of the water, but I'm pretty sure I saw their like elsewhere here too. Maybe they just like big cats. They're friendly enough."

I passed on sharing the bit about the cats being here to eat trespassers, so I simply left it alone and rolled into the manmade river. Several large and small fish looked up from their casual swim. I gave them a wave as we scooted across. "It's well stocked," Ri'Anne said. "But who'd want to eat these things? They're all teeth."

"Oh, they are probably for show," I shrugged and looked up at the inside bank and the row of bushes blocking the view of the inner gardens. "Those look prickly," I said, wondering what we should do. I remembered walking with Jill on one island, our feet and legs becoming scratched and bleeding from simple plants. These were worse.

"What?" Ri'Anne asked climbing out and crossing through them, then looking over at me from the other side. "Oh, go through here," she said pointing to an impassible spot. She showed me by walking back through it to me and gave me a hands up.

"Aren't these beautiful?" she asked, rubbing her hands through the brambles as we went through. "I'd love to have a cutting to take back. Do you think they'd mind?"

We exited the bushes to a pristinely trimmed yard before the house. Several of the bushes carved into fantastical creatures that a kid might like. The grass was well-kept, and a few colorful birds strutted across the grounds.

Just then we heard a high pitched squeal, and then a pair of kids ran around the corner of the house, looking back over their shoulders shouting with glee. They were half-way to us before they looked up and slid to a halt, breathless, laughing and staring at us in wonder.

The girl, probably nine, skinny as a pole, bright eyed with black hair, looked pertinent. She was about to ask us what we were doing there when they heard a noise from behind them around the corner of the house and they dodged past us and kept going. Turning in a whirl we watched them sprint off away from us up some brick steps and down the other side, disappearing from view. We looked back the other way but there was nobody there.

"What was that about?" Ri'Anne asked and I shrugged. "At least we know there is someone here."

Feeling a prickle on my neck, I felt about, turning with a smile and reached for Ri'Anne, but she was saying, "Hi," when I'd finished my turn. Good, she was learning control too.

There was a man there. He gave Ri'Anne a quizzical look and then cast his eyes on me. He was a short fellow. It being in the nineties and super humid, I thought it strange that he wore all black in this heat. A conical hat shaded his face. I suspected he was the source of the noise the kids had been running from, but the guy sure could be quiet when he wanted to be.

He was miffed at our being there, though he was trying his best to hide it. He had this look that said, "You should not have seen or heard me." If I was reading him right he was perturbed with Ri'Anne for having discovered him. I was surprised too. I admit I was lax, but so far the place had been peaceful and quiet. I hadn't been keeping my attuning up.

Attuning really was our only defense and it didn't do any good if we weren't using it. But it wasn't like this guy was going to cast a spell. And if he was, wouldn't he have already? He looked to be the gardener, probably the one responsible for sweeping the sands and such. Dusting off his hands I saw some leaves drop from his fingers, confirming my suspicion.

"Sorry," he said extending his hand with a smile, "We weren't expecting anyone." Ri'Anne looked at me for a translation. I shook his hand, saying, "I'm sorry, we should have …" Oh, it was hot. What had I been saying? I looked at my hands there was something wet on them. "Ri'Anne …"

Seeing spots, it was a moment before my eyes focused. "Water," I breathed with parched lips. Were we poisoned? *That wasn't smart Melanie*, I chided myself. Apparently attuning prevented spells, but not something natural.

"Here," Ri'Anne said with a moan, passing me something to drink from. "Careful, it's sharp."

I let her hold the water to me, but instead of drinking it I stuck a finger in, sucking it up that way, purifying it first. "Ah that's better," my eyes cleared up and I looked around at the dark place. Attuning, my head cleared and I felt we were in an old cistern. I could sense that the only way out was up. It was solid earth around us, but we weren't alone. Beside us lay a dozen skeletons, one not too old. The sky was winking at us. Not even any bars to keep us in.

"They're not very friendly," I said and looked over at Ri'Anne, she was holding her head. "Let me look at that," I asked, getting up to kneel behind her, but it was too dark and my fingers discovered little. Reaching in to her with my senses, there was nothing broken, but she was sore in several places. The gardener I suspected had physically forced her here.

Figuring that water could help heal the bump on her head, I let some of what was in me come back out my hand onto her head. "Oh, that feels good," she said and I felt the swelling go down. She then added, "So I say we leave this place and never come back."

"But why? We just got here," I said in all seriousness.

Ri'Anne laughed, "You're kidding right? Look around you! They don't like strangers."

"We're not strangers," I said. "We met their kids and shook hands with that fellow. After a meal we'll be fast friends."

"Ok, what's your plan? I don't think I can fly, my head hurts too much, but we might be able to climb these vines."

"You climb," I suggested not liking the idea of another climb. The vines were tiny threads as it was. They probably wouldn't hold me anyway. "I'll fly. Race you…"

"Not fair!" she cried as I took to the air with a laugh. At least I didn't have to fight crosswinds as I flew upwards. Kicking gently, I floated to the rim with Ri'Anne a dozen feet below me and rising rapidly. I pretended to climb out in case anyone was watching, but I sensed no one. We were in the back parts of the old grounds. The cistern probably dated back to the pre-electricity days. Ri'Anne finally joined me after finishing her climb.

I told her my thoughts as she sat in a huff and I pointed out, "I suspect the kids don't venture here."

"Well let's go. Be careful, the guy is quick. I'm not sure how he dropped you, but you collapsed within seconds of his handshake. A poisonous sap I think that knocked you out on contact. It had no effect on me, so he resorted to knocking me down. It bothered him to have to use force. He thinks himself too civilized to have to resort to it. The house is this way," Ri'Anne added, jumping down from the edge of the cistern. I landed beside her. "I had a chance to see some of the place as he led me here and then he went to get you."

"How did he get us down the hole, a rope?" I asked curious.

She nodded, "Yeah. Made me untie myself and then you at the bottom. I could hardly stand, but I didn't want anything else bad to happen, so I did as he said. So why is it we're going to bother them again?"

I smiled to cheer her up, "We're going to use their phone, remember?"

"Why don't we just go 'home' use our phone there and then come back?" she asked confused.

"Hmm, I hadn't thought of that. But we're here anyway. We might as well accept their hospitality," I was entirely too cheerful about it.

Going up an old white stone step we arrived at the back of the regular backyard gardens. Stepping out into the yard Ri'Anne rejoiced and spun about in the sunlight. "You forget how glorious sunlight is until you're locked away from it," she said, spinning to stride along with me. Stepping past a hedge we saw the house and fountain in the center of the backyard surrounded by flowering bushes.

Seeing the fountain, I angled towards it expecting at any moment another meeting with the fellow, but sensed nothing. There was a hedge of bushes around the fountain, but this time we got to use the paved stone path to get through them. Sitting on the edge of the fountain I put a foot in and felt my senses go out all around us. The poison had left me weak, but in a moment the water refreshed me and I was able to see further. Soon I had the location of the fellow. He was headed out towards the cistern along another route. We had some time.

"Here, sit. Let's tend to your hurts," and as she sat I bathed her lightly in the water. As a gentle wave, I sensed her pain washing away and with it her muscles relaxed.

"Thanks," she said turning back to face me, her eyes clear of pain. "I didn't know you could do that."

I shrugged, "I've never had to do so much before. Honestly I've only banished sunburn..." I turned my head, facing the way we'd come. The fellow was running, moving fast diagonally. He bent beside a stepping stone, pried it up and pulled out a heavy pouch.

"He's coming isn't he?" she asked, seeing me still.

I nodded, "But he doesn't know where we are. We'll be ok. Let's go inside." The back entrance through tall columns was wide open to an inner courtyard. What was I doing? This seemed foolish. Demanding that they be nice?

"You're persistent," said a girl's voice from behind and to the left. We'd entered the inner yard surrounded on four sides by the house and the wall to the outer yard. "Papie doesn't like visitors," she said. As I turned to look at her I could see she was assured of her safety.

"I gathered that," I said looking over her shoulder to her brother holding a wooden toy soldier on a horse. "It seems a shame. Such a lovely house to be all alone in."

During the short conversation I'd lost track of the fellow, but not Ri'Anne as she turned a bit more back the way we'd come. Then with an elbow, she knocked me aside and I turned, "What?" Ri'Anne was staring back towards the fountain. "Hold these," she said handing me a pair of throwing knives.

"I don't want these," I said dropping them. They bounced on the brick path with a clang before coming to rest. "Where did you even get such a thing?" Then my jaw dropped as I saw her reach up and pluck another from the air. It had been sitting on an invisible shelf. She dropped it to land with the others.

"Can I have them?" asked the boy coming forward. "Sami will be wanting them back." Ri'Anne said it was ok, and the boy bent to retrieve them.

"Wanting them back?" I asked as I finally understood him. "Why's he leaving them…" *how do I say this*, "hanging in the air?" That seemed like a reasonable explanation for a six year old, let alone for me. Sure enough, Ri'Anne pulled another from an air shelf. It seemed there were a dozen such shelves, only visible when she opened them, like chocolates on a Christmas calendar.

20

In the Spider's Lair

Thinking of chocolates, my stomach rumbled. It had been forever since we ate. The girl was standing there, like she expected us to fall over at any second. "Hey," I said, getting her attention. "I don't suppose you have anything to eat?"

"Hum, ok, I suppose. This way," and she walked out into the yard. "Normally people don't get this far, so maybe I can offer you something. I never get to really, play host – you know. I only ever get to entertain my dolls, and they aren't much fun. Come along Gian, bring along Sami's things, and be careful not to cut yourself."

"I'm not a baby Kyria," he complained to his sister, dragging along his toy with one hand and holding the knives in his shirt with the other. I turned to Ri'Anne who was holding the remaining knife, reflecting sunlight off of it back at the fountain. The glare she was creating was more than I'd expect from a simple knife. Reaching back towards the fountain, I saw the gardener hiding behind the bushes, rubbing his tear-stained eyes.

Becoming a mermaid was done by experiencing it. But Ri'Anne was going in a direction that was unfamiliar. A mermaid worked with water, but Ri'Anne was working with air and now sunlight. How could I teach her when I was learning from her?

At least her methods were nonviolent. He meant us evil, and she'd returned it with bright light. The courtyard led through a wide veranda to the inside of the house, on foot-wide brown tiles we walked through the courtyard. Passing a pair of pillars and a delicate fountain, we climbed some stairs onto a veranda with comfortable outdoor chairs. Entering a pair of tall glass-paned doors, we came into a tall entry.

"Hey, I thought I told you two to play outside," came a soft Italian voice.

"We're not playing Papie, we're hosting. Well, I'm hosting, Gian is following along." The girl had gone still at the voice, and we waited for whatever came next.

"You can entertain your dolls outside, Samuel can get you whatever you need, but don't spoil your dinner." The speaker's voice carried well from upstairs.

"Papie, they're not dolls. These two girls asked me for food, and you always told me that I'm to entertain those that ask. It's my first time, Papie, it is ok isn't it?"

"Samuel?" called the speaker, and from behind us stepped out the man with the conical hat, but he'd removed it and was holding it before him in deference to whoever was speaking. "Sir?" he answered the speaker.

"See that Kyria's guests are well treated, but I'm not to be disturbed. I'm still trying to figure out what Jill is going to do with the reporter. Stupid mermaids, up to no good I tell you. Anyway, I have to think this through. Wait, Kyria dear. You said two girls?"

Standing tall the girl cleared her throat, "They're my guests Papie," the young girl said, defying the speaker.

"Yes, yes dear. You told me that already, I'm just curious to their names dear. Promise you'll tell me later."

"I promise, Papie," the girl said, and then apparently the conversation was over. Turning on the gardener, Kyria told him, "Light food for our guests Sami."

"I'm hungry," Gian said reminding his sister that he existed.

"You're always hungry, love, but we have guests. Ok, ok. Food all around Sami, but we're not to spoil our dinner."

"Your will, Miss," the man said politely. "Please have a seat," and he gestured towards a table in the dining room. I expected another knife with the gesture, but I was disappointed.

When we were seated the girl rounded on us with a whispered, "Don't tell me your names and I can say I didn't ask." Not wanting to get mixed up in their family affairs, we agreed. "But why?" I asked.

Looking down at the table and her hands, she contemplated how to answer, and then sounding remarkably adult reasoned it out to us, "I've waited my whole life to have guests. Papie says we must be respectful where we can, but you can't feed every mouth that comes around. I don't understand it all, but up until now if I said 'we' have guests, then they are his as well, and he makes off with them. I never see them again. I expect they're dead, honestly. So far it is working saying you two are 'my' guests. I want the moment to last. As to your names, those are important. Papie is always working on his book, a work of fiction he says. But every time there are guests, he knows people's names before I say them, so I'd rather not know and then he can't say. It's nice to have some surprises in life, you know. Besides, what is the fun in giving him everything?"

On that note, Sami or Samuel came out with plates of cheese, meats and milk, which he set before us. Kyria leaned across the table and picked something from each of our plates, and swapped our milks with those of hers and her brother's. "You can't be too careful with Sami, always trying to off the guests," she said while the man was standing there.

"Not the guests Miss," the man corrected her, "Only the intruders."

"Same difference," she said, sitting up on her heels in the chair. Both she and Gian were too short to sit in them comfortably. "Whatever," she said waving him away. "I want to talk privately with the guests then, Sami."

"As you wish," he said turning and going a distance away so he couldn't overhear, but he kept us in sight.

The girl was clearly upset with the situation, which was understandable if they were stuck here cooped up with an elderly grandfather and the groundskeeper who may play with them, but was hardly a friend.

"So, what can we talk about?" she asked. "I'm not very good at this, never having done it before. Oh, go ahead and eat," picking up a piece of cheese to place in her mouth. I followed suit, not knowing when I'd get a chance to eat next. Ri'Anne looked at me funny. True, the fellow had recently knocked me out with some kind of contact poison, but I had to eat sometime. In between bites I asked the girl what she did around here. She explained about their schooling, and in their free time playing with Sami.

"Well, we were wondering if we could use your computer," Ri'Anne jumped out, seeing that I wasn't going to bring the conversation around to it.

"Oh, sure. Gian?" Kyria asked her brother. "Why is it always me?" he complained, jumping down and dashing off before anyone could answer. "It's always him," Kyria filled us in with, "Because he's always playing on it." Gian came back after a little bit carrying a tablet. He set it on the table, hopped up onto his chair in imitation of Kyria's pose and then started eating.

"Here," Kyria said pulling the tablet across to Ri'Anne, who nodded towards me.

When I had it, I turned it on and started looking for a way to notify Dad and Uncle to our location. Using their Google Earth app I was able to get a link and then send Dad and Uncle an email saying we were ok. Then remembering the reception we'd received, I asked, "Is it ok if I give away our location to my Uncle? He'd have to pick us up in his boat. It would be nice if Samuel didn't treat them, my uncle, Dad and Gigi, our cook, as intruders."

Her eyes grew real big, and she shook her head saying, "Honestly, I have no idea. This would be the first time anyone's been invited here that I've ever heard of. Perhaps, if you met them on the beach it would be ok. Though you probably ought to let Sami guide you. I've rarely been across the river we have around the property, but I'd like to come."

She waved the gardener over, "Sami, their friends are coming." On "friends" his eyes grew wide and he just about blew a gasket. So when she said, "We'd like to go with them to the beach," he laughed and relaxed.

Still chuckling he said, "If you can get past the flesh-eating fish, the ever-hungry tigers and the scorpions on the beach, sure you can go. You might as well swim with the sharks out in the bay we feed to keep around. By the way, how did you two get in here?"

Kyria didn't bat a lash at the list of terrors, but said to the last question of his, "Now, now Sami, don't be impolite. I'm sure they petted your kitties on the way in, didn't you?" And we over exaggerated our nod of yes in imitation of hers. "Oh and a swim sounds delightful. I've never been swimming, but it looks fun."

Ri'Anne observed, "I didn't see any sharks, scorpions, hungry tigers or flesh eating fish. Did you?"

I shook my head no, "Of them all, if you consider the playful yearlings ever-hungry, yeah, I guess I did. But the rest, no." On seeing his expression I asked, "It was ok to play with the kittens right?"

He looked like he had holes where his eyes went. It took him a moment, then he laughed again but this time without mirth. "Haha, right. Played with the kittens, ah-hah. I get it." Sure that he'd made his point, he left us alone to go tend his gardening.

"So can we really go swimming?" Gian asked.

"I don't see why not," Kyria said. "You two done?" she asked looking at our cleaned plates. "This will be better than sitting around talking," she said getting up and dusting off her hands. "You two wait here, I'm going to go get my suit on. Come along Gian, let's get changed. I wish I had swim suits as pretty as yours."

"So, any word?" Ri'Anne asked looking over to me.

I nodded, "They are on the way, a few hours or so. They have to pull up the equipment we'd placed, I guess. It's not like they were that far away to begin with."

Since we had a moment, I thought about the trip. "What I'd like to know is why we're here? Since we landed in Papua New Guinea, it has been kind of slow. Normally, I'm a roller coaster of adventures, helping here and going there."

"You don't think getting stranded on an island, running for our lives, being thrown in a pit and playing with tigers an adventure?" Ri'Anne asked and I shrugged at that. "And what about the guy that owns this place, mentioning mermaids? Pretty strange, especially mentioning Jill in the same breath."

"I'm sure it's a coincidence. Jill's a pretty common name, besides what would she be doing talking with a reporter? What I mean, is there haven't been any sudden transfers." Then remembering how I felt about being sucked out of a jetliner at fifty thousand feet, "It's just as well." I still hadn't told anyone about that. "The last time wasn't very fun…" there were the sounds of running bare feet, and so I held off on telling Ri'Anne about it.

"We're ready," announced Kyria as the two of them ran around the corner holding towels.

"Good," I replied jumping up. "So how do we get back to the beach, if not through all the deadly obstacles we were warned of?"

"Oh I forgot!" Kyria remarked turning in place and sprinting off again.

"She's going to get the Fairy Dust," Gian said. Our eyes went up at that.

"Real fairy dust?" Ri'Anne asked. She looked at me, and I thought she might cackle in glee while clapping her hands.

"Well I suppose. I'm not sure I would know fake dust from real dust," he admitted. "We rarely use it. That's all I know." He sounded proud to know that much at six years old.

A bright light preceded Kyria's return, and I wondered what she was doing using a flash light during the day. She rounded the corner, and I had to cover my eyes, but Ri'Anne jumped forward staring right into the light, "Oh, bottled sunlight!"

"It's dust," Kyria corrected her. "It'll enable us to fly over to the beach. It lasts for a couple hours, but it's really boring. I want to swim. So here, hold out a hand," and she went around to each of us. When my eyes had adjusted, I saw she was holding a glass salt shaker in which appeared to be a tiny sun. I did as she asked and held out my hand. I could already fly, but she didn't know that. When the dust hit my hand, the flakes burst onto my skin. The bright golden glitter spread over me, until I was floating off the ground. Oh, this was more the thing. It seemed I'd only pretended at flying before.

She did Gian next. He, too, started floating. Then she moved to Ri'Anne. As the sunlit fairy dust hit her, a similar light gathered on her shoulders and ran down to her hands. It happened so fast, and then the room burst with light, brighter and brighter. When the spots cleared from my eyes, Kyria was looking at the bottle saying, "It's never done that before." Ri'Anne was floating like the rest of us and looked embarrassed. "Ok, my turn," and she held out her hand and sprinkled it with the sunlight powder. In a blink she zoomed as a shooting star out of the room, her voice echoing away, "I'm putting this away, be… right… back." And there she was floating before us, one leg extended and one bent, bobbing up and down slightly. She was back before she even finished speaking.

"Ok, let's go," and she led us out. Before when Ri'Anne and I had flown, it had been ponderous in comparison. This was like swimming at full mermaid speed times a hundred, and I could tell Kyria was holding back waiting for us to get our air legs. We flew out into the central courtyard, then straight up and arching over the front of the house. It took more time to think about it than to do it and it didn't seem hurried. We were moving faster than thought.

Ri'Anne picked it up fast, challenging Kyria before we were halfway across the front yard towards the beach. Kyria got a determined look, and here I thought we were going fast, but the two of them shot ahead and I saw only their contrails disappearing ahead of me, leaving me like I'd been standing still.

Twin sonic booms rolled back over us. Ri'Anne had been the first to fly, and anything I had was with her help. I cheered her on and hoped she was keeping up with the pipsqueak.

Gian pouted, "Kyria's a show-off. Good luck with your friend keeping up with her. Papie is going to be upset. He doesn't like it when the windows rattle. So how do we swim?" he asked as we stilled out above the bay.

"Are you sure you want to?" I asked. Swimming seemed kind of pathetic compared to the flight we were experiencing. "It's wet and we move a lot slower, but it is kind of like flying."

Gian sighed, "She's doing it again. Look that way, and you may see her coming," he pointed back the way we came.

"Doing what again?" I asked confused. He'd noticed something I hadn't seen. "Wouldn't they come back the way they came?"

"You don't know anything," Gian was getting upset. "Kyria is going around the world, can't you tell?" When I shook my head aghast at the revelation, "Time is slowing. You can tell if you feel for it. The sense comes with the dust, it doesn't just let you fly but it messes with time. A real fairy can time travel."

My jaw dropped to my feet, "Time travel?" I sounded dumb to my own ears. He shrugged, "That's what Kyria says. You see there?" and he pointed, "That's us coming here."

Sure enough, there were the two of us moving backwards, and then in a double brilliant flash, two bright spears of light hammered by to hit our retreating selves, but they materialized into Ri'Anne's joyous self and Kyria looking perturbed at someone pressing her for supremacy of the sky. Then the four of us "were flying backwards towards the house," but it wasn't us, but our earlier-in-time selves.

"How come we didn't see us sitting here?" I asked, pretty sure that I would have.

"Kyria says, we are still moving forward in time in our own way, even if we are moving back in time relative to everyone else." He shrugged again, "It doesn't make sense to me either, we should have seen ourselves hovering here."

"Yeah," I said unable to explain it myself. "So they'll be here any second?"

"Hmmm, I think so. It depends if they fly it straight around," he was sinking towards the water already forgetting about his sister.

"Let's start in the shallows," I suggested joining him, "Over there, away from the scorpions and such."

"Ok, I was just hoping we could swim among the ruins." My eyebrows rose at this. Uncle Arlo I'm sure would like to have a look at them. "Somebody used to have a place on land here, but it sank forever ago. But you can see it when there is no wind to stir up the sand." Forever ago could be twenty years to a kid, but they could be worth exploring.

"Well, we could go in anywhere you'd like. But I had thought to teach you traditional swimming, you know where we travel across the top of the water and look down at everything. Over there, we could practice swimming where we can stand in the shallows. Then after your sister gets back, you'll be better than her. What do you think?"

I think I got him with the last argument, he nodded and zoomed over to the sheltered cove that I'd spotted from the air. It wasn't good for big boats, being too shallow. Debris was everywhere, like one of the several shanty homes had exploded, appearing more a swamp than the delightful cove it had been at one time.

Gian agreed with me, "The water looks gross. How does it get so dirty?"

It was easier to explain that. "The tides clean the ocean, but if we put in dirt faster than it can clean..." and I shrugged to say it was up to people to stop polluting, which would be impossible. "It just needs our help. As fairies, we can use our magic to clean the area."

"Really?!" his voice rose two octaves in excitement. He wanted to do something productive, sounding bored being a kid with no responsibilities.

"Sure, you walk the beach. Think of letting the fairy magic clean instead of flying. I'll start in with the water. When the beach is clean, come join me. I'll need your help."

"Ok…" and Gian blinked across the cove several times before he burned real bright like a lightbulb about to fail, and then his light spread out into the surrounding bushes, trees and grasses. So my idea wasn't as far-fetched as it sounded.

Taking my turn with the water, I set my feet down on the grimy sand. Eew, this was gross. My magical nature shivered at the touch. Closing my eyes, I felt out as I attuned, letting the magic in me expand outwards to my surroundings, especially the water. Together, it was as if a dark cloud parted to let the sun shine through; sand crabs came out of the goo onto newly cleansed sand, cheerful birds swarmed into the trees and flowers came out everywhere.

The fairy magic was working better with the plants and trees, their leaves regaining their sheen and uncurling to capture the sunlight. Trees that hadn't bloomed in ages suddenly had life coming up from their roots and they shouted in exultation, their limbs bursting with flowers.

I frowned, seeing a bird land on one of the crabs, pecking and cracking its shell and pulling out the crab meat with its beak. All life was benefiting, even at the expense of another's gain. Just as the pelican in port had explained, it would eat the fish that came around when I was near.

Stepping through the shallows, I worked deeper. Where I went, the magic went out around me, and the oily water gave way. Just a few days ago I'd answered Jill's summons to help clean Denver's river, but this was my first time to experience a disaster on my own. Ri'Anne should be here to experience this. I hoped she would return soon to lend a hand.

Hearing Gian walking into the water, I turned with a smile to encourage him. Looking back, I was surprised at the change taking place, it continued on without prompting. But I turned my attention to Gian, and explained the basics of swimming. "It's like flying, regular flying, not magic flying. If you have ever ridden a bike, you know that the quicker you go the easier it is. It's like that with swimming too. I know that sounds complex, but as you can see, just standing here going nowhere, well, we're not swimming are we?"

"The body floats a little, and even more in salt water, see?" and I sat down, pulling up my legs, but I was sinking and flapped my arms to stay up. "I have to use my arms to stay afloat. In deeper water you can use your legs in a scissors-like motion too," and I demonstrated it using two fingers going back and forth like they were walking. "Ok, let's go a little further in and I'll help you while you practice floating. Then we'll get into actual swimming. And keep cleaning, you're doing a great job."

I would have thought he would be bored with floating, but he was enjoying it. We were both enjoying his progress when the girls returned. Ri'Anne asked our whereabouts, and then they were flashing out of the sky to "stand" on the water beside us. "Go ahead and get started," and I waved them over and away.

When they went away, I heard Kyria asking Ri'Anne, "How'd you know they were over here? I would have chosen a cleaner place."

Would she have? The open bay might be cleaner, but here there wasn't a strong tide to fight. If we stayed long enough it might become a pleasant enough cove again. Besides, Sami had said there were sharks in the bay. Their lives were already mysterious enough without adding in mermaid stories.

"Can we do more swimming?" Gian asked in a whisper. "I want to get a head start on Kyria."

For the next couple hours Gian and I swam around the tiny lagoon, getting more and more adventurous. Kyria wasn't picking it up as fast, but she was enjoying the water anyway. I could hear her and Ri'Anne laughing from time to time.

"I'm hungry," Gian reported. Pointing to shore he said, "They have oranges and bananas. Can we get some?"

There on the beach were seated several people, three women and two older men. The women sat cross-legged with baskets filled with fruit on their lap. Just then there was the sound of The Lazy Cloud's horn in the greater bay outside the lagoon. Ri'Anne and I exchanged glances.

"We're going to have to go," I told Gian and I saw his hopeful face crash.

"No, no, no – please stay!" Gian begged. Ri'Anne and Kyria joined us on the heels of that outburst. He was pulling at my heart strings, and I gave in and he saw it. Jumping up into my arms he cried, "You can't go. I have no friends."

"Let's go see what they want," I temporized, knowing we couldn't stay.

"They're ignorant savages. They spoil the land and live in huts," Kyria said, clearly upset, with little love in her heart for her neighbors. She was reluctant to go over to them, but she followed after the three of us.

"Hi," I said coming up out of the water. I looked at the women as they stood. At first I'd thought them to be old, but as they came to their feet nimbly I saw they were teenagers. They all had dark complexions, but the girl who stepped forward first had a smile in her eyes as she happily lifted her fruit to share with us. I could see she liked to dance in the way she moved.

"Such beautiful …," she started, waving at our flowery swimsuits not knowing what to call them.

"Swimsuits," Kyria finished for her sarcastically, then in aside to us, "See, barbaric. Their language is so old, even I have a hard time following it and we share the same island."

I saw that Kyria was keeping her hands to herself, even though her brother was picking out several fruits for himself. Her bitter attitude was keeping her from enjoying what was being freely offered.

"… swimsuits," I filled in for the sixteen-something teenager, since she didn't understand Kyria. It was little wonder that Gian and Kyria had no friends with the way she acted. But it may not last for Gian. He was seated under a tree by the two men, speaking to one of them. The two of them were in an animated conversation which soon had the two older men laughing.

Feeling more confident, the other two girls came alongside their friend, one of them reaching out to touch my hair, fingering it, and I could see in her eyes she wanted to play with it. Ri'Anne said from behind me, "Was she complimenting us on our swimsuits? I can't understand anything they are saying. But you know, what are we going to do about our suits? When we left the yacht we weren't wearing them."

I saw in the girls' expressions that they didn't understand Ri'Anne. "Great," I thought out loud, I'm the only person that understands everyone. Having an idea, I turned to look at Ri'Anne, asking her, "Do you think you could make them similar suits?"

"Me?" Ri'Anne asked her eyes going wide. "Hmm, I suppose, why?"

"I want to offer a trade," I said and Ri'Anne looked past me to what the girls were wearing. She'd been wanting some native clothing. She shook her head no, "It's not the clothes, but I'm hesitant – think of the fish. Would you give them to just anyone?"

I had to agree. Jill's rule was not to share our abilities without care. By having Ri'Anne create garments for these girls out of thin air would be going in the face of that rule. No, she was right. "It looks like we are going to have to go back the way we'd come. Can we at least give them what we're wearing?" I asked her.

But Ri'Anne shook her head, "You saw what happened to mine. They'll turn to dirt the moment they are removed. They are beautiful and alive while we wear them, and only then." She shrugged.

How strange, I thought. These flowery suits that came from plants were apparently drawing life from us. "There should be a story for that, but I have no idea what it is," I shrugged and laughed.

"You know what?" I said to Ri'Anne, nobody and everyone. "I'm going to try," and I ran a fingernail across the stem that connected the flowery top with the intricate vine bottom with its explosion of tiny flowers. A cloud suddenly surrounded the two of us. I couldn't see anyone else. Then, peeling off the top, I thought to give it whatever life I had as a mermaid, singing to it. I wanted the girls to have it. Ri'Anne followed my lead, and when we held the suits, the cloud that had been enveloping us and giving us privacy became our new suits. It had worked! They didn't crack away into dust. I'd thought to not show off my mermaid abilities to the kids. But how was I to know the clouds would do that?

"Here," I said to the girl that had liked it so much. Then, with a bow to her and her friends, I presented the garment to the girl. She looked incredibly surprised, and held it close like I'd given her something too precious for words. Ri'Anne followed my example, giving her suit away with reluctance.

Having just acquired them, I'm having problems letting go, Ri'Anne explained. She was having her own separation anxiety as I'd been experiencing earlier without my fish. To calm her fears, I attuned to the suits we'd given them and explained it to her. They retained enough magic to fit the first person that wore them, but after that they'd be regular suits without any magic properties.

Together we turned and about bowled Kyria over, planning to run for the water and dive in.

She looked up into my face and saw my intentions, "No, you can't go yet. Please, don't leave." Her eyes traveled over her neighbors, and then back to me. I caught her meaning. She wanted to say something, but she didn't want them to hear. Gian put his sticky hand into mine, "You can't leave," and I picked him up and held him.

"She's going," Kyria said to him, "But we can give her something for being so nice and to remember us by. Why don't you think of something you'd like to give her."

Gian's face lit up, he kissed my cheek, "That's my gift." And I hugged him close telling him, "That's the sweetest gift, thank you." I had tears in my eyes and when he leaned back, he wiped them away with his tiny hands. We smiled at each other.

Suddenly I saw a duplicate of Kyria standing behind herself, holding the Fairy Dust jar. She held a finger to her lips. It took me a moment to realize I was seeing Kyria as she'd be in her own future. This fairy magic was something else… time travel.

The present Kyria was squirming in place, fighting with herself on a decision and waiting for me to put down her brother. Turning her toes inward, she said with a huff when we were done, "I, um. I can only think of one thing. So before I change my mind, I'll be right back," and she literally disappeared. I knew technically she flew away, but it appeared to me as if she'd transferred.

"Oh wow," said Ri'Anne and I think she saw Kyria fly away. Ri'Anne grasped flying better than me. I preferred flying in water, which I liked to call swimming.

The Kyria that had been waiting stepped forward, holding up a small plastic Easter egg. Swiveling it in place, she showed how it resembled the larger Fairy Dust shaker. Handing it to Ri'Anne she said, "My gift to you for racing with me."

Waving her hand, Ri'Anne begged off, "Oh, no thank you - I'm good. Give it to her, she'd enjoy it more."

Nodding, Kyria stepped before me and held it out saying, "For fun. It's got enough for a burst of speed the likes of which you have never imagined." Then to the both of us she said, "Thanks! You've both brought my brother and I real joy. We'll treasure this day always." Then her serious grown up behavior broke down and she stepped forward, hugging us both.

"Thank you," I told her, not quite sure what to make of the gift. I couldn't see any use for it, but then it would have come in handy when I'd fallen out of the jet. So maybe.

Then Kyria took her brother's hand, "I'm not a baby," he said but they both took to the sky still holding hands and zipped out of sight towards their home.

Turning around to thank the ladies for the fruit, I saw we had the beach to ourselves. They'd mysteriously disappeared as quickly as they had come.

"So that was cool," Ri'Anne said. I had to smile at her, this had been fun. "Fairy magic," and she ran in place so excited her legs blurred. "I can hardly believe it. They are real!" Then looking at the tiny sun in my fist she asked, "So what are you going to do with that?"

"I'm not sure," I said, holding it up between my thumb and forefinger. "Getting it back aboard The Lazy Cloud is going to be a trick. It's not like we have pockets."

Ri'Anne looked at me like I was being silly, "Of course you have pockets. You come and go between places, some of them not of this world. You're trying to tell me, you can't just 'tuck' it somewhere within 'easy' reach?"

I wanted to be like, "duh" but – sure, it sounded easy when you weren't the one that had to do it. She was right though. If it had been Jill and me, I'd have said something similar to her. "Ok," I said thinking out loud. "If I needed a place," and I let my attention go to connecting with that place. At first I thought it could be my dresser at home, but I needed someplace more secure. Even if this was only fun dust, it could potentially be used for something crazy.

"Ok," I said again, feeling the connection between me and the place I wanted to hide the fairy dust. It was a place with a bunch of cubbies like post office boxes. Internalizing the request to the Lord of the Water, I felt it was ok. Like he ever told me no. Then it was only a matter of "dropping" the egg within and it was gone. I was surprised with how easy it was, though I felt parched at the attempt. It had drained me more than I wanted to admit.

21

Fumbling the Ball

With the beach to ourselves, Gian and Kyria having gone home and the mysterious islanders having disappeared, it was time that we got scarce too. I looked over at Ri'Anne, she was examining her new cloud suit.

"This is too much," she said. "Who is it that 'gives' us suits? Why is it so important to them? It happened to me on the submarine then too, the plants becoming my suit. I'd thought it was your magic rubbing off on me then..." Ri'Anne let her thoughts go, playing with the cloud of her top, her thumb disappearing into it as she pressed on it.

Feeling the heat of the sun on my neck, I debated taking to the water to explain. Was it time I explained to her how magic worked, and better yet who was its source? I'd probably left her in the dark too long, but it had never seemed appropriate. Unlike when Jill had taught me, when we'd been moving around a lot and I'd needed to know. I wanted to get back to The Lazy Cloud, but once aboard we'd have all the duties there and I should tell her where nobody else would hear. Deciding to go for it, I sat facing the water with my knees up. Ri'Anne automatically sat with me.

"It isn't my magic, or your magic," I started with the basics, getting her attention. "We believe and use someone else's magic. It has a source in The Lord of the Water. It is he that approves its use, and gives us the, how shall I say it… the natural uses of it, because it seems natural. The more you move in the use of it, the more he'll use you, and sometimes, like now, with these cloud suits without asking us for permission. But as you can see, he has our best interests at heart because it's in his best interests."

I gave her a second to let that sink in. She had a hundred questions and before she could voice one I went on. "When I attune… When I look around, needing water to do so, in general I'm making a connection to the here and now. The vision is down to cellular levels, and is as expansive as I have need for. Like looking for the herrings when we were in port. Attuning is the first step in doing magic."

Committed, I quickly told her the rest, "The second is petitioning The Lord of the Water for understanding of the magic you want to do. If he grants it, and Jill tells me he always says yes, and he always has for me, then you have what you need to do the third step. Which is to practice it, which isn't like the name implies. You aren't practicing, but it's more like putting it into motion. In everything I've taught you, and what you've figured out, you are using his magic at his behest."

"You make it sound like we're accountable for our actions to The Lord of the Water," Ri'Anne said, looking like I'd slapped her. "But this explains so much. How do you attune?" she asked, switching moods with her thoughts.

"I've never thought about the accountability, I suppose I do things as they are presented, doing the best I can and letting things fall out as they may." Thinking of the sailboat rescue, I told her, "The Lord of the Water obviously provides us with things, but he uses me, us. If you continue to learn," *mermaid things*, I wanted to say, but how was I to explain the things Ri'Anne had been doing? Plunging ahead I said it a different way. "…magic, you become his agent to the world. As for attuning, I think you do it already when you work with plants. Try to apply it to people and what is around you." Ri'Anne nodded, I was making sense.

"Actually I do that already," Ri'Anne said jumping in, "but so far only for what a plant needs – like its soil, light and air." Then brightening she said, "Oh, and it cleanses as you do. The air I've noticed gets better." Gripping my hand she said, "I'm glad to have a name for it. Thank you. This is going to help so much. I've felt like I was missing something in the work Gigi was showing me."

"Be careful who you share with," and I held her hand until she stopped to look at me to see that I was serious. "We've paid a price with Uncle, one I hope to somehow fix. Let's not create one with Gigi."

"She's a good person Melanie," Ri'Anne said trying to assure me, but she would be cautious, I could see it in her expression. "Gigi is a mystery for sure, she has a wealth of information for someone her age. She talks about things in history like she's lived through them." I nodded. Do I tell Ri'Anne Gigi's secret? I decided against it. Gigi should be the one to tell her.

"So these suits…" I thought they were interesting. They felt like actual clouds with weather, especially wind. They were the lightest feeling of any suit I'd ever worn. I had to smile at that. In essence, I was wearing air.

Ri'Anne, taking up where I left off, said, "I expect they will be to casual viewers, like your family and Gigi, white suits. But to us… I think my suit is storming on me," and she laughed as it tickled her. I laughed along with her as I felt like I was flying in the cloud as it blew cool air across me. Real air-conditioning suits, how delightful.

"To The Lazy Cloud then?" Ri'Anne asked. I nodded, and together we held hands, got up and ran into the water. The water never felt better, and I was again full of energy and ready for anything. With a last pulse of magic cleansing for the cove we'd been swimming in, since the villagers that had been so nice to us, we swam out into the bay proper.

At about a hundred paces, the shallow sandy bottom dropped away surprisingly clear of human junk. The clear blue waters welcomed us. Out there we could see the yacht, but I needed a swim. Teaching Kyria and Gian to swim had given me a powerful urge to go deep.

Halfway down, Ri'Anne called after me, "Hey, wait… You're going too fast. Melanie wait up!"

Laughing I turned to look back at my friend, thinking she was joking and she was only just behind me. But I'd gone and out swum her, until she was but a spec in the distance, rising to the surface, frustrated. It wasn't like her to be slow, but I was enjoying the swim. It beat flying for me hands down. Waiting for Ri'Anne, I watched her swimming on the surface. It was so nice to be out in the sea. Large and small fish gathered around me for a little while, and then swam off to do their thing when they saw I didn't need them.

Wondering at Ri'Anne's pace, she was slower than before. She'd lost none of the beauty that came from being a mermaid, but it seemed her mermaid talents were disappearing instead of increasing. I was concerned for her. I wanted her to have everything I had and more, but she kept displaying abilities that were so different than my own. I had to admit, she'd liked flying with Kyria more than anything. Maybe that was causing the problem, but it didn't make sense to me – I'd flown too.

I was hardly an expert at what it meant to be a mermaid. She took to flying as easily as breathing, and loved everything that grew. What else? She'd asked for butterflies instead of fish at the beginning. And what did that matter? I'd worn a butterfly. Ri'Anne breathed water as she demonstrated once she was over my head, diving down to join me. I knew I'd demonstrated different things than Jill had, but they seemed to be shades of the same watery traits. I shrugged, so what if Ri'Anne had different mermaid abilities. She was my friend.

"Hey," I said when she hovered before me, out of breath.

"You swim so fast!" she said disgruntled. "Do you think I'll ever swim that fast?"

I wanted to say yes, but I wasn't sure. Still, I tried to encourage her, "Think of flying fast… underwater."

"I tried," she said sounding hurt. "The water is like a brick wall to that. Out of the water, I know I could go faster. But with The Lazy Cloud so close I didn't think I should try, and we'd agreed to hide our talents."

"Well it seems like the better we're at flying, the worse at swimming – at least of the extra fast abilities we have."

"Yeah," she said defeated. "So what are you going to do – fly or swim?"

"Me?" I asked, doing a loop. We were now under the yacht over a deep hole that was so close to the island. It had dropped rapidly off. The hole looked like an inverted island, as if a volcano had gone down instead of up. I wondered if the ruins that we'd been told about were at the bottom of it. We should mention it to Uncle.

I told her, "I'm going to be the best swimmer I can be."

On that note, we heard a splash, and looked up the thirty feet to the surface. There was Dad orienting himself in the water, looking around and then with quick kicks descended towards us. "Uh oh," I said looking at Ri'Anne in panic. We'd forgotten about the underwater cameras. Uncle had to have seen us and told Dad.

"Hold on," Ri'Anne whispered. "You don't have to admit to being a mermaid. Just what is obvious, that you can breathe underwater."

"And see underwater, and probably a dozen things that I take for granted." It was my turn to be upset. I'd screwed up, royally!

"Like," and she was looking back over my shoulder, "those sharks homing in on your dad. How come they don't bother us?"

"You heard the eagle?" and she nodded. "Well, he as much said sea life helps me." And looking at them, I knew their intentions. They were cruising, not straight, but it was obvious their line of travel would have them scaring the diver back into his boat.

"Do something," Ri'Anne urged me.

"You do something, you're just as much a mermaid as me," I countered, but I knew she didn't have the confidence. So far she was hesitant around animals. With the eagle though she'd been secure, but maybe because it had walked on her.

"Hey," I called out to them remembering talking to the sharks when we'd met the submarine. I'd felt insecure then, not really knowing my place. But, sea life were really my friends as they'd demonstrated over and over again, as the eagle had said they should. The three of them changed directions and headed towards us.

"Mistress," they grinned with a toothy laugh arriving around us, "So good to *see* you..." These South Pacific sharks sounded like surfers. I could easily see them in Hawaiian shirts and shorts, flicking their sunglasses up with a single finger behind the ear. They sounded like they wanted to talk dirty. But when I didn't respond, they swam around the two of us and changed their tone to flirt with us, "What can we do for you beautiful ladies?"

I couldn't hear them, because they were still eyeing Dad, hoping I'd sick them on him. Them and their blood thirst. The casual way they were scaring Dad, threatening him. All of it was starting to make me boil over.

My anger was going to my head! I was not used to being enraged and I was close to losing control. My hands were resonating...

Glancing down at them, tiny lightning bolts zipped between my fingers, I was close to blasting them. It was the same way I'd felt with the jet-ski jerks, but there had been a better solution. I tried to push down the anger, but it had a life of its own.

Sensing my turmoil, they responded, offended, "We were only going to smell him. He intrigues us. Besides, the Sea Lords use us as guards from time to time. Surely that is still the case?" That wasn't the whole of it. I'd sensed their real intentions. They were hedging, afraid of me and knowing they shouldn't be. Like I might whip them for being bad "dogs," and they'd done nothing to deserve it.

Their words penetrated to my pride, *Of course Sea Lords should have guardians, it was only fitting.* That thought was as destructive as the anger.

I couldn't think through the anger, so I thought around it. But the last thought was bothering me, a simple mermaid girl like me could use bodyguards, as had come in handy with the submarine divers.

"Ok," I admitted. "As guards true, but …"

"Mistress, we can't do our job if you don't let us!" No more hedging. They had a right to be who they were, especially to me. They counted it a badge of honor.

I frowned. "How am I supposed to get things done if you come between me and guests?"

"You only have to say, Mistress," they said coolly. The word *guests* rang in my head until I remembered Kyria and Sami talking about guests and intruders. The difference to Sami had been those that had been labeled guests. The sharks were my version of Sami the Gardener, friendly and helpful, but they were also protectors.

"Hmm, thanks," I said and then added "Well he's a guest."

"You'd seemed like you didn't want him around," they said cutting to the point.

"Well I don't, but he's my Dad – so I also don't have a say in it."

They sniffed, tipping their heads Dad's direction. "He doesn't smell right, but if you say he's a Sea Lord…"

"He's not…"

"No need to explain lady. He's a guest, that's all we need. Call if you need anything further and we'll come… below water of course. Water has yet to grant us legs."

Heaven help people if sharks had legs. But then maybe not. People had a way of making whole species extinct.

Remembering how I'd thanked Shrremmm the sand shark for swallowing me whole in France then spitting me out, I turned my charm onto them. "Well thanks, but we'll be fine. I'll be sure to call if I need you."

"As always Mistress, may your waters be blissful and trouble free." With that the three of them turned on their tails and sped away.

Ri'Anne hadn't seen what the problem was, and Dad was between us and the yacht, uncertain whether to come to my aid or wait it out. But now with the sharks swimming off he came out of his shock and swam down to us.

I'm in for it now, I sent to Ri'Anne.

Dad arrived and quickly grabbed Ri'Anne and I around the waist. With great kicks of his flippers he moved us nowhere. I wasn't being stubborn, but we needed to talk. He was just being protective. Straining, I could see the muscles on his neck, like he was trying to lift a large rock – he finally gave up.

Struggling through his mask and air-piece from the scuba tank he wore, he tried to make it clear that we had to go up. With his hands taken up with holding us, I reached up and pulled on his mouth piece.

"Stop it!" he complained, and then his eyes lit up on hearing himself. I knowing he wouldn't be able to breathe, and kept the air piece near. He grabbed it with his teeth, inhaled and then, "We have to get aboard the yacht!" he egged us on to help.

"Are they in trouble?" Ri'Anne asked looking at me. She'd been freaked out about the sharks, but this wasn't her first experience with them. I should have been logically trying to see it from Dad's point of view. But now that I'd gotten over my anger, I saw that the sharks were cute, I wanted to hug them and rub their bellies. They were not to be feared, at least to mermaids and their guests.

Dad, shaking his head, "No, but those sharks. What did you do?" he accused Ri'Anne, looking sharply at her.

"Me?" she asked helplessly.

"Dad…" and he looked over at me. He hadn't let go, but if anything was holding me tighter. "Ow, Dad, let go."

"Hun, I'm never letting you go. You'd have to pry me away after what I saw…" He stopped to get some air, then continued. "Do either of you need this?" he tipped his head at the air, as if just realizing we were down there without air tanks. We shook our heads no. "But how?" he asked.

"Magic, Mr. McKenzie," Ri'Anne told him.

"Magic," he said flatly. "I would have said that you would have to show me for me to believe." Inhale. "Is it you?" he asked Ri'Anne again, knowing for sure it couldn't be me. I wanted for her to say yes, but I didn't want her to lie. But she held out, she didn't want to get in an argument with Dad either.

"It's me, Dad," I admitted after seeing Ri'Anne wouldn't say anything. He looked down at me, and our eyes met. In that second I knew he wasn't his brother. His eyes begged the question.

Ri'Anne was shaking her head, wanting me to say what she'd said before, only saying that we were just able to breathe water. Realizing I would be jeopardizing her if I admitted that we were mermaids, I'd have to say something else.

Before I could though, Dad's eyes went round and he said, "I'm going to kill him." His arms letting go. He made to swim up again, but again he didn't move. I could feel the water beside me holding him in place. That shocked me, "The sea and everything in it," echoed in my thoughts. The sea had greeted me in Papua, at the port.

"Melanie, let me go!" Dad turned on me.

"I'm not doing it," I told him sliding away fearfully. He was so fierce, he'd never yelled at me like that. When he looked at

Ri'Anne, about to accuse her, I told him, "And neither is Ri'Anne. You need to calm down Dad and tell us what this is about."

He paused and then looked at me with new eyes, "When did you grow up?"

"What are you talking about?" I asked him. "Spending a night on a beach doesn't make a woman out of me…"

"Look, I'm not happy that you swam off and disappeared like that yesterday. But no harm's done, so no foul. I used to spend nights out under the sky too, my parents none the wiser. I can't expect my child to behave differently," but he looked at me seriously. "But there are dangers in this world and I'd rather you not encounter them."

"Dad, we're not children."

"Melanie, you're not listening."

I waited for him to take a breath from his air tanks. "Dad, I don't want to argue with you." He'd probably end up grounding me and then where would I be?

"Then don't talk back. Your uncle had this planned all along didn't he?"

"I don't…"

"Don't play stupid with me Melanie McKenzie. You've known all along what Arlo was up to, what he was about – what he'd do if he saw you like this." I could only hang my head. Nobody ever said Dad was stupid, and he wasn't about to let me get away with it either. But then something in what Dad said made me hope.

“He doesn’t know does he?” I asked when Dad didn’t go on. The fear of what Uncle would do if he got a hold of Jill, or any of my friends made me certain I didn’t want him to know.

“I think he does. He hasn’t said it, but he wanted me to invite you and a friend. Don’t tell me, but I think Jill is involved. He was upset when he learned she wasn’t coming.”

“But…” that would mean the Syreni procedure didn’t take. Or he left before they could do it. Or he’d talked with Dad before they’d done the procedure. “He’s been nice to both Ri’Anne and I. Even encouraging us to help him with his work.” Which led me to believe he didn’t remember, and he’d told us what he had remembered and it hadn’t included anything about a mermaid rescue. I felt if he knew, we’d be searching for “her” and not the missing island. Unless he expected to find her there, but so far that didn’t add up with what he’d been saying. Nor was he requiring either Ri’Anne or myself to do any extra mermaid like activities and had expected us to use masks and fins for installing the cameras. And for looking for the lost camera. So far Uncle was acting like the Syreni procedure had worked, and it was worth keeping Dad from having his talk with him.

“It’s true,” Ri’Anne said coming alongside me. “I didn’t know what kind of reception I’d have on coming, but he’s made me feel welcome.” Not counting him yelling at her yesterday to be careful with his equipment, and the sending while on the island… Maybe I shouldn’t defend him so much.

“I’m still going to say something,” and Dad started to swim up. The water having let go of him.

"Dad wait!" I called after him and swam up to put myself between him and the yacht.

"Melanie, out of the way," he said in a tone that ended any argument. I moved, surprising myself. He was still my dad.

Rising up with him, I told him. "Dad, there's a chance he doesn't know about me and Ri'Anne." But he didn't stop, so I tugged at his arm. "You confronting him will only make him suspicious." Still that wasn't enough for him.

"Dad, he's had his memory of the event changed..."

"What event?" Dad stopped, looking back down at me.

I shook my head, "I can't say."

"We're going to have to deal with your attitude," he said resuming his swim. He put his hand to the underside of the yacht, reaching for the ladder.

"It was my decision Dad, you can't be mad – at whoever."

"I can if I want too," he said not looking at me, but he'd stopped.

"Dad, Uncle can't know. Your reaction proves to me that the decision I made for him not to know was the right one. If you go storming up there, it will raise all kinds of questions with him. The rest isn't my place to say. Ri'Anne and I breathe water, that's all you need know. But you mustn't tell anyone."

"But you do other things, like sending off those sharks."

"I was afraid of having this conversation, and they were protecting me."

"Protecting?" He paused, and I felt he might understand. But I misjudged him, "You're wrong about him. He won't bottle you up, or cage you. No, but he'll not get over being lied to – that runs in the family," and with that he climbed out of the water ending the conversation.

Ri'Anne came and put a hand on my shoulder, "I'm ok," I told her which surprised us both.

"I'd be a wreck if I'd just had that conversation with my dad," Ri'Anne said and I nodded. Jill had hinted at these decisions when we'd agreed to have Uncle's memory erased. It hurt more now than it did then, but at least I wasn't crying.

"We should go up," and with her nod I watched her climb out. And then after another few seconds I followed after.

"About time," Uncle said exasperated. "Layabouts, good for nothing… You," and he pointed a finger at me, "Fishing pole up front, we need to eat."

Then he turned his finger on Ri'Anne, and I waited to see what he'd do to her. But he waved me away, telling me to get going. And I got. I picked up the shirt I'd been wearing earlier and pulled it on and climbed the stairs to the main deck. I couldn't stay around to hear what he ordered Ri'Anne to do. Honestly, I was glad to have an assignment. He was right, we'd been goofing off.

22

Have Us for Dinner

Walking up to the front of the yacht, I was happy to "fish," sliding my hand over the railing and glancing over the side. I shouldn't have looked, I felt a tug to slip over the side into the wide undersea world that was mine to visit anytime. My heart was there and I'd just left it. I was still dripping wet.

Hearing thunder, I glanced upwards at the evening clouds. There was a bit of rain happening back on the island, but nothing here. Again there was thunder, and a flash of light from my t-shirt. I glanced inside. The swim top had transformed into anvil shaped cumulonimbus clouds and they flickered with light. The thunder was coming from them.

"Shhh," I told them with a finger to my lips. "Are you trying to get me in trouble?"

What I thought I should get was an apology, but instead I felt a sizzling across my chest and my hair at my neck stood on end, followed by louder thunder. I smelled smoke and it took me a second to realize my shirt was on fire.

"Hey, hey!" and I pulled it off, tossing it overboard. It drifted in the air trailing smoke before hissing in the water when it landed. I looked down at the floating rag and sent some magic at it and watched it disappear. Turning, leaning my elbows on the railing, I looked at the flickering clouds. "Easy," I complained.

"The t-shirt was 'too tight,'" I felt the clouds say. "This is much better – we need air to work."

"Then chill already, it's gone." Now I was talking to clouds, and water was running down out of them. "You are gross," I told them as they rained on me.

"Ah better," the clouds sighed in relief as the rain ended. "You take us swimming again we're going to rain…"

Hearing a splash, I looked back over the side. "Come play with us," the fish that had jumped called, jumping up again out of the water as high as it could. There was a whole school with it looking up out of the water at me, hoping I'd join them. The cloud suit would get upset if I did. But then I was a mermaid, swimming was a part of that and they'd have to live with it. Or I was going to have to do away with them and change into another suit.

"I'm supposed to be catching you," I replied to the fish, expecting them to flee.

"Then come catch us, if you can…" and then they dove and returned when I didn't follow right away, causing the water to roll with their hopeful excitement. They waited around, frolicking with colorful flashes as I made up my mind.

"Uncle's going to be mad if I go for another swim," I said to myself, glancing over at the forlorn fishing pole leaning up at the prow beside the fish bucket. A hook seemed a cruel way to bring up a fish. On the deck beside the pole was a bucket and a fishing net. Looking over the side, I thought if I swam with the net, I couldn't be accused of shirking my duty – and the fish were challenging me to a chase.

Picking up the pole, the seagulls that had gathered for the feast scattered in anticipation. I wasn't calling them in, but they didn't seem to care. Well, I wanted a swim with the fish, and diving over the side, I called to them. In a flash of silver scales they surrounded me as I dove between them. The seagulls cried their dismay as we disappeared down into the cool depths.

"I needed this," I thought aloud. The water calmed my nerves. I may not have cried as a result of my talk with Dad, but I was still reeling from it. We'd fought, and I didn't see any way to fix it. He'd implied I'd been lying to him. Well, then, I was lying to the world by not telling them everything about me, and I didn't see how that could possibly be true. They didn't have a right to know everything, or anything.

Trailing a long dress of fish, we swam for shallow waters. At last I settled beside an old anchor that was alone, its rope having long ago disintegrated. Sitting on a decaying scow, I pondered Dad's words. He felt I should share about myself, but how was I going to tell Uncle? His incessant need to be have data troubled me.

In the quiet, the fish were content to spiral around me. For a time I forgot they were there, but as I finished my inner debate – not knowing how to end it, I realized they were shielding me from prying eyes. It was kind of them, like the sharks had been protecting me. There was nobody about, but if anyone had been they'd have seen only flashing fish. All my concerns about swimsuits seem unfounded. Never was I in need; a butterfly provided when I was careless, and clouds when I was reckless.

I didn't think I could be Ri'Anne. She felt mermaids wore nothing and had been comfortable with her suit disintegrating on her. Maybe, if I ever had a mermaid tail, I'd feel different. Still, I had to smile at seeing Ri'Anne. She wore her flowering suits completely proper. It may have been the swim time talking, but I'd gained her appreciation for a time. Still, if I wanted a tail I'd need fish… if my dream with Uncle had any basis in fact. He'd wanted to take the fish that had been my tail.

With that in mind, I knew my rain clouds would have to go. But did I have to have fish? I didn't think so, at least I hoped not. I was liking these different outfits. It must be something about me and not the fish, as it had been true with me being a mermaid independent of the fish. So I could have clouds, temperamental rainclouds if need be. Still, "How about something new?" I wondered aloud. "An octopus, a turtle, a killer whale suit?"

A thousand "Me's" came from the fish that drifted around me, and they flashed their scales, reflecting the sun so that I was nearly blinded by their rainbow.

"Hey, sorry," I apologized shielding my eyes. They'd gotten my attention. It was unfair to be thinking of another kind of suit when I had them with me. While swimming, I'd felt I was an undersea princess, in the long trailing fish gown that was at least twice my length. Even though I'd told Ri'Anne I could do without the princess treatment, I couldn't get away from it.

Letting go of the rainclouds, I invited the fish to become my suit. Singing, I tried getting the fish to stay with me, which only attracted more fish, so I had to choose. Looking among the smaller fish, I sang out the pink and silver.

Amidst them all, a space formed around me as the pink and silver fish flung themselves, smashing themselves into an organic whole, a shimmering pink diamond dance suit with top-hat and walking stick. I laughed at them, "A swimsuit of pink and silver candy canes would have been sufficient," I remarked.

They flashed, and that is what I had. In a second I looked like a candy cane of pink and silver, trailing down my legs, fading out to just a few dots at my knees. "Nice! But, how about a wave?" Then the suit was back to being one piece, but as a colorful, mostly pink wave. I had the thought they could spell out words, but what they'd made was everything I could want and more.

Newly outfitted, I swam with them through the rock field that was overgrown with undersea fronds and came upon several wrecked boats. Drifting over one, an uncountable number of black fish the size of my hand darted out and around it to swim up and spiral around my silver and pink ones. Then they dispersed before diving back within the vessel.

Settling on the prow of the wrecked boat overlooking an old pleasure craft, I twirled the hat on my new cane. Seeing an old pleasure boat, its dance floor mostly intact, I could imagine people dancing upon it. The fish conveyed to me by expression that they always missed the show, for by the time a dance deck got to them, the people were gone.

"Ok, I'll dance…" There should be music. I sang to them. "What is it you want to hear?" I asked getting to my feet and giving them a flourishing bow, replacing the hat on my head, then tipped it forward with a push from the back of my head. The fish gathered, making rows of "seats" for themselves. Creating a stadium around me and the dance floor. Pinpoint light spots circled about me and I glanced up. Silverfish had created a ball of themselves reflecting the sun's remaining light downward.

"Anything," called a blowfish from the third row. "Yeah, anything!" sang out a yellow and blue striped snapper.

"Well… I don't know…" I said spinning on my rosy pink diamond heels.

Kicking out a leg, I twirled, kicking high. Maybe it was time to tell them of my reason for being here. I thought they'd run and hide when I told them of my errand. So I entertained them as I winged a song:

Stomach's a rumbling – bellies a
complaining, what's for dinner? – the bells a
ringing. Do tell us, don't keep us in the dark!
Jellyfish stew? Tiger-shark potpie? Eel soup?

Tapping their fins, the fish that had challenged me to catch them sang out in reply…

You want a fish – don't you serve no blister
spoiling stew. Pick me, I'm long and
handsome. I've the right color, size and

weight. Serve me raw, wrap me in a blanket.
A little rice and lettuce – I'm the best to you.

Hmm, sushi. I wondered if Gigi had any rice. Then a big fat purple fish swam up into full view, suggesting an alternative, not wanting to be left out…

Sizzle in the pan, I'm your flan – Eat don't
speak, spell me a sauce, tell me a tale. Toss
me a spinach, dice me a tomato, cut up a
carrot – have no plates? Serve me out of a
can.

"Very funny," and I gave the purple fish some applause. Then up came the biggest silverfish of the bunch, and it made its case…

Salmon is king, roll the lemon. Fillet me
upon the grill, bounce, dance, summon a
thrill! There is no tastier dish than the king.
Pop a cherry tomato in the mouth, make me
sing. There is no living unless you've tasted a
king.
It is pink that you want and don't forget the
lemon…

Salmon is King!

Cymbal crash, drum roll… "Oh," I sat holding my stomach. "You all are sick to be telling me how delicious you are." I moped out the next verse, no longer feeling like dancing. Staring into the darkening sea above,

How can I be thinking of eating, when you
all are saying you're a delight. You are too

kind, is life so choice that I dare come up with thee? Instead, tell me a tale, speak me a rhyme, weave me a song, or I just might.

Swimming to the fore, the giant salmon sang a low note, making their case:

Have us for dinner, we'll be the center – fun, delight, belly laughs – it won't be wrong. There is no greater pleasure than to love so fair. Sit back, enjoy the evening. Play a hand of cards, speak of the day. Plan the event, be the poet, write us a song. Have a feast, we'll delight, be merry, it's no slight.

"Lemon's the best," echoed several other fish when he finished, affirming that the salmon was right and I knew I had my "winner." I didn't feel like I'd won anything, as the poled net came to hand. Then the salmon swam and sat inside.

Swimming up to the swim deck with my "catch," I saw Uncle sitting watching the water to the west. "I'm in for it now," I told the king salmon.

Surfacing and trailing my long wet hair, I made the best of it, "Hey Uncle, mind giving me a hand?" And I held up the net with the heavy salmon in it.

"You're getting good at freediving," he said with a lopsided smile coming to lift out the fish. "Nice catch… I like it."

"Uncle, I think I prefer the fishing line approach," I admitted, letting go the net. He looked at me with a question in his eyes, so I explained "With a fishing line, you get whatever bites. With a net you choose..."

His eyes stopped me, he was looking to the side... "Wait, what did you say?"

"Well, I was going to fish, but I thought a hook would be cruel so I figured I'd try and catch one," holding up the net.

"But you said you prefer the hook approach."

"*Now* I do Uncle..."

"And you were 'fishing' this whole time?" At my nod, did I just admit to being underwater all along? He stood up and leaned on his crutch, looking off at the horizon.

"Uncle?" Thinking he was wondering where I'd gone, since under us was the deep hole I told him, "I was swimming out around those rocks over there. There's a couple smashed boats and lots of fish." His eyebrows rose at the mention of the wrecks, but he didn't stir.

"Well, as long as you come up as needed," he said again, not meeting my eyes but kept looking off at the open sea. Then coming to a decision he said, "You should get the fish to the cooks, and then maybe you and I can check out the wrecks."

"I'd like that," I said ascending the stairs taking my gasping friend to Gigi and Ri'Anne. While hopping down the stairs to the lower level I wondered if uncle meant in person or using me as we'd been practicing. I wasn't sure I could take another of his... *Oops, keep it positive Melanie.* It will all work out. Dad had said he wouldn't hurt us, at least intentionally.

Well, I should have kept my mouth closed. He had me hauling a few things out to the dingy, including all the dive equipment, "just in case." Some of them were awkward and heavy, but I kept my chin up. After all, this is what I'd signed on for. Once we were loaded up, he turned on the electric motor and we skimmed over the surface to where I'd been fishing.

"This is a nice place," he said, shutting off the motor and holding up the anchor for me to take. "Place it someplace where it won't disturb the site."

Taking the anchor, I slipped over the side, trailing the rope. Diving with a kick, I scooted down to the bottom. The fish were quick to join me, a different group of dark blue, greens and big oval orange swam along with me. When I reached the bottom, a few smaller red fish came out of their hiding places in the coral to see what I was doing. They directed me to some sand, making sure I didn't place it anywhere near their homes. Then when it was set, they flipped on their tails back into their holes while I went back up to the arrowhead-shaped dingy.

Hoisting myself up to rest my chin on my arms, Uncle was muttering, "Where'd she go?" He was looking threw a view finder.

"Uncle, who are you looking for?"

"Yah!" And he rocked back, his legs going up and the boat rocking his way. I had a second to realize he was about to tumble into the water with all of his things. Taking a hold of my side, I tried to counterbalance him so he wouldn't fall. Underestimating my strength, I pitched the craft down and almost sent him rolling my way before I stopped.

Getting his feet on the bottom of the boat, he looked up sharply, "Make some noise next time."

I apologized, but he should be hearing me, and I kicked my feet but there was no sound. I had to really try for there to be a water splash – the sea pulling away from my legs for a second.

Uncle fumbled around for his crutch, and then started in on the gear, his hands shaking.

"Is something wrong Uncle?" I asked, lifting myself up to hold to the top of the boat, I put my head on my arms and looked at him.

"No, no," he said wiping off some sweat with the back of his hand from his brow. Then he dropped one of the devices he was pulling from a bag. He'd yelled at Ri'Anne for being so careless yesterday. "No, nothing's wrong," he emphasized as if I'd asked him again. "Here," and he upended the bag over the edge. "So you don't have to return."

I was looking down, watching them fall into the depths and seeing fish dodging them. My eyes must have bugged out at his carelessness.

"Set up the site like you did the other day. Then tomorrow we'll return for a thorough dive of the find," Uncle said dropping over the other sacks. "I'll be waiting, so don't bother coming up." It seemed to pain him to say it. "Go on Melanie… While we have the light."

I slid down, confused, and hovered under the boat before diving down. Hovering over the equipment, I wondered at Uncle's words. Picking up a corner piece, I turned and swam over to where I thought it might go. Flicking it on, suddenly I was surrounded by fish.

"Hey, I can't see," I told them, but they wouldn't budge. I had to attune to search out the rest of the equipment. The fish had packed in around me. As if they were protecting me, but I couldn't see what they were protecting me from. "Calm down, I'm ok…"

Then on my word, they swam in their big school away and I saw the bag. Going for the next one, I held it up, pondering the fish. Around me was clear water, there was nobody here. It wasn't like the other day when we'd encountered the other divers, and even then the fish hadn't swarmed us until asked. Arriving at the next corner, I placed it and flipped it on. Afraid the fish might my swarm me again, I ducked but none came. *Odd.*

Swimming quickly, I put out several more cameras before I remembered I should go up for air, but then I remembered Uncle saying, "Don't bother coming up."

No, he couldn't know... I'd been so careful, and I was pretty sure Dad wouldn't have said anything. Then he'd figured it out, but how? If he knew me to be a mermaid, then going up for air… would be a waste of time.

I was crying, reaching for the bag, "Well there's no use worrying about it," I said aloud trying to reign in my emotions, and failing.

"No use worrying about what?" asked an octopus fingering our gear.

"My uncle finding out that I'm a mermaid. He'll study me, I know he will," I cried sinking to a rock. With eyes closed, I pulled in my knees, and rocked back and forth trying to figure a way out.

A dozen light touches on my arms and I opened my eyes to see tiny sea horses dancing along my arms. The lead mare floated before my eyes saying, "You should sing. It'll be good for you."

"But I can't," I said choking back sobs and not a bit amused by the idea. "I'm not much of a singer," I admitted. My song for dinner had been so-so.

"We'll start," and the sea horses got some clams to clap a beat.

"Oh that's good," said the octopus gliding around above, and in his deep baritone set down the base track, "Bum, bah, bum, bum."

I tried to beg off saying, "Come on guys, I don't think I can…"

But the sea horses wouldn't have anything of it, getting the tall tubers to blow as flutes. "Now you," they said encouraging me.

I didn't really feel it like I'd felt at other times, but they were persistent. And it really might help me get my mind off the disaster my life had become. I found myself humming along with them, and then I found the words,

> *Silly clams, all a clap. My life set to collapse.*
> *Just when I'd begun to hope that we could*
> *play, the stage is set, there must be another*
> *way…*

Too fast, it was all jumbled. How to say that I just wanted to be me?

Out into the sea I wanted to swim, but I sat scooping up Uncle's cameras and pulled some out. Flipping one on, I set it down. Looking at it, I brushed back my hair, watching it float in lazy swirls over my shoulder. The camera reminded me of the surface above, but this was my life. Taking the camera, I swam for the far side of the field, watching its light change colors, feeling my life a similar swirl of colors…

I tried to explain to Uncle and anyone else who might judge me – all from the bottom of the sea where they couldn't hear me…

> *I can't change, no, I don't want to change. I want to dance, I want to play and sing. Was there no end, no sight too far. Listen, I am a mermaid, and I play. This is my freedom, down among the coral, sea horses on my left, a mighty octopus rhythm and bells. I hear the great blue whale on my side, his friend the green shelled tortoise, inside, that's life.*
>
> *Why do I have to live to your rules? Who made you the decider of my fate? Am I not free to choose, to ride, to sing, to laugh? I don't want to disappoint you Uncle, Dad, friends… But I'm lost down here in the sea without you here with me. I want to celebrate, instead I'm fleeing and hiding who I am from you.*

A big eye in a field of blue winked at me – and his turtle friend lying on his tongue tipped his hat up to see. They and the seahorses sang back to me,

Sea Lord, come play us a song. Lift the sands to the sky, rain down on us – part the sky, butterfly. The waves spray, the serpent lays, around and dive, where is the manta ray? Sunlight glance, mermaids dance – be yourself butterfly. Over here, down under there is – dance, sing and prance. We're going to ride, through the sky – there goes the line.

I laughed at their chorus. Were they singing about a fishing line there at the end? This singing was making me feel better, but above me was the dark underside of the dingy – Uncle was up there!

I'm down, there's no going back up! I'm going to swim, fly, drive, cry and there is no friend, foe, to reel me back. I'm friend of the whale, shark, seagull, spider, rat, tiger, lark. Breathe water, make a wave, I'm in place, I've arrived and I'm going. Don't stop, I'm gone. I came, don't you hear the sound?

I've been found, don't you see? Life is under, I'm around. Trying to seek, to find, I'm trying – the sea cries. I'm singing to hear, my heart laid open, my time don't you stare. Undertow take me down, rise me sunder, lift me choose – in me life, soon, sight, fly.

The last became my chorus as I sang through the song again, over and over until it was near dark. I was alone in the black sea, holding to some of the rocks that broke through to the surface, eyeing Uncle in the dingy over yonder. I was torn between never returning and going straight to his side and telling him everything. Falling off the rock with nary a splash, I wanted to curl over and sleep beneath the sea, but my stomach rumbled. I couldn't avoid my choices.

Glancing down to the wreck, the equipment lay where I'd placed it. Somewhere during our song, the work was done. I didn't really remember doing it, but it was ready to go for the morning. Swimming over to the dingy, I glided over the surface, being sure to be loud enough not to startle Uncle again. Putting my hands on it I felt for the life within, and then resigning myself to my future I lifted myself to put my chin on its side, afraid of the greeting I'd receive.

On seeing me, Uncle asked excitedly, "Did you hear it?" Reaching out a hand, he helped me over the rim, and seemingly all was forgotten. Had I misread him before?

"Better yet," he continued in a rush, "did you see the lights dancing in the sea? I wish I hadn't thrown all the equipment overboard. I do hope some of the gear recorded what was happening. The entire bay was glowing, but it's gone now. You should've seen it. As much time as I spend on the sea, it never fails to surprise me. In any case, The Lazy Cloud was recording! Smell the sea Melanie. I've never breathed in air so clean, so fresh, so full of life. I'll be up all night." Then spinning the dingy around, the electric motor whirring to life, he headed us back to the yacht. I helped him store the dingy in the storage under the main deck and plugged it in. The others were sitting at the table, and the candles had burned low. The three of them were sipping tea and talking.

"Hey you two," Ri'Anne said standing and giving me a hug. "We were getting worried. I'm afraid the food is cold, but I can reheat it if you want." Uncle said that would be great, and Ri'Anne disappeared down the steps with the pot.

Dad said to Uncle, "Did you see the fireworks? The sky is alive with shooting stars. I don't think I've ever seen so many at one sitting. Let's go down to the lower deck," and he turned Uncle around, leading him back to the swim deck where they sat out under the stars and talked.

This left me with Gigi. I'd felt uncomfortable with the woman since our first meeting. Even though she'd let go the active pursuit of trying to figure out how I spoke her true language, I knew she hadn't given up. I didn't know what to say, and a simple "thanks for dinner," hardly cut it. How was I supposed to relate to a three hundred-year-old woman? I didn't have Ri'Anne's flair with plants that the two of them shared either.

"You two were out a while," Gigi opened with. It was noncommittal. Since I could only shrug or nod, she continued. "We've been getting to know one another. Your dad is proud of you, and your friend Ri'Anne is one of the sweetest girls I've ever met. What I don't get is your carefree life. All of mine has been spent going from town to town, city to city, just trying to survive. Rarely do I get opportunities to sit and enjoy music. Especially in the company of cab drivers and kids that are *so* grown up."

With a light laugh she thought a second before saying, "Life never stops surprising me. I'm good with," she said leaning forward and putting a finger on my hand, "you having a secret. I know you know something. It may not be what I want to know, but I've lived a long time and I'm in no hurry. Most important is that you can trust me. I'll prove myself to you, be your devoted friend."

I wanted to say she could start by removing her finger from my hand. But just then Ri'Anne returned with the food. She saw Gigi and I engaged in conversation, turned to put the food down on the counter and dished Uncle and I out a couple plates. Ri'Anne set mine down before me, which gave me a chance to withdraw my hand from Gigi's touch.

Dad laughed at something, and Ri'Anne disappeared that way for a second with Uncle's plate. Gigi gave me a nod. She meant what she said. Then she got up, picked up some empty dishes and went down to the galley where I heard her singing to herself.

"Anything I should know?" Ri'Anne returned and sat, making sure our legs connected, wrapping her foot around mine.

"Uncle knows something," I said, leaning into her. "He's discovered… I don't know what, but something. When we went out..." I couldn't bring myself to say everything, my emotions coming back. "But then after all the equipment was placed and I returned to the boat, he acted as if nothing had happened."

Reaching out and holding my hand she said, "It'll be all right – you'll see."

Squeezing her hand back, "I do hope so."

"That's it, remember we have to hope. We have to redouble our efforts to help him see that it is a benefit. That people benefit from there being…" and she whispered, "mermaids."

"How?" I mouthed. Uncle and Dad were just below us. We could hear what they were saying, and them us.

"Just like we've been doing," she continued in a hushed whisper. "Increase the frequency, like now," and she closed her eyes and I felt her reaching out and letting Uncle "feel us."

I did feel Uncle then. He was a little surprised to be brought into our midst. He wasn't there to guide, or help us and it seemed strange to him to just be there with us. In us, and through us, he saw and felt us holding hands.

Knowing I had to continue our discussion, I told her, "We set up, well *I*, set up the equipment for a dive tomorrow. I think it'll be fun." Then deciding that Uncle should know my heart, if he was listening, I told Ri'Anne, "But when I dove, I was crying - crying under the sea. An octopus talked to me, and tiny sea horses too. They said I should sing to cheer myself up."

Scooting forward more, Ri'Anne said, "I want to hear it. Tell me, can you remember it?"

"Well, to get me going, the clams started clapping so I made that my first line," and I sang again it all coming back to me.

Silly clams, all a clap. My life set to collapse. Just when I'd begun to hope that we could play, the stage is set, there must be another way...

I can't change, no, I don't want to change. I want to dance, I want to play and sing. Was there no end, no sight too far? Listen, I...

And I couldn't go on. The night air had come alive with the song. Down under the sea I could sing my heart to the sea. Here in the open air, I wasn't sure if I wanted to sing *I am a mermaid.*

"When you sing, I feel like the world around us joins in, in harmony. That's so beautiful. I wish I could describe how I feel. You have a gift," Ri'Anne said shaking her head amazed.

"I don't sense any of that, except I feel my heart expand. But that seems normal," and I held up my hands palm up. It seemed everyone else got to experience the magic of what I did.

She asked, "That was all of it?"

"Hardly any of it – but I can't right now." And I hooked my head towards Dad and Uncle. I forgot for the moment that they could hear us, and Uncle could even see me through Ri'Anne. "Alright, alright. We should make the dive a whole family dive. Even Gigi. All she does is play with her plants. Though I'm not sure she can even swim."

"Of course I can dear," Gigi said coming back up on the heels of that. "I've been around the world a few times, and some of that has been under water." Then she grabbed more things to wash and went back inside.

Hooking her thumb towards Gigi, Ri'Anne said, "If it's only Gigi that doesn't know, why don't we just say and end all this fooling around?"

"Know what?" I asked. Until now I could pretend what we were talking about was a joke shared among kids. "I sing with fish, so what? Doesn't everyone?"

"Ok, but I think you're being foolish," and then she sat there and watched me pick at the fish who had served himself up so readily. Reaching out for a wedge of lemon, I squeezed it tight over him spraying his fillet, remembering his promise. Hearing his refrain again, I sang it for Ri'Anne while I ate…

Have us for dinner, we'll be the center – fun,
delight, belly laughs – it won't be wrong.
There is no greater pleasure than to love so
fair. Sit back, enjoy the evening. Play a hand
of cards, speak of the day. Plan the event, be
the poet, write us a song. Have a feast, we'll
delight, be merry, it's no slight.

23

The Ghost of Future Present

Going to bed that night, I thought I'd have pretty strange dreams – eating the fish I'd sang with. The king salmon had sang true, we did have a pleasant evening with it being the main dish. We sat up talking on the back swim deck until very late. I had been pretty tired after finishing dinner but then when I called it a night I lay awake thinking about the songs I'd sang. The singing had helped me feel a little better. Luckily, the rest of the evening went without incident or conflict, so I was able to sleep pretty well. Until, that is, Ri'Anne's sunny little cloud woke me up.

I shielded my eyes. "Hey, cut it out," I complained. "Ow," it was bright and right in my face, and I jumped up moving to the door to avoid it. But I stopped in mid-stride, looking at the source.

A "cloud" floated over her, and a bright light was coming from it. Where it hit Ri'Anne its light reflected about the room. My bed was covered in overlapping triangles of light. Ri'Anne was floating over her bed, asleep oblivious to her miracle sun lamp, singing softly.

Reaching out to wake Ri'Anne, to show her, a hand gripped my wrist, I saw the girl this time (me), and she said, "Melanie don't…"

I screamed seeing who touched me, flinched and fell back onto the floor… but the floor was now grass.

Shaking, I looked around at my surroundings. Tropical paradise, beautiful garden. It felt familiar though I'd never been to this particular place before. I heard that girl's voice, my other self, talking, crying, sniffing back sobs. Coming to my knees, I looked over a rock and some flowers to see a beautiful island home and knew where I was, the Island of Syreni. There was myself talking with an elder of the Syreni.

This was so strange, and I thought it at first a dream, but it was so real. Sometimes in dreams you see yourself in third person, so that is what I thought was taking place. But there was a third person present, "I" was holding Ri'Anne. I choked back a sob on seeing her, blood all over her and on "my" arms. Because of my sob, I ducked down behind the rock, afraid I'd be discovered.

Ri'Anne had been horribly hurt. I couldn't help myself but flung my sight towards her to see what I already knew. She wasn't moving, breathing… My friend was dead. I knew in an instant that this was no dream. This had to be a vision of the future, but what could have happened? And why was I being shown this?

The elder was crying, touching Ri'Anne. Running her hands over Ri'Anne's garment, it wasn't a fish suit, and not her normal flowery plants, but a tight woven gown of plant fibers. They didn't speak for a little while, and then I heard "me" say, "Is there nothing that can be done?"

"Death is final, dear one. Only a Sky Lord can undo the past, and …" she broke off and cried some more.

"A Sky Lord?" I heard my other self ask.

"You would know them as Fairies," I let out a breath at that revelation… Fairies were real. "Now, you'll be wanting her presentable." The elder almost sounded like her usual calm self, but I could tell she was deeply shaken. Picking up some plants, she plucked them up, roots and all. Then she laid them on Ri'Anne. With a wave of her hand, the plants grew in and down into her until she was whole, but still lifeless. Then, still crying, she bent to her gardening, not really seeing it. She tried and failed to till the soil while "I" held Ri'Anne awkwardly.

I watched my other self turn away and then for the first time saw a transfer with my sight. Inside the transfer my other self set Ri'Anne down, pulled out the bright fairy dust we'd kept hidden, and doused herself with it. Then she disappeared, but the vision remained.

I still sat behind the rock, and when I heard a light footfall, I knew the elder had found me. "This is a surprise dear one. Didn't you just…"

And I shook my head without looking up. I told her over my own tears, "I think this is my future I'm seeing."

"Oh most complicated, but not beyond my experience," she said with a light laugh. Brushing back the last of her tears with her hand. "Honestly it gives me extreme joy to be seeing you dear one then. The girl you saw yourself carrying, do you know her?"

I nodded, "She was sleeping when I … I'd been about to wake her, when a hand touched mine and told me … to not." I knew their reluctance to use our names, so I couldn't repeat it wholly.

"And you saw who stopped you?" the elder asked, and I expected she knew the answer, but wanted me to say it.

"Myself," I heard myself say. "But how? You said only a Sky Lord could, but I'm a Sea Lord."

"It gives me great pleasure to hear you say it dear one. But onto your question. You know we can't guide, but only a Sky Lord can do it, true. But what is rarer still is a Sky Lord can give her essence to another in the form of fairy dust. I only say this because I believe you possess some or soon will – otherwise you wouldn't be seeing your future self."

"So that's what I saw…" I said aloud. "When I left with," sob, "I saw into a transfer. Me, I mean my future me, put down … and doused with light before disappearing."

"So that's it then," the elder said getting up.

"What?" I looked up with hope.

"That my dear, I cannot say," and she dusted herself off and left me.

"Wait, if my future self is trying to change the past – if it worked, why are we still talking?"

Giving a laugh over her shoulder she said, "Because it hasn't happened yet."

Then I remembered little Gian telling me about time traveling with fairy dust, was that you continued to move forward even if you traveled into the past. So that must be what is happening, or has been happening. My future self had been trying to get me not to do something, and it involves Ri'Anne. But whatever I did, or will do, still happens and therefore this future remains where Ri'Anne is dead.

What a nightmare! Doubly so for Uncle and for Dad – if Ri'Anne died. If? Since? Was the past changeable? Talking to myself, *Be glad, Melanie, that you are a Sea Lord and not tempted with messing with history.* But then we'd been gifted with the very fairy dust given by Kyria I'd seen my future self use in an attempt to alter the past. Here I'd thought the gift a waste, thinking only of traveling with it. Well, I shrugged, I still thought it useless…

"What's useless?" Uncle asked from the sun couch beside me on the front deck.

Blinking, I tried to get the sun spots out of my eyes. I'd been staring at the sun for too long. Once they cleared, I sat up and looked around. Then, remembering Ri'Anne in "my" arms, I called out "Ri'Anne!" sending as well as yelling and went running to find her.

I'm in the galley, she sent back. **And you don't have to yell. Ow! Breakfast will be ready in a minute...** "Hey, I'll spill."

I'd dove down the central stairs to the lower deck and flung myself into her arms. "You're all right," I sobbed. "I saw, you…" and I couldn't say "dead."

"It was just a dream," Gigi said from behind Ri'Anne. "Frightful things sometimes, the sight. Risky it is to see the future. The present is tough enough. Take life one day at a time."

We both turned to stare at her. "What?" Gigi asked, shrugging. "You're the one who sees things. So what did you see? Ri'Anne dead? It hasn't happened yet – and as merry a bunch as we are, it isn't likely to happen. Besides, forewarning is dangerous. You will be second-guessing your actions from here until tomorrow. You must live for the moment."

"That's good advice," Ri'Anne said turning to me, but I wasn't so sure. But, seeing that they were fixed on it, I shelved my emotions and nodded. "Help me carry these, then," and Ri'Anne started passing me things to carry up to the table.

I still wanted to cry, but having Ri'Anne sitting next to me at lunch laughing merrily away at something Dad said soon had me smiling too.

"You back?" Ri'Anne asked on hearing me laugh. I nodded, but my eyes were still sore. "Good, then let's do the dishes and let Gigi have a break."

24

Troubling Waters

"Dad let me help you with that," I said with one foot on the swim deck and the other in the dingy. Our family scouting expedition had gone rather well.

"Thanks Melanie," and he handed me the first of the containers we'd collected from the ship wrecks we'd scouted this morning. Uncle's plan to scout for aquatic samples had us lifting out bucket after bucket of swimming treasures, trying not to spill. The boat was loaded to the brim with the relics Uncle had wanted to keep.

"Me too," Ri'Anne said, jumping up from where she'd sat with her feet over the side. She dove into the water and came around, pulled herself up onto the swim deck to form the third person in the chain to get everything out of the dingy.

"You know," Uncle said lifting his eyes from his logbook as we set the last of the finds in the study, "It says here that I couldn't find my way, that none of my instruments worked around that island. I had all but given up on being able to go back to that place, but this dive has rekindled my desire to find it." Uncle hadn't mentioned the island for a while, but being around these wrecked boats and seeing some of the interesting creatures we found has brought back the fire inside him to find that special island.

"You'll find it Uncle, I'm sure you will," but it seemed that unless I brought him to it that he never would. Yet, he'd found it once, so I wasn't sure. If instruments didn't work there, then it had to be like Ri'Anne had said on Kyria's and Gian's island – it was in another place shut off from our world. There were enough magical places in story lands besides ours. Peter Pan has his Neverland, Jack and the Beanstalk had the giant's land above the clouds… why not mermaids their place of paradise?

Scooping the creatures out of the buckets into jars, Uncle smiled, helping me place them out where he could examine them, "You continue to be positive Melanie, and I appreciate that. It's tough to see how it can work out, but I like it." He gave a little chuckle. "I didn't used to 'believe' for things, always determining what to believe based on what I could measure. But this trip is changing that. Thanks."

I laughed on my own, "No problem Uncle. But let's open one of these and do some measuring anyway…"

"After lunch," he said and we went to find the others. With the sound of the yacht's engine revving up, we knew where to find Dad, or so I thought. I climbed the steps to the command deck and found it empty. Looking down, I saw Dad, Ri'Anne and Uncle looking at dolphins that were jumping and swimming in our wake. I'd passed Gigi on the way up putting things out for lunch, so I went back down to help her with it.

"They're pretty funny," Uncle was saying as they joined us at the table. "I've always thought dolphins to be fun, but hey, listen to this Melanie... What do you call two dolphins lying on a beach?"

I thought about that with the egg salad sandwich half-way to my mouth, "I don't know Uncle, what?"

"Two porpoises without a purpose," and he started laughing at his joke.

I smiled. It was "punny," but it wasn't exactly hilarious. "Nice one Uncle..."

"You're not impressed?" he asked and I shook my head no. "Well, we thought it funny, didn't we?" And he looked to Dad and Ri'Anne and they both nodded.

"You all thought that funny," Gigi looked up from her book, asking "Then who was telling the joke?"

"The dolphins," Dad said. "Apparently Arlo can hear them now."

I looked to Ri'Anne, but she, on meeting my eyes, shook her head slightly. So if it wasn't her, then Uncle was learning to do these things on his own. Interesting, and I wondered if this was the hope we'd been hoping for, or the destruction the eagle had forewarned.

Uncle leaned forward, full of excitement saying with a smile – already laughing at the joke he planned to tell us. "The dolphins had another one, one I've been saving until now. They said some seagulls told it originally, so that's the clue… What do you call two crayfish lying on a beach?"

I smiled, immediately knowing the answer, saying "Seagulls have one thing on their minds," I laughed, as the others turned towards me. "Anther hint?" And by their expressions I added, "Their next meal..."

"Fish," Ri'Anne jumped in with.

Gigi leaned forward, correcting Ri'Anne "Now dear, 'fish' doesn't make sense. What do you call two crayfish lying on a beach? Fish?"

"Do you know it?" Uncle asked of Gigi, and she shook her head. "How about another hint, Melanie…"

"Ha ha," I laughed. "Ok. We are all sitting down to…"

"Lunch!" Dad guessed.

Ri'Anne held her head, "That is so lame!" to which the rest of us laughed.

"That was lame," I said to Uncle afterwards, leaning in to his shoulder.

"Yeah," he said, scratching his head. "So dolphins tell lame jokes. They seem to enjoy them."

We were coming up on another dive site and Dad had slowed us down. I sat on the edge of the yacht, by the winch, holding onto it as I leaned out and looked at the sea. It was so clear, and I couldn't wait to get my feet wet. The dolphins continued to shadow us, and if you weren't a mermaid you'd think it was the same group that had followed us from the island. But these were bigger, liking the deep waters.

"Come swim with us Lady!" two dolphins rose up under me, tittering in their high-pitched squeals.

Before I could respond, forgetting that Uncle was standing behind me, he said, "They like you," which shocked me into letting go of the winch and I tumbled off the yacht with a splash.

"Man overboard!" Uncle shouted, practically falling over the side himself in laughter.

The two dolphins came up on either side of me laughing along with uncle, and I put my arms out so they could pull me. "I'm Mini," said the dolphin on my left.

"And I'm Mimi. That was pretty funny, sorry about that. But you have to admit, it was funny, huh?"

"Yes, it was funny Mimi," I said quietly. It was yet to be determined if Uncle could hear me, like he could hear the dolphins, though the yacht was a ways off now and was moving away. It took a while for the thing to come to a stop.

"Can I ride you?" I asked her, taking her dorsal fin and pulling myself up on her nod of yes.

"This is going to be fun," Mimi squealed her delight. "Nobody swims with us out here."

Putting one foot fore and aft of her dorsal fin, I stood up balancing and she took off at speed towards the yacht that had gotten ahead of us. "Banking left," she warned me as we came up on the back of the yacht. Dad was in the process of lowering the swim deck. I leaned to my left, but at the sound of the deck lowering Mimi was frightened and turned hard, diving. I went over, cartwheeling across the top of the water before coming to a stop. Mini appeared beside me, lifting me up as I choked for air, having had the wind knocked out of me.

The other dolphins of the pod came and joined us then as Ri'Anne and Dad jumped in. Uncle sat on the edge of the swim deck, dropping his good leg in and stretching out the other one. I heard him saying "Hi," to each of the dolphins as they swam by. They were talking to him while they picked up Ri'Anne and I, letting us surf before sending us flying.

Ri'Anne caught herself in midair, and then realized she was floating said "Oops," and fell into the water.

"I feel weird," she said coming up beside me. She was floating half in the water up to her waist. Steam was coming off her neck and shoulders.

I looked at her, "What's the matter?" I asked concerned. So far I hadn't told her that I'd seen her floating over her bed in the mornings, with light as bright as the noonday sun shining on her. I hoping it was just a phase.

"I don't want to swim," she admitted and floated out of the water. "Meet me around front of the yacht," and then blurred out of sight. I had a glimpse of her shooting forward around the yacht, it was one long streak of light bright as the sun. She was now flying like Kyria did without the dust. What did it mean? And now I wondered if my vision of her being dead had to do with her flying into a wall at that speed…

Mimi had rejoined me, "Lady… What's going on?"

I shook my head, "I don't know Mimi, but I'm going to find out."

Reaching the front of the yacht, I surfaced to see Ri'Anne sitting cross-legged with her head in her hands. She didn't give me a chance to speak, "I'm sorry for the way I'm acting, but I really thought I could do it. The dive this morning was wonderful, but I feel like I'm faking it. I'm done trying to be your kind of mermaid..."

"And, Uncle's research? You were saying just a couple days ago that you wanted more."

"I know," Ri'Anne said sounding stressed. "But it seems the more I embrace plant work and flying the less I want to swim." She looked around, "If only he had something for me to do above water."

I nodded, it made sense. But I was hoping it was only a phase, and that she'd snap out of it soon. This was a setback for all my plans. We'd done so well, and today I was hoping we'd get our first real research dive. "I need you," I finally said. "Uncle expects the two of us," and I thought she might fly away at my tactic. So I tried one other, "Is the swim team to expect you back?"

"Yes," she said standing to bob in the air. But then she looked to the sky as she thought about it, and finally answered, "I don't know." She gave me an apologetic glance and then flew up and over the edge of the yacht and out of sight.

I swam lightly back around to the others, the dolphins rejoining me. What was troubling me the most was that I expect I would be doing the same as her had our interests been reversed. I wanted to side with her on this, and desperately hoped it was just a phase and we could her get back to being "my" kind of mermaid soon. I suppose I should tell Uncle that Ri'Anne was feeling ill…

"C'mon Melanie," Uncle was calling when I returned. "Where's Ri'Anne?" he asked looking over my shoulder.

"Back aboard already," I said grabbing the swim-deck and pulling myself up.

"But I've been here the whole time," Uncle looked about, feeling inept at having not noticed. I wanted to go look for Ri'Anne, but Uncle stopped me. "Hold on," Uncle said. "The dolphins reported a sailboat in need of help, will you tell the others?"

"A sailboat?" That stopped me in my tracks, a dark cloud covered the sun for a second. I glanced up, feeling dread, and then looking back at Uncle and asked, "Three girls?" It couldn't be, please no.

"That's right…" Then seeing my expression he asked, "What is it?" But I shook my head and he added, "How'd you know?"

I didn't reply, holding the railing, and feeling the water where it lapped against the boat as I attuned. The water on the wet deck drained into my feet. It ran upward as if the top of my head was a magnet for it, but my mind was elsewhere. I reached out for Jordan, I saw her lying face down beside Billy and Lorin. Their hands tied behind their backs…

Hoisting Uncle up, Dad gave him a hand to the stairs I was blocking. He said from behind me, "Melanie knows things sometimes. You're in the way Melanie, go on up."

"Sorry," and I dashed up the steps. I had the connection and almost stepped through to Jordan, but they weren't alone. Two men guarded them, one of them being rough. Releasing the connection, I leaned against the wall, catching my breath. My heart was in my throat, I wanted to cry.

Banging my fist against the yacht, the whole yacht shook and I looked at my hand in surprise. "Did something hit us?" asked Uncle coming up behind me. Dad went to look over the sides.

"I don't see anything," he said. Before he could ask me to get a move on again, I went down the stairs wondering what was coming over me. I found Ri'Anne standing beside Gigi working on one of their plants. I went in and sat down.

"Did you feel that?" Gigi asked looking up as I walked by.

"Yeah," I said from my chair. "I did…"

"The whole room shook," she continued.

"Uncle says we're going to go help a sailboat in trouble." I said, and Ri'Anne finally looked at me, maybe it was my tone of voice. But then she went to looking at the plant again, humming and I saw a green glow under her hands and the plant grew a foot.

Oh Ri'Anne why did you have to pick now to be difficult? I think I was supposed to be happy at what I was seeing, but I wasn't. This trip was turning into a disaster. I didn't know what to think, but I did know one thing! I was about to be in a fight. Two guys had Jordan, Lorin and Billy! That made me mad. I was pretty sure I could handle them in the water, but what was I to do if we met inside?

The yacht's motor revved up and I knew we were on the way. Should I warn Dad and Uncle to stay clear? But I wanted to help the girls. Dad and Uncle could help with the two guys, but what if they were armed, what then?

Deciding not to spend the time wringing my hands below decks, I went up to see if I could be of help. Coming up beside Uncle he said, "Do you really think they are leading us somewhere? The intelligence of dolphins has always been debated. It's true they help people a lot, but that could just be a good nature. I wonder what they are thinking."

What could I say? I knew the limits of supposed animal intelligence, but so far on this trip I've spoken with spiders, a bird at the airport, a rat, seagulls, pelicans, fish and dolphins. I had no idea if creatures around me were more than they were normally, or if they were always smart but lived limited roles except when I was near.

"Why don't you ask them?" I asked, "Since we're doing this based on what you heard them say."

"They don't understand me, I've tried. It's so frustrating. I feel like I'm on the edge of a breakthrough." Leaning over to confide he added, "I also wonder if I'm losing my marbles. Talking with animals." He suggested we go up to the command deck.

Since he was slower, he let me take the lead. I turned on the stairs up to give him a hopeful look, "I'd be willing to bet the dolphin leading us is taking us somewhere important to it. I bet we learn something beyond what we would have discovered on our own."

Arriving at the top of the steps, he gave me a smile and a surprise hug saying, "I like your faith. I've lost childlike faith in the simple things of life. I'm with you – we should do this."

I laughed at him, "Even though it will cause a delay, Uncle?" I asked skeptically.

Chagrin crossed his face, and I think he almost decided to call off this search, but then he mellowed. "I almost lost my life. These others may be in similar peril. It shouldn't take us out of our way, much." Stepping up beside Dad, he picked up the binoculars and scanned ahead of us.

"I see a sail," Uncle said lowering his glasses. "But there is another boat."

"Here," Uncle said handing me the binoculars. "It looks desperate, but if they have weapons there is nothing we can do."

"This doesn't seem right," Dad said backing off the throttle as we came closer. The other boat wasn't another longboat, but a yacht. This one bigger and definitely more luxurious than The Lazy Cloud.

Stealth might have been the greater thing to do, but it was too late. At the sound of our engine, a man appeared on the deck of the sailboat wielding an automatic weapon and fired it in the air to warn us off. Dad peeled to the left, slowing and keeping us out of range. "Well, we tried… Oh look!" and Dad pointed to the sailboat.

There we saw a girl (it appeared to be Jordan), come up on deck while the man was distracted and dive in towards us. My heart went immediately for her, and before I knew it I'd run out the back and over the side. "Melanie!" but it was too late, I was down, going under some twenty feet and swimming fast.

I'd never swum so quick, coming across the distance between us in a flash. But it didn't seem to be fast enough, hearing shots impacting the water. I wanted Jordan to dive deep, but she couldn't and would soon be rising. There she was, I saw her swimming as I came up from under her – she needed a fish (no, a mermaid) suit. Why she was swimming without anything, and then I realized these people's purpose. I felt shame and disgust at their actions, as if it was my fault. The seas should be safe from such predators.

I rose up under Jordan, and she jerked back in surprise at seeing me, then threw her arms around my neck. Giving her air was my first concern, and I so wanted to give it with my heart, but ended up doing it as we had before. We "kissed" as I gave her air, feeling a stirring in my heart and hoping it was the start of the magical kind of air, but so far nothing.

"Hi," I said as we pulled apart. "You in trouble?" I felt my magic carry the words to her. I'd changed in the last few days and she was able to talk back.

"Oh! It is so good to see you," she said squeezing my hand and testing her underwater voice. I could see Jordan wanting to ask how, but she had already asked me before – and she knew I didn't want to talk about it. She started to cry as she was going to say what was really going on, and I hugged her back giving her air again.

"Give it time," I told her.

The shots stopped and we had a moment's quiet. Apparently the kidnapping mobsters hadn't noticed her going overboard yet. The sea was clear and beautiful, her sailboat floating some fifteen feet above us. The fish had come and I was glad for their presence as they shielded us from above.

"You live an interesting life," Jordan said trying to derail her emotions. Yeah, what could I say to that, so I shrugged, hoping she'd continue. After another exchange of air, she asked, "Your swimsuit, is it alive?"

"Yep," and I thought the scatter like thing Ri'Anne had done, but for me I wanted them to show Jordan instead of hide. And they swam in a school around the two of us and Jordan's jaw hung open as they came back around and settled back in place on me. They gave me a tingle and I knew they would help her with a suit if I asked. But I wasn't sure if she was going back up or wanted safety. If I brought her to The Lazy Cloud I'd give her the fish.

"Alright," she said trying to explain between breaths, "They came back. I figured it to be the box we disconnected that drew them the first time, but you and I had unhooked it. Unfortunately with so much time on my hands while sailing, I tinkered with it and they returned once I gave it power. I blame myself, but there are too many of them. This time they've brought a yacht… Even if we were to get away."

"I can bring you to my uncle's yacht and see about rescuing Lorin and Billy," I suggested. Hearing the swish sound of a fast boat, I looked up to see a speed boat launching from the larger yacht. "I think they've discovered your absence. So what's it to be?"

Jordan looked up torn, and together we saw two divers jump in from the small craft near the sailboat. She looked at me in fear, but then fish swam to hide us and she looked at me in surprise wanting to ask me again if I was the cause. Not directly, no, but now wasn't the time.

"To your sailboat or our boat?" I asked urgently, as the divers I felt were scouting through the fish that had doubled in density and now swarmed about us.

"I can't..." *What?* I wanted to ask, but just then a metal diving dart flew between us narrowly missing the both of us. The speedboat was now above and I could sense more divers joining the other two.

"Ok, to The Lazy Cloud then and we sort this out later, ok?" And I looped an arm around her. With her nod, I let the fish of my suit join with her, and in a burst they had her beautifully attired. "Hold on," and she grabbed me amazed at the fish doing her up in a like swimsuit.

She had to have air. If there was any time I needed to give her air magically, it was now. Drawing on the feeling I had for her each time we held to exchange air, I examined it with my attuning. I saw a swirling white funnel between my heart and lungs. I poked at it with my heart, and saw it respond. Using all my heart, I opened myself wide letting her in deeper. But I was holding back, I realized, as we "kissed" for air again, and it was the kiss that was bothering me. Deciding to really embrace her, I felt a whistle of air flow from my heart towards hers. "Yes!"

It felt like the first time I'd transferred, a magic I was now well acquainted with. But the first time it had seemed so unreal, and once I had the connection back home I'd felt more alive than on any moment prior. Now I sensed Jordan's heart beating, and knew, as in a transfer, I needed to make myself a part of the place I was going. Letting her heart into mine and mine into hers, I was feeling Jordan's heart beating, thunderous in my ears. Then the kettle-sounding whistle free flowed and her lungs had fresh air.

"Jordan!" And she opened her eyes to look at me, "Breathe normally," I encouraged her. She thought she was going to die here down deep with me, but hearing me she let go and opened her mouth, exhaling first. There were the expected bubbles, and then she breathed in. I felt the water pass her air, seeing the funnel of air that was within me, expand to include her heart that was within mine now. There were no more bubbles when she exhaled again.

"What? How?" she asked, and then another metal arrow flew past wide, having speared a pair of small fish.

The divers were closing in, they could see us now somehow, though the fish about us were as thick as ever. I could take us deep, but Jordan might not be able to handle the pressure. Raising my left hand, I pushed towards the diver that had shot at us, making a wave motion with my fingers. Out from my hand passed the wave I'd once created to bodysurf on, but this was underwater. He tumbled, dropping the next arrow he was loading into his gun.

With a grin of success, we turned to flee but there were too many of them and circling in quickly to hem us in. Down and out seemed the only way. I tried kicking, buy my feet wouldn't work. I lost precious seconds as the divers closed in. My legs felt like they'd been wrapped in chewing gum.

"Let's go!" Jordan urged me, but I was glancing down seeing a huge beautiful fish tail rippling in all my favorite colors, and following it up, I realized I was looking at myself.

Giving Jordan a happy smile, which she looked back with a bemused, we're about to be captured, look. With a fist pump, I exclaimed, "Yes!" She had no idea how happy this made me feel to finally have a tail and to have figured out how to give her air! I could be captured now and my life would be complete. But I wasn't going to sit idly by and let it happen. I flexed my "feet" together, swimming with this fin was going to be awkward. How to go about it?

I knew the butterfly stroke, and had practiced being a mermaid before with a long tube shirt tying my feet together. But this was no shirt holding my legs, my tail being stronger than my own legs and very flexible. It would take some getting used to. I tried a kick and sped to the side, and I had to curve my back to get us going down. Then another, and another kick, darting this way and that accidentally. Luckily it had the unintended effect of dodging all the arrows they shot our way.

The speedboat continued to match our pace. Without the tail I knew I could swim faster, but I wasn't ready to get rid of it yet. It didn't really matter, I'd have to shed it soon, since we had only one destination, The Lazy Cloud.

Swimming along slower, I was able to keep us moving steadily. "You came back," Jordan said making conversation, giving my shoulder a squeeze where she held on with her left hand.

"I wish it didn't have to be like this," I told her.

"How are we going to get past them?" she asked of the motorboat that kept up its hovering. We were nearing The Lazy Cloud. Dad was lowering the swim deck. I'd forgotten the cameras again that were underneath the yacht that Ri'Anne and I had installed. Not only that, but my family was watching a mermaid and a young woman swimming without scuba gear. Again I'd let it get away from me, as I'd been doing every day. Uncle may have known, but he knew now. At least now he could understand what was happening to him. I hoped it was the right thing to do, and now if they were watching he'd know I was sending Jordan to them.

Arriving under The Lazy Cloud I was hoping for a hatch on the bottom of the yacht, but the swim deck would be the quickest way up. The thug's boat was skimming around, keeping me from surfacing. "I can distract them," I said pointing upwards. "You'll have to go up without me. My family see us, so they'll be expecting you," and I let her go. As Jordan swam to safety, I set my eyes on the speedboat, thinking of ways to get rid of them.

Seeing them aim for her, and thinking of my unexpected knock on the hull of our yacht, I swam towards the bottom of the speedboat to "knock" on it, hard. Angling to come up under it when it was overhead, I swam, tail-kicking with everything I had, my normal speed coming back to me now since I wasn't hauling Jordan. Plus the magic of the tail. I failed to figure in. Flashing up, I barely had time to fold my arms over my head before I hit the bottom of the boat, expecting to be flattened and then gobbled up by the propeller.

A gong went through my head, and I lay stunned in the water feeling like a flash bulb had gone off in my face, gently sinking. Orange light flickered behind my eyelids. When my head finished swimming, I opened my eyes to see burning gas or oil floating above my face. The remains of the speedboat scattered all about.

And Uncle swimming to grab me around the waist, "Uncle..." and I put my head on his shoulder as he pulled me out from under the boiling water.

"That was the stupidest thing I've ever witnessed in my entire life," he said as we surfaced. "What were you thinking?"

"I had to stop them." The water was reviving me and I turned in his arms. Even with only one good leg he was an excellent swimmer. "Uncle, I have to go back." He gave me a look of "No way!" Had it been Dad, he would have defeated me.

"Her friends need help," and he let go, nodding. And I was glad he was Uncle and not Dad.

He tread water with his arms, looking with big eyes at my tail. "Uncle, you can't tell anyone," I told him as I looked back towards the sailboat.

"Can I record it?" he begged. I looked at him in surprise, he was truly asking.

I shrugged not wanting to say no and said catching his eyes, "That will only bring trouble, and you know it."

Nodding towards the large yacht he said, "They'll leave us alone after seeing their boat go up in smoke, but you be careful." Then in disbelief added, "What am I saying, you rammed a motorboat with your head!" He then turned and swam to the ladder.

I almost looked at the people watching from above, but I realized if I caught Dad's eyes I wouldn't be going through with this. With one look he'd restrain me.

The dolphins that had led us here suddenly joined me. "How can we help Lady?" They sounded tired, but wanted to help anyway.

Putting my arms around a pair, "To the sailboat to scout this out."

There was a longboat patrolling about, helping their divers. But when someone spotted me, they gave a shout. The captain of the little craft jerked around trying to spot me. There wasn't anything I wanted to do about them at the moment, but if I didn't get this thing going there would be divers to bother with again. Ramming them would be foolish. Those in the water would capture me if I lay unconscious.

A seagull soared overhead, spotting the dolphins and me it cried its forlorn song, "Fish, fish…"

"What can fish do?" I asked the dolphins, thinking the seagull was a sign.

Mimi rubbed up against me, rolling her eyes in delight, "They fill the belly round, yum!"

"Fill the belly. Could they fill a boat?" I asked in return. But the dolphins had given me their best answer. I knew how to talk to animals, but it always seemed like chance if they'd hear me. But every time they responded, much to my surprise even so.

I was called Sea Lord by everyone, Mistress, Miss and in every way honored by those I spoke to. Even the sea itself had greeted me. I felt so humbled by it all that it felt presumptuous to ask for help. But right then, if I was to do this, I needed a boat load of fish and something else for the big yacht. So I tried and reached out to the sea, and called, "Need some big fish, anyone?" A pulse of magic went out from me at the request.

Would this really work? But when I spoke to the sharks, they'd responded quickly enough. And what to do with them once they came? Knowing that the fish would willingly be grilled, I was ready to test them with another task. I could picture them filling the sailboat and pilling on top of the gunmen.

"Coming," I heard an echo and realized they were all about.

Now for the yacht, I really had no idea. It was bigger than The Lazy Cloud… I wasn't ramming my head into it.

Well, the fish had responded to my call, I suppose there were other creatures out there that could help me with a bigger boat. "Hello, I need some help." I shared my need aloud, speaking to the water, feeling a similar pulse go out from me again.

I felt a slithering and goosebumps as something huge disturbed the depths, an answer I think. Then what sounded like a fog horn, but felt like a giant belch, said "I come." The water rose up and then settled. I watched the wave of its words pass us by.

What have I done? Well, whatever it is, we better get ready.

"Dolphins, think you can take out the driver and diver of the small boat? Swamp them or something?"

"No problem boss, just say when. What about the sailboat? We could get the man wet…" Then arriving in great profusion were the huge fish I'd called for. Marlins, tuna, mahi-mahi and others. And again the sea rose as that other thing spoke, and I felt my tail tingle at his voice as he said, "Here." Glancing down, the seafloor had risen upwards. It was the thing. The name Leviathan came to mind. He sure looked the part; a giant's body with a serpent-like shark tail instead of legs and having huge octopus limbs for a head.

Diving under, I swam over to the large yacht trailing a host of fish, dolphins and a slithering monster. Hearing music aboard, I wondered what was going on. Unsure I wanted them destroyed, but knowing whoever was in authority aboard needed to be dealt with.

Turning to speak to he who had come, I told him, "Bring it under." It was going to be the only way I was going to go within, "but try not to …" *damage the yacht,* I was going to add, but it interrupted me.

"I know what to do Mistress." The sea boiled at its speech.

The fish swarmed about me, eager for a purpose.

"Marlins and friends, knock down the gunman and get inside the sailboat, but don't sink it. The girls need to be safe from the men. Go dolphins, let us do this. When the yacht …" All my orders relayed thoughts with the words. I felt that every dolphin, fish and even he who was huge knew what I wanted.

I thought about Dad and the others, but there was no time to warn them as a creature the size of a fifty story building stood up from the seafloor, reached up with giant cable-sized tentacles and wrapped itself around the yacht. It could have done that to an ocean liner or given an aircraft carrier problems. Then, pulling downward it brought the yacht under water, its lights seen through the windows shining in the darkness as it went down. The sounds of screams came from within.

By vision I saw that the dolphins had capsized the small craft and the fish were leaping aboard and down into the hold of the sailboat. It might stink for a while, but there would be nowhere to move. They were packing themselves in like canned sardines.

Swimming in between the massive tentacles, I marveled at his great strength. Three out of how many had pulled the thing down in a loose grip. I had a few seconds to scout it out as the water rushed in, to determine who to save. Those that could were swimming for the surface, but those within were held back by the rushing waters. Then the lights went out as the engines were flooded. There were cries for help, but I held back, afraid to go in alone.

I felt Uncle's touch then, strong and sure. Ri'Anne was next to him feeding him water. Oh Ri'Anne what are you doing? But with Uncle's presence I was able to enter the yacht, knowing I wasn't alone in my task. This is what we'd been hoping for, Uncle serving another's cause. I welcomed him, wondering if this was the end to my suit problems.

Each person we came to, we judged by how they were dressed. The well-dressed were bosses (or worse, customers), then there were the toughs, in various outfits. Some tried to grapple with me, but they were easy to avoid. I found the main room, and what I saw filled me with sorrow. Floating about the room were all kinds of pillows, garments and people wearing next to nothing. There was no way we were dealing with this many aboard The Lazy Cloud.

Well, there was only one place I could send them where mermaids were understood and were bound to help. I thought of the elder from the vision of the future and winged a message to her. She was the elder I had spoken to on the beach of Syreni once.

Incoming... I told her, and she sent back immediately and clearly, **Send them here...** and I had a vision of a football field near a school. I knew the place. She joined me in spirit, stronger and sure of herself and helped me determine friend from foe, interrogating their hearts instead of their outward appearance I'd been going on. I felt other elders join in, and together we began to shove them towards their island.

It was with sadness that I came to the few remaining pockets of air. The brutes were pushing the victims down to drown. But it was going to be they who drowned as we sent the others away.

On the way out, the yacht now on the bottom – the giant Leviathan hovering nearby, still having a couple of its tentacles resting over it, their weight alone keeping it in place and amazingly upright. His other tentacles were packing in coral and rocks to support it. He was a little OCD in my opinion with his attention to details, happily busying himself making of the yacht his personal pet, but I couldn't argue with his results.

I watched as a few toughs tried to swim for it, shooting up and rising fast. But then a couple tentacles plucked them around the legs and dragged them down. I shut my eyes as I saw where he was taking them, and then looked upwards. There were swimmers up there, making for the sailboat.

Dear One, said the lady elder I had contacted. ** Why don't you send us the yacht? There might be something the survivors could use...**

I thought that rather brash, they never instructed. But it was a good idea, and they wanted it in their harbor.

"Sir Leviathan. I don't suppose you can bring it to the Syreni intact?"

"Of course, but could you send me? I'm lazy…" and a mountain of water rose up and sank again, knocking me back before I turned to swim with his swells.

Send like I'd just sent a dozen people, and then, well if he believed I could do it, then I would. I felt for the harbor. It had a pier wrapping one arm of the harbor, a river flowing into it, a nearly perfect place, but deep. Would it be deep enough? It seemed an old crater. Ugh, he was massive, and eew squishy. This trip was one for the books. Diving to him, I touched him, feeling his warmth.

Gathering myself, I reached about him and began the transfer. I harmonized the two locations, feeling the resonance of a song, and then sensing it, sang out to The Lord of the Water, "By your leave," and "shoved." The great Leviathan shimmered and then was appearing in the harbor. The hole left by his bulk sucked me in and then I was alone, the yacht gone leaving only the V shape of rocks and coral he'd created to support it. I collapsed from the effort. It was a moment while the sea and its song revitalized me. Time for a song if I ever heard of one, but later…

Time to finish this up. The boat the dolphins had capsized had swimmers all over it. It was the survivor's contested ground, the sailboat had drifted out of their range and those swimming for it turned back to the little bit of life the capsized boat represented. Rising, I saw a young lady among them, who probably by her appearance was an 'owner,' wearing a fashionable swimsuit. None of the other women had been wearing anything so fine. Surfacing, I ignored their desperate cries, and left them.

Surveying the sailboat, I felt sorry for the suffocating tuna and marlins, but they had their reward. Unable to reach those aboard without revealing myself, I turned and swam for The Lazy Cloud, thanking all of those involved. The sea cleared of its teaming life, leaving a wide beautiful blue sea. I was going to have to do some explaining, but then seeing that The Lazy Cloud was closing with the sailboat, perhaps I could sneak aboard, or transfer. Who was I fooling, everyone had watched me, but I went in quietly anyway.

I sensed that Ri'Anne was up driving, Dad and Uncle getting ready to tie up to the sailboat and Jordan being tended by Gigi in the lower main room. The stairs to the lower compartment were clear. I opened myself to it, stood there a second to be sure, and then stepped, feeling my legs crystalize and the tail disappear by the time I took a step. Stepping down into the room, both heads swiveled around, Jordan's the faster. I wasn't sure what to expect. Though, I had thought part of it would have been recognition, but I was looking at a blank face.

"Hey!" Gigi jumped up and came to me, and then holding me at arm's length, "What, where have you been? Your dad is beside himself," she asked when she wasn't getting the expected explanation. Though she was the only one who didn't know, and I thought I should tell her. It seemed "fair" for all she'd done for Ri'Anne, but I couldn't make myself open up.

"How is she?" I asked in return.

"Always the cool customer, aren't you? Then I suppose you know, of course, don't you?" Giving me a look and then turning on the young twenty something woman, "Do you know each other?"

I thought, *here it comes.* Jordan was sipping at a drink and looking nervous at the two of us. She searched my face and then said, "I've never seen her before." Which shocked the two of us, but fortunately Gigi wasn't looking at me and didn't notice my expression.

By the time Gigi turned to look at me, I'd cleared my face. Explanations later. I asked Jordan, "Are you ok?" Jordan shook her head, but Gigi hadn't noticed, turning her whole body to stare at me in surprise. Then Gigi crossed her arms, her expression slowly turned to accusation.

"What?" I asked Gigi. There was no way Gigi knew we'd met before, I hadn't told anyone of my stop-over to help Jordan, Lorin and Billy. But I thought I recognized Gigi's look, I'd tripped up, but I couldn't put a finger on how. Why did she have to pick now to have it out?

But instead of addressing Gigi, it was Jordan that I cared about and asked her, "What's the matter?" I went to sit with her.

Jordan turned and put her hands on my wet arm. "It's my friends. They are being held on our sailboat. I had to leave, I couldn't stay a moment longer. They hurt us." Why was Jordan saying all of this, I knew this already. Couldn't she say it better? And why did she have to lie about not knowing me?

Gigi stood there hovering, but to comfort Jordan she said, "I heard the men speaking, they'll be over to help your friends." Then she crossed her arms saying, "I could help, but you have to tell me how you know each other." Gigi looked from Jordan to me.

Jordan sat back further into the couch, taking her hands from my arm and putting them in her lap. She was looking down, but I wasn't looking at her but at Gigi, when I told her, "How can you say…" and she slapped me. Gigi's hand was a blur, so fast that I didn't see it coming.

I reeled back into the couch, my cheek stung and tears came to my eyes. Gigi looked at her hand in surprise and I thought she might apologize, but then she railed on me, "I can handle your smart lip, your disrespect, but I'll not stomach lying!"

How dare she? Gigi didn't know and, "Jordan is in need…" and at Gigi's raised hand I gulped and kept my tongue. Then I realized I'd just said Jordan's name and covered my mouth, afraid to say another word. I was a liar, but Gigi shouldn't know that. As far as she should know, we hadn't met. I should have avoided the truth, or said it was none of her business. Still, what was there to hide? Jordan had shown she'd keep my secret.

Jordan jumped to my defense, "It isn't her. I'm the one that lied before about not knowing her." She looked pleadingly at me, but my head was bowed and I couldn't respond. "She swam and saved me. I dove overboard. She came and helped me."

"That isn't all of it," Gigi said, "But I've a question for our secretive friend here," and Gigi turned on me. "*Jordan* doesn't know your name, does she?" And Gigi emphasized Jordan's name, and I gulped again afraid to look, but my vision since getting the tail was stronger and came without my wanting it. I could see her piecing things together. I'd been ill-treating Gigi, and now it was coming full circle.

I shook my head no, and Gigi demanded, "But you know her, and her friends?"

I didn't dare lie to her again and nodded once.

"And Jordan, how does she know your friends' names?"

"Because she saved us before," Jordan looked to me and I gave her a nod that she should tell Gigi. It was time she knew the truth.

"We were near to capsizing. These guys that have taken us, had captured us before. I don't know where she came from. We were north-east of here a few hundred miles, in the middle of the ocean. But she came and set us free. We wanted her to stay, but after a meal she stood up saying 'good-bye' and dove over. We never expected to see her again. Nobody does that and lives, but I understand now." Jordan apologized to the side of my head.

"You understand what?" Gigi prompted gently.

Jordan struggled with finding an answer. I waited breathlessly for her to say what I knew was coming. "She's a mermaid," she finally said.

Gigi held up a hand, but she stopped herself, "I should slap you for lying, but you're telling the truth – at least as far as you know it." Gigi then looked sidewise at me, her mind finally clicking over. "Show me," she insisted.

"Uh, uh. No way," I said shaking my head, meeting her gaze. "This isn't a dog and pony show. I don't perform on cue." She might have caught me out, but she didn't own me.

"I can't believe this, you're admitting it." Then glancing upward at the ceiling, indicating my family and Ri'Anne, "Do they know?" I shrugged, *Sure, they did now. Even Uncle.* "They haven't always known, have they? No wonder the secrecy, this is rich. How old are you? Never mind," she waved the question away. "You're a kid, I'd bet my life on it. No older than you appear."

Then moving to her reason for traveling with us she finally asked the question I'd been expecting since we met, "So do mermaids speak all languages?" She was reading my face as easy as a page now, but I nodded anyway. It hurt to admit it, I felt so horrible, but I'd been careless. "That explains how you communicate with Jordan so well."

I looked sideways at Jordan, "I…" It never occurred to me that they might not be English speakers. It had only ever been them and me.

Gigi continued to ramble, "You could drop me at the next port, but I expect there is more to this story. Maybe you can help me find the answer to why I'm the last of my people," and Gigi was referring to her secret. I truly had no answer for her on that, it was a mystery.

Then hearing the boat's engine quieting and the sound of another boat close, I assumed we were coming alongside the sailboat. Looking out to port, I did see it. "Let's wait to see what the men find," Gigi said glancing out a window. We gathered to watch.

Jordan said, "They shouldn't. They are armed, they…" and her eyes glazed over remembering things that she would live through forever.

"Shall we go help?" I offered, trying to change the mood.

"You go," Gigi said. "We'll stay here," and she steered Jordan back to her seat.

Turning, I went to see what I could do, sure that there would be a thousand questions once Dad and Uncle saw me. I walked out on deck, and looking to port saw the sailboat, but nobody on deck. Then I heard a sound, but before I could react, arms grabbed mine and something hit me on the head. I had a last thought of, "stupid" before I blacked out, having forgotten to look to my surroundings.

25

Captured by Thugs

I moaned, awakened by a splash of water.

“Oh,” my head. That was stupid. I’d gone up on deck without “looking.”

“Hold still, don’t move. Let me,” the golden sunny water said to my barely conscious mind. The water trickling down around me, slowly soaking into me and my things, pooling on the floor. Was I dreaming as it lent me eyes? The hurt I felt I saw wasn’t so bad. By it I could see Ri’Anne on my left and Billy to my right, with the others not far away. Everyone seemed ok, the water revitalizing us all. The swelling on the back of my head decreased to the point where I was aware of being face down, arms and wrists tied, and the feel of the floor on my face.

I heard another pair of buckets dumped on us, and relaxed into the surprising water waves that carried away the hurt. I examined my family and friends, especially Jordan, Billy and Lorin; we'd all been gathered together. The three of them were physically none the worse than I'd last seen them. The water sight was limiting, I couldn't see our captors clearly, I didn't try to look on my own. Not yet.

Someone was boasting, "Oh, this will do fine. Not as nice as the Sunset Prince, but until we get to port it will do. I can't believe our fortune. These idiots waltzing in thinking they all that, and leaving their swim deck down for us to waltz up while they go aboard the sailboat and leave girls to secure their backs."

"It's a good thing they didn't pop Franz and Petri," said a second man, dumping another bucket on the others, and I felt a bit of it.

"I'll say," said one of the two. "Dumb hicks, though this one," and I heard a grunt as he kicked either Dad or Uncle, "gave us a fight. He'd be good in a fight, but they're protective of the girls. Best to get rid of them boss."

They were speaking openly, probably thinking none of us spoke their language. I couldn't believe I'd tripped up in front of Gigi on that score. I knew better, but that was water under the bridge. I tried to hear the sound behind their words but my head was still ringing from where they'd hit me and I couldn't tell what language it was. I would have to be doubly careful with them. It would be best to pretend not to understand.

"No, keep them. We lost all our cargo when, whatever that thing was dragged the Prince to the bottom. Selling them will help us recover our losses, especially this one," and one of them pulled at my suit, probably hoping it would break but they couldn't get a grip on the strap. I did my best not to react.

"One of them is cute, can I keep him?" asked a woman. Curious despite myself I "looked." It was the woman I'd seen swimming before, the woman I'd figured to be a boss. She had Uncle Arlo turned over and Dad lifted to his knees, Uncle looked miserable and Dad was having trouble focusing.

"This woman is awake," said someone, a new voice and thinking he meant me, but then he was lifting the arm of Gigi.

"She's the cook," said one of the others that had spoken before. "See the apron?"

"Good, get her up. I'm hungry, as I expect everyone is after the disaster that has become of our day. A full belly will help." Then when Gigi was standing he told her, "Fix some food, and no tricks," he explained in heavily accented English. That time I was able to hear the real language, the water they were splashing on us for no reason was helping. "You'll sample everything we eat first." Gigi disdained the comment, but when she had her hands free, she went to work.

Gigi was old enough to have been in similar circumstances and I wondered if she would abandon us to them to preserve her hide. She probably wouldn't sell us out, but who knew for sure.

"Kennedy, go get us underway, and cut loose the sailboat. It's dead weight with all those fish aboard, and what a stench that will be." A grizzled figure disappeared up the back steps to get The Lazy Cloud into motion. That left three thugs, the lady and the boss. Would they notice me transferring? I couldn't help if I didn't have my freedom. But I couldn't chance it, if they noticed, I'd be giving myself away. I hated being helpless.

"What I'd like to know is what happened. Anyone?" the boss asked. He stared around at the thugs.

"You always hear about giant sea creatures, but it was like the whole sea turned against us in an instant. Dolphins swamping us, fish sacrificing themselves to paralyze Franz and Petri by pinning them by sheer numbers. Something hit the jet boat, I'd swear it, maybe a rocket launcher, but I didn't see anything before it was hit."

"That sounds like tactics, but nobody, I mean nobody commands the sea," said another.

"Unless," said the only one that hadn't spoken. He sounded superstitious as he said it, "you consider the old gods." There was a round of laughter at that.

"You mean like Neptune?" said the lady in a cultured voice. She wasn't laughing and was actually thoughtful of the idea.

"I mean the other guy, Poseidon."

Her laughter trilled, "They are the same person. Poseidon is his Greek name, Neptune is his Roman name."

"Ok, supposing we're dealing with a 'god,' we're screwed, but since we're underway and have suffered nothing else, I'm going to say it was a freak accident. Did you see the way the water rose and fell before and after? I'm guessing the dolphins and fish just got scared and acted strangely as a result."

"Ha, that's the best explanation I've heard yet," said the boss, relieved at having something make sense even if it had no basis or fact to it. But then, they didn't know what I knew. "Gods, Petri, you had us all frightened of shadows. Ok, time to organize the rest of these before they start waking. I'll have none of the beatings of before, no bruises. Separate them as best you can, but keep the guys apart. The girls will give us little problem, but be sure to keep an eye on them all the same. We'll make port by tomorrow evening, if the weather holds. We can get rid of them then. And no escapes, we'll be among islands and they'll try to break for it given half a chance."

"And the cook?"

"She stays, we need to eat and I've eaten your food Pedro," and they all laughed at that. Apparently he didn't create edible dishes.

"I want my assistant," said Gigi on seeing what was happening. Surely she meant me, knowing I was a mermaid, and my hopes went up, but then they pulled up Ri'Anne and it was my turn to be surprised. Then I was being hoisted and I had to feign sleep or unconsciousness as they carried me up and down onto the swim deck, along with Jordan, Billy and Lorin and released our hands.

"They aren't going anywhere, and Kennedy can keep watch on them from the wheel house." Then kicking my arm, "Time to stop playing at being asleep," the guy spoke English, laughing. Then they went up and out of sight.

So much for keeping an eye on us. They apparently meant to check on us from time to time. But before I could act, the girls were moving and removing the ropes on their feet. Jordan skipped her own ropes and was working on mine, though her attention was on the sailboat disappearing over the horizon behind us.

Lorin and Billy, once free, jumped up and mugged me. "You scared us leaving us like that! Where did you go?" Billy cried, burying her face in my shoulder.

Shaking my head, I passed on giving an explanation, "There isn't time." Then I pushed Billy back, telling her, "As you can see, I'm fine."

"Fine? You're caught in the same mess as we are. How are we going to get free this time?" Lorin asked.

Billy slid back beside Lorin, and absently played with her ponytail, straightening it out and saying, "I couldn't understand a word they said, but I expect we're hostages. They sounded upset."

Jordan sat next to me, and took my right shin in her hand, saying in such a way that left no doubt to her intent, "I'm with whatever she decides."

Billy and Lorin looked at one another, and then Billy looked to Jordan and finally to me asking, "Ok, but what can we do? I'm not for being their captives, but every time we've resisted they've beaten us."

Lorin explained, "They take us by surprise, coming up from under us. We never see them. I don't think I have it in me for another beating, so we have to get away this time."

Billy told me what she, Joran and Lorin had been thinking, "We were as surprised as you that when you found us a few days back they were gone. Then they come back when we're cleaning things – the wind had slacked off. They were just suddenly there. I fear what they are going to do with us." She looked at Jordan, specifically at what she was wearing. I was reminded that I'd given her fish for a suit. It angered me thinking of what our captors intended. It hurt me to hear the girls had been treated this way. Thankfully, Billy and Lorin had their sailor outfits, so I didn't have to give them fish on the spot.

I offered them a way out, "I can send you away… The question is, do you want to go to your boat or elsewhere? On your boat, you 'should' be free and clear, but I can't promise that."

"She understands them," Jordan said, leaning into me.

Billy and Lorin looked from me to her, "What aren't you saying?"

"Put the pieces together," was all Jordan would say.

"You were as upset as we were when she jumped off!" Billy said getting up on her knees frustrated that Jordan was holding back from her.

Holding up my hand before they could argue, I told them, "I go where I'm sent. I was 'told' to help you, so I did. Then it was time to leave, and I did. Would it not have been awkward had I stayed?"

"We would have made room," Jordan said sincerely squeezing my leg. "We would have," the others echoed.

"I have a place," I said looking at Uncle's research vessel, the converted yacht I'd been thinking of as home for the last week. "Though right now it is a little confusing."

"I'm for staying with you," Lorin said, sitting down next to me. "Me too," echoed Billy scooting forward to put her knees against mine.

I looked to Jordan and she looked into my eyes and I knew she'd stay if I asked, but I knew her heart was with the sailboat. Jordan said, "The problem is once they discover us missing, they will probably return to the sailboat, so that doesn't give us much hope of escape. And there's no way we can outdistance them with a hull full of fish."

Lorin took my hand, and I saw her willingness to help against the men, but her fear was plain if we were to fail. Speaking from her heart she said, "I can't Jordan, I'm going free if that is an option. I hate to lose The Dancing Lady, but we're so far from Hawaii, or home. We don't have enough supplies to make the journey back across the Pacific."

Jordan said and touched her head to my shoulder again, "Where will you send us? Just not home, how would we explain it?"

That they had such confidence in me was surprising, but I didn't have all the answers. The only thing I knew is they couldn't stay here. We'd come to help them, and I was setting them free. Maybe the Syreni could ease their pains, and I told them, "I don't know what is best, you decide, but I know some people that can help you forget these past days…"

"Oh, I want to forget…" said Lorin but Jordan said, "I don't want to forget you, and I would repeat the foolish journey again if I didn't know."

I sent to Ri'Anne, **I'm taking the girls to safety…** hopeful she'd respond. There was silence, I wondered if she was ok. We haven't had a chance to talk since she skipped out of swimming with the dolphins.

I paused when I heard men talking, and attuning I saw the coast was clear for the moment. Turning my attention to Jordan and the others, I held out my hands saying, “Ok, quick, they are returning, take my hands. You can’t tell anyone about me. Where to?” And when they didn’t respond fast enough for me, “Let’s continue this talk on The Dancing Lady, we’ll have more time to decide.” Gesturing for everyone to hold hands, I went for the sailboat, taking us all through together.

There was a moment of disorientation in the rush to arrive, the piled fish causing me to slip and do a face plant among them. “Sorry Lady,” the fish apologized flapping their tails in an attempt to move out of the way. Billy and Lorin screamed scrambling for ropes and tiller to try and get their craft under control.

“God what a mess,” Jordan said helping me up. “You ok?”

My mind whirling. I was seeing spots. “Water,” I croaked holding a hand to my face. *Someday I’ll get smarter about transferring with a bunch of people.* “Help me to the water.”

“Yes, right water,” Jordan hauled me up, put my arm over her shoulder and carried me through the fish. Slipping and sliding, we reached the edge. I sat, putting my feet in the water. Immediately I felt its coolness flood through me and fill me right up, but it was a second before the light headedness disappeared.

The others looked at me, saying with their eyes, “If you’re going in, we’re coming too.”

“Stay with your boat,” I urged them.

“If it goes down we’re dead. If we’re with you, there’s hope,” Billy explained.

"Stay with your boat," I repeated. "I'm going to check its undersides. I'll be back in a second." Then diving, I swam under the sailboat and set to inspecting it for damage. Or any more devices. But there was nothing apparent.

Reaching for the side, I lifted myself up and out with a kick. Getting up I went to sit beside Billy while she put up the jib sail. Once they had a sail up they were able to get the boat under control.

"I don't get it," Billy said sitting down beside me to pull on the rope the wind in our hair, the breeze carrying with it mist from the top of the waves. They had the main sail up now. "How you do it?"

"Sit here enjoying the wind in my face?" I asked.

"No, I've been doing that since I was a child. That's why I'm here. Twice now you've pulled us out of the most horrific of situations, then put your feet up and act as if nothing has happened."

"I don't think of everything," I admitted. "They clubbed me over the head too. I didn't see that coming."

Billy asked, "Does it have to do with being 'sent' someplace, like you said before?"

I thought about that. There was some assurance that came from knowing I was in the right place, even if the circumstances were against me. "It does, I feel like I can relax, and not have to worry about details, but it isn't like I don't have a role to play."

"That sounds confusing," Lorin said sitting down beside us. "Don't you get to decide for yourself, or are you always at the will of this thing?"

"Can you guys sit back here?" Jordan called from the tiller, and we got up to go sit with her.

"It is both," I tried explaining as they sat. "They were asking me about how I can be so relaxed. Is it because I'm sent places, and if I have any say in it." Remembering falling out of a jet, "There are definitely times when I'm kicked out, made to appear somewhere."

"That sounds so horrible," Lorin said. "I'd rebel in a second."

"You'd be dead if I had," I explained.

Lorin's eyes glistened at this, "You're not kidding, are you?" What could I say? I was definitely glad that I'd met them. There was no taking our friendship from us now. "But, but that means I'm indebted not only to you, but to your… Who is this person?"

"It is the Lord of the Water," I explained. "From him I have the abilities…"

"Wait," Billy interrupted, "What abilities?"

"To breathe water," Jordan added.

"And to bring us from, it's a blur. I know we were on your yacht, and then we were here. I'd assumed there was a boat, or something…" Lorin tried to express her confusion.

Jordan shook her head, "No, she brought us, though I cannot explain how she does it."

"Breathe water, you're kidding?" Billy asked.

"You didn't find it odd that she could talk to us underwater either?" Jordan asked.

"But that's supposed to be impossible," Billy said. "She was doing that?" Billy looked from Jordan to Lorin. Then lastly to me, saying, "I find that hard to believe."

"Then how do you explain that she speaks Danish? I might add, natively as well." Jordan said.

"But... Why are you picking on me?" and Billy went silent.

"Danish?" I asked, "But I figured you guys for Americans."

"We are," Lorin and Billy said at the same time. Lorin went on to explain, "Our parents and grandparents moved to America before we were born. We were raised speaking our home language before we were taught English."

"And you are speaking it better than we do… I'd just assumed," Billy said. "So you're not from Denmark?"

I shook my head, "No."

Lorin returned to the previous topic, "This Lord of the Water… Sounds like something out of a fairytale."

I smiled, "To do my stuff, I need permission. So yeah." I couldn't bring herself to say *magic*. I wasn't supposed to share the knowledge, and so kept my lips sealed on the subject. I'd slipped up enough as it was.

"We were talking about relaxing," Billy said uncomfortable with the topic. "I was trying to find out how come she takes it all in stride."

"It helps," Jordan said, "If you're not in the circumstance, but above it."

Uncomfortable with talking about myself, I changed the subject as well and asked them, "Where to go so you can park The Dancing Lady?"

Billy giggled correcting me. "You don't park a boat, you port a boat."

"But isn't port the left side of a boat?" I asked. "I'm confused."

"It is," Jordan agreed. "I imagine, in the old days you 'ported' the boat on the 'port' side. Or maybe it's just a coincidence." Then she looked at the others and back to me. "I don't want to seem ungrateful, but I'm having a hard time relaxing."

"Is it the fish?" I asked, they were all about us, up to our knees.

"Honestly I expect 'them' to be back. I have no desire to be one of their slaves. Then I want to head for home. And lastly, I want to clean out The Dancing Lady and take her out again. I want to work her sails. To rise above a huge wave and then hurtle down into the channel between the great waves. I want the sound of the wind as it snaps the sail, and the feel of a stiff rain as it stings my hands."

Looking to the horizon while Jordan talked, I thought about my home in far-away Colorado. Somewhere over the sea, a dry desert and across giant mountains was a little shack that had a bed, some dolls from my childhood and a pile of swimsuits I hadn't touched in a couple of weeks. Funny, I didn't miss them at all. But then I hadn't endured the same trials that they had.

Taking my eyes from the horizon, the three of them had separated to their tasks. I looked at their life. Jordan was wrestling with her tiller and some ropes of the main sail. Billy sat with gloves she'd pulled from somewhere holding to a sheet rope, with her feet braced as the front sail tried to come free. Lorin had gone for food and returned holding food for the four of us, though I knew they didn't have much. I knew them to be the hungrier and let them have the lion's share.

Jordan then came and stood with me. Hugging my neck, she buried her face in my shoulder a second before taking a breath and letting go. She was smiling as she said, "We have enough food for three days, we can make it on our own. You don't have to stay."

"You'd continue with what you've experienced?" I asked. "I'd be for home and the comfort of family."

Jordan looked at me confused and asked, "What are you saying? I'm hearing you, but your words make no sense. Our homes are thousands of miles away, on the east coast of the United States. We've sailed half way around the world." Then with a half-smile Jordan added, "And seen things that none will believe."

Hearing something, she looked up. I followed her gaze, the sails were billowing. They were no longer snapping. "The wind has slackened," Lorin explained joining us. Which I guess wasn't good news for a boat that relied on the wind. If the gang of thugs were coming back we were in trouble.

Billy looked to Jordan from where she sat. They had a disagreement with their eyes, and then Jordan looked away.

Billy said to me. “I overheard what you said, can you really do what I thought you were saying… take us home? Like you brought us here…” I could see Jordan tense up at that.

Now I knew how to read Jordan. She had fought a thousand battles to arrive to this point and I’d be taking that all away from her by “instantly” taking her home. No wonder my idea didn’t make sense to her.

But it was Billy that was asking and she needed to know. I gave her a nod, giving her my promise, “It is true, I can,” then looking at Jordan I told her. “The three of you need to make the decision together. I’ll not force any of you.”

Getting up, I went to the bow while they sat and talked. I sat down on the bowsprit, letting the fish of my suit remake my lower half into the tail so it could trail in the water. The fish of my suit were a surprise. In the last couple days I’d changed them several times, they kept dying on me. But since Uncle had helped me, these hadn’t faded more. Though, I expected Uncle and I would need to have a chat.

Leaning over to look into the depths, I sighed, feeling a captive of people’s expectations. And my family was in trouble. I wanted to be with them and couldn’t understand why Jordan didn’t want to be with her family. Though I could understand that there was a benefit to a struggle, and a benefit to overcoming the difficulties.

The things in life worth having were only achieved through a struggle. I thought of my swim events, none of them came easy – and my victories. Always they required me to give everything to place my hand first, a half second before another. If it didn't take effort then there was no victory.

I could hear the girls talking, but I didn't listen in. They were arguing, talking, discussing their triumphs, the joys and their fears. I'd given them the option of help. A possibility to reset, to cheapen their journey and at what cost? Recapture meant enslavement, I guessed Jordan thought that the existence of that consequence was better than any life she could have with me "fixing things." It seemed she preferred being beaten, tortured and forced to do things for which I had no words if only she got to choose her own destiny in the end. I was for sending them away, anywhere, far from here.

Creating a fist, I would deal with their captors, our captors. Some people thought they could do whatever they wanted in this life and get away with it. But I had to wait and finish this.

The girls came and sat behind me. The fish raced over me as I crossed my legs, still sitting on the prow. Now it was my turn to be difficult. I wasn't ready to face them. They waited while I debated. I knew I'd be as bad as their captors to force them to be "free."

Jordan spoke, "Going home doesn't mean giving up." There was my answer. "My friends and I would like you to take us home." I heard her love for her friends in her voice. I didn't have to turn to know they had their arms about each other. But I turned to look them in their eyes, meeting and focusing on each to be sure of their decision. I was aware I was attuned to their hearts, sensing within the best I was able. Working with the Syreni elders on the others had helped me read hearts. I should be smiling, happy. But now my eyes had been opened to the reality of decisions. I didn't want to make a mistake and force them to anything, it was too important to me and our friendship. Eventually I saw what I wanted in them, they were of one mind in the decision.

I saw in Jordan's eyes actual relief that their trials would be over. She'd been bucking up under the pressure for so long that she'd forgotten how to let go, to love and be free with her affections. She smiled at me, but her kindest emotions were reserved for her friends. I was in no way jealous and was happy that she was ready. She was a fine leader, and her friends respected her.

Billy, her long auburn hair flowing over her shoulder, was relaxed. She liked the sea and its challenges, but she was emotionally drained from their experience, though she hadn't given up. Tackling the globe had been one of her life long dreams. I could see in her that she was already preparing for their next attempt.

Lorin, tough and lanky. Her golden blond curls escaped her braid. She gave me a wink, and I knew next time she'd take me up on a mermaid excursion, but now she was for home. She looked the most tired, but she was also the most resilient.

I'd known them but a short time, it was hard getting to know them only this little bit to be sending them off so fast. If anything, I wanted what they had experienced, what Jordan had described, but it was time to go. I felt the Lord of the Water blessing the journey before I had really even begun to ask. It just seemed right.

Feeling in me, as I had with the rain clouds for clothing, I looked to the sky, saw the wind waiting to be called and gave a hand signal. "Man your sails," I gestured at the giant white sheets as they filled with wind. The girls jumped, spinning about and raced back to their duties. The wind struck, and I felt fire race along my body.

Standing, I held to the jib, feeling a thrill run through me as I felt the moment ripe. "Ready Melanie?" I asked myself. Turning to face forward, the nose of The Dancing Lady ducked into a wave crest. Water doused me and I laughed.

Seeing a spray of water ahead that formed into a rainbow. "There!" I yelled back to the girls. "Aim for the rainbow!"

The Dancing Lady heeled hard to starboard as they brought in sail as they followed my lead. Holding to the jib, I enjoyed more splashes before the rainbow stood before us. A blue iris pulsed between the rainbow and the sea. We were coming at right angles to the rainbow, and I thought we might sail pass it. But then the Dancing Lady again heeled over as Jordan steered her into the wind. Waves hammered over the bow. We were tacking straight into the wind.

Then the rainbow was above us and passing over us. There was a moment of being in two places at once, and then as we moved forward I saw a beautiful east port cape revealed. The girls shouted and wept, immediately recognizing their home. They abandoned their posts to gather around me. I'd walked with the rainbow as it passed overhead and was back among them behind the cabin.

They were looking at me in awe, but I explained to them, "It was the Lord of the Water that brought us through. I'm a passenger on this ride, the same as you."

They wouldn't take that for an answer, and each took their turns picking me up, hugging me and saying, "Thank you." I could hardly breathe from the depth of their crushing hugs. The wind had slacked on our transfer, but then it was back and we ducked as the boom about knocked us off.

26

Cape Port

Now I had a glimpse of what The Dancing Lady could be like as they brought the sailboat around towards the cape. A lighthouse winked at us from a cliff. I could easily understand their love for the sport. Driving around on Uncle's yacht didn't compare to being moved by the wind. There was a keen thrill to the exercise of skill in keeping the boat at just the right angle to the wind and desired direction. I sat with each of them, and they handed me the ropes or tiller so I could gain some understanding to what it was all about.

As we got closer to the cape, we were passed by others lighter on their feet. The girls waved to those they knew. "Hey, it's Hank!" Billy called as a squat dirty white motorized vessel approached, heading out on the evening tide. The girls all waved, calling out, "Hank!"

They stood frustrated when the fisher went on by ignoring them. "It's Hank, but he thinks we're just being nice," Jordan said slouching beside me. "Is there anything you can do? He could use a haul like this," and she waved at the fish. "They'd go to waste with us."

"Why not use the radio?" I asked, surprised by the request.

Jordan frowned as remembrance of their captors surfaced. "They didn't want us calling for help. If they couldn't destroy it, it went overboard. Thankfully, anything worth keeping was saved online. All our pictures are safe."

"Wait, what did you say?" I'd been only half listening, thinking of all they had gone through. Something she had said was important.

Jordan repeated it, looking at the departing fish hauler, "All our data, including our pictures are saved to the web, online."

"Online. Hmmm, that's got to be it," When she looked at me in question I shook my head, "It's too long of a story." That had to be how Uncle had figured it out. The Syrenis had said they'd erased or modified his data. But knowing Uncle, he'd have backed them up. Somewhere, somehow he'd found a discrepancy, had checked his backups and noticed the difference. One mystery solved.

"So your radio is busted?" I asked and she confirmed it with a nod. "And no horn either?" She shook her head, pointing to the wrecked console. "How do you navigate?"

"My dad taught me to sail long before I knew computers. Besides, a compass helps," and she pulled out an emergency compass. It was obvious she was confiding in me her remaining secret.

"Ok. I'll be back," and I rolled over the edge, letting the fish have their way with me, remaking me with a tail. It was much easier going as I entered the water. Smelling the water though, I knew it had been a while since a mermaid had visited. Thinking of how Gian and I had cleaned up at the island, I smiled, today one was visiting. I attuned, letting the magic it contained clean outwards from me. I wanted to sing again, and I hummed, singing the first few bars of my new song, "clams clapping." The song summed up the last few days, for both me and everyone I was meeting.

I was dawdling, flicking my tail, and I hightailed it towards the fisherman. The fisher was rather old, but its name had fresh paint, "Billy's Eyes." It didn't take me long to figure out why Billy had been the first to notice the boat.

Thinking about Billy's eyes, made me wonder why "Hank" thought so much of them. I swam up beside the hauler and pulled myself up to rest my head on my arms to look for him. The boat had seen better days, but it looked functional. The smell of the sea was masked by old fish, and I wondered how they could stand it. They'd spread sand on the grimy deck to make it less slippery. Why not a good scrubbing to get rid of the stench and slime? A host of seagulls swooped above them hoping to be there when they started their fishing. Their cries of "Fish!" went unheard by the fishermen.

There were three guys preparing their drag nets near the stern. I wondered which was Hank. Was it one of the two with the beards? Or the clean-shaven high-school guy? I kind of ruled him out as being too young. Perhaps it was the guy driving. I could only see his back and the olive green ball cap he wore as he scanned the horizon.

Then one of the bearded guys glanced my way, did a double take and then got the attention of his mates. "Hey, what are you…" he stepped towards me quickly and I dropped off the boat floating away. Thinking he might dive in after me, I dove under quickly.

I was being coy. Examining my feelings, I realized I'd started acting this way when I'd read the name of the fisher. I was jealous and that brought me up short. Was I jealous at the boat's name? Or was I jealous of Billy?

I wasn't sure, but it had stirred my protective feelings for her. I was in a mood, and hoped these guys were honorable towards the girls. They'd driven on as I thought about it, and I sped to catch back up, coming up on its other side to lean on the gunwale again. I heard them as they talked looking back behind the trawler into the wake hoping to see something. They were saying words like, "mermaid," and "did you see that tail?"

"Hey," I said to get their attention, my word was everything they were listening for. The three of them spun to stare. I attuned this time hoping to ease into their graces. The magic must have worked, they stood there frozen. "Which of you is Hank?" I asked glad that they weren't going to jump at me again.

"Hey Hank!" the two bearded fellows yelled to the captain.

"What?" he roared back.

Why the yelling? The air was magically quiet, the attuning having quite an effect. The boat filled with magic as I kept it up, the sandy grimy deck was starting to sparkle. The engine made a gentle purr as it stirred up the water driving the boat forward. More strangeness, because the effect hadn't happened on The Lazy Cloud before.

"We have a guest!"

The driver pitched around to peer back over his other shoulder, his eyes quickly finding the odd girl hanging to the side of his boat. He stared a second and then reached for the throttle. I thought he might gun it forward in an attempt to shake me, but then he was pulling back to idle.

He peered around looking for other mermaids and then came to the ladder down. Holding to both handrails he slid down to the deck in a single bound. I measured him, fisherman through and through. The attuning was telling me that he had generations of sailor blood flowing through his veins. There was deep lore to his glance, but it wasn't displayed on his boat in the form of trinkets. Someone had raised him on tales of mermaids. It was as if at long last he was seeing the answer to a prayer. Keeping his hands to his sides he walked around to the back of the boat to sit on the gunwale there. He gestured for the others to sit on the opposite side of the boat from me.

Seeing no shadows about him, I thought I could trust him and lifted myself up. Sitting with my back to the wheel house, legs and feet stretched out on top of the gunwale, I waited for him to open the conversation. The sea had gone quiet. Even the seagulls had stopped their cries and had settled in the rigging nodding to one another.

He spoke saying, "Sea Lord."

I about teared up at that. Letting out a breath, I paused, gesturing back towards The Dancing Lady. "You passed Billy, Jordan and Lorin."

His eyes went wide at the mention of their names, but he didn't turn to look as the others did. "I thought that might have been them," he said pulling off his cap and twirling it in his fingers. He believed me, I could see that in his expression. But he felt like he must explain, "They're supposed to be southwest of Hawaii. And their boat was riding so low that I couldn't read its name."

Daring to take his eyes off me, he peered back towards The Dancing Lady with longing in his gaze and then back to me. Now he really didn't want to be sitting here having this conversation, but he was doing his best to hide it. I was intrigued by his knowledge of mermaids. I'd really like to meet his teacher. Though his respect seemed to be based on fear. Knowing what I'd done, I could understand the fear aspect. But I wasn't here to frighten him.

Saying casually, "Billy and the others could use your help." Then with one of those, I don't know where the words come from and they're out before I can stop myself sayings, I told him, "The Lord of the Water brought them home early."

He nodded sagely. When I didn't go on he asked, "That's it?" he asked. When I nodded he smiled, overjoyed. He was going to see his girl. Getting up, he gave me a slight bow and then turned to his crew. "Stow the nets gents, it looks like it's an early night for us."

"But," said the kid. Then getting a glance from Hank that I didn't see, he shut up.

Climbing the ladder two rungs at a time, Hank went to his wheel and roared the engine to life spinning his vessel about. Gone was the "purr" of the engine, the magical moment over. I stood holding to a rope and debated swimming back to the girls. But a ride with them would serve the same purpose and so I walked along the gunwale forward, seeking a seat up front. Reaching the bow I sat beside the anchor and put my feet over the edge.

It bothered me a little his ready willingness. Hank would have done anything I'd asked, no questions asked – even if it meant hardship for him. He'd been relieved I was sending him to Billy. Was this a case of "forcing" someone to my will?

I shook my head trying to reason it out. I wouldn't have been "fine" if he'd said no, but I wouldn't have done something drastic about it if I hadn't gotten my way. The girls would have had to live with the fish, but Jordan had said they would go to waste. She'd already thought of that, and was willing to bless her friend with the haul instead. Still, he had made his decision based on my interference. Maybe if I'd told him there was a haul of fish waiting for him he'd have been more willing.

Hank had called me "Sea Lord," giving me respect. His willingness to do whatever had me stumped. The eagle had called me a Shepard of the Sea. Did that extend to sailors and fishermen? Hank's fear had me feeling goosebumps along my back and down my arms. But we had a blessing in mind for him. I hoped that would ease his fears of mermaids.

While I was thinking, we'd come up on The Dancing Lady. I stood and waved to the girls who were waving our way. Seeing the girls standing there in stinky fish goo-covered clothes, I dove over and swam quickly to them as the fisher slowed to come alongside. I could cleanse their clothes for them, I hoped they wouldn't mind. Outwardly they were happy to see the guys, but inwardly they were anxious. It had been a while since they'd trusted men.

I arrived and Jordan told me, "You did it!" Then the girls took a look at themselves, Billy yelling, "Clothes, hair, we're a mess!" The two of them dove into the sea of fish in their cabin to return a minute later with something barely recognizable as "nice" clothing.

"You'll need these back," and Jordan ran a hand over the lovely suit she'd been wearing. "I will miss them, and you," and then the fish leaped to me as she put on her things.

"Gather close," I told them, attuning, and I let the cleansing effect do a miracle on them and their clothes. They smiled at seeing their clothes go from fish grime to newness, and their hair freshen out. Again they had tears in their eyes, but they banished them as ropes were thrown to them to tie the vessels together.

I smiled seeing Jordan, Lorin and Billy as they should have always been, respected by Hank and his men. The girls were tentative at first, but they warmed up when they were treated as equals. I relaxed at hearing their easy banter, they would have time to heal now, and I was tempted to slip over the side and leave. It was best to go when the job was done, but I wanted to be absolutely sure and stayed.

There was no mistaking me sitting on the outside of their group, but I didn't really care, knowing I would be gone soon. Though several times one or another of the girls came to sit with me. The guys stayed distant, even Hank.

Once they were working offloading the fish, I went and joined in. A couple of the guys started up a song, and working beside Jordan I saw her wince at their tone. Their wounds were still raw, but I knew a song. I drew on the sea, the wind and the waves to guide our efforts, trying for a melody that fit for the fish giving their lives for the welfare of the women. As the others picked it up, I felt strength flow into our arms and backs. With many willing hands the work went quickly.

Then there was the last fish from the cabin and it went through the chain of arms up and out. The tune died out and we were looking on the burnished sunset lit sea. "That was a tune the Norse would sing," came Hank as he swung back aboard. "I've not heard its like since my 'ole Pappie passed on. And what work, the deck is shined, the railings glisten!" Well, I had no trick for getting fish to jump boat to boat, but the least side effect of a rousing good song could be its cleansing effects. Especially on us girls when rags came to hand. "It looks like you are just setting sail, not the coming home of a long voyage. You must tell me sometime about how the tuna and marlins jumped aboard, but we must put in if we're to get this to market."

Before I could reply, he and his crew disappeared over to the low-riding trawler, carrying their heavy catch. "Now I must be going," I said and the girls all burst out, "No, please stay. Please," and it was all in earnest, "It's too dark, and we can't see to make port."

"Can't you follow them in?" I asked of the disappearing fisher, but I too could see Billy's Eyes was moving too fast and they needed the wind and it was dying away. I couldn't ask, "What would you do if caught out after dark normally?" They would have camped out under the stars, but they wanted their moms even if they weren't saying it out loud.

"Ok, I'll point, and you haul sail, but I don't know where we're going. And I still don't know much about sailing, only what you've taught me." They got down to business, and I worked alongside them, doing my best to guide them. It wasn't like we were sailing blind, there were all sorts of port lights to guide us in, and the wind did quiet down, but there was enough of an evening breeze for them to make it in to their berth. There were cars waiting, and people jumped out shouting.

Lorin said, when she saw our expressions of "How did they know?" she said, "I called using Ted's cell."

The mothers were doing enough screaming that the girls were able to be quiet. The two groups ran into each other's arms. After a moment Jordan came back and took my hand, drawing me forward, saying into the ears of a weather-worn man, her dad I presumed, "This is who saved us, twice."

He said with great affection, "If you ever have need of a sailor, sailboat or anything, you need only ask." The girls had gathered behind them, agreeing with him.

Then they were talking again, sharing many of the details that had been left out since their equipment was damaged. My feet drew me to the sea, and I walked back onto the jetty where the boat was tied up. Their boat looked tiny next to some of the others.

I heard Jordan saying, "She says the Lord of the Water brought us home."

"I don't get it," said one of the parents.

I wondered when their questions would come around to me, but really sitting there close to the water, on the pier next to their boat – I didn't care. Millions of stars glistened above, obscured partially by the port's lights, but I could feel their song. I felt the change from girl to mermaid, but I relaxed feeling at ease. The song of the night twirled around me. In that moment I forgot about everything but the feel of the sea only a short drop below me.

Exulting in the moment, I heard them coming, but it didn't penetrate. I flexed my tail and heard gasps from around me. I turned, scarlet-colored, what was I thinking? Seeing the parents staring with mouths in the shapes of O's, I forward flipped off the pier laughing merrily at their astonishment and dove under some fancy boats.

Now what? I'd been gone long enough to be noticed if I returned to The Lazy Cloud. Sensing the girls' concerned searching eyes, I rose up by the light pole at the end of their pier, waving. When they saw me and they rushed out to me, wanting a last hug goodbye.

"How can we reach you?" the three of them entreated. It didn't seem like they were asking because they were still afraid – though maybe some of it was there.

Umm, I didn't know, but I asked the one who did. With his understanding, I told them, "Say my name to the water. I'll hear if I'm near water." I had this image of water bottles all pinging around me from the hands of my friends. I added with a lopsided smile, "I'm sure that'll work."

"But we don't know your name. You've been terribly secretive about it." They gave me cross looks.

"Right! Hmm, there really hasn't been proper greetings has there? Things were kind of busy, I'd quite forgotten. Hmm, well, I'm Melanie," I said lightly with a smile. Their parents were hanging some twenty feet back, but I wanted only the girls to hear and came up to whisper to them.

"A beautiful name for a mermaid," Jordan said, and we smiled together.

Yep, a mermaid, "Thank you." How cool is that?

"It must be great, being a mermaid," Lorin said.

"There are benefits, like this," but then I frowned thinking of the guys I'd drowned. They shared my expression. I cheered up saying, "It is always like that. Just like it is fun to sail, right? So beautiful as you've shared with me. I'll always remember."

"Any time," Billy said and the others echoed her.

It was an awkward moment and it really was past time I left. "I should go. I have friends in trouble yet…"

"You should go! We're sorry for keeping you."

Still, we hugged one last time. Then I was diving. While coasting out into the channel, I thought I should check on those I'd sent to Syreni before I returned to The Lazy Cloud. It would be the only chance I would get. But I swam for a little bit first exploring the underwater world the girls called home. I was met by a horde of fish who welcomed and swam about me. Following them, they showed me wonders while I cried at leaving Jordan, Billy and

Lorin, silly girl that I am. Then I was transferring to the Isle of Syreni and to the field I'd sent the ones I'd rescued.

27

Being Human

It felt good to be back on the tropical island the Syreni called home. They kept their island clean and beautifully appointed with flowers. The fragrant botanical perfume drifted under my nose and I had to pause to breathe in the aroma. Breathing out I lifted my eyes to the steady giant statues that surrounded the field. Their eyes seemed to look down from the ages on the football field surrounded by a running track and upon all of us here. They seemed to be saying that *everything would be ok.*

Everywhere between me and the statues were the Syreni, gathered around each individual I'd sent here. Looking at the pockets of kids, it wasn't hard to pick out those that I'd sent. Even though the Syreni had gifted the new arrivals with clothing as needed, it wasn't their appearance that set them apart. The arrivals had something in common, a stunned look. The Syreni were very much in their element – preparing all their lives for such events.

Those I'd rescued could hardly believe that they'd gone from a self-serving society, where they were the servants, to the Syreni who were dedicated to helping them. I smiled, yes, this had been the right thing to do.

Still, if I were one of those I'd rescued, I tried to imagine what I would have done. What would be my reaction? Would I fight against these new people? I imagined swimming for my life, desperate for air and then stumbling onto this green football field. It was a fruitless exercise trying to imagine it and turned my thoughts to the Syreni.

The Syreni always made me feel comfortable. They assigned me kids my own age to give me everything. It was the same with what I saw. Here and there, those kids that I'd sent aged thirteen to seventeen had kids their own age sitting and kneeling beside them on the neatly trimmed grass, helping them feel at ease. They didn't speak the same language, but the Syreni had their ways and had made these new arrivals feel welcome.

Standing amidst the others, nobody at first noticed my arrival. But it wasn't long until a Syreni girl did, and then she touched the arm of another beside her, nodding in my direction. I didn't pay them much attention, I knew they'd find me girls my own age soon enough, but I thought I might talk with one of the kids I rescued first.

I called them "kids," though they were all older than me. I couldn't help but think of them that way. Until this point in their life they should have been experiencing the delights of growing up, instead of being slaves to another's desire. They'd been robbed of their childhood, and I was so glad I'd brought them here in the hopes of something better.

Walking by one group, the fifteen-year-old boy there looked up on seeing me. He recognized me, but it took him a second to realize I was the same girl that had been the swimming mermaid that had saved him. By then I'd walked on, to stand with some Syrenis caring for a girl too young to be anywhere near those predators. My heart went out for her more than the others, but none of them were less deserving than her. I could see in her the kids I knew at the gym, happily squealing as they sought to climb all over me and my friends.

Torn between the memory and this girl, I failed to see the boy jump up from among the Syreni and push his way forward to throw himself at my feet. Surprised, I had nowhere to move as he hugged my foot. I didn't know what to do. My foot became wet, he was crying on it. I knew it to be salt water, I was absorbing his tears.

His island boys joined and knelt beside him, encouraging him. I was shocked at their tenderness, for I would have expected boys to mock or at best be standoffish. Instead they helped him up and led him back to his place, but not before others that I'd rescued came forward to do the same. Soon I couldn't move for being packed in by these "kids." Some didn't recognize me directly, but they saw perhaps in me their rescuer through the eyes of the others that had seen.

How was I to respond? But there was nothing I could do but let them show their thanks in their own way. Even the adults I'd rescued that had been sitting trying to figure it out, came and joined those with me. After a time I realized I should ask for help and lifted my hands to the Syreni. It was a while before they could pry them away.

Once I was free of the rescued, I wasn't free of the Syreni girls that stepped in to replace them. They had tears too, and I realized my cheeks were wet as well. It was a little while as I breathed in the delicately scented breeze before I could wipe my face with the backs of my hands and have them stay dry.

"An elder?" I asked when I was settled again. The elders were ancient among the Syreni, born among them, but through some ritual seemed to live forever. It was obviously a rare privilege and honor. All the Syreni respected them. Requesting one of them was like asking to see the President, something I shouldn't do, but they served mermaids, not the other way around. That was another thing I didn't understand - why they did so. I should ask Jill about it sometime and see if she knew, but it never seemed important enough and I'd forget to ask.

One of my companions said as she brushed back her straight dark island hair from her eyes, "I heard something about one of the great sea creatures down at the dock, but if need be…"

"No that is fine, I guess that's my fault," and I sighed. It was because I asked that she couched her words so. If I "ordered it" they'd go out of their way to make sure it was done.

Examining the wreck I'd made of their day, and the scene at the docks, I wondered how these people handle one of us let alone a world of our kind? So far as I knew, there were few of us, but that wouldn't last as more became mermaids. Which of course pivoted my thoughts to Ri'Anne. I'd resume with her as soon as I could. Somehow we'd integrate what she liked with what I thought were mermaid activities. And at some point I should introduce her to the Syreni, but by then we had to have her sorted out.

So what was I going to do? The "kids" were being taken care of, but I still needed advice. If I couldn't have an elder maybe there was someone else among them that knew the answer to my question. "It's just my friends and family are still in trouble by armed thugs, and I..." I was rambling, and cut myself off.

One of my girls gave voice to an idea, "I think I might know who can help," and she took off to speak with someone else in another group, her mostly pink flowered skirt kicked up by her high flying heels. In a minute she returned with her, an older girl, recently back from college if her modern blouse was any indication. I repeated what I'd said, that my family was in danger. Nodding, she said, "I've told my brother." Did she send? Her expression didn't change and I sensed nothing. "He serves and will come and discuss."

He serves. I've heard that before. It underlined their whole way of life. Their "We'll do it, or die trying" phrase, that it will be done as I've requested. Maybe not as nice as an elder calling me "Dear One." Still, it was too easy to order these people around. I'd done that by requesting aid. And they were all serving, waiting with me for orders, being with me as companions, for as long as I stayed. It was a little unfair – what did they get out of the arrangement?

They were friendly, though we were strangers to one another. To find out about us, did they subscribe to the mermaid magazine Fins? Listing all the top mermaids? Their wants and habits, and best of all whether they preferred star fish or clown fish for their mermaid suits? And who we were dating, the scoops and breakups?

With a twinkle in my eye, I nodded. Maybe, just maybe...

With time to wait, I felt for water, saw girls sitting by a stream that I sensed and crossed the football field to join them. I could hardly be there and not put my feet in. Immediately its cool waters slipped into me as I sat and put my feet within. The surface of the water looked like glass slippers as the water curled around me. The illusion lasted even when I lifted my feet, the water sticking with me longer than what was normal. With swishes of fabric, my companions settled about me.

Having just had my mermaid tail, I wanted to see it again. I'm a mermaid for real now, everyone was saying it and I had the tail to prove it. Through the attuning I felt for the mermaid tail and watched with amazement as my legs disappeared, replaced by the tail. There was a quiet gasp of delight from the girls, and I couldn't help echo it in my heart, it *was* beautiful. Seeing it reminded me of Uncle actually swimming with me while I had it, no judgement. Just chiding me for being an idiot. I couldn't help but smile at that. And then Dad, who I'd avoided looking at. *Oh Dad...* I wasn't complete without my family. I couldn't forget for long, wondering if they, especially Dad, were ok.

I tried to focus on Dad, to bring him into view, but unless I started a transfer he was too far away. Frustrated at not knowing, I turned my thoughts to how accepting he was of my changes. But then he'd lectured me under The Lazy Cloud... I decided *accepting* wasn't the term I should use. Uncle seemed more forgiving than he.

I couldn't just sit here with the victims of the people that now had Dad and the others. My legs back in a flash, it was time I did something. I stood up, but then had the thought, *You're safe Melanie, stay put...* and sat back down. Dad would be relieved at having me "safe." I wondered if he even knew I'd been back on The Lazy Cloud before it was captured. I didn't want Dad to worry for my sake. And how he'd worry if I took on the thugs directly.

It didn't seem like there was anything I could do without going in blasting, and how would that work out of water? The one time I'd done that, using an electrical current like an electric eel, I'd shot forth a lightning bolt that had zapped my friend Jill too. But that had been in water where stretching my abilities was easy. I needed something smaller, but I suppose if it was between me getting gunned down… I'd have to think of something. As much as I wanted to do that to these guys, it would be messy and could I take on so many while they held hostages?

A luxuriously warm breeze filled with the fragrance of jasmine and frankincense whisked across my nose and I turned to see where it came from. An older girl had joined my quintet. She sat unobtrusively, and began teaching the girls with me. I wouldn't have noticed her except I was bored. It was difficult to sit idly by, waiting on others. Talking gently with the girls she was explaining the complicated twirl she was applying to my hair to hold perfume even after it became wet, which was surely to happen.

Another time that may have been interesting, but I turned my attention back to the people I'd saved, "What's to happen to them?" I asked the girl with a tray of fruit kneeling before me. Those I'd rescued all wore various expressions. Some were glad to be out of there, but others had come to accept their life. It may have been better than at home, even if it had been slavery.

"What would you like that we do for them Mistress?" I heard the silent "or to them" inherent in the question.

I explained what I'd been wondering, "Sending them 'home' could be worse, but what options are there?"

"You already chose to interfere in their lives," said the older girl, "You have to decide. Ours is only to care for them enough to recover their bearing, and then send them back if possible, starting with their last situation. If you don't give us instructions."

"You would send them back to those I'd freed them from?" That was a shock.

"If they are capable of making a decision themselves, they will be asked of course what their desire is. Some will want to return to family, some will not. The world over people sell their kids in hopes of better lives for themselves, it is a hard truth. So you can see, their masters may have been better for them, but ultimately the decision is yours. Yet, if left alone, we will do the best we can to transition them back into a life they are familiar with and are most comfortable with."

I sighed inwardly, thinking of them as American kids - with playgrounds and team sports - was a mistake. Being sold by your parents, I couldn't imagine. Why would a parent do such a thing? Weren't children precious to them? How many little girls had I seen holding a doll as if it was the desire of "all" mothers to have and to hold a little one, as I had done? My bed at home still had the dolls of my childhood leaned up on the pillows. Too many questions and no good answers.

I didn't like the Syreni's casual attitude either, but I had interfered in the kids' lives. So I had to say something, "Thanks. I'm new to this, so that is good to know. I don't suppose this is an adequate place to send people in the future?"

"Sea Lord, we are raised from an early age to serve. What you see here nobody had to supervise. We who serve, as you may not have been told, were in the midst of normal daily activities of study when these people began arriving. You'd be surprised how quickly word spreads and hands jump to helping. It is joy to serve you this way.

"But if you are bringing violent types, send them to the training grounds or the pits if they are armed. I can show you but you should have their locations from me already." She was right, when she mentioned each place I picked them up from her, knowing them as she said them.

I hoped never to have to use either the training grounds or the pits, but it was worth knowing. Having just experienced those thugs it seemed a possibility. It would be better if I handled it better than I had at the onset. I'd been too squeamish to directly kill them myself and left them liberty, thinking they'd drown on their own and my hands would be "clean." We'd paid the price for my stupidity.

Time to issue my "order." "Them," and I gestured to the field, "They get better than what they had. If you need my help in determining what, the elders know how to get a hold of me." The older girl stuck her arms out from her sides at shoulder height and gave me a bow, and the others with me did the same.

Their reaction got me to walking. It was too easy to give orders. Hank had acted the same way as the Syreni just had, I realized that now. Actually it wasn't exactly that, he'd been afraid I'd issue an order. One he'd be compelled to do. As I had with Jordan when we first met, I'd assumed the lead without recognizing it. She was unable to resist me and I didn't realize that she couldn't act without my lead – she couldn't even speak. Gigi had called me out on it, saying I spoke with authority. I didn't want to be feared.

Walking helped ease my mood. The sound of the wind in the trees made me think of all my favorite summer days. Growing up in Colorado I didn't have much experience with forests, but the peace that came from walking along the stream quieted my anxiety. The path beside was soft to walk on, feeling recently tilled. In places we walked across emerald green moss, and it felt like something alive. It was so distracting that I soon forgot all about my problems.

Every so often along the path were additional brooks, places to sit with beautiful and artistic windmill structures that spun lightly in the breeze. Between them and the occasional pretty lady or masculine statue, so lifelike that they appeared a moment ago to have been moving, and delicate benches on which to contemplate the presented art. I finally asked to those who walked with me, "What are these places?"

The girls were carefree, dancing along the path and stooping to pick flowers. One of them asked, "Do you like them?" When I nodded, I thought they might explain – but they seemed to want me to get an understanding on my own. I could see sitting there for a long time, each place having its own design, view of the forest and delicately tended gardens. But there was nobody contemplating the forest at any of these places. We had this part of the forest all to ourselves.

Seeing a wide stream, I thought we could wait there for the one who serves to arrive. It would be fun to dive in, and I took off running and then dove thinking it would be deep. In mid-air I realized that the stream was shallow and tried to put on air-brakes and fly. But I only managed to cross my arms before my face before I hit bottom. The water's coolness surprisingly surrounded me, with no sudden mineral stop on the stones of the bottom of the stream.

Opening my eyes, I gazed about in wonder. I was in deep over my head. I'd gone into the brook much deeper than seemed possible. Glancing up, I could see the rocks of its "bottom" were above me, transparent but I could see their edges as well as the sand and plants growing "in" the stream. But from there, it was as if I was in a canal dug out to a much greater depth, but only as wide as the brook. There was a name for it, Underriver; the name coming to me unbidden.

The name explained the place only a little. There was the expected river bottom below, but instead of walls of dirt or sand, the sides appeared to be a movie screen that stretched as far as could be seen in any direction, on either side showing a different view of the shore than the one I knew to be there. Floating over to the side I put my hand to it. There was but a soap bubble membrane separating me from the vision I was seeing, but my hand didn't go through when I pushed.

Beyond were trees of light within the field we'd been in, and coming and going from them were the occasional shooting star. Some flew like lightning, and others were quietly hovering and talking or drifting with Syreni girls like those who had been walking with me. These "shooting stars" had to be Sky Lords, the other lords that the Syreni served. In a second there were additional splashes and I looked up as my girls joined me, and like me swam to the edge to examine what I was seeing.

"So it's true," said one of them and then she went up to the surface to look, before diving down to look again. "Though we haven't heard about what we're doing, what is this place Lord?"

"It's the Underriver," I said as if that should explain everything. "What are you seeing?" I asked hoping to draw them out.

"Great giant light trees," she said in awe. "We've been taught the Sky Lords create life from light, and of course they love trees more than any of their realm. We are either looking at the past or the future. I'm sure the Elder Archivist could tell us which."

"The past or future," I mouthed. "You say it so calmly."

"Mistress, all our lives we've been raised on tales of you and yours. Since the Sea Lord has returned, our abilities are returning as well. For example, we can join with you here without you needing to exert yourself. As you learn more about who and what you can be, we will increase as well. For example…" and she held her hand upright and a spot of light formed on her palm in the shape of a snowflake and then it floated from her hand upwards before it melted. "It lasts longer in the air," she apologized. But the other girls were doing likewise, and it was snowing upwards out of their hands. "And it's prettier at night."

"Oh look," one of the girls cried and we turned in time to see the two girls with a Sky Lord morphing into dots of light to fly with the ball of light and zoom off across the clearing with the light trees and rise high up into one before settling at the top of its branches. "I hope this is the future, I can hardly stand it!"

"Where can I learn more about myself?" I asked them, and the four turned to face me and looked as if I'd poked them with a stick. It didn't take me long to realize, "You don't know do you."

"Not that, Mistress," said one of them, "It's just that we are forbidden to teach, but we can help and I know that's a fine line, but we dare not trespass it. You should seek someone that can teach you, one of your kind or a human that knows your ways."

At her words, it was like light turned off in my head and it became dark. I felt my world go wobbly and I had to ask, "Did you just say I wasn't human anymore?"

"That's a question you have to answer for yourself Lord, but since you were sporting the Sea Lord tail, I thought you'd made the decision already."

I knew what she was saying, but somehow I thought I was still human while embracing mermaid things. It was a subtle difference, but it was like her not being able to teach. Helping was so close that it felt like teaching sometimes. I was being rocked by the revelation, every sense I had was diminished as I thought I was losing my humanity.

Feeling out of breath, I kicked for the surface suddenly afraid. I found stepping out of the creek simple, but my thoughts were not there as I took to the path and walked. I'd wanted to be a mermaid more than anything, but at what cost? Would I be losing my family and friends, possibly forever? Well, not Jill, my best friend and mermaid (though she fought it!) No wonder she didn't have the tail, it came by wanting it, all of it. I wondered if I could bring it back in the mood I was in.

Stopping in place so suddenly the girls walked into me, I ignored that as I looked back at the stream thinking about what I'd seen. As a mermaid it was a life of magic and fairy tales (and those shooting stars… Were they real fairies?) And as a human, I had a life of technology and coffee shops, cell phones and a future career for so many years and then I would die. Put that way, it seemed obvious to me that I should choose to be a mermaid.

In the balance was my friends and family. The truth was, I couldn't help them if I became Melanie the human; they would be more victims in the hands of the oppressive. Even if I chose a career in trying to help through mere physical methods, I would be years from being able to help. Before me were the Syreni, I felt their care for me as I debated. Gentle fingers reached out, they were with me in whatever I decided, but I had a feeling I'd be shipped back home if I said I was human, never even knowing of them anymore. They'd go on serving whether I chose to be Sea Lord, mermaid and their friend, or a human without all of this.

Jill had always resisted being a mermaid, thinking herself a freak. I'd never understood my friend's struggle, but now I had the full taste of it. Being a mermaid meant helping others, how wonderful it could be! As I'd told Lorin, by surrendering to do what was asked of me by the Lord of the Water, I'd been in a position to help them. But at the cost of my humanity! How had I missed it?

What would I have been doing at home, being simply human? Manning the desk at the gym, being nice to people and swimming with friends. All good things, but nobody would be throwing themselves at my feet for that or wetting my feet with their tears. Not that I wanted that, but it showed the depth to which they loved me for being a mermaid doing her job.

With a sigh, I looked at the girls. They were waiting quietly, not even meeting my eyes purposefully, so they wouldn't yank my heart strings one way or the other. "So, what's it going to be?" I asked myself aloud, but I couldn't decide. I walked into the field, picturing in my mind's eye the trees of light. What had they been like close up, tangible or truly light? I stared into the sky, trying to see them but I was only looking at clouds and a blue sky.

Just then a trio of bluebirds swam the sky above and around us, circling one another. "Sing with us," they were calling in their sweet voices. My heart ached too much to voice a word, but I held up a finger and the three immediately came to sit upon it and my hand. "What am I to do?" I asked them. They sang to me, but it was only chirps I heard, losing their words in the moment. Then they flew off when I didn't respond. Despondent, I wandered off.

Finding one of the benches I'd noticed before, I sat, but I wasn't contemplating the view. In only moments I'd become Melanie that recycled, swam on a team and looked at the fireworks from Folsom Stadium on the Fourth of July. The grass felt brittle, the sky blank. Was I going to go home in a boat, or was I going to watch girls create fireworks from their palms, swim in oceans and use attuning to return life to nature. It really didn't seem like much of a choice, but there sure was a choice, and it was probably the biggest in my life. One that I would have to make every day. So far I'd been stumbling along, enjoying a ride not really sure of the consequences of my actions.

Could I believe in it enough to want to share it? I'd invited Ri'Anne along to experience it, sure at the time of what I believed. I did believe that mermaids were real now, but it was up to us to choose it, which meant to not be human. What a choice! I guess, what I wanted to know was, was it a greater choice? There was nobody to coach me, to tell me I was making the right decision.

Ok, what's next then? It was either call home… but there was nobody there, or go home and fight for it. Calling home felt like death, a gray existence, and to stay was life and wonder, excitement, thrill and possibly a lonely grave. Doing what I'd done today had taken bravery I didn't know I possessed, diving into a sinking ship, with people that would have killed me given the chance. Instead I'd returned the favor. *I'd killed people today!* The thought just came to me and sank in.

I had purposefully had their yacht dragged under with the sole purpose of stopping them permanently. Then I had left others swimming in a sea without a life raft, knowing, or thinking they would eventually succumb and drown. I felt ill as I was overcome with emotion and stood leaning on the back of one of the benches. I felt my gorge rise and I puked over the back of the chair, tears mingling with the vomit as I wept.

I felt the fingertips of the girls as they gathered close, but my heaves and tears did not stop as I imagined the floating forms that were dead at my bidding. I'd not seen their faces while performing it but now I couldn't forget them. Then, remembering what they had been doing enabled me to close my eyes to their accusations. *But did they deserve death for their actions?* I convulsed in a sob and knelt, still facing the back of the bench, my mouth tasting like a sewer. But I did not want it to go away. I should be feeling this pain! *It meant I still had a heart.*

After a bit I curled up in a ball generally praying for the dead, the sobs relenting to become gentle tears. Which got me to wondering what kind of lives their families led, were they dark like them, or did they not even know the darkness that was being sown through them?

Sitting up, I sighed and looked at the girls now kneeling before me in their pretty flowered outfits. Gone was the magical sense we'd been experiencing together, but not their warm presence, truly wanting to be with me, to experience the life that had been coming from me as their Sea Lord. How could I deny them that? It seemed mighty selfish of me to want to stay normal Melanie.

So far it had really been because of my friend Jill that I'd chosen her way. We were closer than sisters, Jill and I, whatever she wanted I wanted and vice versa. The funny thing is, she and I had been becoming mermaids together, encouraging each other, it was natural for her and for me it was a choice, but it hadn't been a difficult choice. She could resist it and still be a mermaid. Me though, if I resisted I would lose it all, and I didn't want to resist it. But it had been… changing me into something else. With a start I realized I had become like my friend, unknowingly, but I'd only keep it if I held to it.

Could I accept that I was no longer human? Being a mermaid had benefits, there were the obvious signs of a mermaid, beautiful hair and complexion, these things had shown up immediately. Then there was water breathing, increased swim speed, greater strength especially around water and instant travel to anywhere. Oh and that stream beneath the stream I'd stumbled into that had led to my current state. I'm sure there were many more surprising things to discover, so did I want to deny myself them? But really, being a mermaid meant making immediate, important and lasting decisions that affected people's lives, but at a cost to my self-willed, self-guided humanity.

People would try to use me, to harm me, to hurt my family. Right now my family was at risk because of me and the longer I waited to return, to help... They could be dead… and I stood up only to sit again, realizing I would have to be a mermaid to help. I was curling up again. Couldn't someone else do it, to help, to be the one to make it right for me?

The answer to that was yes, I could call on Jill. She would come if I called. Though to call her I'd have to be a mermaid to even make the call. To have Jill appear suddenly to my family would be as shock, but so what – my family would be saved! But I'd also be jeopardizing Jill's safety. *No, I loved her too much to risk her being hurt.*

I would have to face this myself and clenching my fist in heart wrenching agony, kill again. Fresh tears came to my face then, free flowing down as I stood determined. Not for me this time, but for those I would harm.

"Ok," I said aloud, though I had to repeat it until I could look into the eyes of the Syreni girls. My skin had turned dry and brittle, a remembrance of my Colorado skin without lotion. Taking a breath I thought to myself, *I'm a mermaid,* saying goodbye to my humanity. I attuned and the surrounding island turned green and bright to my eyes again. My skin became soft again, and the air cleared in my chest and as I exhaled all the tension I'd been feeling left me. I gulped, even the bitter taste in my mouth vanished and my face dried…

Looking at the four beautiful island girls gathered before me, I tried to imagine their life. School, study, but magic too as they had demonstrated. I wanted to go to their school, but I knew I would have to go to Boulder High in the fall. I might not be human anymore, but that didn't get me out of school and homework. The Syreni had a track and field similar to what I was used to. Did they enjoy pizza, movies, books and ice cream? They looked ready for anything, having trained their whole lives dependent on serving our kind. And ready *to serve*, looking their best in colorful island skirts, blouses and beautifully brushed hair.

The whole time they'd been here with me, not bored but sitting with me, touching me kindly, ready with looks of love. If my closest friends were here, they would not be more supportive. I had to repay them in kind. It was time I began by continuing where I'd left off.

"Has the one I asked to speak to arrived?" I asked looking into their beautiful brown eyes.

"Yes, Sea Lord," said one and she went to bring a young soldier forward who'd been in the background.

We sat down across from one another. Then after explaining the situation to him, he looked up, seeking some way to express their ways to me.

"Lord, our protection of you extends to you while you are here, but out there is your world and your problems. Send them here and we will be all over them like army ants. But we can only advise you if you would like to 'take' the ship military style. We can show how we'd do it, but you will be alone. And if you send the whole situation to us we risk injuring your own along with the perps. It is best if you come up with your own solution. Mostly because if we hurt one of yours you would feel like we were responsible.

We'd rather not have that between us. Knowing that, if you send them we will do our best to separate those responsible from those you think of as friendly." He paused like he might go on, showing his youth. I'd been listening to their explanations for a time now, these Syreni. He'd sounded like he'd recited a textbook, but the words were what I needed to hear.

Already Dad didn't like me bucking at his authority, and Uncle was trying to show me trust. Could I really throw soldiers at them? Did I really want my uncle and father exposed to me ordering about soldiers? I shook my head, no. I didn't want that for myself. I would lose them for sure.

No, "It is as I thought," I said, spreading my hands on my legs. I had hoped for someone else to take this from me, but that was impossible. I must risk my own life for my family, but how? Any violent approach would risk injuring those I loved. This wasn't going to be the last time those I loved got in harm's way, but I could minimize the damage by not involving others.

"Thank you," I told the soldier.

"M'lady," he said with a bow, his heart and eyes full of reverent delight. Then he returned the way he'd come. His actions made me feel weird. As if bowing and scraping were the norm and handshakes and tips of the head were the oddity. This was going to my head. I'd best get back among normal men that didn't worship the ground I walked on.

Standing, I waited for the girls to get up before I set off back down the trail to the stream within a stream. Would a transfer work from there? "I'm heading out," I told them. They gave me a look that said they knew. I could see in their eyes they wanted to come.

"Where I'm going, people may die." They nodded, like duh, you're a Sea Lord – of course you kill people. It's expected. *But it was my first time!* Was it supposed to be easy? Would I be ruthless someday? I was about to be ruthless now. Instead of sending the "perps" as the soldier had called them to the island to be free, I could send them somewhere bad, somewhere deep. I'd been told of the Syreni pits, but that is if I wanted them to live. So far they had given me no reason that they could be different, better.

Where did I know a place deep enough? Nowhere really, maybe where I'd met the girls of the sailboat the first time, that had been deep. I really did not like these thoughts, pre-thinking how to kill. I wanted to bless, but what would be a blessing to them, a hundred slaves to do their bidding? Maybe it should be the pits, could the islanders use them, help them reform?

"We know Mistress, we will do our best to stay out of the way." Their pleas were wearing away at my will, but I had one more insurmountable obstacle.

"So far, the humans," I can't believe I just said that of Dad and Uncle, "don't know me fully. I've decided not to show them soldiers, so how am I to explain your sudden presence?"

I had them there. They looked at one another, then back to me with disappointment in their faces. I wanted to be elated, but they looked so dejected that I had to hug them. I almost said, "Next time," but that sounded so adult and so like it was never going to happen that I was about to cave in right there and then.

"Besides," I said releasing them, "one of them was recently here and doesn't remember on purpose. We felt then that he might try to use us, your elders helped us to that decision." They nodded, and I could see they wouldn't ask again. It hurt me to see it, and I felt so horrible at the answer, but I had to return on my own and make my own future. Nobody else would get hurt if I could help it.

I turned to the stream with the Underriver to transfer from. It really was just the water itself that made it easier, so if I didn't go through the top stream it probably would be enough. Being surrounded by water wasn't necessary. Water made it a lot less tiring and I may be doing several out of water activities very soon. I should make use of the water since it was available.

Stepping into the stream, I felt for the rocks and they were there, solid as expected, but dipping a toe revealed the Underriver as well. It was like the rock was painted on solid water, but as my foot "stood" back upon the rock, it was still there. So very strange. The girls were still with me, so I asked them, since perhaps this wasn't considered teaching.

"We told you, we've never seen this before, but it has a familiar feeling. For all over our island, there are streams that run everywhere, but few are deep enough to swim in. It makes sense, so you have access to deep water whenever you have a need."

"Alright then. Thank you so much for sticking by me," and I dropped down into the water underneath. I barely had time to give the girls a wave goodbye. The resulting surprise of the girls was almost worth it as I disappeared without a splash.

But then I was down below seeing the amazing light trees of the Sky Lords and their thriving community. I was hoping it was the future too. It would be fun to see it, but then maybe I wouldn't. There were no mermaids in sight. Would I see myself?

So many distractions. It was time to leave, to head back to The Lazy Cloud, to see what this mermaid could do about the situation. I readied an electric charge, being sure I could get it back as needed, I readied transfers to the pit and lastly an escape back here if needed. I didn't want to be knocked out like before.

Where on the yacht to go? When I had left, the majority of the people had been below deck, and so I decided to check the upper command deck. If I was lucky, I could take out the driver and then work from there. But when I went to attune the location, there was something wrong, I was unable to find the boat. I was seeing a forest instead, like the boat was now in the middle of the tallest weeds imaginable, and there was nowhere to transfer to. The whole yacht from bow to stern, above and below decks was thick with greenery.

Trying for my dad, it was the same problem but worse. It seemed like he'd been run over by a grassy field. Well, if not Dad… that left Uncle. Now that Uncle knew about me, perhaps he was the ideal candidate. Surprised to feel openness near him, I asked for permission from The Lord of the Water, he gave me the understanding and it was not what I would have ever imagined.

28

The Garden of Gigi

Somehow The Lazy Cloud had met a giant beanstalk and the makings of a grass smoothie, and Uncle was out there riding it. I stood on a disc hundreds of feet up in the air. Uncle was wrangling a growing beanstalk like a calf at a rodeo, fighting it with his crutch. I'm not sure he was aware that he was hanging precariously in space. Down below was a wildly growing island of ferns, trees, grass and every plant that had been growing in pots. In the midst of it all was The Lazy Cloud, Dad, Ri'Anne and Gigi, but you couldn't see any of them for the crazy growth.

The Lazy Cloud seemed to be in the midst of a Gaea revolution. Every plant aboard had decided that Mother Nature's method of growing was too slow. The growth was taking place so fast it appeared the plants were being blown in a strange breeze. I'd seen Ri'Anne grow some things, but this had to be Gigi's work. Ri'Anne had been learning from her.

Standing on the transfer disc high in the sky, I had a clear view of the wild growth. Scouting for a place where I might check things out, I saw a grassy knoll below. Deciding to chance it, I aimed to make the transfer lower, and moving the disc down to the knoll, I stepped out. Immediately the smells of every cooking herb assaulted my nose and I sneezed. And all of it was alive curling up around my feet in seconds. If I stood still I would soon be wrapped up, so I shuffled my feet to keep that from happening.

I saw flowers spring up and in a matter of minutes go to seed and then become soil for the next generation. Some mad magic spell had been unleashed, and somewhere at the heart of it was Gigi and her plants. What I didn't get was what the intruders had done to upset Gigi, but whatever it was, it seemed to be their nature to do so. They cared only about their wants and desires so that even Gigi had reacted. I understood, I too had reacted by summoning the Leviathan against them.

Keeping my feet moving I tried to find a way within, but any opening closed up quickly, making me climb up and away as the growth advanced. I called out, hoping that Ri'Anne or Gigi might help me find a way within. Someone must have heard because I head branches breaking deeper within. I strayed closer to where I thought they were coming from. The sounds grew closer, someone was climbing through. I figured it to be one of *them*, since they didn't answer, and I gathered myself up ready for anything.

Then he was there, the growth parting before him. I saw a flash of light and before I could see what he'd done he'd pulled a pistol and raised it towards me.

"Put your weapon down," I said to him, automatically speaking his language. "And we can solve this together."

My knowledge of his language appeared to confuse him. He looked at his weapon hand as if he'd forgotten he'd just pulled the gun out and then looked at me like he should know me, but didn't see anyone he knew. "We know one another?" he finally asked.

I shook my head, "No, you have come aboard my family's yacht..." I stopped when he raised the weapon again. I was a hair's breath from disappearing. Shaking his head he pushed back an encroaching branch and asked, "How is it you speak our language?"

I shrugged waving about misleading him, "How is any of this possible? Perhaps it is part of this."

"Supposing we worked together, what then? Say we freed our comrades would *we* just leave you?" He shook his head, "We're not like that. Besides our boss would have our heads if we just gave in."

"You could be dead," I offered whispering in his ear, easily sliding into a transfer to appear standing behind him on a branch.

He was fast, whirling around in a split second to make a grab at me. It had been my mistake to talk to him after the move, but it was too late for regrets. I had only to touch him while making the connection to the pits on Syreni I'd prepared for. With the ground opening underneath him he fell back, windmilling his arms, at the last second he tried to get a shot off in my direction. The weapon fired but the hole to the pits closed up before the bullet could come through.

Then there was another behind me, "Hey, how'd you move so fast, and where…"

I didn't even turn, I remembering how I'd leapt to Jill when she'd been in the shark's mouth. It was that quick, but it seemed an eternity when I wrapped myself around him and I knew I was tiring. In my mind he was in a tunnel in the foliage that they'd created through it. He was coming from the tunnel, climbing up the way the other had come. I was down beside him, floating in the air.

Stepping off the disc I began to fall, faster than I'd wanted, and before I could grasp flight I brushed his foot. The touch was enough to send him after his friend, and then I was landing in a heap. Shaking my head of black spots, I gasped for air. Desperately trying to clear my vision. I was dead if there was another to attack me while I was down on my knees like this.

Beside me dropped an old fashioned alloy cigarette lighter which was still lit; my eyes drawn to the bright flame. The green 'ground' shrank away from the flame and the lighter dropped. Diving for it, I grabbed up the lighter before the hole could open up beneath it. As I held it the tentacles of growth that was seeking to fill the empty air and curl around my body shrank away from the flame.

"Hmm," and I waved the lighter around surprised at the plant's reaction. Every growing thing shrank back. So this is how they'd created the tunnel, a tunnel that was rapidly collapsing in above me. In moments I was enclosed in a sphere of brilliant green vines, which if I didn't maintain the flame would soon entangle me.

It was amazing that so small a flame was causing the retreat of the growth, but then the plants were more alive than others normally were. For want of a fairy or my friend Ri'Anne to give me a hand, I had little choice but to proceed and threaten them. Momentarily I thought of contacting The Lord of the Flame for some real fire, but that wouldn't be smart. I might just set the whole thing ablaze.

Tired, I had to proceed. Unable to see beyond the growth with my own eyes, I was relying totally on my attuned mermaid sight. Nearby was a buried thug, pinned down and unable to move. He was choking, the growth trying to strangle him. Making my way to him, I touched him while he was bound to send him away, and I dropped to my knees as blackness obscured my vision. *I can't keep doing that.*

On my hands and knees, weak and unable to move, the plants gave way beneath me because of the lit lighter I held and I was falling down through the semi-decayed plants and their roots. I clunked onto something hard, someplace aboard the yacht.

"Did you hear something?" came a woman's voice.

"Kennedy is that you?" called a man.

My eyesight returned, and I realized I was on top of the yacht. There was no place to hide on the top fair-weather deck, it was no more than a flat place to place a chair or towel behind the antennas and radar. The only way down was the ladder to the command deck.

"I don't like this," I heard the woman say. "We shouldn't have sent them away."

"I suppose you'd like it back in your cabin. You know the one I mean, back aboard the Sunset Prince."

"Very funny," the woman said with heat in her voice. Then in a sing-song voice, she told him, "Go check."

I felt her voice, as a wave that bounced across my weak attuning. If I wasn't already on my knees it would have dropped me. My head hurt resisting whatever it was she did, and it wasn't even aimed at me but at the fellow below.

"Alright, I'll check. But you don't have to use your witchy ways on me woman. I'd of gone anyway."

"I'm sorry dear, I'm just so afraid. How was I supposed to know that we'd encounter a fairy? The trap we'd planned was to capture a mermaid. But it happened too fast, and even if one of them was a mermaid, none of the girls reacted to the water we threw on them."

"Hush woman, the enemy is still about," and I saw a light coming through the brush towards the ladder as the man came towards me. Where was I to go? Another transfer might kill me. I had to find water.

"Wait. You're right. Separating isn't a good idea," and I saw the flame in the man's hand pause with him just out of sight, the last of the bramble between him and I parting. Then he was going back down the ladder and I let out the pent-up breath I hadn't realized I'd been holding.

I next heard him beneath me again, "You should reason with the fairy. Your kind and theirs have never been at odds." Fairy? They had to mean Gigi. So that was the secret to her long life. I wondered if she knew or if I should tell her when I get the chance

"Fat chance of that, you saw what Franz tried to do to her. Besides, I think I used up that ace already. It's lucky we got out alive."

"Well we can't stay here."

"Sure we can, she'll tire before too long. Then we'll take their life boat and slip away before anyone's the wiser."

"That's good thinking. Let's go get it ready. It's a good thing they have their swim deck down. They'll never know what happened to us."

I cringed on hearing that, I wanted to make them pay. But there was nothing I could do as tired as I was. It was best to let them go and not let on that I was ever near. When I heard them leave, I crawled lightly to the edge and peered down. I saw his light, but there wasn't much else to see. It was as dark as a cave down there. The greenery around me captured all the light of the sun above.

Pulling back, I paused to think about what they'd said. So Gigi was a fairy. That made a lot of sense. She was good with plants, more than good if you considered the wild growth. Gigi had to have a lot of power to produce these plants. I guess that came from being hundreds of years old, if she was as old as she claimed.

Waiting a few moments, I waited for the way to be clear. Then I went over the edge and down the ladder with quick steps, pausing to be sure the command deck was empty. My eyes lit upon a treasure chest! A case of water bottles. Scrambling for it, I reached in and pulled out several. Fumbling open the first, I gulped. But hardly could I get it to my lips before my body drained it dry. Its water passing right into me. Then it was empty. I needed more!

One after another I drank, replenishing the water in my body, until I felt whole again. Finally I was able to drink one normally and sipped at it, savoring its flavor. I felt so much better as I wiped my mouth of the last bit of water, unable to absorb the water – my body waterlogged.

I decided I should go after the woman and the man I suspected was the boss. I couldn't go as fast as I wanted to with the bramble trying to wrap me up. The tunnel they'd made had since closed up. Arriving at the swim deck, I saw the hatch to the lifeboat up and the boat gone into a well-lit tunnel – sunlight reflecting off the waves behind the yacht. I thought about trying to attune them, but if they had been expecting a mermaid, then I could be alerting them to my presence. I still had to find Dad, Ri'Anne and Gigi.

Going back up I went forward into Uncle Arlo's study. Working my way slowly through the dense forest I found Dad as I'd seen him before arriving. Grass had grown up around him. He'd been knocked out, a bump on his head and the revolver he'd taken from the taxi driver beside him. I tended to his bump, letting some water out to soothe him. It worked as it had on Ri'Anne, but he remained out. A mysterious green glow came from the stairwell nearby. All the growth seemed to be coming from there. Ri'Anne and Gigi the fairy must be below. Leaving Dad, I approached the stairs.

Great roots and plant stalks glowed with the energy, snaking from the stairwell, across the ceiling and out. Climbing over and under them, I nerved myself for what I might find. Stepping down one step at a time, I felt like I was descending into a nature temple. Water dripped from above. The plants here eerily snaked away from my flame, observing me like living things from the shadows. I felt a shiver realizing the vines were taking it personal. They were blocking me from retreating. I hoped the lighter's fuel held out or I was going to have to leave quickly.

Ri'Anne spoke when I rounded the corner into the brightly lit main cabin, "Is there someone there?" I felt relief at finding her. All the plants here glowed with throbbing green energy making it difficult to see. It was blocking my vision too.

"It's me Ri'Anne," I called to her. "Hold still, I'll get you free!" The great green light was spouting forth greenery so fast that at last I couldn't move forward. "Gigi you have to stop," I called. "It's over, please stop this."

"It's not her Mel," said Ri'Anne apologetically. She was near, but I couldn't see her because of the light. "Look up," she suggested and I turned my attention upwards and gasped.

There was the remaining thug, greenery was growing from every orifice, out of his eyes, everything. Glowing beside him, in some kind of trance was Gigi, covered over in crystalized green sap. Ri'Anne was staring at the thug. The boss lady had said he'd done something to Ri'Anne. Probably something I didn't want to know.

"Ri'Anne, look at me." I had to get her to stop. "Ri'Anne! He's dead, he can no longer hurt you," and I finally got her eyes to track to me.

"But the others? I can no longer sense them, and they brought fire." Her eyes glowed green realizing I held fire. *Oops!*

"Hey, hold on!" I yelled as branches reached out and grabbed my wrists, no longer afraid of the fire. I dropped the lighter as they squeezed hard, but it didn't go out. Lifting me off my feet, Ri'Anne put out the lighter in the only way she could, using my shoulder. "Ow!"

"I can be mean too, so stop it!" I yelled, as more branches wrapped about me and began to squeeze. "Ri'Anne, I'm warning you!"

"I'm Life! And you are Death, Melanie, siding with him!"

Barely able to breathe, I grabbed at the water within the plants. They couldn't grow without water. The vines withered, but that only made Ri'Anne go crazy. The whole ship shook as I felt giant tree-trunk sized vines turn from their upward path and spin down through the yacht towards me. Realizing I had but a second before I was flattened, I grabbed at her and her plants. What to do with them? Imagining salt water would halt their actions, I brought us to the bottom of the sea.

"Melanie don't…" and a tiny hand tried to stop me. I reeled back at the touch, feeling myself slipping away. Future Melanie wasn't playing this time, but I had to escape quickly. I already had attuned to Ri'Anne and the plants she was creating around me. It was only a matter of completing the connection – requesting permission from The Lord of the Water to the deepest, blackest water I could imagine. He gave it as normal and I practiced through – taking Ri'Anne with me.

"Too late, future Melanie," I said and then all was blackness as the yacht disappeared – *next time maybe.*

Transferring without water around me and taking as much of her plants with me as I could took it out of me. I blacked out a second before the sea rushed in to give me its strength. *Ah water!* It felt so good as it bubbled through me.

The deepest black ever known to man surrounded me and the water pressure was having its desired effect on the plants. Smashed, they died and disintegrated leaving only a bit of flickering green around Ri'Anne's hands.

Pushing through the growth now that it was no longer trying to attack me, I slid in beside my friend. She was lying limp. I pulled away all the half formed life that had been coming from her. "Ri'Anne!" I called, but she didn't answer. She was in shock, staring sightlessly, and I gave her a moment, repeatedly saying her name. But she didn't respond.

Growing desperate, I shook her, "Wake up Ri'Anne!" I cried. A dark ink came from her suit at my touch and I backed away smelling blood. There was a cloud of blood around her.

I should get her to a hospital immediately! Drawing her close again, I debated where to go? My first thought was the hospital in Boulder, but I had an image of me appearing there and the doctors rushing in and taking her from me. I couldn't have that.

The Syreni had patched up Uncle Arlo in some kind of medical facility. Surely they could help – they had to help! I reached for their beach where I'd played with Jill and the islanders. I felt it come to mind. Opening myself to the place, I gathered Ri'Anne in my arms and brought us through. The white sandy beach glistened, wet from rain. I could see the storm cloud crossing over the island. I stood in about two feet of water, and a wave crashed the beach, passing around me.

I almost dropped Ri'Anne on seeing her face, she looked bad. "Help," I whispered examining my friend. She was bleeding from many wounds. My heart crumbled, "Ri'Anne wake up, please! I'm so sorry."

Calling out again, I cried in desperation, "Hello! I need help!"

Coming Dear One, said a familiar voice in my mind, and then in a shimmer of light out stepped, one, two, and then three elders. They came from the light, stepping into the water and then as each one saw what I carried, tears came immediately.

"No! She's fine!" I denied their response, "She just needs medical attention."

The woman ran her hand over Ri'Anne's garment, it had changed since I'd last seen her. She now wore roots as fine as thread. The elder touched Ri'Anne face, understanding clear in her expression. She said nothing. Them and their rules! What a time to stand on principle. *Tell me what you see!*

"You'll be wanting her presentable," she said, going to the shore and picking some flowers. Hardly able to believe the woman's reaction, I stood there mutely as the woman carefully chose the blossoms she wanted. The other two elders stood in respect, tears continuing to come as they wept.

Her words tickled at a memory, and when she stepped up and laid them on Ri'Anne I was certain. With a wave of her hand, I felt cold to the bone as the plants grew in and down into Ri'Anne until she was whole, but still Ri'Anne didn't move.

"Hold on," I said, feeling ice crawl down to my toes as a freezing sense of déjà vu ran through me. "Wait a second! Were you just gardening?" I asked her.

She nodded, showing off her dirt stained hands. "Were you watching me?"

I shook my head shaking off the chill. "No, but I've been here before – in this moment!" Glancing around I somehow expected something to happen, but nothing. I tried explaining, "I was observing myself holding Ri'Anne, talking to you and you were gardening. Just like this, but not here."

"Your future self," said the young elder. He looked at his hands, debating what he could say, and then told me. "You tried to alter the past, partly succeeding. Unfortunately the result is the same."

"You told me then," I said looking at the gardener, "that a Sky Lord could alter the past."

"It's true. They travel so fast that time bends. They see the future and past, to dabble," the young man continued. "They're not the only ones, as you've recently discovered, that can see the past and venture there."

"I can go there?" I asked surprised, but saw he wouldn't say anything else, having said too much already, probably only saying it because my future self had dabbled already in trying to alter the past, my present.

"It isn't wise, is it?" I asked, but he remained kindly stone faced.

"Our lives are yours, Mistress," the third elder said. "The Lords of the Sky and Sea are the lords of their domain. You must use your best wisdom in the exercise of your realm. We cannot instruct, or in this case make a judgment. If you feel that your cause is best served trying to alter the past, which is your judgment to make, then you must. The decision is not ours. We must not interfere."

I paused at this before I did something rash. Everything in me said this shouldn't have happened. Glancing at Ri'Anne lying in my arms, lifeless, I knew I had to do what I could. My rash temper had brought about this and there was no way I could explain to her parents or mine. How could I face them like this?! But it was more than this. I'd chosen to be a mermaid, and that meant action. Somehow I'd succeed in doing it, I had to! No matter how many attempts it took.

Thinking about it… I'd failed to stop myself already using only a transfer. Maybe in combination with swimming into the past using the Underriver was the key. My future self hadn't known, or used it. I couldn't believe I was contemplating it, but Ri'Anne needed to live. She'd wanted to be a fairy, and had become one. If only I'd seen it! If I could convince my past self not to kill Ri'Anne… It had to be tried. My past self had to be stopped from killing our friend.

Hold on, though. I'd viewed my future self before, being her past self. Would my past self be watching me now? Maybe I could convince her now and be done with it! Oh, but if she was here then that would mean I would have to go back anyway, because I'd already done so for her to be here!

Looking, there were no rocks to hide behind like I had done. The beach was clear in every direction and the closest trees had nobody hiding behind them. Maybe not them, but somewhere else… but where? Turning about, I gazed behind me at the sea and then froze at a movement, there a young girl hid in the water, her face immediately recognized as the face I saw in the mirror every day.

My feet were moving before I even thought about it, walking down into the water, leaving the elders watching from the shallows. Soon I had Ri'Anne floating and I came to stand before Melanie, my past self, her glorious brown hair floating in curly waves behind her, reminding me of how the fish acted as a gown. Her eyes radiated a depth that read my every motive.

"What do you want of me?" Melanie asked of me, tears floating off her face as she looked at Ri'Anne.

"I have to ask this of you," I told her, "Neither of us wants this, and it is too late for me. My future self tried to warn me, and failed. I'm going to go back, and hope that we can work together to prevent this."

"What happens," and she choked up a second before adding "…that results in this?" and she reached out and then took her hand back, unwilling to touch Ri'Anne. Shutting her eyes she said, "Tell me and go."

Knowing the events that lead to this could change, I told her only the feelings, "We kill her. When anger strikes, don't treat her as you would yourself. She cannot withstand what we can."

"I didn't kill her," Melanie accused me, "You did."

I knew she spoke rightly, that is how I had felt when watching my future self, like it was happening to someone else. I sought for an Underriver and sank into a stream, thinking of the time when I'd arrived by the jet plane. There, I saw myself being air sick. No, I had to go further, to the car, to the gym when Dad had convinced me to bring Ri'Anne…

Yes, that is when. I saw Ri'Anne swimming, but not me coming up from below. Then I realized, I hadn't gone yet. It was time. Giddy with hope, I set Ri'Anne down, promising to save her and then I retrieved the fairy dust. Uncapping the dust, I doused myself and then using all my will zipped through the wall of the Underriver at the speed of the fairy.

29

Take Two

As Melanie hopped through the past, she had to go re-do those things her future self had done for her, which burned precious fairy dust time that could have been spent trying to get her past self to listen to her. Past-self was horribly stubborn, which made her realize that she herself was no picnic. Somehow she had to work through that, she was running out of time!

Arriving at the yacht after she left it with Jordan and the others, tiny fairy Melanie watched as Gigi and Ri'Anne played with plants and she looked for an opportunity to intervene.

Gigi watched with silent amazement as Ri'Anne grew the squash plant from a seed to ripe fruit in minutes with her music. Her pupil had far outpaced her simple teachings. If only the girl would be careful in front of the Tangs, the hijacking thugs that had taken over The Lazy Cloud after their yacht had mysteriously been sunk. Gigi still didn't have the full story on that, but she suspected that Melanie was at the heart of it though she couldn't prove it.

Picking a squash from the new-grown plant, Gigi smelled its tender freshness. It seemed so surprising to her that the vegetable had the same ripe texture of one grown over a period of months in the open sun with good soil. Slicing it open, she tasted a sample, "Ah so succulent… Mmmm," and then Gigi scooped out the seeds to prepare it for the dish she had in mind for the evening meal.

Gigi smiled, glad at how life worked out. Unwittingly, Gigi had been drawn into a world of magic and mermaid intrigue because of Melanie's quirky secretiveness. And thankfully so! The girl she'd dismissed of no importance… Ri'Anne… was the real gem. Ri'Anne was so unlike her secretive friend – carefree and fun. Melanie's gift with languages had been a real let down. Gigi had been really hoping that Melanie had held the key to unraveling her past.

Helping Ri'Anne with the remaining squash plant, together they plucked the fruit of the vine and set them in the window for later. Returning from their swim with the dolphins quickly, Gigi was glad she had chosen to join her, though she could see that something was bothering Ri'Anne. Gigi hoped she'd open up to her on it, but the girl was now playing with the empty squash vine, growing it into a giant ribboned bow. Going through puberty was difficult enough. Add magic and these girls were having troubles. Gigi laughed to herself as she watched Ri'Anne, the girl not caring that a Tang was watching her on the sly.

It didn't bother her, the Tang's presence. They'd be gone quick enough, and their life back to normal. The Tangs, with their worldwide crime organization, felt they could get away with anything. But they'd picked the wrong bunch of girls to mess with. Gigi knew enough of the future to see that they got the bad end of the stick, but not enough to see exactly how it was done.

If it wasn't for Melanie, she would see, but at least she knew enough. It was something that girl Melanie did that caused the problem, at least she knew why now, if not how. Sometime she'd like to ask her what Melanie did to block her. But by merely asking her, Gigi would be revealing she knew Melanie did something, and Gigi might be revealing she had foresight. And that must not happen!

So Gigi had tried piecing together the puzzle on her own. Melanie knew things too, predicting their first bad weather before there was any sign. Gigi thought Melanie's prescience was limiting her own, but the blocking was unpredictable. Sometimes her sight was dim near the girl, and other times she would see normally. What bothered Gigi most was that since Jordan had come aboard Gigi was nearly blind. It was uncomfortable and the reason she'd been so foul with Melanie, taking it out on her. Still it had shocked Gigi, her anger. Wanting to make it up to the girl, Gigi was hopeful she could make amends. She knew Melanie wasn't trying to be spiteful. The girl was simply unaware she was the cause.

Holding a stem upright, Ri'Anne twirled it, breaking into Gigi's thoughts. The squash plant she'd been playing with before had turned to dirt in the planter. Gigi picked up a like shoot, twirling it too, drawing on the girl's joyful mood. She was truly delighting in the current state of the plants, more so than making them grow. Gigi could almost hear them as Ri'Anne said they spoke to her of the sun, wind and rain they loved so much.

Hearing gentle wind chimes, Gigi paused to listen. They caught at her attention, making her listen hard to catch their melody. Then suddenly she was feeling something tiny crawling on her neck! Gigi squeaked, jumping about two feet into the air! She came down and twirled, brushing at whatever was in her hair, but there was nothing there!

Ri'Anne gave her a look, and Gigi tried pushing down her shock as she did her apron. So used to seeing her future, never in her life had she felt such a shock. Her heart was pounding, and then feeling the critter again at her neck – she slapped the spot. Nothing!

Gigi hated not being able to "see" what was happening! She'd grown accustomed to knowing the future and living her life from that knowledge. Again, the thing landed on the nape of her neck and Gigi almost screamed. It was payback for all the pranks she'd spoiled in her life. Knuckling both of her fists to keep from freaking out, Gigi took a deep breath and then let it out, her skin crawled as the thing moved. Then in the back of her mind she realized whatever it was had two hands and two feet, and not something with more legs. Some pint-sized human was on the back of her neck and Gigi's knees knocked as she whimpered. *Be gone!* she ordered the thing. But then she heard a girl crying in her ear.

It was the tiny sound she heard coming from the girl at her neck that froze her in place. She was sobbing, and now that Gigi wasn't reacting, the girl crumpled against Gigi's neck. Her own knees went weak when Gigi placed the voice, and she reached out for something to steady herself. It was Melanie. A thousand questions came to mind, but foremost was what was the matter with the girl?

Unable to keep to her footing, Gigi went and dropped onto the couch. As she spun in place to sit, Gigi had a momentary view of Melanie hanging in the air in the classic pose of a fairy. Then in a blur of light she streaked out of the room, rounding the corner towards the stairs up. In an instant she was gone, but not before Gigi had seen dark tear streaks running down her face. Pondering that, Gigi was glad that at least she'd come to her. It had been harder than expected to get Melanie to open up to her. Maybe some of the ice between them was finally melting. But if she expected Melanie to open up, Gigi felt like she would have to do some of her own.

Hearing wind chimes again Gigi gripped her fingers closed, knowing that Melanie was back hovering behind her ear. How did the girl move so fast, and what was going on? Melanie said she was a mermaid, but was acting in every way like a fairy. Overwhelmed, Gigi slid to the floor, wanting something more solid beneath her.

Then, another Tang entered the room and demanded food. Gigi was too weak to move, so Ri'Anne went to get it for him. Taking a bowl of the squash chili for each of them, Ri'Anne rounded the corner of the counter where they'd been growing the squash to go to the nook table. Gigi felt a tiny hand on her ear. Melanie was tense and that made Gigi sit up straight. But nothing happened when Ri'Anne delivered the bowls… What was Melanie expecting to happen?

Turning her back on the Tangs, Ri'Anne returned to her plants. Having stopped the quivering in her knees and wanting to watch, Gigi made herself get up and go join her. Not feeling Melanie at her neck anymore, Gigi looked back, but Melanie wasn't in the air where Gigi had been sitting either.

Ri'Anne glanced at Gigi, a content smile on her face. It was difficult returning the smile when it seemed they were on a collision course with disaster. Gigi saw contentment in Ri'Anne. The girl would be happy even if the world could come to an end right then, she had her plants to play with.

"Do you have any tree seeds?" Ri'Anne asked, interrupting Gigi's thoughts. "I'm dying to grow some."

Gigi did, but it was a scary thought to have a tree growing wild in the bottom of the yacht. "Where would you plant it?" Gigi asked, trying to throw the girl off. "How about some beans? We could use some."

"Alright, you start them," Ri'Anne suggested, encouraging Gigi to use magic. Then Ri'Anne rounded the counter to go back to the guys to retrieve their bowls. One of them requested more, the other leaving up the central stairway. Again, Gigi felt tiny Melanie behind her, pulling at her hair. Her presence made Gigi nervous.

Feeling like time was of the essence, Gigi worked quickly to get the seedlings started. It required only the barest touch of their song to move them out of their seeds.

"Oh, well done!" Ri'Anne said coming to stand beside her. "Here," and Gigi saw Ri'Anne touch her magic to hers, and the plants became full size in a blink. Giving a gasp, Gigi felt a well inside her open up. The girl had drawn on a reservoir of strength that Gigi hadn't known existed within her.

"I knew you could do it," Ri'Anne said. "We're so much alike, you and me." Leaning into Gigi, she whispered, "You're a fairy, aren't you? Do you fly? I'm a fairy if I'm anything, but don't tell Melanie. She'd be upset – she wants me to be a mermaid. I'd wanted to be, really I did. But deep down I've always longed to be a fairy." Then Gigi watched the girl fly over the counter and Gigi reeled back and screamed in shock. Feeling blood rushing to her head, Gigi knew she was about to faint and bit her lip hard to keep from falling over.

At her scream, Ri'Anne tripped and splashed food on the man. Before Ri'Anne could react, he exploded, wheeled back and slapped her hard. Feeling tiny hands give her a push, Gigi came around the counter to try to ease the situation, unwittingly holding two of the tiny bean stalks in her hands. The look of pure fury on Ri'Anne's face stopped Gigi in her tracks. Seeing the plants, Ri'Anne's eyes turned with an idea. Suddenly, the plants in the room sprung up and wrapped themselves around the guy.

Then in cold fear, Gigi stood transfixed as Ri'Anne took the beans from her and stuck one in the man's mouth and the other in his shirt. They immediately started to grow. She was going to kill him by making the plants grow into him. Because it was Gigi's magic that had started them, she felt Ri'Anne tap her for their growth and she'd be responsible

"No Ri'Anne, don't," and Gigi clamped down on the power. "He only slapped you."

"They intend worse, admit it," she rounded on Gigi, her fury diminishing. "I'll not become their plaything when I can do something about it. If you have a better idea, I want to hear it!"

Gigi saw in the man's eyes that given the chance, he'd repay Ri'Anne ten times what she'd done. As much as Gigi wanted to deny it, she knew that Ri'Anne was right, but that didn't justify killing them. Feeling hands on her neck, pushing her, she suggested, "Wrap them all up until the authorities can be notified."

"I can do that, but I'll need your help. You have a well that's infinite." Gigi nodded reluctantly, since it had been her idea. She abhorred death, the thought of it made her feel ill at ease.

Feeling Ri'Anne knocking at the door to her mind, Gigi opened the door a little for her. The plants in the room tripled in size in minutes as the power within her flowed to Ri'Anne and the girl shaped them. The plant in his mouth had grown to occupy the space it had. The man struggled to breathe around the wad of bean sod in his mouth, held in place by a pair of tough roots that he failed to chew through.

With him bound, Ri'Anne turned her attention to the rest of the Tangs. The cabin filled with growth as she readied herself. It was a delight to see so much life, even if its purpose was to hurt others. Tentacles shot up the front and back stairs seeking to bind the Tangs above. There were sudden shouts, and Gigi suspected that Ri'Anne's plan was working. Then she heard, "Use fire." It was the woman. "They can't stand fire, as a forest fears fire, these unnatural plants hate fire even more."

Ri'Anne screamed suddenly, and Gigi glanced at her. Fury had replaced her calculating look, the fire seemed to be working. The calculating look came back and Gigi heard a man shout in pain, and then suddenly Ri'Anne froze. She'd taken her eyes off her captive. He'd gotten loose and had put a knife to her throat drawing blood. His intention was clear, that she stop all her efforts.

The plants stopped their upward spiral, and without Ri'Anne giving them strength, Gigi knew it was only a matter of time until they found her out. In a minute, Gigi saw bright light boring down the stairwell towards them. The plants shrank back as quickly as they'd grown, retreating from the foot-long spike of fire. Following the flame into the room, one of the Tangs held a mini torch, waving it around until the plants withered to their roots.

It hurt Gigi as much as it was hurting Ri'Anne as their plants were burned to the ground. Then they had Ri'Anne and bound her hands behind her. When the knife was withdrawn, Ri'Anne collapsed in relief, though her eyes continued to track the torch. Her captor stepped away from her for a second to take up the flame thrower. Then, kicking back on the couch he put up his feet and sat to guarding Ri'Anne. Her shoulders finally slouched as she capitulated.

When the tension faded, the others left. Gigi followed them up to get away to have a look at the sea and get some fresh air. The Tangs up there gave her a look, discussing Melanie and the girls from the sailboat. Apparently they'd given them the slip. *Way to go Melanie!* They talked of having backtracked to search for the sailboat, but neither them or it had been found.

Gigi wondered too, but she knew Melanie was safe. But what had Melanie done with the girls? If she hadn't seen miniature Melanie she would have thought the worse between Melanie having Gigi jump at shadows and having her "somewhere" on the yacht as a full-sized gal. Gigi didn't really know what to think. Or had Melanie shrunk them all down? But why the tears, especially on seeing Ri'Anne? Did it have something to do with the "vision" of the future Melanie had seen? They'd gone through that, and Gigi thought that Melanie had accepted that the future wasn't predetermined. Gigi should know, because the future wasn't certain, she knew her decisions affected the outcomes.

Hearing a pair of familiar male voices, Gigi turned to see Arlo and Jeb. She was surprised to see them. Arlo hobbled along, and he sat beside her while Jeb came around Gigi and put his hand on her shoulder. She surprised herself and leaned into him, even though her old habits wanted her to shrink from the touch. It felt good to finally let go her ancient habits and let someone in. If she were to become entangled with anyone, the widowed father of a mermaid sounded about right.

Deciding to give into impulse, she responded to his touch as she'd seen Melanie do so readily and turned to give him a hug. The wall she always kept up suddenly came down and she wanted to put her head on his shoulder. It felt so good to have someone so close, she'd forgotten what it could feel like. Trying to keep her emotions at bay, she asked him quietly, "How did you get free?"

Jeb pulled back, gave her a look and a shrug. "Our bonds were suddenly loosed, and the room opened." *A tiny Melanie could have done that.* Then turning about he said, "I don't see them,

Arlo. Gigi, do you know where they put the girls?" His concern for his daughter was written on his face.

"I don't know," she admitted. "Though I don't think the Tangs know either. Melanie and the three girls from the sailboat are missing." Should she mention tiny Melanie? "While I've been up here, I've been listening to them. Apparently when they learned of their disappearance they went in search of the sailboat - but they found no sign of them or it."

Arlo said, "But there's no wind. They couldn't have gotten far without it, even if they had made the swim to the sailboat."

"Mermaid…" Jeb started and then looked sideways at Gigi. Did she know about his daughter being a mermaid? She gave him an assuring glance, not wanting his distrust. Now that they'd hugged, she wanted more of his attention, not less.

"Oh come on," Arlo said on top of his brother's statement. "There's no way… No hold on, when Jill rescued me, the last image I had of her is her swimming away at the bottom of the sea and then disappearing…"

"But I thought you rescued yourself," Gigi interrupted him.

Arlo nodded, "That's the version I remember, but the data backups show something entirely different occurring. It has been tough believing that what I see on them actually occurred, because I'd rather believe what I remember. But it explains so much, and makes way more sense than me simply rescuing myself with a broken leg."

"I know people tend to remember things differently than what actually occurs. Are you saying you don't remember at all?" Gigi asked.

Arlo shook his head. "My memory of the events are different than what is on my backups, but the scientist in me knows the backups to be the real deal. I'd really like to know how they changed me and my equipment… Everything, logs, notes. Even my own handwriting, changed to match what I know to be 'true.' Yet I found copies that were different. All the data on-board as of a few days ago has been altered. But they aren't gods, since obviously they missed my pending saves. It can only be when I was stuck at the island without satellite coverage that I'd saved everything. But without the satellites, the data just sat there until some later time. I'm not a computer guy, so I can't explain it more than that."

Gigi looked to Jeb and he just shrugged. Protective dad that he was, he was accepting this part of Melanie as if he'd always known. Gigi had noticed the strange father-daughter bond they shared, Melanie fiercely loyal to her dad. But now she saw that it flowed just as strong the other way.

Going back to their discussion on the missing girls, Gigi thought out loud, "So you think Melanie did this disappearing act with the girls? Then they are still aboard, but invisible?" It sounded far-fetched to her own ears as she said it.

"And the sailboat?" Jeb looked to Arlo. "It was filled to the gills with fish. It's possible it sank."

"Could be," Arlo admitted, but he didn't look convinced. "I don't know nearly enough to give an answer to any of this."

Gigi wanted to downplay Melanie's abilities. A mermaid with a tail she could buy. Even one that swims fast like a dolphin… But invisibility? That was stretching it. Gigi had seen many strange things that when explained were not much at all. The first time she'd seen a hot air balloon, she'd thought it magic. Then airplanes and so much more. But in the end it had turned out to be no more than science. On the other hand, how to explain seeing and feeling Melanie only a few inches tall? And flying about with a quickness. It had to be explainable on some level.

"Science, it's all science," Gigi said into the silence, even if she couldn't imagine it at the moment. It turned out to be exactly what the boys wanted to hear. She could see them relaxing. Two tiny hands grasped her ear tight and Gigi winced.

"I agree," Arlo said and Jeb nodded his head. "Some things go unexplained for decades, but eventually we find the answers."

"I found your daughter, Jeb," Gigi stated and felt the hands on her ear tremble.

"What, where?" Jeb said looking around, "Don't be fooling…"

"Melanie, come on out," Gigi said and waited. The two of them looked around, expecting a life-sized Melanie, but Gigi felt the girl come to sit on her shoulder. Turning to look at her, Melanie looked different, haggard. Worse than before. "Right here," and Gigi held out her hand to the fairy-sized lady. Even then they seemed to overlook her.

Seeing that they weren't going to notice her, Melanie flew into the midst of them and popped. There was a shower of sparkles, and Arlo fell back against the bulkhead and Jeb reached for the railing.

Then before either of them could say anything, Melanie gave them one of her words.

"Dad, get the gun – but don't use it. Uncle, you need to be prepared to stay atop the forest – I'll need you. Gigi, give all you have to its growth – you know what I mean." Then hovering in the air, hands on her hips she eyed them all. "I need all of your help." Lastly, to Arlo she said, "Uncle, you get your yacht back."

"How do you know?" Uncle asked pushing off the wall, still unable to believe his eyes.

Melanie shook her head, and Gigi recognized the silent-faced Melanie. But then she unexpectedly started to cry, hard. Then she dropped the bomb, "I kill Ri'Anne, and I'm here to stop myself."

They all stared at her in disbelief. Her dad said in the silence, "Melanie, I just saw her – she's fine."

Melanie sniffed back her tears, and then bobbed in the air, and spoke with the authority Gigi remembered well, "Dad, in a few minutes the forest I mentioned will explode from the plants below, quickly taking over the yacht and anything moving. I have done all I can to prepare for this moment, but I have to go because my time is not yet. I love you," And Gigi saw a flash of light, and then a brief glimpse of a wall of growth where they all stood and Melanie was gone.

Jeb stood shaking himself off. "So far Melanie has been spot on with each of her predictions. I'm going for the gun," and he turned and left them. Wait, what gun? Couldn't they use it on the Tangs? And if Gigi didn't help Ri'Anne, there would be no forest! And Ri'Anne wouldn't have to die! Turning, she followed after Jeb to discuss it with him. She glanced back to see Arlo staring about in disbelief. He looked to be one surprise away from madness.

Catching up to Jeb, they descended the stairs and Gigi stopped him. One of their Tang guards passed them going up. "Can't we use it?" Gigi asked and nodding up to the guard, "On them?"

Jeb shook his head, "Wait until you have kids," he said, thinking Gigi the thirty-year-old she looked to be. "You'll do anything for them and protect them by handing over the weapon. It's why I never used it before. All they'd have to do is threaten Melanie and I'd be lost. No, we have to do it Melanie's way."

With that he went down and left Gigi standing there. Gigi was a marksman with a gun. But the thought of a gunfight that could injure the others, that swayed her. Yet was Melanie right in her predictions? She sure seemed to be, as certain as if it was now the past to her. That made Gigi tremble. Seeing the future was one thing, but traveling to it or the past, that was something else.

The girl was strong, but she was still a young girl and so was her friend, plus Jordan and her friends… Where were they anyway? Gigi wondered if there were more tiny girls hiding hereabouts. At that size, there were hundreds of places to hide on The Lazy Cloud and never be seen.

Deciding Melanie had shrunk them, impossible as it was, it wasn't a vanishing act. Most magic tricks were based on misdirection. So if they became small quickly, it would appear as if they'd vanished. How they got to that size on the other hand was a mystery. One Gigi felt sure Melanie wasn't going to reveal for the asking.

Smelling smoke below near the galley, Gigi went to investigate.

In the main room she saw Ri'Anne and the Tang in a fight of wills. Ri'Anne grew a plant one direction and the Tang would flame it out. The plants had come back and were everywhere. Ri'Anne had been busy. Every niche had something growing in it. With a wide swath of flame, the man chuckled as he burned away the plants that had sprung up beside him. Then vines were winding around his legs, and he kicked screaming, turning on the torch blasting away and turned it towards Ri'Anne. Ri'Anne dove off her chair, but not before she was singed.

"Teach you to mess with me darling," he boasted, plucking up Ri'Anne since her hands were still tied and shoving her onto the couch. A big root shot out from under the couch where it had been hiding under its skirt and wrapped about him like a python. He dropped the torch and it went out. Ri'Anne cheered and stood to watch her pet lift the man wriggling off the floor, he was crying out as she squeezed him.

"Ri'Anne stop it, you're hurting him," Gigi said coming up to the girl, putting her hand lightly on Ri'Anne's shoulder.

Ri'Anne's eyes burned holes in Gigi's with her look, and then she shook her head and Gigi saw the girl she remembered. The man sank to the floor, and the root eased its stranglehold on him. Gigi heard him gasp for air.

"I'm going to kill you," he said to Ri'Anne but she didn't understand him and she looked to Gigi for an interpretation. Gigi wondered why Ri'Anne didn't have Melanie's trick with languages.

"So what are you going to do with him?" Gigi asked her. "He wants to kill you now."

Sassily Ri'Anne sat back on the couch, "He won't. His boss will have his head. Want to unbind me?" and she shoved her hands towards Gigi.

Anything to ease the tension. Gigi went to get the scissors. Returning, she freed Ri'Anne's hands. "Then why don't you let him go?" Gigi asked her.

"Because he'll get all blustery, he'll want to burn my plants and probably a hundred other mean things he could do. I like him just as he is." In a bit of mischief, Ri'Anne made a vine grow up around his head like a crown, and it sprouted big fat pink and green flowers. All the while he glared at her.

Hearing a trill of laughter, the two of them turned towards the stern, the woman was laughing at the Tang Ri'Anne had tied up. She then glanced at them. "Fairy, release my man please and I'll see you go free." Gigi felt the woman's lie, and was about to warn Ri'Anne, but the root had already fallen off.

A look of pure joy was on Ri'Anne's face. "She called me a fairy," Ri'Anne breathed looking so pleased.

Then the man was behind her and before Gigi could warn the girl, he lifted his fist and slammed it down on the back of Ri'Anne's head. Ri'Anne collapsed into Gigi and fell to the floor. He then picked up the torch and clicked it back on. It coughed a couple times before he got it started, and then he went to work on the plants – not missing the growth under the couch. Gigi saw him contemplate burning up Ri'Anne, and then changed his mind yanking the girl aside to burn the plants around her.

Gigi knelt beside Ri'Anne and felt for a pulse on her neck. She lived. So this wasn't the moment that Melanie spoke of. Could it get any worse? Then Gigi was feeling a tug, Ri'Anne had awakened, though she hid it. Gigi knew she had a choice. Refuse Ri'Anne and Melanie, and Ri'Anne would live or let Melanie have her way. In her inner debate, Gigi missed her opportunity because Ri'Anne didn't wait. She grabbed at all the plants that still lived around them and threw them at the man and woman. The lady fled and the man was swept off his feet.

He tumbled, turned and yelled, "I've had enough!" Opening the flame wide, he turned it on Ri'Anne. She started to scream. The swimsuit that Gigi thought colorful started to burn and scream as a plant screamed when being burned. Then Ri'Anne hammered at Gigi's mind demanding her power.

Gigi knew if she gave in the girl would give Melanie what she wanted - the forest and somehow die in the process. But she couldn't stand by and watch Ri'Anne burn either. That would be fulfilling the future too! How was she to know what action stopped her dying? Remembering that Melanie had left, she tried looking at the future and saw plainly if she didn't help Ri'Anne now he'd cook her alive! And if she helped, at least she'd live and return to her beautiful self. Opening up, Gigi felt the power flow towards Ri'Anne and the plants were able to grow to shield her. Gasping, Gigi looked at Ri'Anne, she'd been badly burned. How could she deny her as he turned up the heat?

A glow built up around Ri'Anne as she required more and more power to fight off his attack. Ri'Anne was slowly pushing him back, and then with a shout of triumph he laughed, turning the torch on full and the flames reached towards Ri'Anne again. Gigi had no choice but give her everything. Even so he continued to laugh, fighting the forest back and then he turned the torch at Gigi, surprising Ri'Anne. But Gigi had her future sight and had been ready for it, ducking away.

Thinking Gigi would burn, Ri'Anne defended her by trying to entangle him. The room grew green as plants took over the ceiling and grew across every surface, but they couldn't get close to him as he returned his attention back to her. They just weren't growing fast enough and he would soon have the upper hand. Gigi melted into the flow, feeling herself disappearing and she let Ri'Anne take the controls. It was all or nothing now. Melanie better show up soon or they were dead anyway. The pull tripled and her view grew dim, Ri'Anne was wrapping Gigi in some kind of green shell to protect her from another attack.

Suddenly the torch coughed, flickered and went out. In a shout of triumph, Ri'Anne made the plants go all through him. He screamed and screamed, and it was the worst sound Gigi had ever heard before it became quiet.

Then "together" they were going for those above. All the seeds Gigi had at her disposal sprouted, became hardy plants and shot up the stairwell seeking those above. They met resistance. Those above had flame, Gigi could feel it, but not the torch he'd wielded. No longer constrained to the room, they took over the yacht. The Tangs were retreating to the command deck. Everywhere else, the conquest of the yacht was certain. Already they'd trapped a couple of the Tangs.

Then there was Melanie, life-sized. Arguing with Ri'Anne, and Gigi felt the plants reach out to hurt Melanie. Gigi wanted to stop it, but she couldn't move, couldn't speak. Then suddenly the plants binding her were gone and Gigi sank to the floor, her head swimming. Feeling a soft hand, she tried to clear her vision. Gigi heard her before she saw her, Melanie helping her sit up and getting her to drink some water.

Feeling quickly better, Gigi thanked the girl and waited for her sight to return. When Gigi could see, she saw that Melanie knelt beside her, looking defeated. "Are you all right?" Melanie asked.

"Tired, but ok." Gigi felt like she could sleep for a weak. "Which Melanie are you?" Gigi asked the girl confused.

"I'm the one that killed Ri'Anne. The other is now killing her. It seems I'm doomed to repeat myself in failure…" and Melanie let out a giant sized sigh.

At her words, Gigi felt a thrill of foreboding. It wasn't future sight per-se, but she knew Melanie couldn't give up. Ri'Anne's life hung in the balance. If Melanie gave up, then Ri'Anne was truly lost. If Melanie believed once she could alter the outcome, Gigi had to encourage her to believe again.

"You once told me the rules, 'that the impossible is possible, possibly.' It doesn't sound like you to be defeated," Gigi said watching Melanie carefully. Only a glimmer of a spark shone in her eyes for a second before going out.

Shaking her head Melanie tried to explain, "I've been in the past trying to fix things. Gone all the way back to when we first left home, but it seems all I've done is muddle with time."

"You've done more than that," Gigi said determinedly. "Ri'Anne became a fairy on account of you. All your manipulation has influenced her," and Gigi left off. She was making some of that up, but she felt it to be true. One thing for sure, she couldn't let Melanie feel like she'd failed her friend. "Now you need to go do what you didn't do before."

"But I cannot travel in time anymore." Melanie couldn't say she had no more fairy dust, not to Gigi anyway.

"And you tried that, but what haven't you tried?" Gigi prompted. "Use some of that vaunted authority of yours and order her back alive! Now get to it!"

Melanie nodded wearily rising. A light of determination flickered in her eyes. It could be resignation, but Gigi hoped it was the former. Afraid she had pushed the wrong button, Gigi watched Melanie as she stood to do her disappearing act. It was strange seeing it, as close as she stared she couldn't see how Melanie did it. One moment she was there, the next she was gone.

Gigi sat there with tears coming to her eyes. Even though she hoped Melanie would find a way, the truth that Melanie had been saying for some time now was finally sinking in. Ri'Anne was dead. In the short time she'd known Ri'Anne, they'd formed a bond. It seemed as if all the sparkle in her life would be extinguished if Melanie failed. For once she didn't want to see the future and closed her inner eye to it. The last thing she wanted to "see" was Ri'Anne returned by Melanie lifeless.

30

Bind Them Up

The grass felt especially silky where Ri'Anne sat. The light of the sun warmed her through and through. Around her a wide variety of flowers grew in profusion, all of them brilliant and dazzling in color. As if they were doing their very best to give the world every bit of color that they could. It was so beautiful. Ri'Anne could sit there forever enjoying them.

Running her hands through the grass, Ri'Anne breathed in the fresh air. Never had air tasted so wonderful such that she found herself slowing her breathing just to experience the air in exquisite detail. She watched a pair of birds flutter and dance above. They twined about one another, exulting in the air as well, and then flew off down across the sloping grass and flowers down to a crystal blue river that flowed from her right to left.

She hadn't noticed the river, but now that she saw it – it looked inviting. A swim or a dive to feel its crystal waters sounded blissful. But what she really wanted to do was experience the air like the birds.

Climbing to her feet, she found she was wearing a fluffy white ankle-length dress, with white socks and white slippers like she might wear as a ballerina. She had no formal dance training, but immediately she spun executing a perfect pirouette and then in a graceful leap took to the air like one of the birds. From there she pranced, moving with elegance, enjoying the sky and showing the world her joy. With every fiber of her being she worked the best show she could, just like the flowers were doing, and with every bit of flair she could summon.

Like with her parents when she'd been a kid, she performed. They clapped, approving her dance and ultimately her. Here too, she felt acceptance, someone was watching, delighting in her. On a spin, Ri'Anne glanced about, becoming aware that she was one among many showing off before the Lord of the Water.

All over the world people were expressing themselves in this moment just like her, he made her feel like she was worth it and not as she might expect, him demanding the treatment. Ri'Anne wanted to meet him, to go up to him. But at the thought, she held back – he would be busy, there were so many about him. Then she remembered Melanie's lesson, that he was always letting them do the magic she requested. Since then Ri'Anne had asked for many things, each of them wilder and crazier than before. To fly as she did, to grow plants, to create life and, sourly, she felt guilty about it to take life. It was on her conscience thinking of the man she'd killed in her fit of anger, making her plants grow all through him. She was clearly aware that she could have held back, but gleefully she'd acted to bring him down permanently.

Ri'Anne had been so furious. The reasons were many, he had hurt her, intending great injury to both her and her friends. *Melanie, oh, Melanie – I'm so sorry. In my anger, I turned against even you…* using the abilities he'd given her. Ri'Anne turned to look towards The Lord of the Water with agony in her heart for how she'd hurt him.

Wanting to apologize, she resolutely set herself to walk towards him, no matter how long it would take to get there. There were thousands if not millions between her and him, and many miles to travel, but once she made a step, she was there before him. No distance separated them. He welcomed her, such that she walked right into him before she realized it. Her perspective changed to be third person and she realized she was looking at "his" body from "his" perspective when she thought she ought to be seeing herself.

There was a lesson in this, which she grasped that he saw her by seeing himself. In him there was no fault, and since she was inside him, no bit of her sticking out – he saw himself – perfection, when he looked at her. It was too much for Ri'Anne, she had so many "but"s to say where she didn't measure up to his holiness, but he saw only himself.

His acceptance flooded her, it was so natural that it pushed aside all her doubts. He then took a step from there, and together since she was in him, they were by the river again. He walked alongside it for a while before stopping at her place. Overwhelmed, she wanted to see his face and strangely stuck her head out from his stomach and looked up at him, but she still had his perspective and only saw her face from him. It was clear "she" saw him, but she saw only herself, a bit younger than she was currently, maybe ten or so in age. There was another lesson in this, but she didn't grasp it then.

The Lord of the Water spoke to her, "I'm sending you to bind up the broken hearted."

Then Ri'Anne was hearing Melanie asking of The Lord of the Water, though she couldn't see her, for understanding on how to bring Ri'Anne back. "Call her, command her to return to life," he said to Melanie, but it made little sense to Ri'Anne, because she felt more alive now than ever.

"Ri'Anne," sob, "Come back to me – Live!"

Suddenly Ri'Anne no longer had The Lord of the Water's perspective, but her own and she was underwater somewhere. Her first glimpse of her surroundings had her confused, it appeared like she was under a stream; it was a strange place. The sound of water flowing by her was comforting. They were in a forest somewhere. Melanie was kneeling beside her, running her fingers through her hair affectionately.

Ri'Anne tried to sit up, but she hurt all over and only managed a groan. Melanie, on hearing her, burst out crying and Ri'Anne wanted to comfort her, to tell her, "It was all right," but she couldn't speak. Then Melanie pulled her up into her arms, hugging her tightly. Oh, it hurt so good to feel her friend's arms about her.

Because of the pain, it took her a while to speak. She finally managed to whisper to her friend, "Easy, Melanie." Then when Melanie held her gently, Ri'Anne gave her friend a weak smile, wishing she could do more and hug her back, but her arms refused to move. "What's the matter with me?" Ri'Anne asked confused at her condition.

Melanie went still, her thoughts closing up, and then gently she said, "You've been dead." When that had sunk in, Ri'Anne realized that explained the vision she'd just had. Then Melanie gasped out, "I killed you." Hurrying on quickly, she added, "I didn't mean to, but you were crazy – trying to choke me with plants. I wanted to shock you out of it, but I misjudged things. I've been teaching you to be a mermaid, so I thought you could handle what I can. I went too deep and the ocean crushed you."

"What are you saying?" Ri'Anne asked, it seemed a dream everything she told her. She remembered it all but like it happened to another person. All the anger she'd felt at the time was gone. Instead, she felt peace. The acceptance she felt from The Lord of the Water had removed the stain of her choices.

Slowly, as if Melanie was only discovering it herself, she explained, "Ri'Anne you're not a mermaid. It has taken me a long time to see it, and it is all my fault. The signs were there from the beginning. When I gave you fish, you wanted butterflies. You took to flying far easier than you ever took to swimming the sea as a mermaid. You love plants! I kept thinking it was some alter-mermaid kind of thing that I hadn't experienced myself."

"But… if I'm not a mermaid?" Ri'Anne couldn't help but feel sad at this news. It had been one of her great dreams to become a mermaid.

"I wouldn't think I should be the one to tell you this." Melanie paused, apparently hoping for something. But when it didn't happen, she went on, "Whoever the Sky Lord is should be the one to tell you. But if you don't hear it from me, you're bound to hear it from one of the creatures of your realm." That was mysterious, but it didn't explain anything. Then Melanie dropped the bomb on her, "You're a fairy, Ri'Anne."

But it only made a splash. Ri'Anne knew it, as if she'd always known it. Yes, she was a fairy. How had there been any doubt? Ri'Anne realized this was her vision self-talking. Her other self that hurt so bad wanted to laugh at the suggestion, but the very thought of laughing just then had her moaning from the pain. Her outer self did the talking. "A fairy? But I'm not tiny and where are my wings?" Her inner self winced at the words of disbelief.

"And I didn't used to have a mermaid's tail, but see?" and Melanie unfolded her legs and the fish of her suit did something, swirling down her legs to reveal a glorious mermaid tail, the envy of every schoolgirl. Seeing Melanie's tail revived Ri'Anne's inner self. She had to believe like Melanie believed for it to be true for her.

Then Melanie continued, "I had to make some difficult choices. It took me a while to understand. You've just begun on this adventure and somewhere along the line you'll have to decide if being a fairy is what you want. As you've seen with me, it isn't all lying on beaches looking pretty – though we did get to do some of that."

It was what she wanted, but she knew she'd have to give up some things, like Melanie was trying to explain, and believe in herself. If she was going to do what the Lord of the Water had said, "to bind up the broken hearted," she would have to. That sounded like work, but it could be fun work. They'd made a difference in Kyria and Gian's life on the island.

"Ok," Ri'Anne said accepting the news. "What's next?"

"Everyone's waiting back on The Lazy Cloud for us. The bad guys have been dealt with, but there are plants everywhere..." Taking Ri'Anne up in her arms, Melanie showed her how much she'd changed. She was clearly strong in her mermaid tail and bearing. Ri'Anne couldn't help but wonder if she could ever be so confident, and if she had what it took to be a fairy, but she was wanting to give it a shot. So when Melanie asked if she was ready, Ri'Anne said she was.

To Be Continued

Mermaid Adventures – Book 3

Is currently being written and unfortunately you have a copy that doesn't have the beginning chapters of the next book. On a positive note, there will be a next story. I hope you do get a chance to read it when it is available.

About The Author

I spent my early years in a suburb of Chicago before our family moved to Boulder, Colorado while I was yet a teenager. It was a good move for me, and the town and location is beautiful.

During my early years I was introduced to fiction reading – I think every parent pushes their children to read, but I didn't really catch the bug until my High-School years. Afterwards, it was hard for my parents to peel me away from whatever book my nose was in.

I've never been a "good" writer. In fact I've failed most of my English classes – as may be apparent in the book. A friend of mine constantly complains of my "tense" problems. To date, I still couldn't tell you the parts of a sentence, except for nouns being a person, place or thing.

So… I didn't get any positive feedback from my (English or Creative Writing) teachers growing up, but everyone agreed I was good with computers. So, into computers I went and became a programmer – a very creative career. A career that went nowhere for me.

In my spare time, which I had plenty, I would read. After a while though, reading didn't satisfy my imagination enough and so I delved into writing.

Writing can be very creative, and so different from one writer to another. Complete this sentence and you will know what I mean: "Under the door, I saw a light – when I opened the door …"

… the door slid up into the ceiling – did anyone write that? Then a brilliant cotton candy colored unicorn was revealed. Her name was Tiffany, and she was inviting me to ride her…

… a dump-truck was emptying its content on the floor… It was my kid brother with his toy truck. "Mom! Danny is messing up my bedroom again!"

As you can see, infinite possibilities. Maybe I'll float down a river today, or climb a mountain tomorrow. Or travel on a starship the day after.

I've written lots of stories that sit on my computer, which nobody ever gets to read. Mostly because they are incomplete, some I don't even remember where I was going with the story. What they did for me though, is teach me to write. Good dialog, is not, I looked at Mike's brilliant red race car and asked him, "Hey, how's it going?" but descriptive, "Hey Mike! That's a beautiful race car. How'd you get that color of red? It's brilliant!" At least to me, description through dialog is better than a narrative on the subject.

Writing many incomplete stories can drag you down. I was honestly sick of failing to complete one. So when I got the idea that became Mermaid Rising, I was determined to see it completed. A little over a year later, the book is a reality. And so the series continues with more on the way.

Made in the USA
Charleston, SC
11 July 2016